The Kingdom of Meridian

Volume I

# The Bee Keeper's Daughter

Shiån Serei

# Dedication

*For Masha, the inspiring girl from Omsk, who started it all.*

# Chapters

# Chapters

# Preface

The Beekeepers Daughter is the first of five books in the Kingdom of Meridian Series. The story begins with Maria, a young woman struggling to survive in medieval Russia. Through a series of tragic events, she must travel across Northwestern Russia to find safety with relatives in a distant city. Along the way, her conservative life in a village fades as she navigates a new world filled with danger. Her experience becomes a personal journey in trust, adventure, love and destiny.

You are about to be taken on an exciting journey filled with folklore, Russian history, and romantic encounters. The pace is fast as Maria travels North on the Volga River trying to evade Tatar soldiers seeking to return her to Rostov. Armed only with a handful of items and the knowledge her parents gave her; she must trust her life to complete strangers while learning to survive in a world where nothing is as it seems. Her story unfolds with chaotic twists that drive her to a destiny far greater than she ever imagined.

A word about Russian culture, you'll notice the names shifting a bit during the dialogue between characters. This shift is intentional and is a key element in how conversations take place, beginning with full formal names and then as the familiarity grows the names 'soften'. For example 'Maria' becomes 'Masha' or 'Manya'. Mikhail becomes Misha, Svetlana becomes Sveta and Natalya becomes Natasha or Natalie. This trend continues throughout the book and reveals when the characters are formal, friendly, serious or playful.

It was my wish to make this a historically and geographically accurate tale, but there were some points where a fact had to be sacrificed for the greater good of the story. I hope you can embrace the fictional detours as a means to further enjoy the book.

-Shiản Serei

Language Notes: The story is replete with anglicized words, meant to capture the color of Russian and other languages. These words are written in the way they are pronounced, as a benefit to the reader. You'll find an index at the end of the book with the complete translation of each phrase.

# One Night in Rostov

It is the year 1290 in the city of Rostov. Russia has changed dramatically after being conquered by the Tatar horde. Within months of the invasion, many of the local people had been forced out of their homes or were killed for resisting the army. The autumn sun is setting on a small farm at the edge of the city, where the local beekeeper, Alex, and his family, live.

Alex loaded the last barrel of Mead onto his small cart. His back ached from loading so many barrels, but the order for all his mead and honey was too good to pass up. The Tatars had destroyed so many of his hives and fields during the invasion, leaving him with limited means to pay for safe passage out of Rostov. He walked into his small farm house to bid his wife and daughter farewell.

The room was clad in hand-cut boards, cinched with mud to fill the cracks. A large clay oven filled one corner, warming the house and providing a space for cooking. A small bed fit snugly between the ceiling and top of the oven with just enough space to slide in and survive the coldest nights. A small piece of wood pivoting a single nail held the doors to an angled closet where preserves, potatoes, and onions were kept. A rear door gave exit to the garden behind the house. Wicks dipped in beeswax were cooling by the oven, as completed candles were stacked and prepared for market.

"Lena, I'm off to deliver the mead and honey to those Tatar bastards," he said. "This should bring us enough to get out of here, finally, and move to Neva."

"Ladno, be careful Alex. I don't trust those monsters!" she said as she brushed her daughter Maria's long blonde hair.

Maria was reading aloud in Latin from an illuminated script her Mother insisted she memorize by practice each night. Maria hated learning Latin and paused to respond to her father.

"I will go with you Papa," said Maria. "It will go faster with two people," she said setting the scroll aside and standing to don her coat.

"Net Masha, the Tatar court is not a place for young girls!" Alex said in a determined voice. He turned and walked out the door without another word.

Maria's disappointment was obvious.

Her mother guided Maria to return to her seat, "Nice try, now let's start from the beginning shall we?" said Lena.

"In principio creavit Deus caelum et terram" Maria began sarcastically, without looking at the script.

Lena was the town's school teacher and the only woman who could read and write in 3 languages. Her insistence on developing Maria's mind had been a daily ritual since Maria was five years old. Now at the age of nineteen, Maria was very skilled in linguistics and sciences though her father insisted that she keep her abilities a secret.

As the sound of Alex's cart pulled away, Lena placed her hand on Maria's shoulder. "Your father just wants to keep you safe; he isn't upset with you," Lena said calmly

Then Maria noticed that her father had left his gloves by the door.

"He forgot his gloves!" She gasped. "I'll catch up to him and give these to him!"

She quickly ran out the door before her mother could voice her objection.

Lena sighed in frustration as she picked up the scroll that had fallen to the floor. She carefully brushed the dust from it with her hands. The scroll was sacred to their family; it had been blessed by a priest who regarded it as an icon of the church. She walked to the corner of the house, rolling the scroll and setting it on a shelf Alex had built to keep it safe. Here it could radiate its power over the entire home. Lena turned and began to pack their few belongings in anticipation of their journey the next day.

Maria's freshly brushed hair streamed like ribbons of gold as she ran as fast as she could to catch up to her father's cart, shouting for him to stop. The cart came to a halt as Alex turned and understood what she was doing. "Spacibo Manya" Alex said," You may as well ride along now, it's too dark on the streets."

The cart slowly rode through the decimated town of Rostov, a once proud city now under the Rule of the Tatars. Each day a new rule or tax was imposed by Alchiday the warlord who had declared himself their new king.

"Papa, why did they ask for so much mead tonight?" Maria asked.

"They're having a wedding for Alchiday and some unfortunate local girls," Alex replied. "They breed with the conquered to stop the rebellions against his army. But marriage to these people is nothing more than buying cattle. They take wives and concubines whenever it suits them, but the women are just prisoners for breeding."

"Why don't the women run away then or become nuns?" Marias asked in a naive tone.

"Because they will be executed!" Alex replied harshly.

Maria's eyes grew wide in astonishment, and she realized how dangerous and dismal such a situation would be.

"Have you not seen how they butcher anyone that defies them? Alex continued, "So many families are gone now, and for what? To rule over what remains of our little town? That's why we are finally leaving here in the morning; this is no longer our home!"

Maria rubbed her hand over her father's back consoling him, "Da Papa" she said in agreement.

They rode in silence the rest of the way. Each house and shop they passed showed damage or marking as a witness to the brutality that had come upon Rostov when the Tatars invaded months before. Alex's mind flashed through the memories of his childhood in Rostov and the now empty shell that remained under Tatar rule.

The church in the center of the city became the headquarters of the warlord, Alchiday. His soldiers killed many of the town's people while occupying the adjacent homes and shops. The local residents had been scattered to find shelter where they could, though many died defending their homes. Those, like Alex, who worked on the outer part of the city were permitted to keep their farms to serve the army's needs.

Maria was sad to see the town she had been born in become so dark and dangerous. For nineteen years she had believed she would grow up and live a simple life of farming or perhaps meet a handsome man from a big city and raise a family there. Now, every young man in the town, every classmate or friend she knew was now gone. Only her cousin Dmitri had survived the invasion of the Tatars, and his life, like her father's, was spared because he could provide a service to the army, hauling freight on a river boat.

As they drew closer to the large stone-built church, the horse's hooves were the only sound on the street as they clacked on the hard clay and rocks. Alex pulled the reigns slightly, stopping the cart near the door of the church. They both began to leave the cart, but Alex stopped Maria before her feet reached the ground.

"You stay in the cart, ponimayesh?" Alex said firmly.

Maria did not reply she simply nodded and remained in her seat. Alex knocked at the large heavy door of the church and began putting his gloves on as he waited for an answer. The sound of music and shouting grew much louder as the door opened.

"Ah, Ermolenko is here." Said the guard.

A few words were exchanged with the guard before Alex returned to the cart and began unloading it.

The horse blustered as Maria sat in the cart listening to men cheering, sounds of laughter and drunkenness and the clang of iron swords. It sounded like someone was pretending to fight in sport. Her fingers traced through her hair as she sat patiently waiting for her father to return.

Alex carried each barrel of mead inside; each trip seemed harder as he grew tired and winced at the weight of them. Finally, he finished and walked inside to collect his payment. Several minutes went by, and Maria wondered how long he would be.

Her curiosity became unbearable as she began to wonder what was happening inside the brightly lit church. The sounds and smells of food felt like an invitation to explore what a Tatar wedding looked like; she quickly stepped off the cart and walked to the door, peeking inside, hoping not to be spotted by her father.

She embraced the side of the door and carefully tilted her head just enough to see inside. There were soldiers everywhere, drinking, shouting, some pretended to fight with their swords while others ate like hungry dogs.

The middle of the room boasted a large feast of food and her father's familiar barrels of mead were neatly stacked alongside. Toward the back of the room, several women were adorned in veils. Maria struggled to recognize them but could not make out their faces. They were all undoubtedly sad. Some were crying, and others simply sat with their heads down. It became obvious that these were the future wives of Alchiday. Not just one bride but many!

The wind from the street blew unexpectedly through the passageways and lifted Maria's long blonde strands. As she stood in the door, her hair became dancing threads of light that dared to undulate into view. A soldier glanced toward the door and saw the young maiden with big grey eyes peering into the festivities. Within moments the soldier began walking towards her and took her by the arm. She feverishly looked around for her father, terrified of what would happen.

The soldier spoke to her in Turkic, a language she didn't understand as he roughly pushed her through the crowd toward the rear of the room. "What is happening?" She wondered as she felt a cold fear washing over her.

It was surreal; she was in the same church she stood and listened to her priest says prayers every week. Now her feet nervously were shuffling across the dirty floor as other soldiers looked at her as if she was the best catch of a hunt.

Suddenly she recognized her father; he was standing in front of Alchiday as the warlord's treasurer handed Alex several gold pieces for the mead and honey. Alex smiled nodded as his hand closed around the gold. He took a step back from the treasurer and turned to exit at the same moment his daughter arrived in the hands of the soldier.

Maria watched Alex's eyes grow wide as fear transformed his familiar face. The soldier held on to Maria's arm as he and Alchiday exchanged words in Turkic. The noise of the room created a backdrop to conceal the conversation of Alex as he spoke quickly to his daughter.

"I told you to stay in the cart!" He said with his voice cracking from fear.

"I'm sorry Papa, I don't know what happened, I just looked for a second!" she said as tears ran down her face.

"I'm going to get you out of here!" Alex said reassuringly.

Alchiday motioned to the soldier to place Maria with the veiled women, and instantly Alex understood what would happen.

Alex snatched Maria out of the soldier's hand and quickly slapped her face hard enough to knock her to her knees. Maria did not understand what he was doing; she only felt the burning pain of his strong hand on her cheek as she dared not to stand up. Her father had never hit her; this was beyond comprehension as she felt her body shaking in fear.

"My apologies my Lord," Alex said quickly standing between Alchiday and Maria. "This one is a disobedient young child, not yet old enough to honor you in marriage. But I have another daughter far more beautiful and respectful. Let me punish this one at home and I'll bring my other daughter to you this very night!"

Maria was confused; she was an only child. "Who was this other daughter? What was he saying?" she thought.

As her father spoke with Alchiday, she looked at the future brides sitting a few feet away. The veiled women were watching her, she could see them more clearly now and recognized their faces.

"Lilia ... Nadia ... Katya?" She whispered in shock as they acknowledged her through their tears.

These were her classmates, the girls she had grown up with and here they were like prisoners, sentenced to a life of service to the man that had invaded their town and killed their families. In a single breath, everything had been revealed, and Maria understood she was about to added to their sorrow. Suddenly the reality of the situation rushed over Maria, like a burning rain of fear.

# Ya Ne Boyus

Alex abruptly grabbed Maria's arm, pulling her to her feet as she continued looking at her veiled friends. He pulled her faster than she could walk as she struggled to keep up with his pace. The men in the room calmed and watched as Alex pushed and nudged Maria closer to the door while he spoke loud enough for Alchiday to hear him.

"And let me leave my payment for the mead as a token of good will to Lord Alchiday," Alex said, as he nervously took the gold and poured it loosely over the hand of the soldier guarding the door. The coins chimed as they bounced off the paved church floor, flipping and rolling in all directions.

Alex knew the soldiers were obsessed with gold; He watched all eyes in the room train to the coin's movement giving him a moment's distraction. He reached and unlatched the large door, opening it just enough to push Maria back into the street.

Alchiday stood up in objection, shouting in Turkic as the door opened. He pointed at the door, instructing the guards to react.

"Masha, Run!" Her father yelled, as several soldiers suddenly converged toward the door.

Maria stumbled and fell back. She struggled to get back on her feet as she watched her father swing the large door closed with a thunderous bang as it latched against the frame.

Alex knew how barbaric the Tatars were. To deny them anything would mean his death, but he could not bear the thought of them touching his precious daughter.  He had only hoped to buy enough time to get Maria out of the church.

Maria hesitated for a moment, then heard the shouts of them coming toward the door. Now she understood her father's intentions; she bolted down the street with life over death determination.  She could hardly see, as the tears poured from her eyes. Her hands nervously wiped them as she ran harder and farther away.

Then she heard her father's voice, shouting indistinctly in the street. She ducked behind a large tree to look for him. In the distance, she could still see the dim lit street leading to the church. A wounded man was running, limping while being chased by soldiers. It was her father!

He ran directly toward her, surely he could see her hiding ahead, behind the tree, then she saw him stop and turn toward the soldiers.

He shouted and taunted them as they slowed to engage him. "Ya ne boyus!" he screamed as they pulled their swords and came closer to him.

Maria watched in horror as one of the soldiers impaled her father in the abdomen. Her father grunted then fell to the ground.

He kneeled forward, holding his hands over the wound as blood ran from his body.

"Idi! Idi" he shouted as his body collapsed on the street.

Then there was silence. It was her father's last effort to help her get away.

Maria was horrified by seeing her father killed; she couldn't move, she felt terrified. It was like someone had bound every part of her body and no matter what she did, she was trapped, frozen in her place. She felt guilt, shame, and fear binding her without mercy.

She struggled to breathe as the terror took her breath. She stayed behind the tree's generous silhouette as the soldiers kept looking along the path toward her.

Then, she realized, the soldiers knew where she lived. Her father was the town beekeeper everyone knew their farm, and soon the soldiers would arrive to take their land and her mother.

The immobilizing fear left her at that moment, she burst into action, running harder than she had ever tried. She had to get to her mother before the Tatars!

She ran like a rabbit darting down the streets where moments ago she and her father has just ridden quietly on their way to the church. Finally, she reached the edge of town and saw the light in the window of their farm. The distance home never seemed so far. She consumed each step toward the door, running harder and thinking what to say when she arrived. Finally, she felt the clasp of the door to their home in her hand.

She pushed through the door still running and panting, "Mama, we have to go,… now!" Maria said as she began to grab the packed items her mother had assembled for their trip the next day. Her mother slid down from the top of the oven, dressed in bed clothes.

"Masha, what's happened?" Lena said, "Where is your father?"

Maria couldn't bear to say the words, "They tried to take me, Mama, it's all my fault, and Papa protected me so I could get away…they're coming! …we have to go!" Maria said as her voice cracked from the horror she was describing.

Lena, put her hands on Maria's shoulders to get her to slow down, "Masha, where is your father?" she asked, fearing the answer.

"They killed him!" Maria said as she collapsed into her mother's arms crying.

The two of them held each other sobbing, terrified, and lost. Lena now understood the look on her neighbor's faces when their husbands had been killed. How no words could ever comfort such a loss.

"Why?" Lena cried, "Why my Alex?"

Maria felt remorse overwhelm her body and soul. If she had just stayed in the cart, if she had just listened to her father, he would be alive now.

The dogs that lived on the farm began to bark as soldiers approached the farm house.

"We have to go!" Maria insisted as she carried as much as she could hold and opened the back door. Lena followed in shock, quietly behind Maria's lead as she tried to understand what had happened. They walked through the rows of the garden and bee hives to conceal their escape.

The air had grown colder outside as Maria suddenly remembered her mother's coat was still inside. She looked at her mother, following her in bare feet and only a nightgown on as they stood in the damp soil of the garden.

"Your coat, your shoes!" Maria exclaimed, as her mother looked at the ground unaware of anything but the loss of her husband.

Lena looked up at Maria, and as their eyes met, she spoke in a tone Maria had never heard. It terrified her to hear her Mother talk this way. "I won't need them," her mother announced. "Let them come."

Maria started back toward the house to get her mother's things, but Lena grabbed her arm and stopped her. Maria looked and saw that her mother had no intention of escaping with her.

"Maria, go and find Dima, he can get you out of town. Go to my sister in Neva, tell her what has happened." Lena said in a disturbingly calm voice.

"What about you?!" Maria asked in shock.

"Two of us could never outrun them, but you can if you go ... now!" Lena said as she reached and took a thick support stick from the nearby row of green beans.

The sound of soldiers kicking in the front door echoed in the air. Their voices shouted as they quickly shuffled into the house looking for Maria.

"Go now! I'll join you later!" Lena said as she walked back toward the house, stopping in the middle of the bee hives.

Maria, set the bag of their belongings down, preparing to fight with her mother. She reached for an equally sized stick, but her Mother turned and stopped her. "No! You run!" Lena said.

Masha was reluctant but obeyed her mother's wishes, she grabbed the bag and ran toward the nearby woods, hiding in the shadows. She watched as her mother walked into the midst of the bee hives and waited for the soldiers to emerge. Suddenly the back door flew open as the soldiers shuffled out, with swords drawn. They saw Lena standing calmly and began to charge toward her.

Maria's hands squeezed the bark of the tree she stood behind, fearing her mother would be killed just as her father. Then she heard her mother, shouting in anguish as she struck the bee hives, breaking them open, sending thousands of angry bees into the air just as the soldiers got close to her mother. Lena lowered herself into a small ball on the ground as the soldiers stepped into the swarms. She knew very well how to remain calm in the presence of bees and had baited the soldiers toward her.

Suddenly the sound of terror filled the air as the soldiers were defenseless against the bee stings that easily penetrated their clothing and armor. Their bare hands and faces began to swell from venomous punctures until they could no longer hold a sword or see anything around them. They only knew to back away and try to escape the endless assault of the bee's wrath.

Lena was spared the wrath of the bees although she was stung a few times, she kept still and waited for the soldier's retreat. The clever farmer's wife had bought her daughter an escape, but she knew Maria would not go without her. She looked toward the woods, suspecting Maria was there watching, then ran in the opposite direction, leading the remaining soldiers away from Maria.

Maria watched until her mother disappeared with soldiers chasing behind her. She continued with their plan to meet and made her way along the edge of the nearby woods until she arrived at the river. She knew this place well as she often played here as a child. She was undetected by the soldiers as it was quite dark that night and she could make her way easily on the familiar path leading to the dock where her cousin Dmitri worked.

Hours passed as she walked in the cold night air, her mind was a blur of everything in her world changing in an instant. The sun would come up soon, and she knew she had to keep hidden for fear of being caught. Her arms soon exhausted from carrying the heavy bag. She tied a belt around her waist and put as much as would fit inside the top of her dress to keep warm and free her arms from carrying. She reluctantly left behind things that would not fit in her dress but kept the illuminated the scroll, so dear to her mother, as she knew this would have to remain in her possession. She slipped it carefully inside her dress and continued on her way along the river.

She arrived at the ship dock just before sunrise. She knew guards would be at the dock and slowly stepped along the outer wall of the dock, to remain undetected from their surveillance of the main street. Her eyes searched the piers for the ship where her cousin worked. She couldn't remember the name of it, but knew it was a cargo transport with a wide deck and yellow trim along the sides. She began to fear it may not be there and wondered what she would do if she couldn't find it.

She heard footsteps on the adjoining pier and saw soldiers making a check of the ships tied to their posts. A soldier walked to the end of his pier, looking around as he stopped and paused. Maria knelt down and moved to keep out of view, ducking between the ships that blocked the soldier's view of her. She knew if he turned down her pier, he would see her immediately. She held tightly to a post, hoping it would conceal her in the dim light.

The soldier stood still for a moment; it appeared he was trying to listen for any noise as he glanced in both directions. Maria held her breath, wishing to be invisible at that moment.

A distant trickle echoed in the water as the soldier began looking down. Within moments Maria realized, the noise was from the soldier, urinating off the pier into the river.

She nervously turned to see the familiar yellow trimmed ship at the end of her pier. She knew this would be her only chance to escape as she crawled to the end of the pier in clear view of the distracted soldier. She looked back to make she was undetected by the soldier before jumping from the dock to the deck of the ship.

Her feet thudded lightly on landing as she quickly scurried aboard the fully loaded vessel. The soldier heard the noise and finished his business before straightening his armor and walking down the pier. Maria heard his heavy footsteps and rushed toward a tarp, covering a stack of cargo.

The tarp was tucked in tightly, making it difficult to pull out and give her a place to hide. The corner of the tarp slowly unpeeled from the edge as she yanked desperately to get under it before the soldier arrived. She put her foot against the cargo and pulled harder to force it open, making it tear slightly before giving way.

Maria dashed underneath the cover, pulling its' corner back inside. She knew if the soldier saw it moving she would be revealed. She could hear his footsteps coming closer, slowing as he looked around. The tiny amount of space was barely big enough to conceal her as she took the corner and sat on it, with her back to the outside, making the cargo look as it was before.

All was quiet; she tried to keep her panting breath from giving her location away. Then the deck shook as the soldier stepped onto the ship. The boards beneath her vibrated like a hammer against a nail as the soldier stepped in her direction. She held her breath as he came near, fearing he knew exactly where she was. The sound of his sword pinged as he drew it and stepped closer. Maria tightened her back in anticipation of being stabbed by his sword.

"Got ya!" Shouted the soldier as he thrust his blade toward a raccoon, hiding on the pallet next to hers.

The raccoon shrieked and hissed at the soldier as it evaded him and ran off the ship. The soldier quickly followed in pursuit, with each step shaking the boards of the deck as he jumped to the pier and ran toward the road.

Maria's heart raced as she slowly realized she was safe and undetected. She released her grip on the net that wrapped around the cargo. She felt her way in the dark, finding enough room to slip from the deck onto the softer sacks of grain and cotton that were inside. The hidden place felt warm compared to the open air of the river bank, calming her shivering body as she fell asleep from exhaustion.

# Passage to Yaroslavl

The sounds of footsteps and men's voices woke Maria; it seemed she had only slept for a minute, but the daylight peering through the edges of the cargo cover assured her it was now morning. Maria carefully looked through the stitching holes of the cover to see if her cousin was in sight.

She saw unfamiliar faces and realized how dangerous it would be if she were discovered by someone loyal to the Tatars. Then she recognized her cousin Dima's voice; he was speaking with someone else as he walked onboard the boat. As he turned in her direction, she started to move off the grain sacks, but then she saw he was walking with two of Alchiday's soldiers. They were asking him questions and looking around at the cargo holds. Maria could just overhear the conversation.

"Of course, if I see either of them I will alert you, but I doubt they would come here. They're just simple farmers, have you checked the woods?" Dima said confidently.

As he spoke, one of the soldiers stepped on board and went below to look around. The other soldier took out his sword and began lifting the covers off the cargo. Dima began to explain what was in each one, his voice was casual but annoyed at the soldier's presence.

"This is cotton, be careful with the sword, if you cut the bailing it will blow everywhere!" Dima said cautiously to the soldier.

Maria panicked, if Dima didn't know she was there, he wouldn't know to conceal her beneath the tarp.

Step by step, the soldier flipped the covers, as if he would strike the moment he saw anyone underneath.

Maria could feel her breath growing faster; the fear was like hands around her neck. She couldn't get enough air as the sound of her breathing seemed so loud that everyone on board could hear her. The edge of the soldier's sword jabbed beneath the cover, and she knew her life was about to end. Her lip quivered as her body began to shake uncontrollably. She held her breath and then heard the voice of the other soldier shouting as he appeared back on the top deck.

The guard was distracted and turned to speak with him as his sword slid away, leaving the cover in place.

The seconds that went by seemed like a lifetime as she waited for him to turn back and uncover her there. But then the other soldier, who appeared to be in charge, motioned for them to leave and continue searching elsewhere.

Maria could not believe her eyes, just as her life was surely about to end, the soldiers walked away.

Dima returned to tie down each of the cargo covers, his hands quickly lashing them with ropes. He came to the place where Maria was hiding, and as his hands reached to tie it down tighter, she whispered to him, "Dima!"

Dima's hand nervously pulled back, as if he had seen a snake. Some of the other shipmates looked for a moment then returned to their work. He kneeled down, pretending to work on the rope, and slid the cover carefully aside just enough to look inside.

"Masha? Are you and Tetya Lena in there?" he said in a relieved voice.

"Tolka ya" her young voice sighed.

"I heard what happened, sorry about Dyadya Alex, he was a good man," Dima said as he tried to keep his voice from others ears. "They put a reward on your heads where is Tetya Lena?" Dima asked.

"I don't know where she is, but we are too meet in Neva, at your mother's house" Maria replied, wondering if she could trust anyone with these details.

"We are setting sail today for Yaroslavl, can you stay in there until nightfall? No one can know you are here, that reward is too tempting for even my friends to turn down." Dima said as he tied the rope in place. "I'll bring you some food and water, just stay in there.

"Alright, I'll stay here, please see if you can find my mother before we leave?" Maria asked.

"I'll see what I can find out," Dima said, in a doubtful voice.

Dima was an experienced sailor and knew how the Tatars worked. What they could not buy, they took through force. "If Lena hadn't already been captured, she would surely be dead,"

He thought. He stepped off the boat and walked toward town, looking for answers about his aunt's location.

The deck of the ship was made of rough splintered boards that were filthy from endless cargo storage and dirt. Maria shifted her position often, quietly trying to relieve the growing discomfort of laying across thick, coarse ropes and sacks. There were noises and rumblings on the deck as the last of the cargo was placed on board. Maria fell asleep at times, sleeping only from exhaustion, as her mind tried to understand the events in the last few hours. From the moment she stepped off her father's cart to peer inside the church, her entire life had changed forever.

Flashes of the scene haunted her mind. The chilling fear returned as she pulled through the crowd of soldiers in the church. Her father's gentle hands turning to iron when he struck her face to create an escape; the scene of him turning to face the soldiers, unafraid and determined for her to get away; Her mother so calmly doing the same at the farm house.

She had always known her parents love, but seeing them step in the way of death to protect her, made her shake with a sense of unworthiness. She could hardly swallow from crying and running in the damp night air. She tried to silence her despair by thinking of reuniting with her mother.

The men began to come from below deck with bowls of food. They sat on the deck and talked as they ate and drank.

Dima finally appeared, carrying a bowl of borscht and a cup of water. The captain spoke to him as he walked across the deck.

"Ah Dima, missing all morning for the loading but made it in time for lunch?" he said sarcastically.

"Da Captain, I had an urgent family matter to attend to before pulling out, I apologize for my absence," Dima said respectfully.

"I heard, Sorry to hear about your uncle. Any news on your aunt or cousin?" The captain asked.

Maria feared Dima could give information about her or her mother and listened carefully.

"Net, they vanished into the woods. That's all I know." Dima said sadly.

"Hopefully, they will find safety." The captain replied, patting Dima on the back, "Can you handle first watch tonight?" he asked.

Dima nodded and walked toward the place where Maria was hiding. He sat with his back to her and slid his soup under the cover for her, pretending to have the cup still in his hand to avoid suspicion.

"Masha, eat this!" he whispered.

Her delicate, shaking hands slid from beneath the cover and pulled the bowl inside. Dima could hear her gulping it and wondered if anyone else might notice. He coughed to mask the sound and alert Maria to be quieter.

Dima reached inside his coat and carefully lowered a quarter loaf of bread to the deck and tucked it behind him. "Masha," he said in a whisper.

Maria's hand appeared again, just long enough to pull the bread out of sight. It was just bread and soup, but at the time it was a feast. She felt less tense now; her hands stopped shaking, and she focused on finding her mother.

"Dima" she whispered. "Did you find my mother?"

"No" he whispered as he reached to take the cup back into his hand, noticing it was empty.

"Do you want water?" he asked, wondering how he would give it to her without drawing attention.

"Net, spacibo" Maria whispered, "I'll need to pee if I drink anything."

"We are leaving soon. Your mother must have found another way out of town so you should go with me!"

Dima waited for an answer but then realized Maria had fallen asleep now that she had a meal.

The ship cast off, taking the strength of the northward wind into its sail. A cool breeze slid beneath the covers as the boards of the deck creaked from the ships movements along the river. Maria awakened as the sun was setting, and realized the ship was now well on its way to Yaroslavl.

From her limited view, she could see Dima talking to the man who was steering the ship. Dima then came and sat in front of her as before. He slipped more bread to her and told her they would arrive early in the morning.

"I'll have to get you off the ship before the crew wakes up to unload. There won't be much time, but I can make arrangements to get you to my mother's home in Neva." He said quietly.

"I'm going back to Rostov tomorrow to see if your mother is still there," he said confidently.

"Thank you Dima, she is a clever woman; I'm sure she is already in Yaroslavl," Maria said hoping her wishes were true.

"Just be ready when I come for you!" Dima said as he quickly stood up.

Footsteps of the captain echoed on the deck as he walked over to Dima.

"Enjoying your rest while on watch, young Petrov?" the captain snapped.

"Just tightening my shoes, sir, all is well," Dima said in a nervous tone.

"Indeed. Keep an eye out for stowaways. Those Tatar soldiers will be searching every ship coming in or out of port now." said the captain as he walked below deck.

Dima hoped Maria didn't hear the captain's words. He was more like her brother than a cousin and was determined to save her.

Maria began to see her life change from dreams of the future to an unknown existence with each passing moment. The helplessness of her situation crushed her spirit, but her resolve to survive was never stronger. Her parents sacrificed everything for her, and she wanted to deserve the selfless bravery of their deeds, even though she felt responsible for setting those acts in motion.

"If only I had stayed in the cart" her thoughts tormented. "If I could just go back and change that one decision, my Father would be alive, and we would be on our way to Neva as a family."

The remorse and guilt swam around her like a heavy breeze until she could not bear the weight of it. A depressive mood guided her eyes to close as she slept concealed under the cargo tarp as if an invisible hand closed her eyes to sleep, avoiding the pain of her conscious reality.

# Oxana's Tavern

"Masha! Wake Up! We have to go!" Dima whispered.

Maria woke and felt the cold early morning air swirling around her. The ship was tethered to the dock with a town dimly lit in the distance. Dima pulled her to her feet while the crew continued sleeping. She was weak and stiff as she tried to stand after being still for so long.

"I can't walk," she said faintly as she fumbled to stand.

"You have to!" Dima insisted as he looked around to ensure their stealth. He pulled her by the hand and her feet began to step one by one. Her clothes still packed inside her dress, she shifted and adjusted as best she could to keep up with Dima's quick pace.

They made their way down the gangplank and quickly walked toward large stacks of freight, stored at the port.

"Where are we going?" asked Maria

"To see a friend," Dima said mysteriously

Maria had never been outside of Rostov, and all the new surroundings were curious and strange to her. She read the signs above the shops as they walked, Tobak, Producti, Bar. Reading had never been so useful as now with so much unfamiliar space around her. The two of them wove between freight and piles of fishing nets, avoiding lighted areas. They reached the main street and then walked along an alley until they arrived at a strange looking tavern.

Dima knocked at the door, it took a while but soon a woman with short blonde hair and brown eyes appeared at the door. She clearly had been sleeping and was groggy but instantly recognized Dima and let them in.

"Dima? Shto takoe?" She asked in an unpleasant tone as she pointed at Maria.

Dima placed several coins in the woman's hand, telling her to hide Maria from everyone until someone came for her later.

The woman looked at the coins and hesitantly accepted, inviting them inside as she looked up and down the street to see if anyone was watching.

"This is Oxana, you can trust her, she runs this place and will help you. I have to return to the ship before they see I am gone!" Dima said as he hugged Maria. "My friend will come for you tomorrow and take you to Neva. Kiss my mother for me!" Dima said sweetly.

"Spacibo Oxana!" Dima said as he kissed Oxana firmly on the lips, surprising her and Maria as he made his way to the door, quickly exiting.

Oxana watched looking favorably as the sound of Dima's steps could be heard running down the alley. It was clear that she liked him or knew him well. She closed the door and looked back at Maria. She studied her for a moment, a slim girl covered in dirt, wearing a dress stuffed with clothing, summarizing her predicament and thought Maria must be family or slave on the run.

Oxana nodded, feeling sympathetic to the fear on Maria's face. "Idite za mnoy." She said as she led Maria up the tavern stairs. The tavern had a strange smell, a mix of wine, mead and perfume seemed to permeate the air. As they walked down the hall, sounds came from some of the rooms. A man's snoring, two women talking, and distant crying.

"This is my only free room," Oxana said shortly. "There're water and towels there, and the sheets are clean. You smell like a sailor, so…wash!" she insisted.

Maria nodded, "Mda, I've been hiding in a cargo net since yesterday! Thank you!" she said

The door closed as Oxana left, and Maria walked toward the mirror near the window. Her face and hair were filthy. Her hands looked almost black with dirt as she pulled the items from her dress and let it slip off. She reached into the large bowl of water and began to wash away the last few days of suffering and guilt.

She found a brush and began to pull the tangles from her hair. She remembered the last time she did this; her mother had insisted on helping her so they could braid it. Just moments before her father was leaving to deliver the mead.

"Why can't I go back in time?" she agonized.

She changed into a cleaner dress and slid into the bed after washing, the clean sheets and soft mattress made her gasp.

It was such a comfort after so many hours of running in the woods and stowing away on the ship.

She had hardly pulled the blanket over herself before she fell asleep. For the first time since her father's death, she felt safe.

Morning came and went as Maria continued to sleep. Oxana knocked at her door with breakfast but left it by her bed when she saw how tired she was.

Maria woke up as the sun had just begun to set. She saw the breakfast and ate everything at once. Moments later Oxana returned with dinner and marveled that Maria was awake.

"Are you one of those vampires that only comes out at night?" Oxana teased. "Still hungry?"

Maria nodded in agreement as she began to chew on the first thing she touched.

"The ships are coming in from the Volga now; I expect whoever is coming for you will be here tonight," Oxana said.

"Spacibo, Oxana," Maria said as she swallowed and reached for water. "Spacibo bolshoe."

"Well I've got work to do, so I'll leave you to this," Oxana said as she left the room.

Maria finished her meal and looked out the window. The sun set over the city, and she wondered if her mother might be somewhere nearby.

A recurring sound began to resonate from the room next door. It was like the crying she had heard the night before. Maria walked closer to the wall, and could feel a vibration coming from the floor as if someone was jumping or fighting.

Her curiosity drew her closer and closer until her ear was against the wall. "Was someone in danger?" she thought. As her face pressed against the wall, she could see a small light coming through from the other room. She walked towards it and found a hole just big enough to peek through.

She leaned in and started to focus her view into the other room. It was similar to her room, but more candles were lit along with a lantern by the bed. The walls were wooden with fabric tapestry hanging across a wooden rod. The bed had a fancy lace blanket, nicer than anything she had seen in Rostov. A young woman with dark red curly hair was sitting on the bed facing a half-dressed man who moved toward her. He began to slide her dress off her shoulders and slid his hands over her bare breasts.

Maria gasped, she was shocked and intrigued at the same time. She pulled away from the wall, feeling embarrassed by what she had seen. She walked back to her bed and sat there, listening to the woman giggling as the man's voice lifted and dropped in conversation.

Maria understood perfectly what they were doing; her mother had explained everything to her when she was 13, but she had never experienced sex or even seen a naked man. Although she had seen more than expected through the clothes, her classmates wore when they went swimming, in the village. Soon she found herself back at the wall, watching again.

The woman was now on top of the man; his hands slid across her smooth skin as she rode him like a horse, gliding forward and back as he moved beneath her. Her breasts were large, and he caressed them often. She seemed to enjoy him, she smiled and moaned and placed her hands over his, encouraging him to keep his hands in place. Her hair spilled across her back as she tilted her head back and slowed her movements.

The man's body was slightly concealed by the bed linen. Maria could only see his arms and legs from her point of view. He looked rough and hairy in comparison to the woman's smooth skin. They moved together with increasing force until the man pulled at her body, thrusting himself upward and then holding her there as he moaned. They stilled as the woman lay forward on his chest and kissed him as his hands stroked down her back.

Maria was entranced. It was the most erotic experience in her life, and she felt as if she was on fire after watching them. "Was this her husband?" she wondered. "Is this what married couples do?"

The woman then slipped away from him, standing and pulling a bed sheet to wrap around herself. She walked to the washstand and poured water from a pitcher into a bowl, then began to clean herself. It seemed odd to Maria, the woman was so passionate and then washing right away as if removing the experience entirely from her body.

She watched the man stand up and reach for his clothes. His body was muscular, and as he turned to get dressed she saw his manhood hanging between his legs. Her mouth parted in shock as she admired the fleshy shaft he covered as he pulled his pants on. A warm sensation washed over Maria, intriguing and beguiling her imagination.

She heard the woman and man talking and looked to see what else they would do. The whole in the wall painted a different scene when she peered through on the unsuspecting couple. She saw him fully clothed and smiling at the woman as he slid his boots on. He wore the clothing of a sailor and appeared to be an older man. The woman seemed uninterested in him now, a strange look was on her face as she appeared impatient and annoyed.

The man reached into his pocket and handed her some coins. The woman counted them and looked at him with a disappointed face. The man gestured with his palms up as if surprised then gave her two more coins as he walked out. The sound of his footsteps echoed down the hall while the woman went to the candles and blew them out, darkening the room.

Maria was confused and went to sit on her bed to calm herself down as she began to realize where her cousin had hidden her. She was staying in a brothel and had just watched a prostitute render her services.

"The rumors of sailors and harlots must have some basis in fact," she thought, but then she connected the most important point: Her cousin Dima was a well-known customer and must have had some favor with Oxana to accommodate his cousin in so early in the morning. Her opinion of Dima changed instantly. She had always pictured him so proper and hardworking, this was a new side of him but after pondering the idea, she came to accept that if it were any other man she would not be as surprised by the act. He had no wife, and there was no time for love in their world destroyed by war and invasion. Perhaps this tavern offered comfort to her lonely cousin who lived a hard life on the river.

Suddenly there was a knock at the door. Maria thought it might be the woman she had been watching. She put herself under the blankets to give the appearance she had been sleeping, "Yes?" she said firmly.

A man opened the door and stepped inside.

"Sorry to disturb you so late in the evening, are you Maria?" he asked?

Maria panicked, had this man been sent to her room like the sailor she had just watched? "Why!?" she replied nervously.

The man nodded, realizing it must be Maria, "My name is Sergei, Dima paid me to take you to Neva." He said calmly.

"Yes, I'll be ready to go as soon as my mother arrives," Maria replied as she kept the blankets pulled up to her neck.

"Oh, I didn't know about this." Sergei paused, "We have to leave tomorrow morning if we're to get you up the Volga before it freezes. If not, you'll have to wait until Spring." Sergei insisted.

Maria hesitated, "The river won't freeze for at least another 2 months!" she insisted.

"Here, yes....in Neva, by the time we arrive in 3 or 4 weeks the ice will already be forming," Sergei replied.

Maria had not considered the northern track she was on. It made sense that the weather in Neva would turn cold sooner. She had not imagined making the trip alone but understood it was her parents wish for her to get to safety.

"Horosho, I'll be ready in the morning," she said.

Sergei nodded and left the room.

Maria hoped she was making the right decision. She laid back in her bed and looked at the ceiling. The value of the distraction in the room next door faded as the sad reality of the journey ahead consumed her thoughts into the night.

# From Those with the Least to Share

Maria felt the light from the window brushing her face as she woke up. Today she would travel to Neva to find her aunt and hopefully be reunited with her mother. She got out of bed and gathered her things. She took one of the linens from the wash stand, tied it by the corners and placed her belongings inside it. It looked awkward but gave her some convenience in moving about.

Noises emerged from the room next door as she prepared to leave. She ignored them at first but rushed to the hole in the wall to take one last look to see who might be there.

A giggling young woman entered the room, she was slender with brown painted eyes that looked intense and mysterious. Her chestnut hair was in a long braid that looked like a rope twisting down her back. A man followed her inside, pulling at her clothes with an eagerness that made the woman slightly protest.

"Careful!" she said, "You will tear it for sure!"

The man was tall with sandy blonde hair and blue eyes, his clothing looked foreign with Nordic designs on the cuffs and lapels. He gestured to the woman to remove her clothing as he sat on the bed. The woman skillfully turned a button, and her entire dress slipped to the ground.

"Like what you see Captain?" She teased.

The man smiled in silence then sucked his breath in a soft whistle, "Shoo" he said in agreement.

"It was so sweet of you to offer me breakfast, but as you can see I have something else in mind." She said playfully as she walked toward him and began to take his clothes off. Maria marveled as she could see everything from her vantage point, but only the back of the woman's bare body.

She watched intently as the woman slipped his pants off and began to caress his chest. Her hands slowly working lower until she was on her knees.

Maria could not see around the woman, and watched hoping to get a glimpse of the man's body. It was as if they knew she was watching and did everything to block what she wanted to see most, but suddenly he turned into view as the woman climbed onto the bed. The man looked bigger than the last one. His manhood curved upward with a more defined tip. It was beautiful, erotic, inspiring....and Maria's hands began to slide over her body as she felt the return of the warm sensation she had felt the night before.

The woman undid her braid, freeing her curly brown hair. Maria watched in astonishment as the woman took the man into her mouth and slid her fingers up and down his shaft. The man ran his fingers through her hair and moaned deeply as the woman took him into her mouth over and over.

Maria's hand cupped her breasts as she looked on in hunger at the couple's erotic exchange. The man seemed to be in a trance, unable to contain himself as the woman moved faster and took him deeper into her mouth. She had such power over him as if she was placing a spell on him, controlling him as he could only moan for more. The man began to whisper in a foreign language, but the woman ignored him and continued stroking him faster.

He reached and stroked her breasts, squeezing them firmly in his hands as he let out a deep moan and arched his back. The woman held his throbbing flesh in her hands and tilted her head back as his creamy juice began to pulse onto her neck. He moaned again as she squeezed him for more and praised him for giving her what she had worked for.

"That's it, let it out." She coaxed.

The man seemed to collapse onto the bed. Breathing heavily as if knocked down from a fight.

The woman stood up from the bed and went to the washstand, cleaning herself as the other woman had done. But then she returned to the bed and laid alongside the man. Her slim curvy body was so smooth and graceful in the morning light. She was more attentive and tender than the last woman, making him completely yielding to her will.

Maria felt a hunger growing inside her body, a new and powerful mystery of pleasure and intrigue. It was as if a seed had been planted that filled her womanly curiosity to see and experience more.

She felt jealous of the woman's freedom to have a man and do such things as she had seen. She knew she needed to leave this unexpected place and continue her journey, but she felt her view on life, her body and men were awakening.

She took one last look at the couple lying in their bed, naked and draped in tossed sheets. They seemed so peaceful compared to their earlier intensity.

She gathered her things and made her way towards the door. She took one last look around the room wondering if she would ever return here again. After such an ordeal, this room had become the first comfort she had known, and the beginning of a journey not only to Neva but within herself.

Maria walked down the halls remembering her first impression of the tavern and how different everything seemed now. The smells and chemistry of the tavern lit fires of curiosity as she passed each door. She descended the staircase and was able to see the rest of the building which was dark in the early morning hours. There were several small tables and chairs in the center of the room. Large barrels of mead and ale set in the corner where dozens of tankards were cleaned and neatly stacked. She imagined how it must look in the evening full of sailors and working women. She remembered a similar place in Rostov, but she never saw the inside of it. Somehow it seemed so dark and mysterious from the outside, but now she saw it in a very different way. These were not evil beings, conspiring to corrupt anyone who dared come through the door. They were simple people, probably lonely, who were willing to exchange money for companionship, and the women working there had likewise reconciled the act of affection as a service for hire.

After seeing the last couple, she wondered, "Do they ever find love here? Is it possible?"

She walked towards the back of the Tavern, following the sounds that only a kitchen would create. As she entered the room, she saw Oxana cooking some eggs as she spoke with another woman. The relationship of the women intrigued Maria, they seemed to share a sisterhood of sorts with faceless men passing through their lives.

In the corner, there was a small table and three small children waiting for breakfast. A boy and two girls with innocent faces.  As she looked around the rest of the room, she heard a voice say, "Kushet budish?"

She looked and realized Oksana had asked if she was hungry. Maria smiled and nodded in agreement, "Da! But please let me make it, I've imposed enough on you."

Oksana was pleased with Maria's response, and said, "You are welcome to whatever we have, dear. This is Tanya by the way, she helps me run the place."

Tanya was an older woman, she was heavier in shape than Oxana with a modest appearance and clothing. She looked like she had lived a rough life and now stared into the distance rather than at people's faces.

"Can I help you ladies finish cooking?" Maria asked.

"Da, you can make the oats for the children." Said Tanya.

"Yes, of course, I'll get some water," Maria said as she quickly made herself at home in the kitchen.

Maria felt an excitement and energy in the air, it was as if there was no time to think of dark events, she needed to focus on what she was doing to make her life better. All of her thoughts rushed to the positive goal of traveling to Neva and being reunited with her mother.

She set a pot of water on the stove and put the oatmeal in once it boiled. She stirred quickly to keep it smooth and noticed the children were watching her every move.

"Hungry?" She asked with a smile.

The children didn't respond, they were quiet and looked at each other for assurances on not speaking.

Maria felt drawn to them, their innocence and bright eyes full of curiosity. She took the pot to their table and began filling their bowls with oatmeal. "Kak tebya zovut? She asked the little girl.

The children remained shy and did not respond to her. They began eating and kept their eyes on their food. Each of them started to blow on their spoonful's waiting for it to cool.

"Oh!" Maria said realizing it was too hot. "Do you have milk or butter?" she said, walking to the stove to look for it.

Oxana pointed her in the direction of the milk and eggs. Maria brought both back to the table and added them to the bowls. "Does anyone here like cinnamon?" She asked in a voice that reminded her of her mother's.

Maria looked toward Oksana curiously as if she may have done something wrong. "They are shy with strangers and so many coming and going around here," Oksana said with a glance of understanding as she handed Maria a small roll of cinnamon bark.

One of the boys pushed his bowl toward her and waited as he watched her. Maria felt excited, it was the first sign of communicating with them. She reached for a knife and scraped the cinnamon flakes into the bowl.

"Spacibo," he said softly as he began to eat again.

"Pozhalysta," Maria giggled as she brushed her hand over his head.

Maria stood and remembered she had not put any honey in the oatmeal. She looked around the kitchen and spotted a small ceramic pot sitting by the stove. She returned to the children's table and taunted them playfully, "I don't suppose anyone here likes honey?" she said.

All three children stopped eating and pushed their bowls forward immediately.

Maria giggled as she removed the top of the jar and lifted the wooden comb spoon inside as the honey dripped slowly from the combs. "Oh look how dark it is, this is the best honey!" She said as she drizzled some on each child's oatmeal.

The children smiled and happily began mixing the honey into their oatmeal, continuing to devour it.

Maria reached for a bowl and set with the children while she ate her breakfast. She began to realize these children were probably born in this Tavern, not knowing who their father might be. It was such a different existence than what she had known growing up on a farm. She could not imagine what her life would have been like without her father. And at that moment she felt the cold reality sweeping over, that now she would be as these children were now, facing a life without the protection and care she had lost in Rostov. She looked at their innocent faces and quickly wiped her tears away, repeating to herself to focus on moving forward.

There was a knock at the front door as Tanya went to see who it was. She returned with Sergei, who looked like he was in a hurry to leave. His eyes were wide, and he stood as near the door as possible.

The ladies offered him breakfast, but he refused quickly.

"Are we going to miss the boat?" asked Maria as she stood, preparing to leave.

"Net, we have enough time, but if any of my wife's friends see me here, I will be a dead man in the morning," Sergei said in a nervous tone.

Oksana and Tanya burst into laughter as Maria smiled and turned to say goodbye.

"Thank you for your hospitality and kindness, I appreciate everything you have done for me," Maria said as she picked up her things.

Oxana noticed her linen wrapped around Maria's things. "Wait, I have a sack here..." she said sifting through her potato bin, "It's not fancy, but it's clean."

Maria smiled, delighted to have the white linen sack to carry her belongings in. Everything fit perfectly, and the cinch cord made it easier to carry.

"Poka detii," she said sweetly to the children as they looked up at her, not understanding why she was leaving so soon.

Maria and Sergei walked towards the door as Oxana followed them.

"Oksana will you please tell my cousin Dima that I have left for Neva and will wait for my mother there?" Maria asked.

"Of course, he should be here at the same time next week," Oksana replied.

"Meanwhile, he handed me this before he left. I believe it's for...the unexpected" Oksana whispered without Sergei hearing as she placed a bag of coins in Maria's hand. "No reason for anyone to know you have that, dear."

Maria smiled and nodded, understanding Oksana's advice as she carefully hid the bag of coins in the potato sack.

Dima opened the door and walked outside onto the porch as Maria followed. Suddenly the little boy she had given the cinnamon to ran onto the porch and wrapped his arms around Maria's waist. He did not say a word, he only held her tightly for a moment then ran back inside. Maria only had a moment to pat his head before he was gone. She looked toward Oksana in astonishment.

"They don't get treated very kindly in this town, thank you for making them feel special," Oksana said with a quivering voice.

Maria hugged Oxana and felt the warmth of her heart.

"You know, there is a place like this in my town, and I thought the people there were so..." Maria began.

Oxana stopped her and smiled, "Nothing in life is as it seems dear. God speed you on your way."

Oksana turned and quickly walked inside, clearly feeling the emotions of the moment.

Maria watched as the door closed, and she realized how much she had learned about life, people and even herself in this unassuming little tavern. She wished she could have stayed longer but accepted that her journey must continue.

Maria continued with Sergei down the street where a carriage was waiting.

"We have to board a ship on the other side of the harbor where the Tatars control the ships. It's likely they are looking for you from what I was told, so... put this on, you're my wife if anyone asks." Sergei said as he handed Maria a kerchief while they climbed aboard the carriage.

The streets of Yaroslavl were quite different from Rostov. Maria admired the larger buildings and smooth streets. The energy was different in the city, there seems to be more possibility for a future life. She began to imagine how Neva must be even more impressive and have even more to offer.

Sergei handed Maria a small bag of coins, "Dima said these are for expenses."

Maria nodded in confusion. Why would he give money to Sergei and Oxana for the same reason? Then she remembered when her cousin had paid Oxana for her stay in the Tavern. She realized Oksana had chosen to give the money to her instead. She remembered back in the tavern, and how Oxana had taken risks to help her. In a world where the rich exploited the innocent, she had experienced generosity and kindness from those with the least to share and most to lose.

# Kupala

The carriage slowed to a stop as it pulled alongside a large single sail ship, tied to the dock in Yaroslavl. There were pockets in the sides where boat oars could be extended, and each board of the vessel was glued together with an acrid black tar. The ship was taking on cargo, as barrel after barrel was rolled up a plank on the side. The name Kupala was carved into the forward side and across the back in large letters. Maria recognized the name from mythical stories she had heard as a child. Each summer there were festivals where maidens engaged in rituals with flowers and water celebrating traditions in the name of Kupala, but Maria's parents were Christian and forbid her from taking part in such things.

Maria exited the carriage and looked up to admire the overwhelming size of the Volga River. It seemed more like a sea compared to the river she knew in her small town. With each day since her escape from Rostov, the world had become a much larger place, and she was both terrified and intrigued to discover more.

Sergei boarded the ship and spoke with the quartermaster about their travel arrangements. From the dock, Maria could hear some shouting and arguments, but this was typical negotiation tactics in Russia. As she looked around taking in all of the sites, a large group of men walked by her to board the ship. They were poorly dressed and smelled of alcohol but walked like kings of their own world inside an entourage of sweat and muscle.

Sergei returned with a discouraged face that he tried to hide as he explained the situation to Maria. "There is not enough for both of us to take this trip, so you will have to go without me." He said in a slight whisper, keeping his back to the ship. "I told this man that you knew your way around the ship and would be okay without an escort. Can you go alone?"

Maria's hand slid towards her pocket, thinking to offer the money Oksana had given her earlier. But something in the back of her mind told her to go on without Sergei.

"As long as this ship will take me to Neva, I will be fine," Maria said as she reached for her sack of belongings.

Sergei seemed very relieved, "The quartermaster is a good man, he will keep an eye on you. Meanwhile, I'll explain everything to your brother when he returns next week." He said with a smile.

As they walked towards the gangplank, Sergei's voice lowered once again as he whispered, "There are all sorts of people on these ships, criminals, slaves even spies. Do not trust anyone, and sleep with this in your hand." He said cautiously as he placed a palm-sized knife between her fingers.

Maria quickly hid the knife in her pocket and thanked Sergei for his help. "I appreciate everything you've done for me, now go and be with your dear wife, she is lucky to have such a devoted man," Maria said as she began to board the ship.

Sergei watched as Maria found her place on the deck. He marveled at her maturity and character as he was accustomed to the cavalier and insatiable personalities of city women, but this young farm girl seemed wise beyond her years. With intense regret he turned back to the carriage, watching this charming lady fend for herself on an unknown journey.

Maria looked around, taking a long silent view of the Volga River; the view was breathtaking in the morning air. She felt the boards beneath her feet creaking and bumping as men below worked and prepared the ship to get underway. She recognized the boisterous language and tone of the workers who had passed her earlier on the dock. These were the oarsmen who would row the ship to its destination. She found it hard to imagine such an existence and wondered how anyone could live such a life.

A few more passengers boarded the ship as the ropes were being untied. The ship gently floated away from the dock as the creak and splash of the oars began their rhythm to and fro taking the vessel northward. Soon the dock was a small detail on the rear horizon as scenes along the river rolled by. A cold breeze blew from the South filling the large square sail entirely until it whistled at the edges.

The cold air quickly chilled Maria's body as it blew through the open weave of her dress. She saw a portal inside and decided to seek warmth inside of the ship. Her curiosity was peaked, she wanted to explore rest of the ship and find where she would be spending her nights. She had never slept in a cabin on a ship, and her mind began to imagine a spacious room with a window and comfortable bed. She saw the quartermaster directing everyone in different directions; each person seemed to be going the wrong way or had a complaint about their assigned place.

"Excuse me, sir, can you tell me where I will be sleeping tonight," Maria said gently.

The quartermaster turned to answer her as if he were annoyed by yet another question, but he saw the innocence of her big grey eyes and hesitated to answer. His demeanor changed as he smiled, "Young miss, you'll be sharing the forward cabin with our cook. We've no steerage for young ladies, and I can't put you on the deck with the crew. Just walk straight down this way to the door at the end". He said.

"And may I also have a room, kind sir?" Teased an oarsman, faking a woman's voice

The quartermaster quickly returned to his coarse nature and barked at the man, "Get your gear stowed below and get to your post! He said as he pushed the man to the stairwell.

Maria giggled quietly, enjoying the kind attention she had not expected. She walked toward the cabin, keeping her hands along the walls to balance as the ship rocked from left to right. It was an unpleasant almost sickening sensation to have such sway in each step. The massive Volga was clearly not as gentle as the river she had just traveled the day before.

As she reached for the door she feared for the worst of characters, she imagined a fat old man keeping her awake all night with snoring. "Why would they put me in a room with a man?" She wondered in protest.

She took her hand away from the doorknob and decided to knock softly before opening the door. Hearing no response, she felt relieved and opened the door, trying to keep from stumbling in as she made an effort to walk and enter as the ship swayed sharply to one side. At the corner of the room, a naked petite woman stood bent over a wash pan with her hair dipped in the water. She was wrapping her hair in a towel and quickly looked up, sensing the open door and shouted at Maria,

"Close the door!" the woman snapped.

Maria stepped inside and immediately closed the door. "Sorry! I'm looking for the cook's cabin." Maria said awkwardly. "He said it was this way, and I must've opened the wrong door."

The woman fixed the towel over her head and comfortably walked about the cabin as the light from the forward window cast a shadow on her nude figure. She had a slim hourglass figure with full breasts, warm brown eyes, and long chestnut hair. She moved in a hurried pace as if she had to be somewhere else at any moment.

"Relax, you're in the right place, I'm the cook, Svetlana Nikolayevna." She said, extending her hand generously.

Maria hesitated to extend her hand and tried to avert her eyes feeling embarrassed by Svetlana's nude body.

Svetlana's brown eyes looked down and realized her appearance, "Oh, sorry, not used to having guests on voyages. Most of the crew prefer me this way." She said with a loud laugh. Sveta's bright smile was contagious, her teeth looked almost childlike, white and perfectly straight.

Maria smiled and continued to look down at the floor, "It's pleasant to meet you Sveta, I am Maria Alexandrova."

The two made brief eye contact and stood in the middle of the room with awkward silence around them.

"Right," said Sveta, as she reached for her dress. She turned her back to Maria as she pulled it over her head.

Maria's eyes quickly looked noticing how different Sveta's body looked compared to her own. As the dress cascaded down Sveta's back, the curves of her body intrigued Maria. The graceful way her body curved sinuously inward to her waist, then extend outward to her hips. Her skin was smooth and toned with tan and white where her clothing had been. She had bruises and scratches that seemed to tell a story of her hard life as a cook on a ship. Maria felt an awkward interest to see the rest of Sveta's body in more detail but looked away before Sveta turned around.

"I thought the cooks were men on these ships?" Maria asked politely.

"They usually are, but my father died with debts to the ship's captain so it was either take his place or watch them put my mother and me on the street," Sveta replied in a neutral tone. "Besides a kholops life isn't so terrible compared to the nunnery!"

Maria quickly understood the situation and stopped asking questions. She pointed to an empty bunk and waited for Sveta to nod in agreement that she could sleep there. Sveta nodded and continued preparing herself.

Maria moved to sit on the bunk and fell onto it as the ship rocked more intensely with the wind and waves.

"That wind is a blessing and a curse on the river; it speeds up the ship then shakes you all about," Sveta said as she finished dressing and walked toward the door. "I've got to go get started on lunch. Welcome aboard Maria!" Sveta said while closing the door behind her.

Maria looked around the cabin as she sat on the bed. It was very different than she imagined but it was warm, safe and moving toward Neva. She noticed Sveta did not have many dresses or personal things, some of the clothing scattered around the room looked like it belonged to a man rather than a woman.

"Perhaps she is the only woman on the ship, and with so many men, I can't imagine how much attention she gets!" Maria thought as her mind blended the scenes she had seen in the tavern and the site of seeing Sveta naked just moments before.

As the ship continued to lift and drop into the water, Maria felt an overwhelming sickness come over her. It was as if she had consumed a dozen green apples and now they took their toll. She laid down and hoped the feeling would go away. She soon fell asleep in a state of bilious confusion.

Hours later the waters calmed, and she awoke in a disoriented haze, forgetting momentarily that she was no longer in her familiar bed at home, but on a ship cutting its way North on the Volga River. Maria retraced her steps back to the top deck, where the quartermaster and crew were organizing barrels along the walkway.

"These get taken off at the next port" shouted the quartermaster. "Make sure they are secured. Then let's get the other one's below to make more room for the crew to sleep."

Maria saw the men were carrying the barrels toward her as she stood at the top of the stairs leading below. She quickly went back down the staircase and went in search of the kitchen. She made her way below another deck and followed the smell of food and sounds of cooking.

Sveta noticed her and immediately offered her a bowl of soup, "There's my cabin mate!" She said in a joyous tone. "Gospodi, you're green! Is this your first time on the river?" Sveta teased as others laughed.

"First time on the Volga," Maria murmured as she looked at the soup rocking back and forth in her bowl.

"Take some bread, it will help until you get your sea legs," Sveta said as she handed Maria a small loaf.

Maria sat at a table, dipping the bread in her soup. She slowly felt better with a full stomach. She noticed the other passengers, some were eating, others were merchants accompanying their cargo to various ports on the River. For them, this was just another day of work, but for Maria every detail of the ship and people were new.

She took her bowl back to Sveta and tried to wash it, but Sveta brushed her aside.

"Will you replace me?" Sveta teased. "They have cleared the main deck. You can go up and see some of the villages along the river if you like." Sveta said as she began to clean a pile of bowls and pans.

Maria smiled and nodded in agreement. She headed to the top deck and found a comfortable space near the front to look out, watching one group of homes after another roll by on the banks of the river. Each village was unique, some larger and some quite small.

"How many lives, and how many stories each place must have." Maria thought.

The afternoon sun painted the landscape as each new village came into view. A dock with many ships, a quiet inlet leading to a distant village, the trail of chimney smoke tracing a path to a port side tavern. Maria imagined her life if she were to step off the boat and begin a life at this place or the next. With each new scene, she realized her life had become a random direction on an unknown path, but it also felt free with unlimited possibilities. She braided her hair to keep it out of the wind and dreamed of her future life in Neva.

Hours passed, and the smell of the evening's meal began to drift from below the deck. Several passengers and crew went below, but Maria felt content to remain and think about her father. She hoped to light a candle for him as soon and also imagined her mother making her way toward Neva at the same time.

"Perhaps she is one ship ahead of me or took a different route by land through Moscow." She thought.

The wind grew cold as the sun began to set on the Volga. The river was endless, each turn revealed another long stretch of waves and life along the bank. Maria cradled her arms around herself, wishing she had a coat. She looked back across the empty deck as she headed toward the stairs leading below deck.

A man stood at the bottom of the stairs and waited for her to complete her steps before walking upward. He had dark hair and green eyes with a serious face. She stepped off the staircase and looked at him with a nod of appreciation for waiting.

He smiled in return, and his face seemed to completely change. It was as if he was a different person when he smiled. Maria's eyes followed him as he walked past and climbed to the top deck. He had masculine features, his hands were thick from hard work, and his shoulders pushed against his clothing as he moved.

She found herself taking in each detail of his body, as he walked out of sight. Her sudden fascination puzzled her.

"Why am I looking so much at women and men?" she wondered.

She did not feel she needed more to eat, so she returned to her cabin. The few clothes she had were all dirty, so she decided to clean everything while she had the room to herself. She found a wash basin and made use of the water and soap left in view by Sveta.

The cold water made her hands ache as she twisted and squeezed the cloth. She took off her dress, and undergarments one by one until everything was washed and hanging on any available surface in the cabin.

She set the washtub aside, knowing she could not empty it without something to wear. Then she slipped into the bed to keep warm. The feeling of her naked skin sliding between the cold sheets gave her a boost of energy that faded as she grew warmer.

She was soon asleep, as the remaining sunlight faded orange to black through the window.

# Are you sleeping?

Maria awoke in her bed, still naked beneath the sheets as she heard the sound of people talking outside her room. Their voices were growing closer, and the clump of their footsteps announced them before the door swung open.

"Maria?!" whispered Sveta into the dark room as she giggled.

"Maria are you in here?" Sveta persisted as she led a man inside and closed the door.

"I think she's asleep, so let's not wake her" Sveta giggled in a voice that clearly had the influence of wine.

Maria was astonished; she was too embarrassed to say she was awake. It seemed better to pretend she was asleep and perhaps they would go somewhere else.

Sveta came over to Maria's bed and nudged her gently, "Ti spiish"? She whispered in a careless giggle.

The man's deep voice filled the cabin, as he pulled Sveta to the other side of the room, "Ladno, she is asleep, idi suda!" he said playfully.

Maria kept perfectly still; it was impossible escaping now without a tremendous embarrassment. She understood what might happen, and in the dim grey light of the moon that cast the window, she could see them embracing near Sveta's bed.

He was taller than her and had his hands around her waist, pulling her against him. Sveta seemed to resist him a bit, but as they kissed, her arms began to encircle him. Then her hands glided up his arms and shoulders until her fingers were running through his hair pulling him deeper into the kiss.

Maria felt the sensation of arousal building inside her as it had in the tavern when she watched through the wall as the girls satisfied their men. Only this time she didn't have to peak from a distance, it was just a few feet away, making it almost repulsive without wanting to stop watching.

"Davai," the man said hungrily as he pulled Sveta harder against his body.

Sveta stepped back from him and pulled her dress over her head, letting it drop to the floor.

The dim light seemed to caress her body at every curve. Her breasts disappeared into his hands as he touched her, kneeling down to taste her nipples in his mouth. Sveta caressed the back of his neck, holding him to her as he sucked her nipples. She tilted her head back as he held her in his arms, sliding his hand down her back, caressing every inch of her.

Maria strained to see his hand as he stroked his fingers up Sveta's thighs and then slid them between her legs. Sveta moaned as he touched her there, Maria felt her body throbbing as she witnessed the intimacy of the two lovers, camouflaged in the darkness.

She watched him kiss lower and lower down Sveta's body, leaving a trail of kisses that made Sveta's body quiver as he moved. The anticipation built with each kiss, making her wonder if he would continue further, then his eagerness was expressed as he suddenly shifted and buried his face between her legs. His strong hands cupped her round bottom, squeezing her flesh as his tongue slipped inside her wetness. Maria could hear him kissing her there, and the sound of his sucking was rewarded when Sveta gasped.

Sveta dug her fingers into his shoulders, it was too much for her to take and continue standing. She pulled him toward her bed and lay back waiting for him to satisfy her. Maria could see Sveta's body easily as the window was closer to her bed. The light made her skin look ghost like, and the view of her large nipples made an erotic contrast to the shape of her full round breasts.

The man untied his belt and let his clothes fall to the floor as he eagerly pulled his shirt off. Maria admired his masculine shape; he looked powerful compared to Sveta's nubile body. He had broad shoulders and a defined back that tapered slowly toward his waist. She felt on fire as she looked at his masculine buttocks, it looked as if it were chiseled from solid marble and she wanted to reach over and feel it but knew she could not.

He knelt on the bed, ready to take Sveta. Maria quietly turned her face, hoping to see the rest of his body.

"Why doesn't he turn this way?" she thought frustrated from the view. She wanted to see everything, all of him. Then she saw Sveta's hand sliding down his back, coaxing him on top of her. He slowly lowered over her and reached down to guide his throbbing flesh inside her.

Maria felt her breath failing her, as she watched him feeding his manhood to Sveta's hungry cave. Sveta gasped and whispered, "Slowww, you're so big!", As he moved deeper inside her. His body moved closer and closer until he covered her beneath him, Sveta's hands traced down his back and clawed at his ass in ecstasy.

From Maria's view, they were an entanglement of legs and arms, joined in the center. They moved together, like a language without words, only gestures, touches, and gasps between movements. It was beautiful and erotic to watch, and seeing them secretly gave an intensity that excited Maria even more.

The man lifted himself by his arms, hovering over Sveta as she wrapped her legs around his waist. He began to thrust his shaft into her. His back and ass became a rhythm of flexing muscle accelerating in each repetition. He rocked Sveta firmly against her bed and headboard with growing strength.

"Surely they know the noise they are making would wake me up!" Maria thought as her hands began sliding quietly under the blanket, finding her erect nipples with her fingers. She pinched at them, wanting to imagine the pleasures taking place just out of reach. She was so aroused, so eager to feel the pleasure of sex and attention but kept absolutely quiet to maintain her secret view.

Then her eyes caught the gaze of Sveta, who was now watching her as the man continued pumping his body into her. She could see Maria, and kept her eyes directed at Maria knowing she was watching. A slight smile crept over Sveta's face as if she had gotten what she wanted, enjoying the twist of being seen.

The man began to groan more intensely, with each thrust his voice grew louder, building to a final conclusion. Suddenly Sveta pushed the man off of her bed and onto the floor.

"Wait! You have to finish another way!" She whispered as she got on her knees and turned him toward her mouth. Sveta seemed to position her body like an actor on a stage, she had situated herself and the man to be turned just enough for Maria to see their crescendo of pleasure.

Sveta eagerly took his hard shaft to her lips and slid it deep into her mouth.

"Finally!" Maria thought excitedly, as she could see the rest of his body.

His penis was firm and looked massive compared to Sveta's hands and mouth as she pleasured him. His strong legs were like iron that rose up from the ground to present his impressive shaft. She wondered if all men kept such wonders in their pants, and marveled at how big they could grow from a woman's touch.

The man placed his hand on Sveta's head, guiding her to take all of him, it looked impossible to fit so much in her mouth, but Sveta slid him deep inside until her lips were at the end of his shaft. The man moaned in appreciation and stroked his fingers through her hair. He slid his hand to the back of her head and pulled at her hair, it looked almost brutal to Maria, but Sveta seemed to like it, gasping as she slid off of it and quickly returning.

Maria noticed Sveta's hand was between her legs, stroking herself as she took the man in her mouth.

"Finish me, I am burning!" the man said.

Sveta smiled as she squeezed his cock firmly in her grip and stroked him twisting her hand around his shaft. "Shhhh" Sveta moaned softly...reminding him, they were not alone. "I want it in your mouth" he sighed, as she responded eagerly.

Her hands moved quicker as she took the tip of his penis, and sucked it while she stroked him. Her other hand cupped her breasts and pinched her nipple. She was trying to bring him to the point of no return....and then he suddenly grabbed her head, pulling her hair and thrusting his cock deep into her mouth.

He gasped as she tried not to choke from his strength, then she placed her hands on each side of his hips and pulling herself off his shaft with a mouthful of his juice. She let it drip from her mouth back onto his penis and onto her breasts, as he caught his breath. She slowly stroked him as he placed his hand on the wall to keep from falling over.

Maria's hand had found its way down her body, reaching the place that begged for attention after watching the interlude unfold in front of her. As her fingers began to slide between her legs, she felt intense wetness, waiting to greet her welcome fingers. Her pulse seemed to push through her skin, where she began to stroke her fingers, curious and eager to see where this burning pleasure would take her, but it would have to wait until she was alone.

Sveta looked like an enchantress; she had taken him on a journey and made him give her everything she wanted. Maria watched her as she stroked her hands through the juices that covered her breasts; it was like a trophy to Sveta. She seemed content to control him from her knees as she stopped stroking him, and reached for her dress to wipe herself off.

Maria watched in a state of amazement; an entire world seemed to exist in the bedroom that escaped all boundaries of life, time and space. Her interest and curiosity to learn more grew by the minute.

The man dressed quickly and prepared to leave as Sveta retreated to her bed. He sat beside her and quietly placed something in her hand.

"No, it's not right." Sveta said, "You make me feel like..."

The man interrupted as it clenched his hand around hers, to keep her from returning it. "I know the captain doesn't pay you much, take it for your mother if not for yourself." He said, as he kissed her hand and quickly exited the cabin.

Sveta held her hand open revealing a few coins that reflected in the light. She sighed deeply and set them beside her bed. She looked over at Maria, seeing her eyes closed and assumed she had fallen asleep.

Sveta looked at the ceiling of her cabin, it was dark and unremarkable in the night light. She seemed very far away from the place and time she was currently in. She wiped her body once more with her dress and set it on the floor as she pulled a blanket over her bare breasts. She rolled towards the cabin wall and sighed as she drifted into sleep.

Maria quietly turned in her bed, her body still alive with hunger she could hardly contain, but she knew she had to remain silent. She ached to stroke herself but there was no way she could attempt it undetected.

She slid one of her hands to her breast and imagined a man lying beside her, holding her like that. The warmth of his body against hers and the freedom to make him hard whenever she wanted. How amazing the intimacy seemed between a man and a woman, such an escape from ordinary life to something exquisite and sensual.

Her mind raced through the images of men and women she had seen in the last few days. So much to learn and explore and yet, she couldn't imagine herself with anyone unless she loved him. The mix of life as she had seen at home and the world she was now in made all her expectations swim in her thoughts until she too fell asleep.

# Port Mologo

Maria woke up and looked over toward Sveta's empty bed. She had already left to work in the kitchen, leaving everything sorted and cleaned as if nothing had happened. Maria felt a strange awkwardness about facing Sveta after watching her with her lover the night before. But as long as Sveta did not know that Maria was awake, it seemed harmless to have secretly watched their encounter.

Maria's clothes had dried overnight, she folded them for storage and went below to the kitchen to get something to eat. She was starving after skipping the previous evening's meal while doing her laundry. She heard Sveta's voice talking with people as they were given their ration of food. The room was filled with merchants and crew members, all struggling to find a space to sit or stand while eating their oatmeal.

"And here's my sleepy cabin mate!" Sveta said with a cheerful voice, "Slept like the dead last night I think?"

"Da..." sighed Maria as she held her bowl up for a helping of oatmeal.

Sveta filled her bowl until it was almost overflowing, then handed Maria some raisins.

"Shh," Sveta whispered as she motioned with a finger over lips not to tell anyone.

Maria understood that this was an extra kindness that others did not receive, "Spacibo Sveta," She replied.

"Na zdorovie, hope we didn't wake you last night." She giggled as she winked at Maria.

Maria's face ran flush with embarrassment as she tried to pretend ignorance of Sveta's comment and rushed toward the stairs to eat her meal on the top deck.

As she emerged from below, the fresh air blew across her face and through her hair. It was crisp and refreshing with a slight scent of spice in the breeze. She found her comfortable space at the front of the ship and looked at the towns and ships that passed by. The ship was much closer to the shore than before, and more details could be seen.

"We'll be in port for a few hours today if you want to stretch your legs?" came the voice of the quartermaster. He pointed forward to a large pier and harbor where the ship was headed.

"What's the name of the town? Maria asked.

"Mologo" he replied.

Maria thanked him and finished her oatmeal. She wondered if perhaps her mother had made it this far already. Perhaps her mother was also in Mologo, and they could continue their journey together. Her heart filled with hope as she went to prepare for going ashore.

Sveta was in the cabin when she walked in. Maria smiled but had difficult looking Sveta in the eyes. She felt ashamed for watching her and pretending to be asleep. At the moment it had been exciting, but now it made her feel wrong and awkward.

Sveta noticed and asked "Something wrong?"

"Net" Maria quickly responded, "I was just thinking about looking for my mother when we pull into port. It's possible she made it here already."

"Oh, I didn't realize you were traveling to meet your Mother. I can help you look if you like? I know Mologo very well." Sveta said kindly.

Maria started to decline her invitation but realized she didn't know this city at all. "That would be very kind of you, thank you," Maria responded as she turned to look Sveta in the eyes.

Maria felt overwhelmed with a need to confess what she had seen the previous night. "Sveta, last night I..." she began.

"Masha, I know...we were impossible to ignore and I'm sorry about that. I had too much to drink, and he hasn't seen me for several months, we just got carried away" Sveta said, "Besides it made me feel excited that someone might see us, it's more umm...intense?" she giggled as she embraced Maria.

"You forgive me?" Sveta asked cheerfully.

"Konechno," Maria sighed in relief.

They both paused in silence, then Sveta smiled and asked, "So... you *did* you watch us!?"

Maria felt her face turn red again as they both burst into laughter, "mDa!", she giggled as she playfully made a guilty face.

The two began to laugh like sisters, immersed in the excitement at the reception of each confession.

Maria looked curiously at Sveta as the ship listed to one side for a moment, then a loud thud was heard along its side.

"We're in port!" Sveta said, "Let's go look for your Mother!"

The two began chatting as they walked off the ship and headed toward the shops and town square. They felt themselves in that rare moment when new friends are made, and everything feels alive and free. The complimentary mix of blonde and brunette, smiling as they walked in port caught many men's eyes, but they ignored them all and kept a fast pace toward the line of shops along the river bank.

"If your mother is traveling north she would definitely come through Mologo. All the ships stop here because this is where the rivers intersect on the way to Neva." Sveta said confidently, guiding Maria through the busy port.

Barrels and boxes were stacked in all directions as ships loaded their freight. The port appeared like a giant dance of cargo and people, each moving in a different direction at a hurried pace. The smells and sounds were all so foreign to Maria, as she often stopped to see something new or read the markings on the crates.

"You can read?" marveled Sveta.

"Da, my mother is a school teacher." She replied confidently.

"You're so lucky! I only know the ship symbols, never learned text, but I'm good with numbers." Sveta said.

"What about your father, what does he do?" Sveta asked.

Maria paused; it was the first time she had spoken about her father's death since the night he was killed. "He is a...was a beekeeper and farmer until he was  murdered by the Tatars." She said softly.

Sveta realized she had made a mistake in asking such a question, "I'm so sorry, I didn't realize he was..." She said trying to find the right words.

"Thank you" Maria interrupted, "I still can't believe it." She sighed.

The two continued walking at a slower pace as Maria shared the story of Alex's death, how he was a hero for saving her and now she was desperate to find her mother as she fled from the Tatar controlled region of Russia.

"This port is too busy for the soldiers to keep watch, so you're safe here," Sveta assured Maria.

Maria wished to change the subject, "So you seem to be free to go into port, doesn't the captain fear you will run away?" she asked.

"Well, he has the contract on my father's debt and knows where my mother is, which keeps me from running away, but he gives me special privileges because I take care of him when he asks for it." replied Sveta.

"Take care of him, how?" Maria said in a teasing voice.

Sveta blushed as she raised an eyebrow and spoke in a sarcastic voice. "Oh, yesss...you're So big... give it to me! You mad beast!"

"Big?" Maria mused.

Sveta held up her smallest finger, bending it limply, "Enormous" she replied in a high pitched tone.

The two of them burst into laughter as passing citizens walked around them on the crowded streets. They visited several shops, makers of dresses, coats, shoes, confections and pastries. In each place, they received no news of Maria's mother. Maria described her mother and left the store owners with the message that she would continue to Neva, should her mother appear in the following days.

As they walked back to the ship, Maria was sad that she hadn't found her mother or had any news of her whereabouts. Sveta could see her sad face and wanted to cheer her up. She pulled Maria into a nearby store and purchased some honey for her, "To remind you of home" Sveta said.

Maria's eyes filled with tears as she held the clay jar of honey close to her heart. She truly missed both her parents and felt so alone without them. But her new found friend gave her inspiration to keep going and make the most of her days. Maria knew her father and mother had done all they could to get her to freedom, and she didn't want to disappoint them by giving up. She had to continue on the journey to Neva.

As she and Sveta walked toward the ship, she asked Sveta about her life and how she felt about life onboard the ship.

"I'll lose my best years to this crazy life, I know it. By the time I'm done paying my father's debt, I'll be too old for most men to want me as a wife. Although some have said, they would take me as soon as I'm done. I won't believe in that until the time comes." Sveta said sadly.

"But if that's the way of it, why should I suffer and go without a man's attention? Most of them are very generous and bring me nice things. Of course, they have wives back home, I'm just someone to fill in that need for variety while they're away." She continued.

Maria interrupted, "What about love? Don't you want love?" She said kindly as she placed her hand on Sveta's back.

Sveta paused, "Of course I want to be loved and to love. But that time is not now, it's somewhere in the future when I can have a say over where I go and who I'll be with."

Maria could hear the sorrow in Sveta's voice, she knew she ached for love just like anyone would. Perhaps that's why she allowed men to have her in bed so she could feel something other than despair.

"It's a hard life," Maria said calmly

"Indeed it is." Sveta replied, "And that's why I drink!"

They laughed and continued back onboard the ship just as it was making ready to set sail. The new cargo was on the deck, and other items had been offloaded. The captain stood at the mast and shouted at Sveta as she walked toward the downward staircase, "Don't wait till the last line is cast off to come back aboard!"

"Sorry captain - won't happen again!" She replied sarcastically.

"Da, you say that every time!" he blasted as he reviewed the papers for the cargo.

Maria returned to the cabin and placed the jar of honey by her bed as Sveta changed her clothes before going to the galley.

Sveta's naked body didn't embarrass Maria as it had before; she was becoming used to seeing her cabin mate this way. It seemed almost natural to look at her now.

Sveta pulled her clothes off and quickly washed with a wet towel. She stood with a small pan of water on the floor, dipping the cloth in the water then making long strokes along her body. Maria laid face down on her bed, propping herself up on her elbows as her ankles crossed and lifted up and down as she talked.

Sveta told her more about the ship, the crew and the ports that they would see on the way. A trail of water trickled from Sveta's shoulder, down across her breast, following a path unique to her body, slowing as it ran past her hips and down her leg. The cold water made her nipples harden as she finished washing her front.

Sveta noticed Maria was watching her closely as they talked, she turned her back to Maria and playfully asked, "Wash my back?"

Maria felt nervous but stood and walked toward Sveta, "Hold your hair." Maria said as she reached for the wet towel.

Sveta turned and lifted her hands to pull her hair out of the way. Maria began to slowly wipe from her neck, across her shoulders and down her back. Sveta sighed from the cold cloth against her skin. Maria's hand continued down Sveta's back until she reached the curves of her bottom. She paused there for a moment, wondering if she should stop.

She held her breath and continued down Sveta's body, gliding the towel over every inch of her backside. She couldn't help but to look at every detail of Sveta's body. She had never closely seen how a grown woman looked unclothed, her mother had always kept covered, and her friends at home had moved on or died before reaching that age.

Her eyes took in the softness of Sveta's skin, how her legs flowed upward to the soft hair that delicately covered her most intimate flesh. Maria wondered if her body looked the same, so impressive and wondrous.

"I think my legs are clean dear," Sveta said as Maria realized she had remained too long in one place.

Maria quickly stood up to return the towel. Sveta smiled and thanked her, turning toward her to take the towel from her hand. Maria's eyes glanced down and saw that Sveta's nipples were absolutely firm with arousal. She quickly looked back into Sveta's eyes.

Neither lady said a word, they simply realized they had shared an intimate moment that was unexpected and pleasant. Sveta reached for her working dress and Maria returned to her bed.

"See you at dinner!" Sveta said as she put on her shoes and headed for the door.

"See you then!" Maria responded.

The new found friendship between the two was filled with energy to explore and share. It was a comfort that made them feel closer and more confident about their lives. Someone they could say anything to and understand each other as they were, not as they should be.

Maria opened her travel sack and found the small script she had carried since leaving her farm. She whispered the words in Latin thinking about their meaning for the first time, "In principio creavit Deus caelum et terram, In the beginning, God created the heavens and the earth." She reached for a brush and pulled it through her hair as she continued reading in fascination at the creation of woman.

"In the beginning, the last thing God made was a woman, the final crown of all creation, no wonder our bodies are so inspired to look at and touch." She thought.

The light in the room faded as the sun set on the Volga with the Kupala catching the last breeze northward, carrying it toward the next stop along the river.

# Fireflies on the Volga

The smell from the kitchen began to permeate the entire ship like a silent announcement that it would soon be time to eat. Maria decided to get some fresh air before making her way below. She walked up the stairs expecting an icy blast of air but to her surprise, a warm breeze lifted her senses as she took the final steps up onto the deck. She smiled as it still felt like daytime under a canopy of stars.

The cloudless sky revealed the majestic constellations as a full moon sat just above the horizon. She could still see the lights from Port Mologo in the distance, but her eyes were drawn to the river banks where fireflies danced along the water's edge, pulsing their locations to each other in a celebration of the last warm days of autumn.

It reminded her of the stories her mother had told her when she was a little girl; fairies and magic creatures granting wishes to lost children in the woods. She imagined herself encountering such a creature, and what she would wish for. Immediately she realized she would want to go back in time and change one decision, to remain on her father's cart and reverse all the events that followed. She could still see him on the street trying to stop all the guards as they chased her. An unarmed man standing valiantly against an army to save his daughter.

She felt unworthy of such devotion and sacrifice by both her father and mother who had done everything possible to get her to safety.

"If nothing else I have to honor their wishes." She thought. "I have to live a life worthy of their love and sacrifice."

For the first time, it occurred to her that her mother may not be on her way to Neva. "Surely she must have been stung dozens of times while my escape." Maria thought. "Anyone with that kind of injury would not be able to run or hide for very long."

Maria began to recall childhood incidents where children had gotten into the beehives and were stung as a result. Her father had always warned her that her friends should not play near the hives but of course, they didn't listen, hoping to steal some honey and get away unstung. Most of the children recovered from their injuries in a few days, but she remembered one of her friends that almost died from a single sting, like a devil was choking him from the inside.

She tried to remember a time when her mother had been stung, and could not recall it. In fact, she remembered that her mother had always avoided going near the hives. "What if mama had such a reaction or knew how dangerous it would be for her to be stung at all?" She wondered.

She felt the back of her neck tingle with the realization that she may be searching for her mother in vain. "Maybe she never left!" Maria thought as her mind raced through all possible scenarios. "What would they do to her, if they caught her?"

At that moment, a warm breeze with the scent of wildflowers and honey blew through her hair. It smelled exactly like the breezes that came across the fields in Rostov. She felt her fears soothe for a moment, but it left her with such a yearning to be reunited with her family. The once simple life in a small farmhouse had become a faraway heaven, fading quickly in the passing wind.

"She has to be alive, I just know she is" Maria asserted as she turned her attention back to the fireflies.  As far as she could see along the river ahead, fireflies lit the way as an invitation to continue on the journey. She closed her eyes for a moment and wished to find her mother, just in case the fireflies were listening.

The quartermaster and a few deckhands were moving barrels below. The new cargo was transitioned on various decks unless it would be offloaded soon. It made sense to her as it gave more room on the deck for the men to sleep.

The quartermaster noticed Maria sitting by herself and the sad look on her face. "Is everything alright, Miss?" He said calmly.

"Yes, thank you I am fine." She said realizing her sadness was no secret.

She stood to go below and get something to eat but had to wait until the men finished with the barrels.

"Why is it necessary that everything goes below?" She asked the quartermaster "Is it to give more room for the men? Maria asked.

"That and to protect it from damage during storms" the quartermaster answered. "If cargo is damaged the captain has to pay for it, so you can understand why we are so careful." The quartermaster explained as he watched the men working.

"Ah, makes sense," Maria added.

"That won't fit that way! I told you to turn it around before you go down the stairs!" The quartermaster shouted at the men. "I better get back to work, have a good evening, Miss."

Maria nodded and returned to her seat, waiting for them to finish. It seemed a very hard life aboard the ship; everyone was on a tight schedule with very little room for rest. She wondered how people could spend years or a lifetime in such a trade.

The men finally finished, and the quartermaster returned. "You can go down now, Miss," he said kindly.

"Thank you, I was wondering about this trade you have. It seems so difficult, how is it that men can do this for so many years?" She said curiously.

"Ah, well..." the quartermaster replied as he paused, "It's certainly not a job for everyone I'll give you that. But we only work when the river flows. This will be our last run of the year, once the Volga freezes we'll be waiting for the spring thaw."

"The whole river freezes?" Maria said in surprise.

"Da! Ice as deep as a man is tall and jagged on top like frozen rocks! All ships stay in port until spring, then it's a new river, it changes and flows differently each year." He said in a kind voice that reminded her of her father.

"It sounds a lot like farming," Maria said, "Everything is seasonal… So what do you do when the river is frozen?" She asked curiously.

"I spend time with my wife and children in Neva" he replied. "I hardly see them from spring through fall."

"That's important," Maria said in a supportive tone.

"Da, we used to live in Yaroslavl but after the Tatars had come it was no longer safe. Neva is outside of their control, but they allow us on the river to keep supply lines moving."

Maria nodded, understanding all too well the situation he was describing.

"Best you get below Miss, the food will be gone if you wait too long." He said cheerfully.

Maria smiled and walked toward the stairs turning to wave to the quartermaster, "It was nice talking to you, and have a good night… Oh, and my name is Maria!" She said extending her hand.

"The pleasure was mine, Miss, enjoy your dinner." He replied.

Maria continued making her way down the stairs, thinking it odd the man had not given her his name, she walked towards the smell and sounds of the kitchen. She could hear the chatter of the ship's crew and merchants all talking on top of each other in the noisy room.  There was no place to sit, and everyone pushed and shoved to get closer to the food.

Maria felt intimidated to be surrounded by so many men; it reminded her of the Tater court in Rostov. The men had the same kinds of looks on their faces as she pushed by them, some annoyed, some curious and many looking at her with hungry eyes. She felt her appetite fade and turned to leave the room.

"Skatina takoe! Let the young lady through, ya bunch of cows!" Barked the captain.

It was the first time she had seen him face to face. He was shorter than she imagined, with wide shoulders and a stocky build. His face was rough and tan from a life on the river, he had deep wrinkles around his eyes and a white beard that needed trimming.

"Forgive us, lass were not accustomed to delicate young ladies on the ship." Said the captain in a boisterous voice.

"Shto?!" Came a woman's voice from the kitchen. It was clearly Sveta listening in and protesting in her playful manner.

The men burst into laughter and moved aside to let Maria through. She smiled, appreciating the accommodation and moved toward the large bowl of soup Sveta had prepared. She leaned over the bowl, admiring the dark red color of the soup, it was borsch, and it smelled delicious.

Sveta appeared from the kitchen and quickly prepared a small bowl for Maria. "We took on fresh beets in Mologo!" Sveta said excitedly. "This is my mother's recipe, but we've already run out of cream, thanks to all these hungry bastards." She stated in a voice loud enough for them to hear. The men cheered, and it became evident that everyone got along like one big family with playful insults.

Maria felt more comfortable in the room when Sveta was nearby. She smiled and turned, looking for a place to sit.

The captain turned and swatted a man on the back of his head, "Gennady, make room!" He charred.

A young man stood and made eye contact with Maria. He was clearly the youngest of the entire crew and immediately offered his seat without objection. Maria smiled as she walked towards the seat, noticing the young man continued his gaze on her.

"Thank you," Maria said sweetly.

Gennady paused for a moment, appearing nervous, "Preyatnoga apetita". He said quickly.

"Gena, where are my cargo records?" The captain said as he cleared his throat.

"Da Captain, right away," Gennady said as he quickly exited the room.

The captain came and sat next to Maria. "Welcome aboard, Miss. I saw you come on in Yaroslavl, but I had my hands full with these greedy merchants." He said.

"Thank you, your ship is...very nice!" Maria said nervously, unsure what else to say to him. He appeared as if he wanted something from her but she could not imagine what it would be.

"Ah, she was a fine ship in her day, but each year she's more rotten and gone through with worms than the year before. Held together with pitch and patch." He said in a regretful voice. "Are you staying with us all the way to Neva?" The captain asked.

"Yes sir, that is my intention." She replied

"Very good, we'll get you there safe and sound." He added as he stood to leave the room. "Oh, and be mindful of Svetlana, she's a great cook but full of mischief!" He said jokingly.

"Ya slishu!" Sveta's voice boomed from the kitchen.

The captain chuckled, knowing she could hear him.

Maria suddenly remembered how Sveta described the captain's small penis. Her face turned red as she couldn't help but stare at him, this strong man with such a humbling secret.

"I'll be mindful sir, thank you for your advice," Maria said charmingly as she held her giggle.

The captain turned without another word and began pushing his way through the crowd. "Make a hole!" He bellowed as he exited the room.

Maria finished her soup and returned the bowl to Sveta.

"Spacibo, it was delicious, reminds me of home," Maria said.

Sveta smiled in appreciation, "Na zdorovie!" She said.

Maria made her way out of the room, this time, the men instinctively knew to clear the way. She felt recognized and respected by their gesture but kept her eyes down as she felt uncomfortable when she saw how they looked at her.

She returned to her cabin and felt the weight of the day overtake her. She laid on her bed and felt warm and relaxed as the ship rocked its way northward on the Volga. The sound of the oars creaked their familiar rhythm beneath the decks as she began to fall asleep.

# The Power of Words

Maria awoke as she heard Sveta entering the cabin. Sveta appeared exhausted, and her clothes were dirty from cooking and cleaning in the kitchen. She seemed to be in a hurry and frustrated by her tasks.

"You've got the right idea," Sveta said as she noticed Maria waking up. "I wish I could get some sleep."

"You're not done?" Maria asked.

"No, the captain wants to see me, and I don't think it's about my cooking," Sveta replied.

Sveta sorted through her few dresses, in an attempt to find something appropriate to wear. She kicked off her shoes and sat on her bed taking a deep breath. She paused, staring at the floor as if her mind was overwhelmed with thoughts.

"Can I help?" said Maria

"What, you want to go visit the captain instead? Be my guest!" Sveta said sarcastically.

Maria laughed slightly and said, "I meant to help you get ready" as she reached for her hairbrush and walked towards Sveta.

"Oh, that's nice," Sveta said in a relieved voice.

Maria began to comb Sveta's long brown hair, she had to make tiny strokes as the steam in the kitchen had made it brittle and tangled. Sveta turned her back to Maria to make the brushing easier, she was delighted to have such attention.

"You don't have to do this you know?" Sveta said calmly as she reclined and closed her eyes, taking a rest when she could get it.

"I don't mind, besides your hair is very pretty when it's brushed," Maria replied

"And when it's not...?" Sveta jabbed sarcastically.

"C'mon don't be like that," Maria said, knowing how women always destroy their compliments.

"Sveta, I'm curious how it works with him." Maria asked, "Do you just show up and do it, or does he talk to you?"

Sveta felt embarrassed by the honesty of the question but realized there was no intended harm in her words. "Sometimes we talk a lot, others I'm just a servant doing his bidding," She said regretfully.

"There are times I feel more like a wife, or how I think a wife would feel, taking care of her husband. I listen to his problems, rub his shoulders and say it will be fine, that he is clever, and he calms down." Sveta continued.

"He seems kind of rough, does he hurt you?" Maria asked.

"I suppose to some he would be rough, but I am used to such men. His hands are hard, but usually, he is kind." Sveta said as she decided to share more than she intended, "It's not just the sex he wants. Actually, a man with power is very different. He wants your words as much as your body. You can't just lay there and wait for him to finish, that will only make him angry. He needs you to say something to make him feel you...even after you're gone."

Maria was surprised at what she was learning; she had never heard such an idea. The curiosity in her awoke as a thousand questions filled her mind.

"What do you say!?" She asked in an impatient voice.

Sveta giggled as she knew this question was coming, "I try to think of new things to keep myself from growing bored but in general, they are all the same idea. You see, when a man looks at a woman he feels hunger inside him, a craving that he cannot contain. It's like a fire that grows out of control until he has her... or thinks of her until he finishes with his hand." She said as she burst out laughing.

The two of them giggled like school girls as Maria finished her hair and reached for a dress Sveta could wear. Sveta pulled her dirty dress over her head and reached for a damp cloth to wipe the sweat and dirt from her body. As she wiped, she continued her explanation.

"So... I have to think like a man and say the words that are like... perfect breasts for his mind. Words he will want to touch and feel, days or months later. In fact, sometimes, I think it makes them finish so much faster when I talk to them like that!" Sveta said as she dried off and pulled the clean dress over her head.

"Like what?!" Maria shouted, feeling frustrated by the delay in the answer.

Sveta laughed, "Oh you mean exact words? Well let's see..." she paused.

Maria's anticipation was overwhelming; she felt she was learning a great secret that would give her a magic power to use on an unknown future love. Her mind became open to learning as if she was being entrusted with a great mysterious secret full of power.

"I'll tell him I want him or need him, that his body is strong, or he is so big or hard, like I've never seen or touched a man before, and if he is close to finishing I'll beg him to come, but only if he is out of me, because I don't want to get pregnant!" Sveta said, as the two of them sat together on the bed.

"I know it seems strange, but I feel proud when they finish, because I know I did that, I took control of them and made their body produce that magic juice!" Sveta said as her eyes sparkled.

Maria's face twinged, "Eww, that's disgusting!" She said in horror.

Sveta laughed, "Oh believe me I used to think the same way, especially at first, but now I crave it! And if I were married I would want it inside me every day, there is just something about it that makes a woman feel better...more...regular, you know?"

"Really?" Maria said in amazement.

Sveta's eyes lit up with excitement, "Really!"

They both stood up smiling and laughing at their conversation. Maria primped and groomed Sveta's hair and adjusted her dress. The look of a servant had faded away, Sveta's hair had a slight curl as it draped down her shoulders. Her dress revealed the fullness of her body, feminine, elegant and beautiful.

"Irresistible," Maria said with a smile as Sveta changed her shoes.

"Thanks, I don't know what time I'll be back, depends on if he's in a talking mood," Sveta said as she walked towards the door.

Maria smiled and straightened up the room. "I understand; I hope he is nice tonight." She said unsure if it was appropriate or not.

Sveta smiled and exited the cabin. There was such energy when the two of them opened up and shared parts of their life. Maria had never experienced such a relationship except with her mother. But this was different, she didn't feel inhibited to ask such questions and since her time in the tavern, her curiosity about sex had preoccupied her mind.

As she heard Sveta's footsteps walking away from the cabin, she imagined what her new friend's evening would be like. A knock on the door, the captain bidding her come in, and then how he would touch her or what she would say to him. She remembered how Sveta looked on the night she brought the man into their cabin. The way she touched him so confidently and took his hardness into her hand, and his juice in her mouth. It was hard to think of this as erotic or desirable, but she valued Sveta's insight.

"Maybe this was something a woman grows to wish for or demand?" She thought.

Maria felt the eagerness to explore her body, she had the cabin to herself and pulled her dress off. Her hands slid across her body, she felt every inch of herself and wondered how she compared to Sveta. She knew her breasts were smaller than Sveta's, but Maria was slimmer with longer hair. She took the hand mirror by Sveta's bed and looked at it, as she held it out and slowly lowered it down her body. She could see her familiar curves, just as she had admired in Sveta. Her hand lowered and she watched the reflection of her womanhood in the glass.

She felt aroused in her exploration, her hands sliding over her skin as she looked into the mirror as if it were her lover's eyes. She slid her fingers between her legs and felt herself wet with desire. She wanted to visit the pleasure she had discovered while watching the lovers in the dark, the couples in the Tavern and even the hungry looks from the crew.

She eagerly climbed into her bed, blowing out the single candle lighting the room, greeting the cover of darkness like an invitation to go on an erotic journey in her mind. She felt her nipples harden and pinched them noticing how it made her body tingle all the way down to her wetness. She pinched harder and harder to see what would happen until she found the limit where the pain was greater than pleasure.

Her fingers eagerly rushed between her legs. The slippery juices of her body made them glide quickly over her flesh. She spread and pulled her lips wide to expose the firm spot that cried out for attention. Each time she pressed it, she felt shivers of pleasure echoing through her lower body. She stroked it and teased it as it became firmer and aroused. Her other hand slid down and found the opening where she felt such a desire to be taken. Her finger slid inside her warm body, dripping wet and eager to be filled.

She carefully slid her finger inside her inner walls, it was exquisite and filled her with desire. Both her hands worked feverishly, circling and pressing as she ventured deeper inside her wetness. A warm glow began to spread across her body as she felt her breath escaping. It was as if she was flying, higher and higher, faster, stronger with each stroke and everything in her being urged her to keep going and find how this journey ended.

Images of the man she had watched with Sveta raced through her mind, his powerful body, his muscles and large member penetrating her over and over, and then she imagined what it would feel like inside her own body...that throbbing flesh, filling her as her hands squeezed his arms and held on to him until he came inside her.

Suddenly her face felt hot, she was shaking with excitement and hunger for more as she curled her fingers deep inside her wetness, feeling a pleasure so intense she couldn't contain it. Her fingers were soaked in her juice as she made her body into a playground for pleasure. The thought of a man, coming inside her suddenly felt amazing, to have that pleasure of his hard shaft thrusting and bursting like an explosion of power made her quiver and moan.

Then she felt something new, terrifying and wonderful at once, taking over her body as she moaned out loud in ecstasy.

There was no turning back, no escape, only complete surrender to the demand she felt as her body tightened around her fingers and squeezed in wave after wave of incredible pleasure. She held her breath and suddenly the world stopped as she felt her soul escape for a moment then slowly transcend back into her body, carefully, lowering her back to the bed in ecstasy.

She raced to catch her breath as if no air was left in the room. She gasped and slowly rested her hands, ceasing all movements as her hips arched and twisted from the echoes of her orgasm. This was heaven, paradise, and she wanted to remain in such a trance of pleasure. She closed her eyes and imagined a man, softly kissing her body now, touching her and whispering things in her ear. How his body would feel next to her and the warmth of his touch. This was more than sexual exploration now, it was a secret way to visit her future lover. And she couldn't image denying him anything he wanted.

Maria's thoughts faded into dreams as she laid in her bed. The ship gently rocked and cradled her into a deep sleep where she drifted in images of a man's bare body and his hands on her. It was the first time she had dreamt of such erotic and powerful sensations. As if a fire had been lit inside her soul that would not easily be controlled or extinguished.

# A Storm at Midnight

A rushing sound crashed and knocked at the sides of the ship as Maria awoke in her bed. She felt the room spinning and dropping as she realized something was very wrong. A few seconds later another crash from the opposite side followed by creaking boards and shouting from the deck above.

She quickly got dressed, stumbling about the cabin as she tried to keep her balance. She looked out the small window, but there was no light only the loud crash of waves knocking the ship in all directions. She could hear the oarsman moving things about on the deck below, everyone clamoring and shouting.

The door burst open as Sveta returned. "Good you're up!" She said quickly.

"What has happened, did we crash into something?" Maria asked.

"It's a storm; it came in fast before we could get to the port so we will have to ride it out," Sveta said as she put on her coat.

"I have to get to the kitchen and secure everything, or it will be a mess in the morning! You can stay here or come with me, but it's dreadful at the front of the ship." Sveta added as the floor seemed to drop from under them and suddenly boom as it caught the next wave.

"I'll go with you!" Maria replied as she grabbed her shoes.

The two made their way down to the kitchen where pots and pans were rolling in all directions. It was dark and confusing as people shouted at each other to act quickly.

"Can we light a candle?" Maria asked in frustration as she stumbled over the cookware.

"No it's too dangerous, no fires are allowed when there is a storm, it turns the ship into a burning prison if it gets out of control!" Sveta replied as she reached and felt around in the kitchen blindly searching for the nearest object. "I know it seems impossible but grab everything that moves!"

Maria felt a large pan rolling towards her and put her hand out to catch it. Her fingers were greeted by a tumbling iron pot that rolled into her grasp. Piece by piece they held on to the walls for balance grabbing the tumbling cookery until the sea of clanging metal was silenced. They sat on the floor of the galley, listening to the ship creaking against the thud of the river's waves.

Sveta sighed, "I knew I should have locked everything down before I left the kitchen." She said with a sarcastic laugh. "Thanks for your help, though!"

"You're welcome." Maria said, "I think the storm is calming!"

"We're lower on the ship, it's not as noticeable down here," replied Sveta.

The captain shouted orders from above the decks that were repeated by the quartermaster through the hallways down to the oarsman, "Hard port, only port!"

The shuffle of extending and retracting oars drummed through the ships timbers in response to the orders. The crew was in complete unison with every word that came from the captain's lips.

"What are they doing?" asked Maria.

"The storm is pushing us toward shore, so they drop the sail and steer us into the current to keep us straight." Said Sveta as she motioned for them to sit against the wall.

Their eyes adjusted to the limited visibility in the dark galley. The clouds moved quickly, letting occasional moonlight work its way through the windows and stairwells.

"Are we safe?" Maria asked nervously.

"Sure, it's a lot of spinning about but the captain's good at keeping us away from danger. You realize why he is the captain at times like this." Sveta said admirably.

Maria listened to her words and began to realize Sveta had feelings for the captain, regardless of her objections to being his servant. She thought to ask about the evening's meeting but decided this was a question that should wait.

Flashes of lightning silently lit the hallways followed moments later by explosive thunder that shook every part of the ship. Maria had seen many thunderstorms during summers on her farm, but she had never heard one so fierce and close. She moved closer to Sveta feeling safer near her friend.

Sveta put her arm around Maria, "Ladno, just another day on the river" She said as she patted her back.

Maria's arms wrapped around Sveta, she couldn't help the fear of such an unknown experience as it shook and terrified her. Sveta realized Maria was still a young girl, tender and easily frightened. Her womanly instincts to nurture took over as she held Maria in the dark.

Lightning flashed again in an almost blinding brightness then absolute silence. Finally, a dark distant roll of thunder echoed across the sky booming and shaking with less intensity. Sveta kissed Maria's head and patted her back, "It's moving away from us, we can go back to the cabin soon," Sveta said reassuringly.

Maria looked up feeling encouraged and felt calmed by Sveta's words.

"Thanks." She replied, "I've never experienced such a storm in my life."

The ship began to slow its hard shifting and soon the sounds of the oarsman returned to their normal pace.

"Those poor men, we probably lost half a day's progress up the river. They will be rowing extra tonight." Sveta explained.

The ladies soon returned to their cabin, the waves had calmed slightly but continued to batter the ship. Sveta was extremely tired, but Maria wanted to know how it went with the captain.

As Sveta took off her dress, Maria asked, "So, how was it … with him?"

Sveta paused, "I'll tell you in the morning, I'm exhausted." She replied.

As Sveta's clothes dropped to the floor, she fell to her bed, exhausted. Maria looked at her in the dark, she looked cold and didn't have the strength to pull the blankets beneath her over herself.

Maria went and took the blanket from her own bed and returned to Sveta's bedside. Without a word, she draped the blanket over Sveta's body and lay alongside her.

"Such a paradise," Sveta whispered as she fell asleep instantly.

Maria felt such an appreciation for all Sveta did for her, and wanted to return her kindness in some way. She curled up behind Sveta and let her arm drape over her. Sveta shifted slightly then took Maria's hand, holding it to her breast.

It was shocking at first, Maria wanted to pull her hand away thinking it was an unconscious mistake. But the sensation of Sveta's breast, so warm and soft in her hand, felt very different from her own. She dared not to move a single finger, feeling the tender impression of Sveta's nipple against her palm.

Maria felt awkward, speechless, uncomfortable but also aroused as she had admired Sveta's breasts since the moment they met.

"Was it wrong?" Maria wondered. "Surely Sveta knew this was not a man beside her."

Maria searched her mind, trying to find an answer but realized her objection was to the idea of touching a woman, not how it actually felt. In fact, it only felt feminine and natural to touch someone so familiar and kind. Maria let out a deep breath and laid her head on the soft curtain of Sveta's hair as it spilled across the pillow as they both drifted into sleep.

# Weft Threads

Things moved slowly the next morning; Maria awoke in Sveta's bed to see she was already up and getting dressed. Sveta seemed late for getting to the galley and said very little before quickly slipping her shoes on and heading for the door.

Maria felt guilty for not having a task to perform, she could hear people all over the ship working, moving things about and shouting for help with this or that. She got dressed and headed for the top deck to see what the ship looked like after the storm.

At first glance, everything seemed normal until she noticed a few barrels were missing from where they had been lashed the day before.  Then she turned and saw several members of the crew looking at the sail, it had a large tear at the base where it had been pulled hard against the grommets and was split completely open from the breeze running through it. Her eyes grew big at the idea the wind could be so violent.

"We didn't get it down in time." The quartermaster said as he saw her looking at the damage. "That storm caught everyone by surprise." He added as he rubbed his hand over the back of his neck in frustration.

"Can you fix it?" Maria asked.

"In the next port we can, but that's bad news for the oarsmen, they have to push upstream against this current." He said gritting his teeth in anger.

"Well get it down before it rips sideways as well!" he shouted at the crew.

Maria stood in a trance, as she watched the breeze flickering through the loose threads of the torn sail. She instantly remembered her mother teaching her how to make blankets on a loom. Each winter the snow would cover the doors and windows, burying the family inside for days at a time. They always had a fire, food, and tasks to keep their mind off the harsh cold that imprisoned them.

Maria's mind immersed her in the scene of her mother guiding Maria's hands across the loom, teaching her how to stretch the main threads in the loom before completing the piece with a shuttle and fill thread. The process took days to complete as they wove blankets and sewed quilts from scraps of cloth.

Maria slowly blinked, staring determined at the sail as she walked toward it. "I can fix this!" Maria said excitedly.

The quartermaster looked up from his tools, feeling annoyed by Maria's interjection. He searched for a reason to excuse her from the task. "Oh, I couldn't impose on you miss, you're our passenger, and mending a sale is a very dangerous job, the weight of it alone is..." he continued in a patronizing voice.

Maria could sense she had to prove her abilities and felt the school teacher voice of her mother emerge in complete authority, interrupting the quartermaster before he could finish speaking.

"Look right there! See how the tear is perfectly straight?" She asked insistently.

The quartermaster sighed and nodded, hoping she would stop talking.

"Those are weft threads, they just the fill the sail, the stronger ones...the warp threads that go up and down are fine! I can patch on both sides through the warp threads, all I need is a needle, thread and a piece of canvas....do you have that on board?" Maria said looking up from the sail at the stunned quartermaster.

The quartermaster stood speechless as the young lady spoke in a language he had only heard among shipwrights and riggers.

"You have the tools, yes?" Maria said confidently.

The quartermaster turned and shouted at one of the crew, "Fetch me the sail gear in the tackle box and the old sail from down below!"

A member of the crew rushed down the stairs, returning moments later with the items.

The quartermaster placed his hand on Maria's back gently and spoke quietly in her ear, "If it's not done right, the sail will be ruined. You're sure about this?" The quartermaster said as he handed the tackle box to Maria.

Maria nodded confidently and walked toward the sail rigging. She felt she was being taken seriously for the first time, rather than a helpless kitten with no value to those around her. The crew unleashed the base of the sail and lowered it for her. They laid the old sail out on the deck and stood like an audience, watching a performance. Maria immediately went to work measuring the tear and size of the patch she would need to cut from the old sail.

The quartermaster watched from his post with a smile as she had all the deck hands helping her. Each man seemed eager to be her hands and teased each other in the process.

"Those are weft threads there." said one crewmember to another, as if he knew it already.

Maria giggled and corrected him, "Actually weft threads go up and down, those are the fill threads that go across, they are the weaker of the two." Maria said as the man nodded in embarrassment.

She walked out the length of patches to be cut and looked around for a knife. The quartermaster stepped down from his post and pulled a blade from his belt, working it along the sail where Maria pointed.

He cut a large set of patches and placed them over and under the main sail to be sewn together. The men held the weight of the sail as Maria set out to stitch the patches in place, ignoring the attention she drew from each man watching her. Her long blonde hair dancing in the breeze as she knelt and turned over and under the sail.

She looked up and saw their blank faces, all looking at her. "Sorry gentleman, I know it's heavy, I'll go as quickly as I can." She said keeping her eyes on the sail.

"It's not heavy to me!" One man said, "Nor I!" said another, as each of them wanted to boast of their strength in hopes of impressing her.

After two hours, the stitching was complete, and the quartermaster returned. "Well I'll be!" he said as he inspected the work, pulling at the edges to test the strength. "That's excellent work!"

"Thanks, we still need a grommet." She said still focused on the task.

"Now that I can do!" said the quartermaster as he motioned to one of the men to cut a whole and clamp a ring around it for reinforcement.

Moments later, the sail was lashed to the cross arm and hoisted up as it caught the wind, and the ship made a familiar pull forward. The patch held and took the weight of the breeze as before.

Suddenly the oarsmen, covered in sweat, began to appear on deck, one after another in a long line. It was evident they had been told the news and were all looking at the sail with an inspired smile. Then the quartermaster began to clap as he walked toward Maria acknowledging her with a big smile, the entire deck began to cheer with applause as the men felt relieved to have their sail back.

Maria didn't understand how important her contribution was to the ship, the southern currents of the Volga routinely made hard work for the oarsmen, but without a sail to help propel the ship it would have been almost impossible to travel North. She was their hero.

The captain also joined in and patted Maria on the back,

"U Nas Kupala!" he shouted, "U-ra!"

"U-ra" the crew responded in unison.

Each member of the crew looked Maria in the eye, thanking her and nodding their head in appreciation before returning below.

The captain remained to speak with Maria. "You've done us a great service young lady, and saved me a substantial amount of money in repairs." He said in a grateful tone.

"Normally we give some money to each of the merchants if we are late getting in but we'll back on schedule now." Added the quartermaster who listened in as he packed up the repair gear and old sail.

"Ay, and that as well." The captain continued, "I'm returning your fare for the trip and hope you'll continue with us to Neva, but of course you are free to pick another ship at the next port if you wish." He said as he handed Maria a small bag with gold coins.

Maria's eyes grew wide with astonishment as she held the coin purse in her hand. "Thank you! I just wanted to help, I didn't expect all this!" She chirped.

The captain nodded and continued on his way, returning to his duties and shouting at the crew, "Back to work! We're underway and making time to Cheropovets!" he said in a boastful voice.

The men scattered like ants devouring a piece of bread, all with a destination of haste and purpose.

"That was really sweet of you," Maria said to the quartermaster, knowing he had spoken to the captain and brought the men on deck.

"Miss, you never asked what the benefit was to you, and on the river, everyone looks for their reward before the work. The captain and I both appreciate that." He said as he rolled the remains of the old sail. "Thanks again." He said as he turned to complete his tasks.

Maria stood on the main deck in astonishment. She felt truly valued and respected from people who had every reason to ignore or dismiss her. There was a lesson in the experience she wanted to hold on to, she had asserted and proven herself when she would have normally backed down. At that moment a small part of the shy farm girl faded away, and the woman inside her began to emerge.

She headed below eager to share the news of her adventure and reward with Sveta. It was as if the entire experience had not happened until she told it in full detail to her new dear friend. She stopped in her room to store her gold, packing it in her sack and storing it under her bed before making her way toward the kitchen.

She could already smell the scent of something sweet in the air, there was no mistaking it, Sveta was making blini, her favorite!

She rushed down the stairs and raced into the kitchen before the crowd had formed.

Sveta saw her and immediately waved for her to come inside the cooking area. Maria smiled and came around the other side of the wall separating the crew mess and cook space.

"Blinchiki!" Maria shouted excitedly.

Sveta laughed, "Da, my favorite." She said as Maria agreed on the same.

The two ladies nibbled at their Russian-style pancakes covered with berries and honey as Maria shared the story of mending the sail and the captain's generosity. Maria detected a hint of jealousy in Sveta's eyes but quickly dismissed it. She knew Sveta had been the only woman on board, and this meant Maria presented a competition even if it was not intentional.

Sveta sounded genuinely happy for Maria, even though her eyes were a bit far away.

Then Sveta surprised Maria in response, "Well that's good news, now you can pick a better ship with your own cabin!" She said half laughing.

Maria's eyes filled with tears, "You want me to go?", She said in horror. "I thought you liked having me there, but yes, of course, I should respect that it's your home, and I'm imposing…" Maria said trying not to be offended even though she was clearly hurt.

Sveta quickly put her plate down and moved next to Maria, wrapping her arms around her. "Ignore me!" She said apologetically, "I'm a stupid jealous woman." She said as her voice softened, "I don't want you to go!" Sveta said as she squeezed Maria tightly.

It was the first time Maria saw Sveta's softer side, she was not as tough as life on the ship had forced her to be. "I want to stay on board until we reach Neva," Maria said assuredly.

They wiped each other's tears and quickly finished their meal as the sounds of the men came into the crew mess looking for their meal. Stools slid across the floor as utensils, bowls and plates began their routine distribution among the hungry shipmates. "Davai Blini!" the men shouted in a playful manner. It was wonderful to feel the positive mood of all after a hard night and exhausting recovery from the storm.

# The Unexpected Barber

Sveta and Maria were sitting in their cabin, sharing stories from their childhood after the evening meal. Each of them took turns revealing intimate details about their experiences and adventures while growing up.

Sveta talked about the son of the town blacksmith, his strong hands, smile and piercing blue eyes, and how one night while her father was away at sea and her mother fell asleep, she snuck out of the house to see him.

"Of course, I was only 15 at the time, my mom would have killed me…and my father would've killed the boy for sure!" Sveta giggled as she continued the story. "I remember it had rained that day, but it was summer time so there was this misty, light fog in the air. We agreed ahead of time to meet behind the stable where he worked.

So there I go, taking all the back ways so no one can see me because everyone in Neva knew my mother.  Finally, I make it to the stable and head to the back where he is supposed to be waiting for me. But it is so foggy I can't tell if he is there or not, so I start walking through the straw, getting closer to the door that leads inside the stable. And he isn't there! Of course, I'm frantic, I've come all this way and nothing! "

"Why didn't he show up?" Maria asked hanging on every word Sveta spoke.

"He did! Just as I was about to go home and never speak to him again, I see a shadow moving in the stable, they always keep a fire going to heat the iron, so it's lit up with this orange glow. But what if it's not him, right? I leaned back against the wall, hiding in the shadows, just in case it's his father or someone else.

"Was it him?" Maria asked as she leaned forward in anticipation.

"Yes! He steps out and whispers my name, and I decide to wait to see what he does because he can't see me yet! Then his head drops and he says, "Bleen!" Because he thinks, I didn't come!" Sveta expressed in an excited whisper.

"So of course at this point I can't stand it any longer, and I say, "What kind of language is that in front of a lady?" Sveta says as they both burst out laughing.

"So what happened, did you kiss him?" Maria said anticipating more of the story.

"Oh yes, we kissed! I wasn't sure what to do, but I didn't want him to know it was my first time. He walked over to me, looked in my eyes, and without another word he kissed me, just like that." Sveta said as her eyes sparkled with enthusiasm.

"And you know, I liked it! He wasn't shy or afraid to offend me like most young guys are. He just did what he wanted! I can still remember how his tongue felt in my mouth, it was so erotic!" Sveta said.

"So he kissed you, and that was it?" Maria asked as she imagined every detail.

Sveta paused, "Well...no, there was more" she laughed, embarrassed and covering her face with her hands.

"We must've kissed for an hour or more, and we kept getting closer to one another, I could feel his hands were eager to touch me more but he kept them right at my hips, or he would run them up my back kind of playfully. Then during the kisses, I noticed his fingers would just move a little closer to my breasts or lower down my back right above my bottom. So, of course, I'm pretending not to notice but how can you not, right?" Sveta teased.

Maria's mouth fell open as she knew this story was going to get more interesting by the second.

"I decided to see what he would do if he thought I was in agreement for more, so I hold my breath and just...pushed my tongue deep into his mouth, daring him to be bolder. He starts to moan a little bit, so I know he likes it. And I don't know where the idea came from, but as I pulled away from the kiss I sucked his bottom lip real slow...pulling it between my lips as I slowly let it go.  And that must have done it because he pressed me against the wall and his hands went right over my breasts squeezing me like there is no tomorrow. I could feel his hardness right through my clothes, like a rock down there pushing against me!"

Maria smiled imagining every detail, "Then what?!" she snapped wanting Sveta to continue.

"Then I pushed him away and told him I needed to go. I mean...as much as I liked it, I was young, and it felt a little wrong if you know what I'm saying? It was wonderful and terrifying for a first-time." Sveta said looking for Maria's agreement.

Maria nodded, disappointed that the story had to end, but she completely understood. She could not bring herself to confess she had hardly experienced such things with a man yet.

"I remember my first kiss." Maria began, then a knock suddenly came at the door.

They both looked at each other curiously, not expecting anyone.

Sveta went and opened the door, and two of the oarsmen entered the cabin.

"Well...back for more, both of you?" Sveta teased.

"Da." they both nodded

"And you already washed?" Sveta commanded.

"Da." They quickly agreed like children agreeing with their mother.

"Alright, which one goes first while the other one watches?" she replied seductively as she walked toward her bed.

Maria was shocked, it seemed so businesslike and crude.

"Two men at the same time!?" she thought as she quickly put her shoes on and said, "I'll go get some fresh air!"

"Don't be silly you can stay and help!" Sveta replied calmly.

Maria looked horrified as she turned to Sveta in shock. Suddenly, Sveta understood what Maria must be thinking.

"Ah! Net dorogaya, it's not that." Sveta gasped and laughed as the full weight of the scene began to unfold in her mind. "They are here for haircuts." She added with a riotous laugh as she reached behind her bed and pulled out a small sharp knife.

Maria's sighed in deep relief, "Konechno, haircuts" She said as her face turned red in embarrassment.

"Have you ever cut hair before?" Sveta asked.

"I watched my mom cut my dad's hair a few times," Maria replied

"Well come on I'll show you," Sveta said as she placed a small stool in the middle of the room and looked at the men waiting for one of them to sit.

The larger of the two men stepped forward and sat on the stool like an obedient child.

"They like their hair really short because it gets sweltering hot when rowing and with everyone so close together down there, head lice can spread like wildfire," Sveta said as she ran her fingers through the man's hair pulling it out word for examination. "I leave just a little bit to keep them from getting a sunburn and cut the rest." She said as she began pulling the knife through the man's hair.

Maria watched as the man offered no objection as Sveta cut his hair vigorously with a knife. She pulled hard, yanking and hacking away at his locks, causing his head to bob from one side or the other while the man looked completely calm.

"Now you try!" Sveta remarked while handing the knife to Maria.

"Oh I'm not sure am ready, I think maybe I will just watch this time." Maria contested.

"Nonsense, you patched the mainsail today, we learn by doing not by watching, just like sex!" Sveta said as the men laughed.

Maria jabbed her elbow at Sveta for embarrassing her as she stepped behind the man and began to cut his hair.

She ran her fingers through the long last part of his hair and carefully began to cut. Her touch was so gentle the man's eyes lit up, and he smiled. His friend noticed and decided to tease him.

"Vse normalno Victor?" the other man asked.

"Da, ochen horosho" Victor replied.

Sveta could see what was happening, and nagged Maria to work faster and be firmer.

"Right, we're cutting hair tonight, not seducing the crew, get on with it!" Sveta said as she placed her hand over Marias to guide her to pull harder and finish.

Maria had no idea her touch was so gentle in comparison, but she enjoyed the reaction that she saw.

Victor stood and turned to face both ladies. "Spacibo!" He said as he rubbed his freshly shorn head.

His friend laughed as if he looked ridiculous. "Davai, ti tozhe" Victor snapped as he pushed his friend into the seat.

Sveta looked at Maria and shrugged her shoulders, "Go ahead." She encouraged.

Maria was determined to cut in the same way Sveta did, this time, she ran her fingers through the man's hair and quickly pulled the knife through make stronger strokes them before. She was so intent on doing it the way she had been shown that she did not see the young man's face wincing in pain by her firmer technique. She was done in seconds and tapped him on the back to stand.

He turned and faced both ladies to thank them, and at that moment Maria could see the tears in his eyes that he tried to conceal by quickly blinking. "Spacibo," the man said weakly. As he and his friend turned to leave the cabin.

The moment the door closed the two of them burst into laughter, "Did you see his face?!" Sveta said as she covered her mouth in surprise.

"So awful, he must think I'm a butcher!" Maria said regretfully.

"Serves him right for making so many jokes." Sveta said, "Don't worry they will be back in a couple weeks."

Maria shook her head in disbelief, but couldn't help but laugh about the situation.

The two of them pushed the hair into a pile with a small broom.

"What do I do with this?" Maria asked.

"Use it to fill your pillow," Sveta said plainly.

"Eww!" Maria recoiled.

"I'm joking! I'll throw it overboard!" Sveta replied as she laughed, taking the pile of hair in her hands and heading toward the door. "When I get back I want to hear about that first kiss."

Maria nodded and waited for Sveta's return. She washed her hands and began to rehearse how she might tell the story. Perhaps she would add more detail to make herself seem more experienced than she was. She felt the simplicity of her first kiss was not worthy of being told after hearing Sveta's amazing erotic story.

Sveta returned, jumped on her bed, and said: "So, the first kiss, go on!"

Maria hesitated; her hands writhed in anticipation, trying to find the best way to tell the story.

Sveta could understand what was happening. "Masha, it's okay to go slow in life and take your time with men. You know?"

"I know," Maria said, "I just haven't experienced things like you have yet."

"You're still very young, you have all the time in the world for that, and I hope it's not just sex but love that you find."

Maria was surprised by Sveta's comment, "I thought you didn't care about love?" She said.

"Of course, I care, but in my situation, it's not likely to happen anytime soon. So I would rather believe it's by my own choice instead of the luck of the draw. You think I don't dream of only one man touching me? Having his children? Of course, I do! But not here, not like this." Sveta replied.

Maria nodded and felt she actually understood Sveta's character.

Maria smiled and began, "So, during the harvest my father hired local boys to help bring in the crops. Since I wasn't as strong to help in the fields, my job was to keep track of their work and at the end of the day I'd give them their payment."

"I like this story already," Sveta said encouraging her to go on.

"My mother was in town teaching in our school, and my father took the horse to go and pick her up because it was getting late. This one last boy comes to the door and asks for my father. I told him he wasn't there, so he said he would wait until my dad returned to collect his payment. But I had already paid everyone for the day and did not know who this boy was. So we are talking, and I am checking all the names and transactions because I think there is a mistake. Finally, he looks at me and says "To be honest you can keep the money if I can have a kiss. "

I thought wow, he worked all day and would trade that hard work for something so simple? I felt like all my friends had already kissed a boy so...why not me? And I said yes.

He stands up and walks towards me, he was a little taller than me with dark brown hair and brown eyes, and he had these irresistible dimples when he smiled. Uff, so handsome! He placed his hands on my face just before he leaned in to kiss me. And that warm sensation of his hands went through my whole body just at the moment his lips touched mine. It was soft and gentle and...eternal." Maria said as her eyes looked down, remembering the moment.

Sveta perked up, "Such a story teller you are! So what happened? Did your father come back?"

"Da, my father, and mother came back on the horse and passed the boy as he walked down the path away from the farm. My father walks into the house and asks who he was, and I said, 'Wasn't he one of your workers? He came to get paid.'

My father shook his head no and said he had never seen that boy before, and I was smart not to pay him! Can you imagine? That boy was so clever! I was angry and flattered at the same time!... But I never told my father the rest of the story!" Maria said.

They both laid on their beds talking late into the night as the ship creaked and rocked its way along the river.

"Tomorrow we will be in Port Cheropovets, they have the best fruits there!" Sveta said.

She waited for a reply and then realized Maria had fallen asleep. She reached and blew out the beeswax candle by Maria's bed, "Sladki snov, Manya" Sveta said as she returned to her bed and felt herself like a big sister watching over her innocent young friend.

# Cheropovets

The morning light appeared into the cabin as the nearby sounds of the port grew closer and louder. They both awoke at the same time, "We're in Port!" Sveta announced as she sprang from her bed rushing to prepare the morning meal. Maria pulled her blanket around her as she stood up and walked to the cabin window to see what the port looked like.

It was much smaller than Mologa and appeared to be less interesting, making her wonder why Sveta had such energy about this stop. Maria shrugged her shoulders and returned to her bed, draping her blanket onto the mattress as she stretched and yawned. She reached for her brush and quickly fixed her hair into a braid. Then she slipped her nightgown over her shoulders and let it fall to the floor.

She wiped herself down with a hand towel, dipping it in the pan of water that was kept in the cabin. She imagined the pleasure of taking a bath in the creek that ran by her farm in Rostov. The water would still be warm this time of year, and the feeling after a long swim was so relaxing. She remembered how her mother would scold her for taking an entire cake of soap and using it for her bath, but that was Maria's passion, she loved to lather and wash until the soap was gone.

As she finished cleaning herself, she paused to dry before putting her dress on. The air was becoming colder as it circled around her. It felt as if she was riding further away from summer as the ship moved northward each day.

She slid her palms over her skin to feel warmer and dry faster. A chilled wind blew from under the door as the top deck was opened and the sounds of offloading cargo began. She shuddered and donned her dress and shoes, then reached for the small bags of coins in her sack.

"I hope we have oatmeal today." She thought as she headed to the galley.

Sveta was clearly in a hurry to finish her duties when Maria arrived in the kitchen. She was washing dishes and cooking at the same time. Maria noticed and quietly asked her, "What's the hurry?"

"Were only in port for a few hours today, not much time to go ashore. I have to purchase food for the crew and get it all back here before we leave." Sveta said in a loud whisper as she continued working.

Maria nodded, understanding the situation but she was still very curious about Sveta's excitement.

"Do you want to go with me?" Sveta asked as she picked up the last large pot to clean.

"Yes, of course!" Maria said as she took a small bowl of oatmeal to eat. "I want to see if anyone might have seen my mother come through."

"Ladno, finish your breakfast, and I'll be done here in a few minutes," Sveta said as she reached inside the still hot pot to clean it as water sizzled around its edges.

Maria's eyes grew big, but Sveta nodded in disagreement that it was as hot as it looked, and smiled.

"There is definitely something or someone in this port that she wants to see." Maria thought.

The two ladies emerged from the ship half an hour later, Sveta walked at a brisk pace lightly pulling Maria by the arm to keep up. They made their way past the cargo and fishing nets until they arrived at a small market filled with vegetables and fruits grown in the local village.

The farmers recognized Sveta and quickly took her order as she picked through their produce, tasting and questioning how fresh it was. She ordered large quantities of potatoes, onions, carrots, cabbage and a few spices.

"This is where we fill up for the rest of the trip, it's much cheaper here than in Mologo." She said as they worked their way through the market. Sveta talked like a spoiled girl to manipulate the price, pretending to walk away until the farmer gave in to her demands.

A large display of apples caught her eye, they approached, and Sveta handed an apple to Maria motioning for her to take a bite, "What do you think? The other ones were better right?" Sveta asked.

Maria did not understand the question at first, then she remembered how her father would sell produce in Rostov where everyone had to bargain to make a sale.

"Oh yes, absolutely, the other ones were much tastier. I think they were just picked this morning." She said with enthusiasm.

Sveta smiled, happy that Maria had caught on to her negotiation tactics, "Let's go back and talk to the other man then." Sveta demanded in a voice loud enough for the farmer to hear. They turned to walk away and within two steps they heard the farmer say "Devochka, podezhdi!"

They both grinned and then changed their appearance to be more serious before turning around to face the farmer.

"Da?" Sveta replied in a coy tone.

"Davai, let's make a little business. You need good apples and mine are the best. Don't trust these other guys, they are all from small villages." He said in a rural accent as he quickly began to put his apples in a bucket. "How many do you need? For you, I will make a special price."

Sveta didn't hesitate, "120 from the top, none of your bottom ones with all the bruises, and no worms!" Sveta ordered. "Have them on board the Kupala within the hour... horosho?"

"Horosho, konechno, horosho," the farmer said, delighted to have such a large order.

Sveta took Maria to meet Aleksey, the market manager, who worked with all the ships that came through the port. She knew if there were a chance anyone had seen or talked to her mother, he would be the most likely person. Aleksey was a shrewd businessman, but he was always helpful to patrons in his market.

"Aleksey!" Sveta said, "This is my friend Maria, she is looking for her mother who may have come through here in the last few days. Have you seen anyone?"

Aleksey looked at Maria for a moment as if he was annoyed by Sveta's request. "How I should know who her mother is?" He said in a contemptuous tone.

Maria immediately tried to help, "She looks like me only older, we are the same height, but her hair is darker and about this long." She said pointing toward her shoulder.

The man stared into the air for a moment then spoke, "That could be any woman." he said sarcastically. "In last few days, only my frequent customers came through. It's the end of the season, so not as many boats. " Said Aleksey.

Maria's face became sad, as she feared her mother would not make it up the river before all the ships docked for winter. "Thank you for your time," She said in a broken voice as her eyes teared.

Sveta glared at Aleksey for being so rude and careless, as Maria turned to wipe her eyes. He realized this was a more serious matter and didn't want to offend Sveta as she often bought a lot of their end season crops.

"Dorogaya," he said gently to Maria as she turned back toward him. "If your mother comes through I will tell her you are looking for her." He said looking at Sveta for approval.

Sveta nodded as Maria shook her head in agreement, "Thank you, and please tell her I am on my way to Neva on the Kupala."

"Konechno" Aleksey replied as the two of them exited the market.

They walked away as Sveta guided them toward a farm house farther away from the port. "What's next?" Maria asked.

"Meat!" Sveta replied "We can only take on so much per stop because our salt box isn't very large, so we have to fill up often. And this guy has excellent pork and chickens."

They walked along the path leading to the farm house in the distance. Sveta had a smile on her face that grew as they approached the door.

"Vanya, ti zdes?" Sveta shouted playfully as she knocked.

Moments later the door opened, and a tall, handsome man with blonde hair and brown eyes emerged, "Lanochka!" He shouted as he picked Sveta up in his arms.

Maria now understood the mystery of Sveta's excitement. She had a boyfriend here who was clearly her heart's desire.

Sveta laughed as Ivan put her down, and introduced Maria to him.

"Maria this is Ivan," Sveta said proudly.

"Ochen priyatno!" Ivan said as he shook her hand.

"How much time do we have?" Ivan said impatiently as he looked at Sveta.

"Maybe one hour," Sveta replied.

"Only One?" Ivan said, "Maria can you help us? There are chickens and pork already butchered in the barn, just tell my boy, Jenya, which ones you want."

Maria turned towards the barn and saw the open door, "Sure I can do that, how many should I?..." Maria stopped talking as she heard the door close and turned to see they both had gone inside.

She paused, thinking maybe they did not understand her, and perhaps she should follow them inside. As she placed her hand on the door latch, she realized, Sveta was probably naked already on the other side of the door. Maria giggled and made her way towards the barn, shaking her head in disbelief as she walked.

The barn was a large structure with big doors to move cattle in and out. Grotesque masses of animal flesh were hovering by hooks over a smoking fire, while fish were skewered on sticks to cure in the sun.

Maria cringed at the sight of the dead animals and how they looked so disgusting during the process. She remembered such scenes around the farms in Rostov and always felt uncomfortable seeing such brutality. She and her mother did not eat meat, and her father seemed content to have fish or chicken on rare occasion.

She stepped inside the large door but didn't see anyone inside, then she walked around the back side where she could hear hens cackling and scratching for food. She could see their nests at the side, and a large basket filled with eggs that must have just been collected.

"Izvinitye? Jenya?" She asked as she looked for someone to talk to.

A teenaged boy holding a bucket of seed turned and walked toward her, kicking his way through chickens as they jumped at the seeds that had spilled on his shoes. The boy had brown eyes and looked like a younger version of his father, Ivan.

"Privet." He said kindly, "Can I help you?"

"Yes, I'm here with Svetlana from the ship Kupala, she asked me to get some chickens and…"

The boy nodded and immediately headed back inside the barn, "She usually gets the same thing. 10 chickens, half a pig and all our eggs!" he interrupted as he walked.

Maria was relieved that she didn't have to guess what to request. She stood out near the chicken pen watching them feed as Jenya went to prepare everything. It was a nicer view than what awaited her in the barn.

The boy stuck his head out the barn door, "Are you taking it with you or do I need to take it to the ship?" he asked.

"Oh if you could take it for us, that would be great!" She replied.

He nodded and returned to the barn where he salted and wrapped each item. Maria could hear the sounds of his knife as it hit the cutting table like a woodsman chopping away at a tree, only she knew it was an animal carcass being cut for their order.

She shivered at what it must look like and kept her eyes on the chickens. Jenya continued working while Maria reached for the seeds in the pail and fed the chickens. It had been some time since she had done simple tasks like this.

The peace of life on a farm made her feel calmer inside. She walked toward the wood pile and pulled an axe from the stump where larger timbers were cut into firewood. She brushed the stump with her hand to make sure it was dry and sat down holding the axe across her lap. It reminded her of home, the river in the distant view, the trees and the fields loaded with produce as the last harvest was coming.

A warm breeze rushed through the fields, moving the crops like waves on the river, moving closer and closer until the scent of everything brushed by her. She closed her eyes and felt herself in Rostov, remembering how her mother would be making candles at this time, and her father bringing in vegetables to be stored for winter. For as long as the breeze touched her face, she could be home again.

Jenya returned and picked up the basket of eggs as he walked toward a small hand drawn cart where the other items were placed. "That's everything, I need to get these to the ship, are you coming with me?" He said in an impatient voice.

"Um no, I'll wait for Sveta, she's...talking with Ivan..." Maria said feeling uncomfortable with the details.

The boy looked toward the farm house and smiled, "Talking? Da ladno!" he chuckled as he lifted the cart handles and began pushing it toward the port.

Maria knew that they needed to return soon. She wedged the axe back into its resting place and walked to the farmhouse door, knocking lightly, "Sveta, it's time to go dorogaya!" She said in a motherly voice.

She waited, but there was no response at the door. She looked around and decided to lean her ear to the door mischievously hoping to hear what was going on inside. She could not hear a single sound; it was as if no one was there. Then she heard voices coming from the back of the house and walked around thinking they must be outside having something to eat.

She stopped in her tracks as she rounded the corner of the farmhouse. Ivan had a small banya built there, and they were both inside it with the door open. She didn't want to disturb them but at the moment she had stepped into view, she could see them easily.

Their naked bodies were golden in the glow of the fire inside the banya, it made them look like living statues coming to life. Ivan was behind Sveta as they both stood, his hands wrapped around her, holding her hips as he pulled her back on to him. Sveta had her hands on the walls as she leaned forward and pushed herself back onto Ivan. She was taking him deep inside her and enjoying every movement he made.

They had such a hunger for each other, she reacted differently to him than she had with the men she was with before, this was not just her way of placating a man for her own benefit, it was more romantic and passionate.

Maria began to back away from view as she could see Ivan's scarred bare body starting to thrust harder and stronger as Sveta moaned for him to give her his juice. Maria stopped in shock, the woman who was so careful not to get pregnant was begging this man to finish inside her? Surely she knew the risks but, "How could they not give all to each other with such a passion between them?" Maria thought.

As she stepped back around the house and walked to the front door, she could hear them shouting and moaning as they climaxed together. It made Maria wonder how it must have felt at that moment but at the same time, it was such a risk for Sveta to let him do that. She knew she would have to ask about it, but was not sure how to bring up the question without admitting she had watched them.

Ten minutes later, the door opened as Sveta and Ivan emerged. They were both drenched with sweat as Sveta tried to quickly dry her hair. Her clothes were sticking to her body revealing her bare nipples beneath the material. Ivan tried to pat her dry, but she knew it would not help. "I'll be dry by the time I reach the ship, there is a good breeze today." She said sweetly.

Maria smiled and looked toward the river motioning they needed to return to the ship.

"Just one more minute, Mom!" Sveta teased as Maria began walking toward the path.

"Promise you'll come see me this winter?" Sveta asked.

"This time, I will," Ivan said as he pulled her into his arms until her feet lifted off the ground.

They kissed, and Sveta rushed to catch up with Maria on the path.

At first, they walked quietly, then Sveta sighed and returned to her former self, "Did Jenya take the pork and chickens to the ship?" she asked

"Da, and the eggs also," Maria said with a smile.

"Oh great, everything is done then." She replied in relief.

"Ivan seemed very nice," Maria said, hoping for more details.

Sveta quietly agreed and didn't seem very talkative as they walked along the path back through the port towards the ship.

"Is something wrong?" Maria asked, thinking Sveta may have seen her watching them and was angry.

"No, I'll just miss him. It's our last trip through here until the spring. He promised to come see me in Neva during the winter, but without the river, I don't know if it's possible." Sveta sighed.

"I'm sure you won't be alone in Neva, there are lots of men there, right?" Maria said, trying to encourage.

"Not like him," Sveta sighed in a lovesick voice.

"Oh, he is special then?" Maria said teasing Sveta.

"I knew his wife before she died," Sveta expressed in a serious tone.

Maria felt embarrassed for her casual remarks as she listened to Sveta.

"I bought food from her in the market and then on one trip she wasn't there anymore, and they told me she been killed. I thought I should pay my respects to her family as she had told me about them. "

"How did she die?" Maria asked sadly.

"She was looking for mushrooms in their field and didn't know that the bull was out of the barn. They say she didn't even hear him until he was right in front of her. Can you imagine, Jenya saw his mother running for her life and called to his father, then here came Ivan right at that bull with only a rock in his hand. He stood between them and told her to run, but the bull had already hit her so hard that she could barely stand."

"That's awful!" Maria said, remembering how her father had come to her rescue in a similar way.

"Da, and poor Ivan, he cracked that bull on the head until he knocked it out, but he was poked full of holes in the process. Jenya said his father was covered in blood when he carried his wife out of that field. She didn't last the night. Jenya helped his father recover from his wounds, but his injuries took away his ability to have more children if you take my meaning." Sveta said.

"Uzhas!" Maria gasped, imagining the horror the man and his son had been through. "I can't even imagine, after seeing how happy Ivan is with you."

"Ay, he's better now. Still healthy and the bull didn't take everything, the important parts still work!" She said changing her tone with a giggle.

Suddenly, everything Maria had seen made complete sense and her curiosity turned to hope for her friend. Perhaps this was the kind of man that would win Sveta's heart and bring the promise of a more normal life in the future. And if not, at least they had each other for a season.

As they approached the ship, they saw Jenya returning with his empty cart. They approached, gave him a hug and thanked him for bringing everything to the ship for them.

"The quartermaster paid you, yes?" Sveta asked.

"Da, everything is on board and ready." He replied.

Jenya picked up his cart and began the long walk to the farmhouse.

"He seems a little uncomfortable with us," Maria said.

"Ah it's not you, it's me. He misses his mother and when his father is with me…" Sveta said.

"He thinks he is betraying her memory?" Maria interrupted.

"Yes, I suppose it's like that. But life moves on and anyone who has died would still tell you to keep moving." Sveta said as she boarded the ship.

Maria thought carefully about her friend's words. Though there was truth in them, they still had a bitter taste so close to the time of her father's death. She took one last look at Cheropovets and boarded the ship as well.

"That's the last of the passengers, cast off!" The quartermaster shouted as the ropes were untied from the dock and oarsmen began pushing the ship into the river's flow. The sail slid into position and caught the afternoon breeze as the ship thrust forward on its way North into the sinuous track of the Sheksna River.

# Dark and Forbidden

Sveta and Maria returned to their cabin as the ships rocked a bit more than usual from the firm breeze on the river. Each of them fell onto their bed, exhausted from the day's events.

"I can't move!" Sveta exhaled as she spoke.

"Da, so much walking today!" Maria agreed.

"Walking… and more." Sveta sighed. "I have to be downstairs soon, we skip meals in port so they will be screaming for dinner in a few hours." Sveta added, "Uff and I smell bad!"

Maria giggled, remembering how she had seen Sveta with her boyfriend in his banya. "I can get some water if you like," Maria said.

"Da, pozhalysta!" Sveta sighed.

Maria sat up and looked across the cabin at her exhausted roommate. Sveta's skin glowed from the time she had spent in the banya. Maria remembered how her whole family would spend time in the banya on their farm, even during winter it was such a fun experience. Her father got the fire as hot as an oven and brought in a branch of birch leaves so everyone could lightly whip their skin with them as a treatment for health. Then they would run outside and lay in the snow with barely any clothes on. Her parents drank mead and got very drunk, but Maria had only water as the mead was bitter to her taste. She felt homesick and sad to think those times would never be possible in the future.

Maria quietly walked to the door with a bucket in her hand to get some fresh water. She headed up the stairs and walked across the busy deck, where the men were sorting through their barrels and putting things below. It was almost a routine for her now as she walked to the barrel marked 'rainwater', and lifted the ladle to fill her bucket.

She noticed a few new merchants standing at the edges of the deck, keeping an eye on their cargo as the crew worked the items into position. Everyone shuffled and grunted in their labor as the farm girl passed between them like a butterfly among a herd of horses. She waited until a barrel was taken below and then made her way down the stairs, trying not to spill the water from the bucket. It was heavy, and it sloshed at the edges with each step leaving a trail down the stairs toward her cabin.

The quartermaster saw her heading to her room and shouted in his commanding voice, "Miss, we can't have water on the steps when we're loading! Someone could get hurt!" He insisted.

Maria felt embarrassed for her carelessness, "Prostiti, I will come back and..." She began.

"...Gena! Grab a mop and get this up!" He ordered to one of the crew as he winked at Maria with a smile.

He reminded her so much of her father, wise and strong but always showing her favor. She turned with a smile and carefully carried the water to the cabin where Sveta was waiting. As she opened the door, she saw Sveta had gotten up from her bed and was taking her clothes off. A pile of material formed at her feet as Sveta's nude body emerged like the stem of a flower in the garden.

Maria quickly closed the door and shuffled her way to the corner, pouring a portion of the water into the wash pail until it was half full.

"Spacibo dorogaya!" Sveta said in charming appreciation.

"Pozhalysta," Maria replied while handing her a wash cloth.

Sveta set the pail on the floor and dipped the cloth in the water. Then she slowly began her ritual of long strokes along her skin, to clean and soothe the day away. Maria returned to her bed and watched as her friend worked the cloth across her limbs and torso like a swan straitening its feathers in the pond.

Sveta dipped the cloth in water then twisted it with both hands, letting the water run down her neck and across her breasts, small streams formed for moments, making their way over the curves of her body. It was as if the water traced the same paths as man's eyes when he looks at a woman. Beginning at her neck and moving with pleasure over every inch of her inward and outward places, slowing in yearning to feel the roundness of her breasts, then rushing down her torso determined to disappear between her legs.

Sveta looked up at Maria's eyes, knowing she had been staring at her all the while. Sveta liked the attention, even from a woman, it made her feel attractive and more feminine. Her hands stroked upward from her waist as she smiled at Maria. "There's enough water here for two." She teased.

Maria felt a rush of heat move through her body, she was afraid and aroused at the idea. She trusted Sveta and felt so comfortable with her that it was more about sharing the moment than some kind of forbidden intimacy. She stood up and walked toward Sveta as she tugged at the tie strings that held her dress to her shoulders.

Her dress slipped off, falling down her arms. She felt each inch of her body escaping the cloth as it fell to the floor. Her senses heightened, suddenly aware of the air in the room, the heat from Sveta's body, everything was more noticeable.

Sveta noticed the fear in Maria's eyes and softly soothed her mind, "This is how women take care of each other. We're made to nurture; don't you think?" Sveta asked.

Maria's clasped her hands over the small, soft curls of blonde hair that drew a line between her legs. She felt nervous and awkward, unsure how to respond as her curiosity grew stronger than her innocence.

Sveta reached and dipped the cloth into the water, then twisted it over Maria's shoulder as the water trickled down her body. It felt cold, and Maria shook as it first made contact.

"Shh," Sveta calmed, "We're just sharing a bath." She said as she wrapped one hand around Maria's hair and held it up so it wouldn't get wet.

Maria didn't know what to say, then felt her breath fade from her chest as Sveta began to wash her back. The slow strokes, so gentle, it felt wonderful. It was as if she was in a trance." Sveta glided the cloth over Maria's shoulders and down her arms.

"Oh to be nineteen again, look at your tiny, perfect waist, you're so slim and beautiful," Sveta said admiring Maria's firm body.

Maria smiled, she hadn't heard such compliments before and wasn't sure how she looked to a woman or a man. She only knew men had said she was pretty, but her body had always been covered until now. And the sensation of Sveta's hands washing her was so pleasant and gentle. The farther down her hands went, the more Maria wanted to feel Sveta's touch. Her anticipation built as Sveta washed further down her back without stopping until finally, she felt the cool cloth gliding over her bottom.

Sveta enjoyed taking her time there, circling and caressing, comparing her body to Maria's. She knelt down and washed Maria's legs, one by one, being careful to avoid her more delicate personal space.

"I can do my front," Maria said as her voice finally returned. She was afraid of how much she liked this feeling and wanted to stop there.

"Of course" Sveta replied, "Can you do my back before I go? "She asked.

Maria nodded and turned to take the wash cloth. Their eyes met, and it was clear they both were enjoying the awkward intimacy. Their breasts lightly brushed together as they rotated positions. It was only a moment, but it stayed in both their minds as if it had been hours.

Maria rinsed the cloth and began washing Sveta's back. She could see light bruises on her ribs, and gently touched them. "Does it hurt here?" She asked.

"No, it's fine. I get carried away with Ivan and make him hold me all kinds of ways. Sometimes it leaves marks from his hands or whatever he was pushing me against." Sveta said, knowing she would intrigue Maria.

"So much passion," Maria said as she imagined such scenes in her mind. "How does he hold you to leave such marks?" she asked, hoping for a detailed answer.

Sveta giggled, "Well, it's when we do it standing up, I climb him like a tree and hang on." She replied. "He holds me out so he can push harder and then leans me back while my legs wrap around his waist?" Sveta asked looking for confirmation of the idea.

"How?" Maria asked, not sure what to construct in her mind.

Sveta turned and put her hands on Maria's shoulders, demonstrating the position. "I'm like this, and his hands are here," Sveta said guiding Maria's reluctant hands to her waist. "I wrap my legs around his waist and lean back, holding his arms..." She stated in an excited remembrance of the position.

"I see, and it feels good?" Maria asked as Sveta turned to let her finish her back.

"Amazing!" Sveta said assuredly, "He can put his shaft all the way in and push really hard!"

Maria felt surprised, "Doesn't it hurt if he goes too hard?"

Sveta paused, realizing Maria was a virgin. "At first, you want to go slow and gentle, but when it starts to feel exquisite...you want them to break you into pieces." She said with excitement in her voice.

They both laughed as Maria began to finish Sveta's back. "Tell me more.", Maria said.

Sveta cleared her throat, feeling the sensation of being washed as she recalled her sexual explorations. "Well, of course, it's nice in bed too, especially when I'm on top. I can ride him all day like that, if the man is, you know...strong." Sveta said.

"What else?" Maria demanded, as her interest kept building.

"I like it from behind," Sveta said. "You can feel the man's power that way, his hands on you, the way he grabs you or pulls your hair." She said as her words slowed with erotic pleasure.

"Standing or laying down, it's great, and I push back when I want it deeper." She said nudging her bottom against Maria's hand as she began to wash her there.

Maria giggled, feeling aroused and full of interest, she wouldn't stop washing now for fear Sveta would stop telling her such details.

"That's a lot of ... positions," Maria said.

"There are hundreds of them, dear, and not just for pure sex," Sveta assured her.

"Normal?" Maria asked.

"Sveta turned," knowing her bath was well over done. "A woman has many places for a man to take care of, you know?" She said as she stepped toward her bed reaching for a clean dress.

"I mean, there's the most obvious, and then your mouth, or between your breasts!" She said, pushing her bare breasts together to demonstrate. "Then there's the dark and forbidden!"

Maria looked confused by the phrase. She tried to imagine what was left when everything had been mentioned. Then her intelligent mind arrived at the only place left, even though it seemed, disgusting.

"You mean …?" Maria started.

"Mmm yes, there!" Sveta grinned as she put on her shoes.

"I'll tell you more about it later, I need to get to the kitchen!" She said teasingly.

Sveta rushed out of the cabin as Maria stood naked by the water pail. Maria rinsed the cloth and began washing her chest and abdomen.

"Dark and forbidden," she thought, "How strange!"

The cold water woke her nipples as she washed her breasts. Her nipples stood firmly from her round breasts. She cupped her hands over them, letting the warmth from her palms radiate into them. She closed her eyes and imagined it was a man's body, his chest against hers, keeping her warm as he made love to her.

The conversation and bath had left her hungry for pleasure. She could feel a yearning between her legs, as she walked to her bed to lay down on the warm sheets. Her hands quickly slipped between her legs as she imagined a muscular man standing before her, she would climb him and hang on tight as he thrust his body inside hers. She needed it just as Sveta described, her fingers were stroking harder and harder, thrusting inside her wetness.

It seconds she felt her orgasm quickly rising, scenes of making love flashed through her mind. She imagined her hands on a man's fleshy hardness, squeezing it and pulling him into her mouth, his hands on her firm bottom as he took her over and over. And then as she felt a hint of her orgasm starting to fire, she let her mind go and embraced the idea of being taken so dark and forbidden. The erotic thought made her orgasm immediately, as she shook from the pleasure her hands had brought to her body. Now she craved a man inside her like never before.

She slipped under the blanket and drifted in the sensation of pure warm light that seemed to bathe her body.

# A Pie for the Captain

The scent of roasted vegetables crept from the kitchen and into every corner of the ship, like a seductive dancer beguiling everyone to follow. Maria awoke and sighed as the scent beckoned her to the galley where Sveta had taken full advantage of the fresh produce they bought that day.

Maria quickly walked down the stairs, passing several crew and merchants who had lined up to eat as soon as it was ready. She made her way to the kitchen and saw Sveta hard at work. She knew how tired her friend was and reached for an apron, tying it around her waist as She said, "How can I help?"

"Ah, Masha, spacibo bolshoe!" Sveta sighed as she covered her hand with the corner of her apron and pulled a hot pan from the stove. "It's almost ready, can you cut the apples for me?" Sveta asked.

Maria nodded and quickly went to work. Sveta had prepared the pork and vegetables in the oven and had set a large pan with a crust laid on top of it. Maria understood Sveta wanted to make a pie from the apples, so she cut them into slices, filled a pot with water and set them on the stove to boil.

Sveta leaned against the counter, she was exhausted but seemed in good spirits. She wiped her forehead and sipped a cup of water while watching the roast in the oven. The temperature was overwhelming, but the smell was heavenly.

"It feels like a banya in here!" Maria said with a laugh, "I don't know how you can do it every day."

Sveta paused as the thought of a banya brought back memories of time with her lover, that day. "Real banya was earlier today, much more fun than here." She said with a smile.

Maria didn't want to admit she had seen her and Ivan, so she was careful with her reply, "When did you go to banya?" She said innocently.

Sveta looked around the corner to make sure the crew couldn't hear her. "Vanya has a banya behind his house, he took me there when you were in the barn." She said excitedly.

Maria pretended to hear this as news, "Really? Sounds erotic...?" she coaxed.

Sveta again checked the corner for listeners, then put her hand on Maria's shoulder pulling her closer to whisper in her ear. "It's the best sex, all your sweat makes your body slide like you're in the water and the heat makes it hard to breathe....it makes me come so hard when I can't breathe." She said as her eyes lit up with mischief.

Maria realized there was more to what she had seen than just two lovers in a banya, it was a secret recipe for intense sex!

Sveta continued, "I like how he tastes when I lick his body, like a saltwater but more erotic!" she confessed. "And because he can't make me pregnant...I take his all his juice inside ... off, such a pleasure!" she sighed as her voice grew stronger.

Maria looked around the corner also making sure no one had walked up. "What about... dark and forbidden?" She giggled.

Sveta reached into the stove with a long spoon and stirred the vegetables. "Vanya is a good boy, he doesn't attempt such things, but there are some other men who like it that way." She said as she winked.

Maria was amazed how many things she was learning, and how it seemed to take so many men to satisfy Sveta's appetite for sex. Perhaps her life on the river was to blame, but Maria began to fear her friend might not be happy with one man at the end of her commitment to the captain.

As the apples on the stove became soft, Maria drained the water away and asked Sveta what she would like done with them, "There are butter and cinnamon there, just add some honey and mix them all together." She instructed.

Maria followed her friend's wishes, then placed the apples into the baking pan. She took the dough Sveta had rolled for the top and put it on top, pinching the corners to seal it up.

"Ready for the oven!" Maria announced.

"Wait!" Sveta shouted as she hastily reached for a small canister on the shelf. "Special ingredient!" she teased.

Sveta opened the canister and immediately gagged as the offensive smell filled the kitchen. She pulled back the pie crust and reached in the can, pulling a few dried leaves out as she crumbled them in her hands while sprinkling them like ashes over the pie filling. She then snapped the lid shut and exhaled in relief."

"What is that!?" Maria asked as she wrinkled her nose and wafted her hand to dispel the intense fumes.

"Valerian root," Sveta said quipped as she set the canister on the shelf and closed the pie crust with her fingers.

"Smells like dirty feet, uff...actually, I think dirty feet would be offended by the comparison." She joked as she waited for the smell to fade.

Sveta laughed with a mischievous grin on her face as she pulled the roast from the oven and set it aside before sliding the pie into the oven.

"This is going to ensure I get the best sleep tonight." She beamed as she closed the oven doors.

Maria stood confused, not understanding the need to put the offensive root in the pie.

"They will devour this like wild dogs!" Sveta said as she began cutting the roast for serving. "But the pie is for the captain, it's his favorite!"

"That's...nice of you?" Maria pondered in reply.

"Well, I value my privileges in port, so it's best to give him something extra now and then." She said with a hint of regret.

"You mean, not just pie?" Maria asked

"Not tonight…I mean, there is no way, after being in port, I could, you know…go again, so a little Valerian root in the pie and he'll be asleep before I'm done with the dishes." Sveta responded with a giggle.

The quartermaster walked around the corner, "Sveta, they are eating the chairs out here, let's have it already!" he demanded.

Sveta laughed and lifted the hot roast with her apron-padded hands and walked around the corner as cheers erupted from the crew. Sveta smiled as she set a portion onto each man's plate as he walked by. The men shoved and pushed each other, eager to get their plate to Sveta's benevolent hands. Some elbowed their way in front of other men, causing them to quarrel over who was next.

"What did I tell you, Masha?" Sveta shouted around the corner. "Wild dogs!" she laughed.

Masha agreed as she rotated the pie in the oven. She marveled at the subtle craft Sveta commanded, she was so clever and charming, it was no wonder the captain wanted to have her, but surely her heart belonged to Vanya.

The heat seemed unbearable. Sveta returned with a pan, moments later. "The children have been fed." She mused. "I saved you some," Sveta said as she reached for a plate.

"Just the vegetables, please," Maria asked.

"As you like," Sveta replied as she filled a plate with potatoes, carrots and onions.

"Spacibo," Maria said as she closed the oven door. "The pie should be ready, soon."

The two ladies stood in the kitchen, nibbling at their meal and talking while the crew devoured their dinner. Everything seemed to be shifting back into the balanced flow of daily ship life. The sounds of men telling their stories of life on the river mixed with the clang plates, pots and pans as the kitchen slowly emptied and all that remained were a pile of dishes to be washed.

"My work is never done" Sveta sighed as she began to scrub and dip each dish into her sink. "If I get to them while they are still warm, it goes quicker."

Maria pulled the hot apple pie from the oven and set it on the counter carefully. The crust had become a golden brown blanket that teased her taste buds with the scent of cinnamon and apples. "He will eat the entire thing!" Sveta exclaimed proudly with a sinister laugh.

Maria began bringing the large pots to the sink and took the clean plates away to be stored. Within minutes everything was clean and drying.

"When do you go see the captain?" Maria asked.

"Soon, I need to change my clothes and wash off again after being next to this over all night."

Maria began to see the endless work her friend had to endure from day to day. She was always working or cleaning it seemed yet she didn't complain or blame anyone.

"You need to rest!" Maria said.

"I will after I visit the captain," Sveta replied, hoping it would take only a few minutes rather than hours with him.

They returned to their cabin, and Sveta quickly wiped herself down and changed clothes. "I'm going to get this over with so I can get to bed soon." She said as she headed back to the kitchen to gather the pie for the captain.

Maria decided to get some fresh air on the top deck. The night air was cooler than during the day which was a welcome relief from the heat of the kitchen. The ship slowly worked its way through the curving channel of the Sheksna. The river was less wide, and lights from the bank revealed small towns and settlements.

The quartermaster approached her as she sat in her usual place looking out at the river." I see you decided to stay aboard", he said.

"Da, I like it here," Maria replied.

"We are glad to have you." He added.

"We seem to be moving slower than before?" Maria asked.

"Indeed we are, there is less wind to work with and more turns on this part of the river. It will be like this until we reach Beluzero at the end of the week." He said, "As we get closer to winter there will be lights in the sky. Have you ever seen them?" he asked.

"No. What kind of lights?" Maria asked.

"It's difficult to describe, like ropes of light dancing across the horizon all night long." He said.

"What are they?" Maria asked.

"There are many legends, but I've always believed the one my father taught me, they are the souls of the dead leaving this earth." He replied.

Maria marveled at the idea of such lights, especially with their meaning as the quartermaster had described. She searched the horizon for the lights, but only saw stars in the night time sky.

"Can we see them from here?" Maria asked.

"No, once we're farther North, you will be able to see them on that side of the ship." He said pointing the right of the keel.

"Will you point them out for me when we get there? She asked impatiently.

"You can't miss them, you will see!" he chuckled.

Maria sat on the deck enjoying the view until the air grew too cold. She hoped Sveta had returned to the cabin and was already asleep, and went to check on her.

The sound of the anchor splashed into the water as the ship came to a halt for the night. The oars rumbled out of the water as the crew made their way to their beds. Maria passed some of them in the hall, working her way to her cabin. She didn't care for their hungry looks and ignored them when they invited her to join them in bed.

The quartermaster stepped down the stairs and all the men quickly dispersed like frightened mice. Maria smiled, as she felt his protection without having to say a single word. As long as he was nearby, she felt safe.

She walked to her cabin and looked immediately toward Sveta's bed when she opened the door. She was disappointed that her bed was empty, and wondered how her dear friend could manage such work and men in a single day.

Maria changed into her bedclothes and waited for Sveta to return. Perhaps she would have an interesting story to tell, or could share more about her erotic adventures. It was clear to Maria that Sveta was the highlight of her days aboard ship and without her, life would be a grim reminder of the sadness that set her on this journey.

# Masha, Run!

Maria fell into a deep sleep, her day at the farm in Cheropovets now like painted memories became scenes of her life in Rostov. She felt her mother brushing her hair as she read aloud in Latin. The feeling of the soil on her bare feet as she picked vegetables in the garden. She walked along the street where all the shops had once been and heard the sound of the horse's hooves echoing louder as she moved closer to the church at the center of town. She looked around and realized she was alone, not a single person in sight. She stepped toward the door of the church, it swung open, and her father emerged.

He was covered in blood and limping as he moved toward her. He grabbed her arm and as he pushed her and shouted, "Masha, Run!"

Her eyes popped open as she awoke, breathing heavily. She was certain it was real. Even her father's voice seemed to echo in the room. She reached and caressed her arm where the sensation of being grabbed still remained. She looked over and saw Sveta's empty bed, realizing she was completely alone, but someone had touched her. This was not imagination, her skin felt cold, her breath was rushed as if she had run for hours.

She sat up in her bed and felt her face become flush as a shiver ran down her back. "What is happening?" she wondered.

Strange noises began to emerge from the top deck, some men shouting in the distance followed by hard footsteps running in different directions. Suddenly the door of the cabin burst open, it was Sveta.

"Masha, wake up!" Sveta said in a nervous voice.

"What's happening?" Asked Maria.

"A Tatar scout ship is approaching, we are getting close to the boundary of Alchiday's control, and sometimes they come on board to look for stowaways or stolen goods. Basically, it's a shakedown, but if we don't give them something, they will take even more." She said as she tossed a shirt and pants for Maria to wear.

"Put this on and your shoes, we need to hide you quickly!" Sveta said nudging Maria toward the door.

"Why do I need to hide? I'm not a stowaway!" Maria insisted.

"Masha, we've told everybody in the ports that a young woman on the Kupala is looking for her mother and is on the way to Neva. Anyone could have overheard that. Those soldiers are seeking to get a reward for returning the girl that escaped from Rostov--Now go!" Sveta shouted as she pushed Maria down the hallway.

The quartermaster was waiting by the stairs, he took Maria by the hand and led her to the cargo hold. "Masha, I need you to do exactly what I say, or we will all be dead." He said as he pushed nets and boxes out of the way.

Sveta was right behind them, "It's okay Masha, we've done this before." She assured.

The quartermaster rolled an empty barrel into the center of the floor. He winced as he pried the top open with his bare hands, then turned, stretching his arms out towards Maria. "Right, in you go!" he said nervously.

Maria looked inside the barrel, she understood what they intended but shook her head feeling it was impossible to fit inside. "Ya ne magu!" She said as her voice revealed her fear.

"Well, they have plenty of room on the soldier's boat. Hmph?" The quartermaster said waiting for Maria to understand.

She nodded her head and lifted her leg trying to step inside the barrel. The quartermaster wrapped his arms around her and lifted her until both her feet could fit down inside. She then tried to lower herself into the barrel, but it was too small. She began to panic, "It's too small...they will find me!" Maria shouted in a whisper.

"Keep trying!" The quartermaster said as he moved more barrels and cargo around.

Maria shifted and tried to fit inside the barrel again. This time, she could lower herself almost all the way, but it was still not enough. She shook her head in frustration and fear as she stood back up.

"Ladno," said the quartermaster, "I have an idea."

He put his arms around Maria and lifted her out of the barrel while Sveta walked up the stairs to see if the soldiers had boarded the ship yet. The captain passed her in the hall, "Did you hide that girl yet?" He said in haste as he walked up the stairs.

"We're working on it," Sveta replied.

"Work faster, they are already alongside!" The captain snapped as he walked on to the top deck.

Sveta ran down the hall into the cargo hold, "They are alongside." She shouted.

The quartermaster could see the fear in Maria's eyes. He put his hands on her shoulders and said, "Don't worry lass, I won't let them take you." Maria nodded as she began to shake nervously.

"I need you to squat down for me, make yourself a small as possible." He said.

Maria squatted down and wrapped her arms around her knees. "Like this?" she asked.

"Da, perfect." The quartermaster replied as he knelt down and picked her up and carried her to the barrel. "Sorry about this." He said as he dropped her into the barrel pushing her all the way down."

Maria shouted in pain as the weight of her body pressed against her knees and back. It felt unbearable, but she was completely inside.

"Cover your ears," he said.

"Why?" asked Maria.

The quartermaster slammed the top back on, hammering it completely shut with his strong fists.

Maria then felt the sensation of the barrel rolling back into the corner, and the sound of other barrels being pushed next to it and on top of it. It was a grain barrel, allowing her to see slightly through the seams between the boards.

She could see the quartermaster and Sveta draping cargo nets and pushing boxes around her barrel, to make it less noticeable.

"That should do it. I've got to head topside; you should be in the kitchen." The quartermaster ordered as they both left the cargo hold.

Maria could hear the sound of her own breathing, she was terrified that she would be discovered by the soldiers and taken back to Rostov. She placed her hands on the sides of the barrel and tried to shift her body to relieve the pressure on her knees and ankles. Even the slightest movement gave her some relief.

She could hear shouting above deck and the unpleasant sound of the Turkic language as the soldiers searched the ship. The captain entered the cargo hold, followed by two soldiers. They pointed at different boxes and barrels as the captain seemed to understand them and showed them his papers for each item.

Then she could see one of the soldiers looking at a barrel filled with wine. He tipped it from side to side and nodded to the other soldier. "I'm sure we could spare a barrel for you and your men." The captain said.

Then the other soldier began to speak in Russian, "We appreciate your generosity but you are too quick to offer us compensation when all your records are in order." He said slowly. Perhaps there is something you do not wish us to find in our search?"

"Not at all, you can search the entire ship if you want." The captain replied.

"I do not need your permission to search your ship." Commanded the soldier. "Alim!" he shouted as one of his men brought Sveta into the cargo hold.

They pushed her onto her knees and held a sword to her throat. Then the soldier looked at the captain, "Where is the girl who escaped from Rostov?" He demanded.

Maria's heart began to beat so hard she could hear it in her ears. "This was it," she thought, they were going to discover her now.

"I know nothing of any fugitive, this is my cook, she's a tho lop from Neva. I have her papers in my cabin if you wish to see..." The captain began.

The soldier grabbed Sveta's hair and pulled her head back harshly, exposing her neck even more to his blade as she cried in fear.

"Hold on! I forgot...we had a young lady on board, she patched our sail and got off in Mologa." The captain said nervously

"How interesting that your memory returns. And if I slit your cooks throat open, will you remember more?" The soldier taunted as he shifted his blade against Sveta's throat.

The captain paused, calculating the resolve of the soldier. "Well, she's not much of a cook." He said sarcastically then laughed in hopes the soldier would calm down.

The soldier looked oddly at the captain, then smiled as he lowered his blade. The other soldiers joined in the laughter as they spoke in Turkic.

The captain exhaled, feeling he had diffused the crisis and would soon be free of the soldiers.

"Where is the quartermaster." The soldier ordered.

"I'm the quartermaster." Came a voice from behind the soldiers.

Maria peered through the seams in the barrel watching the quartermaster as he stepped into view.

The soldier drew his sword and let its blade rest on the quartermaster's shoulder.

"A cook is easy to replace, but a reliable quartermaster...he would be worth his weight in gold to the ship's Captain." The soldier taunted as he began to grip his sword tighter.

The quartermaster looked at the captain with fear in his eyes. The captain knew that these men would not be satisfied if they had to leave empty-handed. "Sir, I told you the truth. The girl is not here. Please take some wine for your trouble and..." the captain said politely.

The soldier gritted his teeth as he raised his blade and sliced diagonally across the quartermaster's chest cutting him open as he fell to the ground. Then he placed his sword on the captain's shoulder as Maria and Sveta watched in horror.

"I'm going to ask you again, where is the girl who escaped from Rostov?" the soldier demanded.

"Sir, she is not among us! She left the ship, and I haven't seen her since I swear to you!" The captain pleaded.

The quartermaster lay on the floor as his blood began to pool around his body. His eyes stayed fixed on the barrel where Maria was hiding. "He tells the truth." The quartermaster said shaking from the shock of his injury.

The soldiers looked at each other and then put their swords away.

"The next time you tell me to take something for my trouble, you will remember what my trouble can be." The soldier said as he turned to the other soldiers instructing them to take the wine and two more barrels near the door.

The captain followed the soldiers out of the cargo hold instructing his men to put the barrels on the ship. As soon as the soldiers left the room, Sveta jumped to the quartermaster's side. "Get some sheets and tear them into strips!" She commanded to the crew standing in the hallway.

The quartermaster's eyes remained on the barrel where Maria hid. He pointed his arm in her direction and tried to talk but was too weak for Sveta to understand.

"I need some help in here, now!" Sveta ordered.

Several oarsmen entered the room, shocked by what they saw. They quickly took their shirts off and covered the quartermaster to keep him warm. "He is losing a lot of blood." One of them said.

Maria began to bang on the sides of the barrel determined to get their attention, she wanted to help her devoted friend.

Sveta wrapped the shirts over the quartermasters bleeding body. A small trail of blood trickled from her neck where the sword had lightly cut her. She heard the noise and remembered Maria was still inside the barrel.

"Go, see if the soldiers are gone!" She said to one of the crew.

Moments later the man returned, "They just cast off." he said

"There, behind the cargo nets, she's inside the barrel, get her out! Sveta shouted.

The men quickly moved the nets and boxes out of the way. "Which one?" They asked each other. "Ya zdes! Ya zdes!" Maria shouted as she knocked and banged the barrel's sides.

She felt the men pull the barrel away from the wall, then a loud knocking and pinching sound came from the top as they forced a lever into the lid and pried it open. The light mixed with cooler air swirled inside as she looked up to see their faces. "Davai, davai" she insisted as she extended her arms out for them to pull her from the barrel.

The men grunted as they pulled her like a cork from a bottle. She could feel her knees and back being cut by the rough wood as she slowly and painfully emerged. Her legs were numb as they set her down. She immediately crawled across the floor toward Sveta and the quartermaster. "I'm so sorry!" She said to the quartermaster who was barely breathing.

The captain returned with the tackle box used for fishing.

"There's no surgeon we can reach in time." He said as he looked at Sveta's neck which was bleeding more heavily.

The crew returned with sheets from their bed, tearing them into strips with no idea what to do with them.

Sveta stood, appearing dizzy but determined to help. "Hand me one of those?" She said as she wrapped a strip around her neck.

"You will have to stitch him up, or he will bleed to death." She said to Maria.

Maria looked at Sveta then to the quartermaster, she was terrified at the sight of such a large cut and the blood that poured from his body.

"Masha, you're good with a needle!" Sveta insisted as the captain moved closer with the instruments and thread.

"I've never stitched a wound before!" She said as she looked carefully at his injury.

"You will try! He protected you, now save him!" Sveta insisted.

Maria felt a calm wash over her body, "I can do this." She assured herself

One of the crew handed a bottle of wine to Sveta, "For the pain." They said.

Sveta lifted the quartermaster's head and urged him to take a drink, but most of it ran out of his mouth and down his cheek.

She then held the bottleneck toward Maria, "Your hands!" She insisted.

Maria quickly lathered the wine over her hands to clean them while the captain threaded the needle. She pulled back a small part of the blood-soaked cloth to examine the wound where it began below the shoulder. It was pulsing slightly and made her feel that she would faint any second.

She snatched the bottle from Sveta's hand and lifted it to her lips, taking a long drink to dull the overwhelming fear and despair that overcame her. She then reached for the needle and held it to his skin. Her hands began to shake as she tried to make the first stitch. She imagined the pain the needle would add to his injury, the moment she pressed it through his flesh. It seemed incredibly cruel to put a suffering man through even more agony as she hesitated.

The quartermaster's eyes opened as he lifted his hand and touched Maria's arm. "Those are warp threads," He said weakly, forcing a smile to his face. Maria felt her heart melt as her eyes teared but she blinked it away and nodded, knowing he was relying on her. As the needle pierced his skin, he shuddered and flexed his body in anticipation of what was to come, but the pain and blood loss was too great, and he passed out.

Maria paused and looked terrified at Sveta, "Is he...?"

"He is still breathing, work quickly before he wakes up!" Sveta said, trying not to agitate the cut on her throat.

The captain pulled a box over for Sveta to sit on as the crew began to fill the room. Everyone watched silently as Maria's began to sew the wound. Her hands shivering as she punctured each side of the cut, sewing it together like a ripped tent. With each repetition she felt the fear leaving her hands, replaced with determination to save the quartermaster.

The captain saw the concern on everyone's faces and knew he had to lead the thoughts of the men before they began searching for blame or cause of the quartermaster's fate.

"That's excellent work." He said. "I've seen men live through much worse when the Tatars invaded my village. He's strong, he will be fine."

"Aye!" the men echoed in agreement as they watched.

Sveta and Maria also sighed in relief of the captain's words.

"Gennady, fetch the short plank, we'll carry him to his cabin." The captain shouted down the hall.

Moments later, Gennady returned with a plank of wood. He brushed the dust and dirt off of it and stood quietly watching over the captain's shoulder as Maria completed the stitches, placing bandages over the wound as Sveta continued handing her more strips of cloth. The pile of bandages slowly became more white than red as the bleeding stopped.

Maria looked up and saw Gennady watching her as she wiped her blood covered hands. He looked pale, almost seasick.

"Is he alright?" Maria asked.

Suddenly the short plank slipped from Gennady's hand, falling loudly on the deck as everyone turned to see what had happened. His lips turned white, and he fainted as the captain reached to catch him.

"Aye, no stones at all on this one! Take him up top!" The captain cursed as everyone in the room burst into laughter.

The moment lifted the mood of everyone as two men carried Gennady from the room. The short plank was slid beneath the quartermaster. Maria gently held the bandages in place as they carefully lifted him and took him down the hall to his cabin.

The captain tended to Sveta, looking at her neck and taking her to his cabin to clean the wound. "I'm all right, it looks worse than it is," Sveta said, declining his attention.

"Let's clean it up and be sure." The captain insisted, "You can't see your neck, but I can!"

The two of them went to the captain's cabin as Maria continued on with the quartermaster. The men helped her in sliding him off the plank and onto his bed. He was still unconscious, but his breathing continued, reassuring her they had done all they could for him.

She looked around the room and at the men. Unsure what to say or do. They simply watched him lying in his bed, covered in bandages and dried blood. Moments passed, and Maria felt she should move things along somehow.

"I guess we won't need the board anymore?" She said as she looked at in in their hands.

The men nodded, eager to help but also glad to have something constructive to do as they guided the plank out of the room and back up to the top deck.

Sveta entered the cabin with a clean white cloth wrapped around her neck. The captain followed, carrying a pail of water. He looked over the quartermaster and set the container by the wash basin. He took a towel and began to wipe the blood from the quartermaster's face and hands.

"I can do that." Maria insisted as she stepped forward.

"It's fine, you've done the hard part, let me feel a little useful." The captain said as he continued cleaning the quartermaster's face.

Maria stood in the midst of everyone, grateful to be safe and to have helped but also feeling responsible for everyone's injuries.

"Thank you, thank you for saving me from those soldiers." Maria sighed. "I have put you and everyone in danger by being on this ship." She said as she reached and touched Sveta softly.

"Nonsense." Said the captain. "Those bastards board us every time we go out of their territory. Last time they threatened to take Sveta!"

"Really?" Maria said astonished as she looked in Sveta's eyes, "How did you stop them?"

"I told them if they took her, they couldn't bring her back." The captain mused as he chuckled.

Sveta reached and swatted the captain on his shoulder, knowing he was joking but still feeling offended.

The captain turned and rinsed the cloth, turning the water red as he wrung it dry.

"Ladno, the two of you could use some rest, and clean clothes." The captain said without looking at them.

Maria looked down at her dress, it was covered in blood and dirt from the floor. Her fingernails were outlined in dried blood that smeared and smudged up to her elbows. Even her shoes were red.

Sveta took Maria's hand and guided her out of the quartermaster's cabin. They shuffled their way to their cabin and carefully sat down trying not to irritate their cuts and bruises. Maria could still see the needle in her mind as she stitched the quartermaster's wound. It felt like she was watching someone else's hands rather than her own.

Sveta sat beside Maria and washed her hands, wiping the blood away.

"It could have been much worse," Sveta said reassuringly.

"I feel like I caused this," Maria said staring into the distance.

"The soldiers will use any excuse to be violent. They don't value any life here because they came to conquer. And once they were in control, there were no more battles to sate their lust for blood. They just chose us tonight." Sveta said as she guided Maria's face to look into her eyes. "They would have come anyway!" she insisted.

"But they were looking for me!" Maria objected.

"They are just after the reward. There will be another person to hunt next week. This is how the Tatars feed their soldiers, to keep them loyal and corrupt. You don't really think you're the only blonde girl in Russia, do you? Hmm? Such a prize?" Sveta teased until a smile came to Maria's face.

Maria felt the guilt subside and reached to touch Sveta's bandage.

"Does it hurt?" Maria asked as she gently inspected the wound. She removed the cloth and saw that the bleeding had stopped, revealing a thin cut across her throat.

"I think it will be sore but in a few days will be gone," Sveta said as she began to wrap the injury.

The two of them pulled their dirty clothes off carefully, creating a pile on the floor as they each slipped into their bed dresses. There were no more words at the end of such a day, only sleep could write the conclusion. Sveta blew out the candle beside her bed as she laid down.

Maria closed her eyes, as her head fell into her pillow. She reached and touched her arm where the sensation of being grabbed by her father had woken her. It was the same place he had touched her when he pushed her out the door of the church in Rostov. The exact sensation, and the last time he would ever touch her. Had he come to warn her?  She imagined him watching over her from the world beyond as her eyes slowly closed in sleep.

# My Name Is Vladimir

Maria and Sveta awoke as the sun lit the room through their tiny window. They had slept for only a few hours and wanted to remain in bed but the crew needed to be fed, and the quartermaster needed his bandages changed. Sveta sat up on her bed, moaning and yawning as she combed her fingers through her hair. Then she fell back on the bed with a sigh. Her bandage hung loosely around her neck, exposing the small scar from the soldier's blade.

Maria slid her feet to the floor, and saw the bruises around her ankles, they were not as swollen as before but were still tender to the touch. She leaned forward to slide her hand over her ankle but quickly stopped when she felt the scrapes in her back aching from such a position. Her knees were red with scabs and her hands still had traces of blood around her fingernails.

"Kashmar!" she sighed, I look like a disaster.

Sveta sat up again, looking over at her friend. "You'll be fine in a few days." She said as she stood and got dressed, removing the bandage from her neck. "I'm more worried about the quartermaster."

"You want me to help with breakfast?" Maria asked.

"No, this morning I am going to put some fruit out, and that will be all until lunch. The men will understand." Sveta said as she hopped on one foot while putting her other shoe on.

"Ladno, I will check the quartermaster. I want to put the honey you bought me in Mologo on his wound, it will help him heal and prevent infection." Maria said through a soft yawn.

"Really?" said Sveta, "I didn't know honey could be used for that."

"Da, farmer's witchcraft," Maria said jokingly as she stood and took the honey from her bag.

"I'll be back soon; I need more sleep before lunchtime," Sveta said as she exited the cabin.

Maria carefully got dressed, being careful of her cuts and bruises. The simplest task became difficult as she tried not to aggravate her injuries. She slipped her shoes on and limped her way down the hall to the quartermaster's cabin. It was still painful to walk, but she knew her suffering was minor in comparison to what the quartermaster had gone through to save her.

She knocked on his door and thought to call him but then realized she had never learned his name. It seemed impossible to her that someone she knew so little about had protected her with his life.

She opened the door and entered the cabin, setting the honey aside as she approached his bed to check his wounds. He was asleep, but his breathing was erratic and shallow. She placed her hand on his forehead and immediately detected a strong fever.

"I'm just going to check your bandages." She whispered as she began to pull the blood-soaked cloth away from the stitches.

He immediately woke up shouting in pain as the bandages pulled at his skin as she removed them.

"I'm sorry!" She repeated over and over as she carefully removed them one by one.

He was breathing heavy and looked at her with shock. She knew it was the pain that he was reacting to, and the fever was making him delirious.

"I need you to drink some water, as much as you can take," She said.

He nodded and tried to sip from the cup she handed him, but it was impossible at this angle. Maria slid her hand beneath his neck and pulled him up carefully so he could drink. He winced in pain from the pressure this put on his stitches but held his position and drank several cups before nodding that he was finished. She carefully lowered him back onto his pillow and began cleaning his wound.

"The bleeding has stopped, and the stitches are holding, I just need to get as much of the dirt and blood off as possible," Maria said as he nodded in agreement. Her thorough and gentle hands worked quickly to minimize his discomfort.

"What's that?" He said as she reached for the jar she had brought.

"Something to make you heal faster." She replied as she drizzled a thin line of honey along the entire cut before covering him with clean bandages.

"You know…" She started, "I never learned your name. All this time you've been "the quartermaster" She said with a smile. "What is it?"

"My name is Vladimir," he said with a rough voice as his eyes closed. He relaxed and returned to normal breathing but was clearly still in a serious condition.

"Ladno Vladimir" Maria said as she gathered up the old bandages. "I'll be back to check on you soon."

As Maria exited his cabin, she saw the Captain coming down the stairs. "How is he?" Asked the captain.

"The bleeding has stopped, I just changed his bandages, and he has a fever." She replied.

"Molodets." said the captain in appreciation, "The fever is to be expected with such a large wound. Will you keep an eye on him? I need to run things top side while he is recovering." The captain asked.

"Konechno!" Maria replied, "He saved my life!"

The captain nodded, pleased with her answer. He made his way down the hall while Maria went to wash the bandages. She returned to her cabin and saw Sveta had already returned and was lying on her bed. Maria quietly cleaned the bandages and laid them out to dry. She did not want to disturb Sveta so she went to the kitchen to get something to eat.

It was the first time she had visited the kitchen without Sveta there. The men had already come and picked through most of the fruit, but she saw the familiar apples she and Sveta had bargained for in Cheropovets. She ate two of them, realizing how hungry she was as she reached for a third.

Her mind calmed, she was out of danger, the quartermaster was recovering, and the bruises on her ankles reminded her that she had escaped the Tatars once again. She felt guilty, as her freedom carried a high cost at the expense of others. "I'm undeserving of such selfless protection, how will I ever live a life worthy of such sacrifice?" She thought.

The sounds of the oars creaked beneath the ship, as it curved its way through the river. She could hear directions being shouted from the top deck to the oar deck below. "Hard to starboard!", "Ease up on port!" As the ship rocked from side to side. She returned to the cabin, and gently laid herself on the bed. She was not tired but didn't feel there was a better place for her at the time.

"How is Vladimir?" Sveta asked from the other side of the room.

"He is getting better." Maria replied, "Did I wake you?" she asked.

"No, I can't sleep during the day. I'm tired, so I will just lay here for a while." Sveta replied.

They quietly laid in their beds listening to the sounds of life on the ship. Maria began to think about the events the night before, "Were you afraid last night when that soldier had his sword to your throat? Maria asked.

"Not really, it's like a game with these Tatars, they always grab a woman or child and threaten them with a knife. It's how they negotiate." Sveta said. "But when they put a sword on a man, its disaster, just like you saw…. bastards, I hate them!"

"Was it true what the captain said about them wanting to take you, the last time they boarded the ship?" Asked Maria

"Da, they thought I was a prostitute working on the ship. They didn't believe that I was the ship's cook until the captain showed them papers of my father's debt." Sveta said recalling the experience, "Can you imagine? If a woman is a prostitute, they can make her a slave. If she is already a slave, then they leave her alone. Such a world."

"My father said women are like cattle to those men. I didn't realize what he meant at the time, but I'm quickly finding out how right he was." Maria said.

"He is absolutely correct!" Sveta replied. "If they had taken me I don't think I would survive a day with them."

"I can't believe the captain said they wouldn't take you because he made them promise not to bring you back." Maria teased.

Sveta laughed, "Da ladno, eto vso, no more apple pie and no more sex! His balls will turn blue before he gets any relief from me!"

Maria grew quiet, "Can that happen?" she asked.

Sveta coughed in amusement, "Personally, I've never seen a man with blue balls, it is just a phrase men use to describe how they get when they don't have sex for a long time." Sveta said as she leaned on one arm facing Maria's bed.

Maria also turned wanting to know more about this idea.

"I've grown to realize that sex is like food for men. No matter how much they have, they will be hungry again in a few hours. And as time goes by they start to starve, and get crazy, doing anything to satisfy their needs. I think this is why prostitutes and hands will always be popular." Sveta replied sarcastically.

"I think women need sex too, but the need comes from a different place for us. We want love, emotion, and of course children." Maria replied.

"A woman who has a good lover, who can make her fly, she will want sex as much as a man. But in my experience, most men only want to finish and then they roll over and go to sleep. Eto uzhas!" Sveta said, "Imagine being married to such a man your whole life!"

"I never thought about it like that," Maria said.

"Of course, most women don't! They just expect the man will take care of them in bed, but if he is without experience, how will he learn?" Sveta asked.

"He can learn from his wife, she can explain what she needs, and they learn together," Maria answered.

"Sometimes yes, I think that can work, but men are so fragile in bed. If she asks for too much from him, he will think she is missing some past lover. Most women are pretending to fly away in bed just so the man will finish!" Sveta said with a cynical tone.

Maria remembered how the women acted in the Tavern, they were so convincing to the man, "Was it all a show?" she wondered.

"So you think it's best to find a man with experience?" Maria asked.

"Konechno dorogaya, why take chances with a naive virgin, when you can fly every night!" Sveta teased. "But I will tell you this, a woman has to know herself better than the man. She can't expect him to teach her how to finish, she should be aware of the places she wants to feel him the most."

"What do you mean?" Maria asked, realizing she didn't know this about herself either.

"Well, sometimes sex can feel good but not enough to finish. You just keep going, but it's not...building." Sveta began.

Maria compared thoughts about her private moments touching herself and tried to connect it with the description Sveta began to weave.

"So there you are, in the middle of sex, and it's just not going to happen. This is when you need to stop and say, 'let's try this, I need to be on top, or I want you behind me', or you can rub yourself down there while the man is inside you." Sveta continued.

Maria felt embarrassed, trying not to show she understood everything in theory rather than by experience. Her face felt warm as Sveta spoke more.

"Sometimes I like it when the man is on top of me, I can feel his body pressing down on me, and I run my hands across his arms or his back! Just...not the same thing every time or it becomes routine, like brushing your hair or cooking." Sveta replied.

"What about dark and forbidden?" Maria giggled as she was still curious about this idea, "Does that become routine?"

"Ah, well...that." Sveta began as she laughed in embarrassment. "OK, I'll tell you but don't think bad of me."

Maria shook her head, quickly agreeing in eager anticipation for more.

"Well you know, a man likes to be sucked down there. I mean, he lives for it." Sveta said.

Maria nodded, although not sure how it all worked.

Sveta noticed Maria's curious look, "Let's start there. For a man, his cock is his trophy. He wants you to admire it and give it so much attention.  Your hands, your mouth, your breasts and definitely everywhere else." Sveta said.

Maria listened intently as she sat up in the bed, paying attention like a student.

Sveta continued, "If you just suck him in your mouth, it will be fun for him, but this is not enough. You have to show you are hungry for him, play with his balls, lick them, let your spit make his shaft wet as you stroke it and look at him with seductive eyes. It's like worship in a way, he is standing there, and you kneel in front of him and show all your affection…. make sense?" Sveta asked.

Maria nodded, as she felt herself getting warm from the ideas she was hearing. "Then what?" she asked.

Sveta laughed, "Ladno, … it's a bit embarrassing to describe but…while you suck him… take your other hand and slide it up his leg. Keep going until you feel his balls in your hand, then let your fingers go back between his legs until you feel his…." She stopped talking as she coughed from unexpected laughter and anxiety.

Maria's eyes grew wide, "No!" she shouted.

"Da!" Sveta insisted. "You can take one finger and put it in there while you suck him …he will finish quickly like an explosion, boom!" Sveta laughed. "Not all men will allow this of course if they are too traditional, but once they try it, they like it!"

Maria tried to imagine such intimacy, it seemed grotesque and sinful to her. "It sounds kind of … evil." She said shyly.

"Dark and forbidden, dorogaya. What did you expect?" Sveta replied.

"Well, thanks for explaining it to me." She said as the images Sveta described raced through her mind.

"There is more!" Sveta insisted. "The man can do similar things for the woman if he is a real lover."

Maria's eyes lit up as her interest grew again, "Tell me."

"It's similar idea, he licks you down there or puts his tongue inside. I really like how that feels." Sveta added, "One time, this guy sucked me down there, right on my little white bump, you know where it is?" she asked.

Maria nodded, understanding all too well this little bump between her legs that made her come hard when she pressed it.

"It was similar to how it feels when he sucks your nipples but ... down there, it felt so strong!" Sveta's voice grew in excitement, "Then he started curling his fingers inside, right beneath that bump and I thought I would die from pleasure. I was begging him to take me, it was uncontrollable!" She shouted.

"Did he do it to you then?" Maria asked as she felt the story moving through her body.

"No!" Sveta replied, "And that's the thing about an experienced lover, he gives you what you need, not what you ask for."

Maria looked puzzled, "I don't understand." She said.

Sveta continued, "He knew how to make my body go up, higher and higher, and he could keep me there as long as he wanted! And just when I think I can't think any more of him down there, he pushes my knees toward my chest and slides his tongue inside me...and not just the one hole but...both!"

Maria gasped in shock at the idea. She was utterly speechless and unable to respond.

"I really thought I would stop breathing, it felt amazing, so erotic and passionate! Then he took me onto his lap and sat at the side of the bed. I wrapped my legs around his waist and felt him go inside, I was so wet for him, and when he slid inside, I thought I would finish right there! Then as we made love, he slid his hand down my back. I could feel where he was going but didn't expect it when one of his fingers slipped into my...ass!" She said embarrassed to use such a word.

Maria's eyes were as big as plates, she couldn't imagine such an experience although her mind was racing with images.

"It was like two men at once, but all from him!" Sveta said as her hands drew outlines in the air of her experience.

"I didn't know what he was doing; I just didn't want it to stop. I have never been so wet for a man, the whole floor underneath us was soaked." Sveta said as she laid back on her bed. "That was the best sex of my life, and I just imagine not knowing it was possible if I was with a less talented man my whole life!"

Maria sat quietly understanding the depth of her new knowledge. It was horrible and fascinating all at once. She had so many questions but felt she had already pushed Sveta too much on the subject. Still, her curious nature emerged before she could refrain from asking, "Did he do more than put his finger there?" She said innocently.

Sveta smiled as she sat back up, "Masha you are so adorable sometimes!" she began, "Yes, he put his shaft in my ass, I wanted him like that after he woke me up down there. I mean, such attention can actually make you crave darker sex."

"It seems ... unnatural to me." Maria replied, "I don't know if I would like that."

"Dorogaya, do you really think we have two holes so close together by accident?" Sveta said sarcastically.

Maria paused, unsure how to respond.

"It feels different, it's more intense, and it can make you finish in a different way than usual." Sveta explained, "But the best is when he is in you the regular way, and you feel him coming inside, like a hot explosion. There is nothing better! These other things are just ways to keep it interesting so it's not the same each time."

Maria nodded, as she tried to process so much new knowledge. She felt aroused, wet and eager to try such ideas with a man, or even by herself when she was alone. "I'm not sure what to say now." Maria giggled. "...Thank you?"

Sveta laughed, "Pozhalysta" I'll tell you, later on, I need to stop now because I'm getting wet remembering all of this!'

"More?" Maria gasped.

Sveta laughed and nodded her head, "Everything I have told you was not even half." She mused.

Maria could not imagine such a possibility. Compared to all she had known, there was an entire planet of unexplored territory, but Sveta had the map. It was as if she had climbed a mountain only to see a larger one in the distance.

"There is so much I do not know," Maria said. She retraced each interlude she had seen in the tavern and in the cabin. It is hard to distinguish what was real and what was done to please the man in the way Sveta had described.

"How many women are pretending with their husbands?" Maria asked.

"Most of them!" Sveta smirked. "It seems unthinkable that a woman would hide her unsatisfied needs but then, how would she explain it to her husband? And how would he react when he finds out she was pretending before?"

"I see your point," Maria said imagining such a conversation.

"Can you imagine how he will feel, knowing he can't make his wife finish? Or that she lied to him and now he can't trust her? He would lose interest in sex with her!" Sveta said.

"Uzhas, even if he did learn what to do, he would not trust her response," Maria said.

"This is why women keep silent about it, too much to lose or explain. I think they just take care of themselves when the man is not around." Sveta replied.

"You mean with their hands?" Maria asked.

"Or another man." Sveta shrugged.

"So what is the conclusion?" Maria said aloud. "To lie and keep the peace?"

"No!" demanded Sveta. "To never lie! Make him satisfy you or find someone who does and marry him!" she insisted.

It seemed so practical and wise although both ladies knew life doesn't offer such simple choices. They talked more, exploring the reality of how life should be and how it actually was behind closed doors. It was as if everyone pretended, playing a role of dutiful husband or devoted wife while secretly wishing for something else. There had to be a better path for finding happiness with a mate, and both were determined to discover it through their conversations.

Their honesty and freedom to speak to their minds created and energy in the room that was contagious. It was as if they were solving the great problems of mankind and would soon emerge from the cabin with all the answers.

# The Giant of Lake Beloya

Maria awoke to the welcome sounds of the crew loading cargo from the hold onto the top deck. This meant they would soon be in Port and after a week of slowly moving up the Volga, she was eager to get off the ship and feel the ground beneath her feet.

It seemed everyone on board shared the same excitement, even Vladimir had requested he be topside to coordinate the port activities. Sveta was already in the kitchen preparing oatmeal for everyone. She and Maria had planned on shopping in the market and searching for information about her mother.

The captain stood on the top deck, waiting for the quartermaster to be brought up for his first walk since his injury. All the men cheered as Vladimir slowly walked up the stairs, gritting his teeth with each step as he tried to masque the pain.

"Come on old friend" The captain shouted, "Can't stay in bed forever!" he said as Vladimir smiled and leaned on the mast for balance.

"I've kept things going while you were recovering," said the captain.

"Nu konechno, which is why everything's such a mess!" Vladimir teased.

The captain burst into laughter and began to walk below. "Welcome back!" he shouted as he walked down the stairs.

Gennady stood by the quartermaster, "Captain says I should do the shouting for you today?" he asked.

"Da Gena, I'll tell you what to say, and you repeat so the men can hear, ponimayesh?"

"Ponimayu!" Gena replied, looking forward to the idea of commanding the crew.

The ship moved quickly toward the dock as the quartermaster began his work, as a conductor of a symphony of musicians.

"Drop the sail." He murmured.

"Drop the sail!" Gena shouted at the top of his lungs.

"Easy Gena, they are not deaf," Vladimir said as the crew began to chuckle.

"Helm to port, prepare the anchor." Vladimir began, as each step unwound in exact precision.

"Secure the oars, cast the first line." He continued, "Quickly Gena!" Vladimir whispered.

Gennady shouted the commands as the ship curved into position in the dock.

"We're moving too fast for this dock," Vladimir said as he looked over the bow.

Gennady began to shout what he heard, then looked at Vladimir... "Was I supposed to say that?"

"Reverse starboard oars in the water, drop the anchor." Vladimir chuckled, realizing how careful he had to be.

The oars quickly extended on one side of the ship, dragging it to a crawl as the anchor splashed off the stern.

Gennady watched in amazement as the ship gently came to rest alongside the dock as if a giant hand had gently placed it there.

"Secure forward and aft lines, set the gang plank, all hands on deck," Vladimir said as he patted Gennady on the back.

Gennady shouted each command, and watched the workers react in exact precision; it was an inspiring experience for the young shipmate.

"What next sir?" Gennady asked. "Shall we begin loading cargo?"

Vladimir smiled, "We have to make room for it first. Let's offload what we have, get paid, and then we take on our next load."

"Right, I knew that!" Gennady replied as he headed to the cargo hold.

"Gena!" The quartermaster called, "Watch these merchants, they will try and renegotiate the price once their cargo is on the dock. Captain's orders are that they pay first, then we offload. Ponimayesh?"

"Ponimayu!" Gena shouted as he turned to see the merchants arriving on deck. "Who's first?"! He shouted. A trader raised his hand and pointed at several barrels that were his.

"Davai, where's your payment?" Gennady snapped.

Vladimir watched the young man so full of energy, eager to do his job, "Gospodi!" He whispered to the crew that was standing nearby.

The men laughed for a moment, but Vladimir wanted them to respect Gennady as well.

"Well go on, get the man's cargo unloaded!" He barked as he held his hand close to his aching chest.

The men quickly dispersed and began unloading. Minutes later Sveta and Maria walked onto the deck. They saw Vladimir standing by the mast and marveled that he was on his feet.

"Vladimir! You're out of bed! How do you feel?" Maria asked as she rubbed his back.

"Like hell!" he laughed, but glad to be out of that bed.

"Don't do too much too soon." Sveta cautioned.

"We're going to the market; can we get you anything?" Maria asked.

Vladimir thought for a moment, "I promised my daughter a new coat for winter. If you could pick something out for her?" He said as he felt in his pockets for coins.

You can pay us when we get back!" Insisted Sveta.

"Of course!" Maria replied, "Oh, how old is she?"

"She will be 13 this year" Vladimir replied

"We'll find the perfect coat for her!" Sveta said.

They exited the ship and headed for the market. The port was enormous, fishing and transport vessels extended to the horizon in both directions.   Sveta led Maria to the market area and pointed toward the clothing and garment shops. "I need to get more vegetables, but you can look for a coat there. They have fine furs here; I'm sure Vladimir's daughter will be happy with one." Sveta said.

"Shall we meet back here or at the ship?" Maria asked.

"I'll find you in the shops; it shouldn't take me too long," Sveta replied.

Maria nodded and turned toward the shops. Suddenly she felt Sveta grab her by the wrist and pulled her an alley. "What are you doing?" Maria asked.

Sveta looked into Maria's eyes and then over her shoulder, "There are two soldiers behind you." She murmured.

"Do you think it's the same ones?" Maria asked nervously.

"I can't tell from here; Tatars all look the same," Sveta replied.

"What should I do?" Maria asked nervously.

"Just stay out of sight, they don't know what you look like, so blend in with the crowd and don't walk near them," Sveta said calmly.

Maria began to walk away as Sveta reached for her again, "Masha! It's better you don't ask about your mother here, ponimayesh?!" Sveta said in a whisper.

"Ponimayu." Maria nodded as she exited the back side of the alley, keeping her distance from the soldiers and stepping around objects and people to block their view. Once they were out of sight, she relaxed and felt more excited by the shops and street life of the port.

She found several fur coat shops, and tried many of them on, imagining how nice it would be to have one for herself. The shop owner brought her several to try on, telling her all about the fur and where it had come from. A small mirror was fixed to the wall, and she turned in all directions to admire how the coat looked on her. The sensation of shopping was an absolute thrill for her, there was so much to see, and it all looked perfect.

Some of the coats still had feet or heads of the animals on them, reminding her where fur comes from, causing her to lose interest in owning a coat like this for herself. As beautiful as the coats were, she could not separate the thought of all that suffering wrapped around her body.

She chose a small fur for Vladimir's daughter and picked a long woven tunic made of wool for herself. "I think this one is perfect, how much did you say it was?" She said as she turned to address the shop owner.

There directly in front of her was the Tatar soldier that had injured Vladimir. His companions stood outside while he had entered the store. He looked directly at Maria as if he recognized her. She could not speak as the fear of being captured rushed through her veins like fire and ice.

He walked towards her and lifted up his hand, she knew she was caught. She could not run, she could not move, she was frozen in the same bondage of fear that had imprisoned her when she saw her father killed.

She closed her eyes, knowing her life was about to change forever. The soldier's hand pushed her shoulder firmly to one side as he walked past her to look in the mirror. She stood still for a moment, realizing he was not interested in her at all, only his visage as he stroked his beard.

She gathered herself quickly as the shop owner returned. "Have you made up your mind?" The owner said bluntly, noticing the soldier in their midst.

"Da, these two." Maria said as she poured coins into the owner's hand, "Is it enough?" she asked.

"D-Da ladno, enough..." The shop owner said stuttering in surprise.

Maria quickly walked from the store, exiting the door past the men who stood outside waiting. She didn't look at them or turn in their direction; she simply plunged into the crowded street to make herself disappear from their view.

She caught her breath as she found safety in the busy streets. The shops enticed her with their clothing, food, wine and books.

She had never seen so many things to buy in one place and felt she would exchange all her money without realizing it.

She noticed a street performance taking place and watched as children lined up to watch it. She walked over and saw actors pretending to be small, while a man pretended to be a giant, stomping around them. The giant picked up a large bowl full of water as if to drink it. Then the children all giggled as the giant went away rubbing his belly.

"That's the legend of the giant and the lake," Sveta said as she walked up behind Maria.

Maria jumped as Sveta touched her shoulder. "Gospodi!" She shouted.

"What happened to you?" Sveta asked.

Maria told her the whole story about the soldier as Sveta's eyes grew bigger and bigger in shock.

"Well, they do know what *I* look like." Sveta said, "So we should go before they realize the Kupala is in port."

Maria's face turned white with fear, she hadn't considered how many people were now in danger. "Maybe we should not walk together?" Maria said.

"Relax, when soldiers are in port they are looking for two things, sex and drinks! We will be fine." Sveta assured as she changed the subject to distract Maria, "That children's play you were watching, I thought it was just a story for children, but Vladimir swears the lake in this town can disappear overnight." Sveta said.

"Really? Oh, I think they he is just teasing you." Maria said.

Sveta shrugged her shoulders as if she wasn't sure if she believed it or not. She touched Maria's tunic and smiled, "Finally, something to keep you warm on the ship!"

"Da!" Maria agreed.

"Is that the coat for Vladimir's daughter?" Sveta asked excitedly, "It's gorgeous! How much was it?"

Maria smiled and said, "Isn't it beautiful? I gave 10 pieces for it."

"Sveta gulped, that's a lot! I don't know if Vladimir can afford this." Sveta said as they rushed back to the ship.

"I'm not taking his money, he saved my life, it's the least I can do for him," Maria said confidently.

Sveta ran her fingers through the coats luxurious hair as they walked. "I wish I had a blanket like this, I'd never get out of bed." She sighed. "A naked woman covered in fur is irresistible to a man!" Sveta teased.

They laughed as they navigated their way back to the ship. Sveta inspected the vegetable deliveries while Maria went on board to find Vladimir and show him the coat she had bought. The ship was preparing to set sail, and everyone was in a hurry to move on to the next port.

Maria saw Vladimir still standing on deck, trying to remain on his feet a while longer. He was looking out over the lake as Maria presented him with the coat. Sveta watched as she told Vladimir she was going to pay for it. He seemed truly touched and carefully hugged Maria for her kindness.

Sveta went below to prepare dinner as the deckhands began storing the cargo below. Maria noticed Vladimir seemed transfixed on the lake, as he continued to stare at it.

"Something wrong?" Maria asked.

"I want to be off this lake as soon as possible, it's cursed," Vladimir said.

"Really?" Maria replied.

"Da! Seriosno, it can disappear overnight and anything in it as well." He said convincingly.

"When I was a boy, my father and I came through here on our way to Yaroslavl. You can imagine our surprise when the river turned into a waterfall, pouring into a giant hole where the lake once was!" He continued. "Several that went before didn't get a chance to tie off their boat upstream, and their ship and all the crew just went over."

Maria was shocked to imagine such a scene. "Is that why they tell that story to the children in town about a giant coming and drinking the lake?" She asked.

"Da, the local legend is that a giant sleeps in the woods. If he is woken up, he comes to the lake and drinks until the lake is no more." Vladimir said.

"The villagers told my father and I that they heard nothing during the night, the lake was simply gone when the sun came up.

I wouldn't' have believed it, but I was there." He said pointing at a corner of the lake where a river trailed off.

"We tied off our ship and walked right there on that bank, the water was simply gone, only mud and ship wreckage down below," Vladimir said shaking his head in disbelief. "We had to wait here until the water returned which took weeks. Ever since then I've always known to move quickly through Lake Beloya." He said.

Gennady approached them as they spoke. "You orders, Sir?" He asked.

"Hoist the sale and dip the oars for speed, we want to be off this lake as soon as possible." He commanded. "I'm done for the day; they are in your hands Gennady," He said.

Gennady turned and echoed the commands as Maria headed helped Vladimir down the stairs. Each step was very painful as he tried not to put any stress on his wound. Maria held his arm and encouraged him with each step, counting them down until he was at the bottom.

Vladimir smiled and thanked Maria for her kindness and for the coat. He was out of breath as he entered his cabin to lie down, but seemed in good spirits. "I'll change your bandages in the morning," Maria said. Vladimir waved as Maria closed his door.

Maria kept wondering how accurate the stories about giants really were. Perhaps it was just a fairy tale, but the way Vladimir's eyes looked out over the lake was very convincing. She began to share the wish to leave the lake quickly and continue north on the Sheksna.

# Scars, Damage, Control

Maria arrived in the galley and picked up some food for Vladimir. She quickly took it to his room and then returned to finish her meal. She sat with Sveta sat in the kitchen as the crew left their dishes to be cleaned. One by one the bowls and plates grew into a pile that Sveta chose to ignore as they talked.

They sipped soup made from the fresh vegetables Sveta had purchased in the market. Maria felt the familiar repetition of setting out from the port, while the mood around the ship focused on getting things underway. "It's interesting how everyone looks forward to being in port, but when it is time to go, there is a rush of energy to get moving," Maria stated.

"This is the sailor's curse." Sveta replied, "Never in the same place too long and always looking forward to what comes next."

"This is the slowest part of the trip because the river gets smaller now. We're heading toward the Karelia region and Lake Onega; it is beautiful there!" Sveta said with a smile. "There is a port there where rocks were carved by the ancients, you can see how they fished and hunted, it's so interesting!"

Maria's eyes grew wide with intrigue. She had never seen anything older than the church in her town. "Do they write stories in the rocks?" She asked.

"It's more like a story told in pictures, and everyone reads them differently," Sveta replied.

The sound of the ship oars began to permeate the galley. The captain and crew were determined to move as quickly as they could upriver while the weather was pleasant and the full moon lit the path. It was a calm night, and the ship moved quickly through the open water.

"The crew seems to have a very hard life," Maria said

"When we are going upriver, yes, the current works against us and sometimes the wind doesn't help. But this is the last of the heavy rowing. After Onega, we have the current and a strong wind to take us toward Neva." Sveta replied. "The trip will go much faster then."

Maria began to realize she would not be on the ship forever, even though it had become a home to her, and her new friends felt like family, the journey would soon be coming to an end. She felt saddened by the realization but then remembered the hope of being reunited with her mother in Neva.

"Do you think we could visit each other during the winter?" Maria asked.

"That would be lovely!" Sveta replied. "I can show you all the interesting places to visit, the beautiful shops and where the wealthy sailors go looking for girls!" She said with a giggle.

"I'm already looking forward to it," Maria added.

The conversation continued with ideas for enjoying the winter in Neva until Sveta surprised Maria, "Masha, someone wants to visit me tonight in the cabin. Do you mind? "She said shyly.

Maria hesitated, "Where should I go?", she asked.

"You don't have to go anywhere, but if you could pretend you're asleep it would be...easier," Sveta said as she poured more soup in Masha's bowl.

Maria thought about the last time she had seen Sveta with a man in the cabin, it was one thing for her not to know she wasn't sleeping, but another if she did.

"I don't know what to say." Maria replied, "It's your cabin, I'm just a guest, but maybe I could stay up on the deck or something?"

"The crew sleeps on deck, you'll be safer in the cabin!" Sveta insisted.

Maria stared at the floor, she felt embarrassed by consenting to such a plan. Her curiosity was already beginning to build in her mind, even though she was sure she would say no.

"You remember how I told you men are different; some are more erotic than others?" Sveta asked mysteriously.

"Da, konechno I remember, why?" Maria asked as her interest began to grow.

"There is this one merchant who came on board, he travels with us often." Sveta started, "He came on board today, and I saw him at dinner."

"What about Ivan?" Maria sighed, "I thought he was the one you wanted to be with."

"Ivan is a good man, the best. But he hasn't asked me to marry him. Besides, this merchant can do things Ivan doesn't know about." Sveta said.

"What things?" Maria asked

"Pretend you're asleep and find out." Sveta teased.

"Oh, ok I'll fake being asleep, but I liked you with Ivan, he seems like the perfect man for you," Maria said in a sad tone.

"One day I might teach Ivan all the things I like, but then he will ask where I learned them. For now, he hasn't asked me to be his wife, so I am free to do as I wish. And I hope for a man who can give me something different." She said as her eyes became far away in her thoughts.

"For me, I want to fall in love and be married, then do all those things," Maria said, realizing how simple it must have sounded to Sveta.

Sveta paused, "I used to think that way too." She said.

"What happened, you seem so free in your choices of men?" Maria asked.

Sveta giggled, "Well that's one way of saying it nicely." She replied as she placed their empty bowls down.

"Masha, no one knows this about me, but I know I can trust you," Sveta said as she became somber. "I like the power of having as many men as I want, whenever I want. It's very pleasant for me to attract and seduce them."

"I understand but don't you worry what people might think about you?" Maria asked.

"Not really. I know it sounds bad but, I like the idea of men wanting me only for sex, no emotions or complications, they just want me so much that they would even pay me for the privilege!" She replied.

Maria felt as if she didn't know Sveta at all. Her words offended all Maria's sensibilities and beliefs. "How can you not want love? And don't act like you feel nothing because I saw how you were with Ivan!" Maria insisted.

Sveta hesitated, "With Ivan, I'm the woman I could be, with the rest, it's who I am now."

"It doesn't seem right to me; it can't just be about the money or the sex," Maria said trying not to offend her friend. "Sveta, I'm sorry, I haven't experienced a man even once, I shouldn't assume to know more than you."

Sveta's eyes sparkled as she fought back her tears. Maria thought she had gone too far, but the darker truth was boiling inside Sveta's memories as she struggled with admitting them out loud.

Sveta stood and walked around the galley wall, making sure the room was empty. She returned and sat next to Maria so she could talk quietly.

"Masha, your first time should be special and with someone you love, and always with someone you love. Sex by itself is an empty pleasure, you mustn't think otherwise. Most men want me out of their bed as soon as they finish, and it feels horrible to be cast aside after they are inside you. The money, it makes it bearable, even forgivable, but my emotions look away because if nothing else, at least I got paid." Sveta said.

Maria reached and held Sveta's hand, "Sveta, you are a beautiful, kind woman, you deserve love and happiness. You don't have to sell yourself just to feel close to it." Maria assured.

Sveta's eyes teared, "It's not that. I just don't feel like I'll ever be pure, so why not embrace the scars and damage and turn it into power rather than a weakness. I really do like sex, it's not a revelation, I know... but it's the idea that I'm in control,  that is what makes it appealing to me." She said.

Maria looked into Sveta's eyes, her words were revealing more than she had intended. "Scars, damage, sex, control...these were not experiences of a woman in love, it was something tragic." Maria thought

Maria ran her fingers through Sveta's long chestnut hair, grooming her in a supportive gesture, as the tears fell from both their faces.

"Something happened to you, yes?" Maria started, "I think it was when you were younger?"

Sveta nodded but couldn't speak. It was sad to see her painful memories running through her mind as she wrapped her arms around herself as if she felt cold, vulnerable and afraid.

Maria put her arms around Sveta, not realizing the depth of the pain she had just uncovered. She felt Sveta shaking as she cried without making a single sound, only quick breaths as if she were drowning and trying to stay afloat.

"Shh," Maria soothed, "You're not there now, and you're safe here. We don't need to talk about this anymore."

Sveta stood and nodded, reaching for a dishtowel to wipe her face, "Da, never going back there."

Maria stood and hugged Sveta, not knowing what else to do. She held her tightly and only wanted her hurt to fade and never return. "Let's talk about something else?" Maria said.

Sveta laughed uncomfortably, "Davai! Now my eyes are all puffy no one will want me like this."

Maria nudged Sveta, "Then they don't deserve you!" She snapped.

Sveta let out a big sigh and looked at the pile of dishes that were waiting for her. "Back to work." She said in a loud exhale.

"I'll help, you have a big date tonight, and I need to be asleep when he arrives." Maria giggled.

Sveta looked at her, "You'll do it?" She said with a smile.

Maria nodded, she wanted her dear friend to feel better, and if this was important to her, she knew her silence was a small price to pay.

"Are you going to watch?" Sveta teased.

"Stop!" Maria giggled, feeling embarrassed by her curious nature. "Of course!" She added reluctantly.

They worked quickly through the dishes, setting them out to dry and be ready for the morning meal. Sveta cleaned the stove, oven, and sink while Maria swept and mopped the galley floor.

"Do they get any of the food in their mouths?" She joked as she worked her way across the dirty floor.

"I know! They leave more on the floor than in their bellies!" Sveta shouted from the kitchen. "I begged the captain for a dog, but he said no because then there would be another mess to clean later."

"Takaya svinya!" Maria joked, "Such pigs!"

"You should see their toilet!" Sveta added as she finished in the kitchen, "One time I had to go in there, apparently getting anything into the pot is optional!"

Maria shivered in disgust as they both laughed and put the room to rest. Sveta blew out the lantern as they headed up the stairs. "Thanks for helping me, you're a good friend," Sveta said.

"Dishes and cleaning don't bother me; it was my pleasure," Maria said kindly.

"I wasn't talking about dishes," Sveta said as she kissed Maria's forehead at the top of the stairs.

They walked together to their cabin, both anticipating what lie ahead for the night. The sound of the ships anchor splashed in the water as the oars came to a halt and the ship came to rest until sunrise. The crew shuffled their way to top deck to rest as the Sveta and Maria began preparing for the arrival of the mysterious merchant.

# The Merchant

Maria paced the floor while Sveta washed the smell of the kitchen from her body.  The merchant would be there any moment, and Maria felt nervous.

"Should I just close my eyes and pretend or...?" Maria said anxiously.

"Masha, calm down. All those merchants drink and gamble the whole night, he will be drunk by the time he arrives, and we'll blow out the candle so he won't be able to see much at all." Sveta said calmly.

"I'm not sure about this now..." Maria said nervously.

Sveta stood from her bed, setting her washcloth aside. She was completely naked as she walked toward Maria, "You've seen me like this plenty of times now, what's the problem? "She teased as Maria sat on her bed and slipped under her blanket.

"I haven't seen him before," Maria muttered.

"Men, they are all the same," Sveta replied in sarcasm.

Maria knew this was not true, each time she had watched couples having sex, the men seemed very different to her. Some were attractive, and some looked like wild beasts, there was no way to predict what she might see tonight.

"You like being watched?" Maria asked shyly.

Sveta waited with her answer as she looked in the mirror to fix her hair and slide her dress on.

"Yes, it excites me. I don't know why. But it does... and you like to watch, da?" Sveta replied turning the question to Maria

Maria felt uncomfortable as her face felt hot while she held her answer.

Sveta laughed, "Ah, naughty girl!" She teased, "I'll try to give you a good show then since you're helping me out."

"How am I helping?" Maria asked wondering if she was expected to do something.

"By letting me bring him in here," Sveta replied. "There is no other place but the kitchen and it's too risky down there."

Maria hadn't considered the kitchen. "Maybe I should go there instead?" She said as the anxiety began to set in.

The sounds of footsteps approached the door, and a knock broke their conversation. Maria looked at the door as if a ghost were on the other side. Sveta walked and blew out the candle and motioned to Maria to be asleep as she walked to the door. It was too late to exit the room now, as Maria pulled the blanket over her face to avoid eye contact.

Sveta opened the door as the man's voice boomed, "Svetlana! My little bird!" He shouted in a slur of drunken happiness.

"Shh," Sveta cautioned as she invited him in. "My cabin mate is asleep; we don't want to wake her."

"Why not? She can join us!", He boasted as he walked toward Maria's bed.

Maria was in shock, she thought for sure he would pull her blanket away, but Sveta routed him to her bed instead. "Misha, come sit here, you know I am all you need."

"Mda, such a spirited woman!" He boasted as she put her finger to his lips.

"If she wakes up, we have to stop, so, shush" Sveta insisted as she began to remove his coat.

"Ladno, whatever you want, just take care of me dorogaya!" He said as he stood to let her finish removing his clothes.

Maria carefully slid her blanket down passed her eyes to see what was happening; she hoped it was dark enough to conceal her point of view.

She saw Sveta on her knees, removing his boots and pants in an eager fashion. Within seconds he was naked, with clothes spilled around his feet, and only an open shirt across his shoulders.

He was a massive build of a man, more wide than tall, with big arms and a round belly from too much wine. His clothing looked well made; probably a wealthy merchant who enjoyed all his money afforded him. Sveta seemed to know what he liked, as she ran her hands up and down his legs and looked up at him.

He ran his fingers through her hair and admired her touch with his soft moans as she traced her hands around his flesh. Sveta kept her body turned to be in view of Maria's bed. This was a performance for her, and she wanted it to be impressive.

The man quickly became hard; Maria marveled how fast his soft flesh grew erect in Sveta's skilled hands. He pulled Sveta's face toward his shaft as she instinctively took it into her mouth. Her face took on a more defined shape in the moonlight that gazed through the window. As she opened her mouth, her cheeks became more prominent and graceful while her hands stroked his hard shaft, guiding it between her lips. The man pulled her onto him, pushing his shaft down her throat. It seemed as if Sveta would choke, but then he released her and let her begin again. The sound was somewhat disgusting to Maria, but Sveta seemed to understand this method, and with each release, she let the spit in her mouth gush from her lips onto his shaft, stroking and working it in.

She played with him and sucked him as he stood with some difficulty. Sveta guided him to part his legs which he did without hesitation. She sat back on her knees and looked up at him as one hand stroked him and the other played with her breasts. "You want to take me?" She teased.

"Ochen!" The man moaned, "You know how I need it."

She pulled the drawstring from her dress, letting it fall down her body as she writhed upward to let it expose her bare breasts. "Da, I know how you like it." She whispered as she slid her hand from her breasts to his balls.

He moaned as she caressed them, then sucked them into her mouth. Her tongue flickering across his smooth flesh as her other hand began to slide up his legs. "Misha, do you know why you like me?" She teased in an erotic voice.

"Pochemu?" He said, moaning as she continued her hand up his leg.

"Because I know what you won't ask for, but crave so much!" She said as she licked her finger, then sucked his shaft into her mouth. She took it deeply, pushing herself to consume it completely while she slid her wet finger into his ass.

"Daaaa!" Misha moaned as she took control of his body.

Maria watched in erotic suspense, Sveta was so intriguing and powerful with him. Like casting a magic spell over him as she did whatever she wanted. The man was out of his mind with pleasure as Sveta gave him maximum attention, making him shake as he reached to steady himself against the side of the bed. His fingers gripped her hair firmly as she sucked him deep.

He was in ecstasy, and she had only been with him for a few minutes, Maria was impressed and marveled how quickly a strong man could be overwhelmed by a woman's charm and skill.

Sveta knew Maria watched her every move, she made sure she could see everything and wanted to share what she knew with her friend. It appealed to Sveta's ego, to be respected for her abilities with men, her knowledge and control of them, and ability to get what she wanted from them.

Misha began to flex his body harder into Sveta's mouth, his buttocks squeezing as he pushed deeper between her lips. He was going to come any second now; Maria was sure of it. But then Sveta surprised her as she stood up and said, "You don't come until I give you permission!" and then she slapped the man lightly on the face.

She thought for sure he would be angry, but instead, he dropped to his knees and kissed her belly as if he were an obedient servant. "Take off my dress!" Sveta demanded in a soft voice.

The man did exactly as she ordered, then Sveta lifted one leg to the side of her bed, and reached to his head. She took his hair into her hand and pulled his face between her legs. "Get your tongue in there!" she demanded. "Yes, like that!" she sighed.

Maria's eye grew big; she had never imagined such a way to be with a man. It was as if Sveta was the master and he was her slave, and he was so willing to be. He enjoyed her commands and did each with eagerness.

Sveta knelt face down on the bed, stretching her legs open with one foot touching the wall and one on the floor as she steadied herself. Maria could see her completely from the back, it was clearly meant for her to view.

"You've been good, Misha!" Sveta said coyly, "I'm going to let you lick my ass as a reward!"

Maria's mouth fell open in surprise, Sveta was an entirely different person with this man, but so in control of him, and such requests she was making! She marveled how the man got on his knees beneath her. His hands sliding up Sveta's smooth legs, then rushing to bury his face so his tongue could reach her forbidden place.

Sveta moaned as soon as his tongue began to glide over her tight little hole, "Yess, deeper, all the way in!" She beckoned as he pulled her thighs against his chest and kept his face between her cheeks.

Maria felt hot from the arousal that was building in her body. She carefully slipped the blanket down some and let her hand glide between her legs, where she was already wet with excitement, and eager to touch herself.

"Misha!" Sveta snapped, "What am I?" she asked as he stood behind her.

"You're a slut!" he said as he swatted his hand on her ass.

"And what do you do with sluts?" she teased.

And at that moment, it was as if the control had been handed back to Misha, and Sveta was now the servant, and both were expected to perform in their respective roles with intensity.

Maria gazed at them as her fingers stroked eagerly between her legs. It was like a fantasy in real life, right before her eyes, and so unexpected from one moment to the next.

Misha ran his hand up Sveta's back as she put her leg down and bent over on the bed. He pushed her neck lower and lower as she turned over to receive him from behind. The anticipation was building, as Misha guided his hard shaft between Sveta's legs.

Sveta moaned as she felt him filling her wet, hot chamber. His body was powerful and determined to break her it seemed, as he began to thrust hard into her. Her body shook with each movement, taking all of him inside only to push back against him for more. He slid his hand to her shoulder to keep her from getting too far from him as pulled her down onto his hard shaft.

Sveta moaned as he was making her feel the kind of intensity she craved, "Da, da, like that!" She said breathing in exhaustion.

Misha guided her to stand and slid his hands around her, caressing her breasts from behind as he whispered to her. "You need to take care of me!" He said as Sveta turned and pushed him onto his back on the bed.

She climbed on top of him and took his hard shaft inside her. She arched her back and leaned forward to kiss him, then guided his face to her breasts, "Suck me." She whispered.

"Mmm mama's hungry little baby!" She moaned as he buried his face between her breasts and sucked her nipples.

Maria was surprised, it seemed an odd thing to say, but he clearly liked it and did as she instructed him. "Who takes care of you?" Sveta whispered.

"You do!" he moaned as he sucked her nipples.

"Who shows me my place?" Sveta teased.

"I do!" He commanded.

Sveta was taking control again, it was such an interesting language they shared, passing the power between them whenever it pleased one or the other. She rode on top of him motioning her body as if in a saddle, rocking forward and back. She moved harder and faster as she pressed her wetness against his firm body.

"Misha, break me!" Sveta demanded as her voice faded through her breath.

Maria studied his hands, he grabbed Sveta's hips and pulled her further forward and pushed her further back than she could do on her own. Her body became weak in his hands as he rocked her against his body as if scrubbing clothes on a washboard. Sveta was like a doll, riding him at his will and completely under his control.

Then she let out a moan, in a voice loud enough to be heard on the whole ship! She was climaxing intensely, and she slowed to catch her breath, gently touching Misha's chest to hold herself up. She looked exhausted but was smiling and looked happy.

"I'm not done with you slut!" Misha commanded as he began moving her back and forth as before. Sveta could hardly speak, she was overwhelmed and within minutes, came again, and again. For an hour it seemed Misha could continue taking her at will, and she was without a voice to stop him, but wouldn't dare as she wanted it like this.

Maria felt her own climax building as she watched Sveta's body, riding this man's intensity. Her breasts shaking and her curves flexing back and forth as he made her come over and over. Then Sveta let out another load moan, and Maria felt herself orgasm, she gasped under the sound of Sveta, keeping herself hidden in sleep.

She watched, so in awe of the way these two exchanged power and pleasure. Then Misha stood up and laid Sveta on her back.

"I want to come," he said eagerly.

Sveta seemed unable to respond, she was exhausted by him. Maria worried this might be a risk for Sveta, but she knew her friend was very aware of such things. She watched him, as Sveta wrapper her legs around his waist and thrust himself inside her again. He lifted Sveta to his waist, as her shoulders remained on the bed. His hands stroked her breasts as he pumped his iron-hard flesh inside her.

Maria watched as Sveta guided one of his hands to her neck, "Do it." She gasped, "You know what I need."

Misha flexed his whole body, forcing himself deep into Sveta as he wrapped his fingers around her neck as if to choke her. It seemed so strange, but Maria was in a trance, each thing they did made no sense at first until she saw the result. Seconds later, Sveta began to moan, her legs pulling Misha harder into her, she apparently liked this choking sensation and wanted more. She could see his arms tightening and flexing, as he was squeezing her neck as he took her.

Then she heard Sveta gasp as her body shook and latched on to him, she climbed up to hold him against her, as he stood. She wrapped her hands around his head and pushed her breasts into his face as she tried to catch her breath. She was climaxing again, but it was different than the other times. She kissed the top of his head with appreciation and care, as she quickly descended to the floor, taking his cock into her mouth once more.

"Now you're mine!" She said in a dark voice. "I want it on my breasts!" she whispered as she spat and stroked his cock with her hands, "give it to me now!" she continued.

Misha's hands ran through her hair. Clearly, he was close, only a nudge would push him over the edge, and Sveta was the master of him.

"You want to finish on my face?" She teased softly... "I'll be really good and clean it all up, just give it to me, I need it!"

Misha nodded, his body flexing and moving, but still he seemed to hesitate, he was holding out for something more, another line to cross, and all Sveta needed was something erotic to push him over the edge.

She slid back on the bed and pulled him toward her. "Come here, my strong man, I'll give you my ass." She whispered, "You know how naughty I am, will you give me your come there?"

Misha held his shaft with his hand, guiding it over Sveta's tiny little hole. It seemed an impossible fit, but she pulled her cheeks wide and demanded, "Do it to me, take my ass!" She begged as he began to push his shaft inside her.

His cock looked enormous as he slid it inside, inch by inch. Sveta didn't know how much of this she could take, it was extremely tight, but the look in his eyes told her he was close. Misha could not hold himself any longer, she had given her entire body to him, and he was boiling with energy to orgasm. Sveta leaned forward and put her hands around his neck and choked him intensely, "Davai!" she demanded, "You come when I tell you, now come inside me!"

Misha's body tensed and twisted as he felt the shockwave of pleasure burst from deep inside him as his body gushed its magic juice into her. She felt him pulsing inside her and lightened her grip around his neck. "Mmmm that's my strong man." She whispered as he gasped for breath and felt his strength fade.

He laid on top of her as he caught his breath. She ran her fingers through his hair and caressed him gently down his back. The intense exchange had softened to something intimate and gentle.

Maria kept silent, but admired them as lovers, even if for only a moments passing, they understood how to give each other something unique and personal, it wasn't just sex, it seemed more like a private language, an exchange of what they needed most but could not admit beyond a smoldering bed.

After a while, Misha stood and got dressed. He was oddly silent, in comparison to how much he talked before. Sveta also seemed a bit uncomfortable, as she wiped herself off and put her dress on. She poured a cup of water and gave it to him.

He drank, and said gasping, "You are amazing Sveta, there is no other woman like you. You understand me better than myself."

Sveta took the cup and drank from it also, "And you, such a power, I think we woke the whole ship so many times..." She said as she walked over to Maria's bed, pretending to acknowledge she was still asleep.

She kissed him softly and groomed his hair with her fingers as he reached into his coat pocket. He placed a bag of coins in her hand, "Until next time then." He said as he walked to the door.

The cabin door closed, as Sveta held the coins in her hand and stared at the door for a moment. She felt something with him, his intensity and strength attracted her. But she knew it was an impossible idea to imagine herself with him beyond her bed. He was wealthy and had many girls like her.

"Are you alright?" Maria asked.

"Da," Sveta said as she turned with a smile. "I'm fine, just tired."

Maria thought there was more to ask but felt it best to keep her words for the night. "That was incredible to watch the two of you, I've never seen anything like it." She whispered.

Sveta nodded as she sat on her bed. She lit a candle and opened the bag to count her coins. They seemed insignificant in her hand compared to the experience she had just felt. She put them away and looked at Maria, "He's really generous, always gives me a lot." She said.

"I don't think it's just about that," Maria replied as Sveta walked over to her bed. She sat beside her with her head down. Maria put her arm around her friend, knowing the conflicts that raged inside.

Sveta didn't say a word. Maria pulled the blanket over the two of them and blew out the candle. She curled her arms around Sveta as they laid down.

Sveta understood Maria's kindness and snuggled up to her, "Stay with me a little while?" she whispered.

"Of course," Maria replied.

They both fell asleep in minutes, keeping each other warm in a world where they would have been alone; they had each other to get through the night. The waves of the Sheksna slapped against the side of the boat as it sat anchored near the river's edge waiting for the sun to rise and the voyage to continue.

# The Girl from Thessaloniki

The next week was a grueling push up the Sheksna River. The captain gave strict instructions to the crew to work extra hours to get the ship up the river and into Lake Onego. The currents seemed to push the ship back faster than the men could row it forward. Everyone onboard had a mood of frustration and small fights among the crew broke out but were quickly stopped. Merchants exited the ship at small docks and ports along the way to deliver their goods, but none were permitted to come on board to keep the ship light.

Sveta's merchant left the ship without a word at the first stop the next day. It was his usual custom. She knew this was his way of keeping her from becoming closer to him, and she accepted his desire to only visit her from time to time, although she felt inclined to stop seeing him as each time he left, she felt abandoned and resentful. It was impossible for her to experience such intense pleasure and not want to cling to the man that she shared them with.

The air grew cold, and the wind picked up as the ship made the final turn out of the river into the lake. Everyone but the oarsmen stood on the top deck to see the enormous lake. Onego looked more like an ocean to Maria, she couldn't see the other side, only water over the entire horizon.

The wind from the lake blew hard against the ship as the captain shifted the sail and let it pull the ship forward. He called for the oarsmen to stop as cheers erupted below decks. This was the end of the hard rowing on the trip. Only navigational strokes would be needed as they tracked their way South to Neva.

The oarsmen joined the rest of the crew on the deck, everyone smiled and greeted the wind as a gift from God that would carry them the rest of the way. Sveta went below and brought a large kettle of soup for everyone to enjoy on the deck. It was the first time she had served them outside the galley, adding a celebratory feel to the ship as they moved swiftly through the open water.

"Where will we stop next?" Maria asked the captain.

"We'll make a stop at Port Besov, ahead." The captain replied as he pointed in the distance. "The crew needs to stretch their legs on land...and take a bath!" he chuckled.

Maria nodded, as she cupped her hand over her eyes to see the bright sun. In the distance, she could see the land curving around from the right to a point just out of view. The lake smelled fresh, even with the colder air blowing it was a welcome change to the slow pace they had endured for so many days.

Sveta took her empty pot below, and Maria followed her. They stopped by Vladimir's cabin, noticing he wasn't topside earlier.

"Vladimir? Ti spiish?" Sveta announced as she knocked and entered his room. As they walked in, they could tell something was wrong. He looked pale, and his breathing was shallow and rapid. Sveta set the pail down and rushed to his side as Maria went to get the captain.

"Vladimir, what's wrong?" Sveta asked as she checked his bandages and wiped his forehead.

He coughed and tried to speak, but couldn't. He was clearly in pain when he coughed, and he seemed out of breath as if he had been running.

The captain entered the cabin with Maria, "Let's have a look." He said.

Sveta stepped aside as the captain examined Vladimir. The captain's eyes were serious as he checked the bandages and wound.

"Is it an infection?" Maria asked, "I put honey on the wound, it should have worked." She said.

"The wound is healing well, it's his lungs that are the problem. Too much time in bed and not enough on his feet." The captain said. "We need to prop him up, so he can cough easier."

Sveta and Maria arranged blankets to help Vladimir rest in a seated position. He was frail and seemed unaware of what was happening.

"If he coughs, the stitches could break," Maria said.

"The stitches are not the worry, he could stop breathing from the fluid that's building in his chest, that's more serious." The captain snapped.

"I'll have Gennady tie some ropes to the bed to keep him from falling out, he needs to walk every day and stay upright until this clears." The captain said as he left the cabin.

Maria and Sveta looked at each other, both were afraid their friend would die from his ailments.

"He's a strong man." Sveta said, "He will fight this."

Maria didn't look convinced but held her concerns inside. "Maybe we should try to get him on his feet, a little walk?" she asked.

They pulled his feet from the bed and turned him to stand. Each taking one of his arms to lift him up.

"Vladimir, we're going to take a little walk. Can you stand up for us?" Sveta asked.

Vladimir moaned in disapproval, he clearly wanted to be left where he was. But the ladies were determined to get him to his feet. They each took an arm over their shoulders and lifted him as he groaned in pain and began to cough.

Maria thought they were killing him, "We should put him down!" She said.

"No! It's what he needs to clear his chest." Sveta insisted.

Vladimir's cough sounded like something was rattling in his chest; with each cough the pain from his wound shook his body.

"The air is too cold here, he needs something to soothe his breathing," Sveta said. "Let's get him into the kitchen where it's warm and I can get steam in the air."

Vladimir protested wanting to stay in his bed, but the ladies were determined to fight him if necessary. They shuffled down the hall and stairs into the kitchen and set him in a chair near the stove.

Sveta quickly set every pot she could fit on the stove and put a small amount of water in each. She pushed coal into the oven and opened the grill to get more air in. Maria stood behind Vladimir's chair and kept him from falling over.

The steam quickly filled the kitchen, until the air was thick with vapor. Vladimir began to breathe easier, and Sveta joked, "We just need to find a banya in port for you."

Soon his cough returned, but it was not dry like before. Sveta handed Maria a washcloth, "He's going to need to spit that out." She said.

Maria grimaced but understood this was necessary. As Vladimir coughed, she held the cloth to his mouth allowing him to spit the fluid from his lungs. It was dark, like tree sap as he tried to work it from his mouth.

Both ladies patronized him, "Good job, spit that out!" they encouraged with each session, but they were clearly disgusted with what it looked like and tried desperately not to get it on their hands.

After an hour, his coughing ceased, and his breathing sounded much better. They returned him to his cabin and met Gennady there as he installed the ropes the captain had ordered. They nestled Vladimir into his upright bed and set the ropes to keep him from falling from the bed in the event the ship rocked.

"The captain has ordered the watch to check on him each hour," Gennady said.

"Excellent." Replied Sveta, "We will be back later to walk him some more."

Maria stayed behind to sit with Vladimir a while, while the others left. Vladimir's color had improved, and he fell asleep instantly in his bed. Maria folded his clothes and straightened his room. He was an organized man, only a few things were out of place.

She saw the coat she had bought hanging in the wardrobe of his room. On his counter, there were a few personal items. A handmade necklace that she assumed his daughter had made for him, a razor for shaving and a single brass coin that was worn smooth with frequent handling. It looked more like a keepsake than spending money.

She looked at it carefully, it was from another country with Latin letters at the edges. She recognized the text, "QEODOPOC ... Theodoros!" She said translating it out loud.

"You speak Latin?" Said Vladimir, who had watched her.

She quickly set the coin down and apologized. "Sorry, I was just curious about the markings on that coin..." She said as she sat down.

"Ah, that coin is my reminder." He said roughly.

"Vlad, you should rest." Maria interrupted.

"I've rested enough; I'm tired but no longer sleepy." He said.

"Go ahead, you can look at the coin, it's from my wife's home in Gretzia." He said.

"How did you meet her?" Maria asked as she sat by his bed.

"I worked on a trading ship as a crewman when I was younger. Loading cargo and traveling all over the world. We came to a port in Thessaloniki where I met this beautiful woman, with long raven hair and brown eyes." He said with warmth in his voice.

"It was your wife?" Maria asked.

"Well, not yet." He chuckled. "She was walking along the dock and a barrel rolled off the plank, it was heading right for her, and I pushed her out of the way. You can imagine what happened, next. I took one look at her and wanted to protect her like that for the rest of my life."

"What happened?' Maria asked, feeling the excitement of the story.

"Her father came running after her, he was an influential merchant in the port, and he yelled at everyone, threatening our captain and the usual things a man like that would say. I didn't pay attention to him, I was looking at her, and she looked at me... We knew... you know?" He said with mystery in his voice.

Maria smiled, "Love?" she asked.

"Da, big love, just like that!" he said as his eyes sparkled from the memory.

"We met later, and she spoke Gretzi, I spoke Russian but each word told us it was simply meant to be, I can't explain how we knew it, we just did," Vladimir said.

"So romantic!" Maria replied. "So you married her then?"

Vladimir laughed, "Well not so fast! Her father had no intention of letting his darling girl run off with a Russian sailor. He had me arrested by the port police, whom he kept in his pocket."

"No!" Maria said in shock

"He wanted to get my attention, so I'm sitting in jail, and he walks in. They open the cell, and he sits down in front of me. He could speak a little Russian, and he explained that only a wealthy man could have his daughter, not someone like me." He said as he paused. "I admit, I felt embarrassed for being less than she deserved. In fact, I remember hating who I was, for daring to think I could have such a woman so far above my station." He said as the regret remained in his voice.

"That's so sad, it shouldn't matter as long as there is love!" Maria said.

"I agree, but that's something we simple people can believe because we have nothing. For the rich, it's a different world." He replied.

"So what happened?" She asked.

"I'll never forget his words." Vladimir said as he pretended to speak with a Greek accent, "My daughter cry and beg me to let her go with you … Then he handed me that coin you're holding and said "take this and no see my daughter again.""

Maria looked at the coin with renewed intrigue. "The price of a daughter's love?" She asked?

"Net, the price of mine. It was more than I made in a month," said Vladimir. "The police let me go, knowing I would take the money and leave port. I walked back to the ship, looking around at all the things her father owned and felt myself a tiny, insignificant man. And all the while that coin was burning in my hand, reminding me that I'd never have a woman like Alexia."

Maria imagined the younger Vladimir and how sad his story was, "There is more to men than money Vladimir. I think you're one of the richest in that way." She said as she touched his hand.

Vladimir smiled, "Spacibo Masha, but at the time, I felt like the poorest. You hear stories of young lovers ending their lives from a broken heart, and I was no different. I really couldn't imagine my life without Alexia, but then there I was, casting off from Gretzia hoping I would never see that island again.

We pulled away, and I watched it getting smaller and smaller, knowing she was there, it just took hold of my heart and all I wanted was to jump off the ship and swim back." He said, "I reached into my pocket and looked at that coin. It represented everything I would never have, never be good enough, rich enough, lucky enough ... and then I heard a voice behind me say, 'Vladimir, I go with you.'"

"No!" Maria said in shock, "It was her?"

"I turned around and there behind me was my beautiful Alexia, with her big eyes looking at me from under a large cloak. She had booked passage to Russia on our ship. Imagine that!"

Vladimir said as his face lit up with pride and love. "The captain married us onboard the ship that same day!"

"Such a story!" Maria said as she felt her heart beating with excitement. "So what happened with her father?"

"Ah, he eventually forgave us, when Alexia introduced him to his granddaughter a few years later." He replied.

"So I keep that coin to remind myself what I have waiting for me, and how she could have been with a richer man, but chose me." He said wisely.

Maria smiled, "You have a romantic heart, Vladimir. Alexia is a lucky woman."

Vladimir chuckled, "I'm the lucky one, he said, "It took a lot of faith for her to trust her life to a man with nothing to offer her."

Maria paused, "She must have sensed you had more to offer than money would buy."

"Prosto tak." He sighed, "When you're in love, you can just tell things about someone without knowing why." Vladimir smiled and stared into the distance, "I think I'll rest a while." He sighed.

Maria stood and checked his bandages before leaving. "When we get into port we will see if we can find a banya to help ease your breathing." She said.

Vladimir nodded as he shifted himself into a comfortable position. Maria set the coin back on the counter and admired how such a simple token could represent a love story like the one she had just heard. She quietly closed the cabin door and headed up the stairs to the top deck.

# The Witch of Besov

The ship moved gracefully across Lake Onega throughout the day, Maria returned topside to see the progress as it moved closer to the port in Besov. The captain was at the mast as she approached him to see how long the journey would take.

"Ah, Masha, how is our Vladimir?" He asked.

"We took him to the kitchen and had him sit in the steam for a while, it helped a lot." She began, "We thought maybe a banya would be helpful if there is one close to port?"

The captain thought for a moment, "Da, there is one, near the glyphs." He replied, "But it belongs to a strange local women there, they say she is a witch!"

Maria was surprised, the women accused of witchcraft in her town had been run off or put to death by the church. "They permit witches in the town?" She said naively.

The captain shook his head, "The world is not a single town full of Christian farmer's, young miss. You'll find there are all kinds of places where people think and do things much differently than you are accustomed to." He replied with caution, "Try to keep an open mind."

Maria didn't know what to think of such a statement. She turned to go and ask Sveta for advice.

"We'll be in port by the late afternoon." The captain said.

"Spacibo," Maria said as she walked below, keeping her arms close to her sides to shield from the cold wind.

Maria returned to her cabin and saw Sveta resting on the bed. "Are you alright?" Maria asked.

"Da, just tired. Misha took all my energy last night." She said with a sigh.

"Vladimir seems better, he told me the story of how he met his wife." She said with excitement.

"Really? I only know bits and pieces. We should take him to banya when we get into port." Sveta replied

"Da, I asked the captain and he said there is one by the glyphs?" Maria said with hesitation.

"Mda I know it, Natalya's farm," Sveta said as she laid on her bed looking at the ceiling.

"Is she a witch?" Maria asked nervously.

"Who told you that? The captain?" Sveta snapped.

"Why is every woman who thinks for herself a witch?" Sveta said with disgust. "Natasha knows more about curing people than any surgeon!"

Maria sensed she had offended Sveta unintentionally, and decided not to add more to the statement.

"So she has a banya?" Maria asked.

"Yes, we'll go there when we dock," Sveta said as she closed her eyes attempting to rest.

The silence and steady rhythm of the ship lulled them both to sleep as the afternoon hours passed. They awoke to the sounds of the oarsmen nudging the ship into port as the anchor dropped off the stern. There was still a tension between them over the discussion about Natalya that Maria did not fully understand.

As they prepared to leave, Sveta stopped and looked at Maria, "Don't say the word, 'witch' when we are around Natasha. To local people, she is a shaman and has kept most of them alive when they would have died at the hands of the surgeons."

Maria nodded, feeling very nervous about meeting the woman everyone was telling her about.

The ship finally docked, and everyone began heading ashore to take a walk or visit the town. Many of the men walked toward the taverns as Maria and Sveta helped Vladimir up the stairs and off the ship.

The captain met them at the gang plank. "Give my regards to Natasha." He said as he called for Gennady to come near.

Gennady rushed over, "The plank is not wide enough for three of them, help Vladimir to the shore." He ordered.

Gennady and Vladimir carefully stepped down the plank as Sveta and Maria watched. "Sveta, tell Gennady what you need from the market, and he will take care of it." Said the captain.

The ladies rejoined Vladimir on the dock, as Sveta instructed Gennady on where to go and order the provisions for the next part of the journey. Her instructions were overwhelming with details as the young man tried to follow her words;

"This one has the best onions, but don't buy his apples, they're always mushy. Get potatoes and anything fresh in vegetables from the last one on that street."

Gennady nodded and began to leave as Sveta stopped him.

"And don't pay the first price, act offended and walk away two or three times until they lower it." She insisted.

Gennady began to walk then turned, "What if they don't lower it?" He asked.

"Tell them the captain is a cheap bastard and that's all you can afford!" She said, knowing the captain could hear them. Sveta looked over her shoulder and smiled at the captain hoping he would not take offense.

The captain laughed out loud, "Damn right!" He shouted.

Gennady rushed off to the market as the ladies walked Vladimir to the edge of the port where Natalya's farm was. It took a while, but Vladimir found it easier to walk after being on his feet for a while. They talked as they made their way to the farm.

"There are carvings on all these rocks along the water; you should see them while you are here!" Vladimir said to Maria.

"Are these the ones you told me about Sveta?" Maria asked as she dashed to see them.

"Da, they are everywhere along the port! "She replied.

Maria marveled at the carvings, she had never seen anything like them. They looked like children's art, but were cut into the rocks; animals, birds, strange shapes, even people were represented in poses of hunting or fishing.

"It's like a story of their life!" She said excitedly. "How long have they been here?"

"They are from the ancient tribes," Vladimir said.

Maria walked along the rocks as Sveta stayed with Vladimir on the pathway. "You're right Sveta, they are like a language, I can see some things more than once in the way some letters appear more often in books." She said as she returned to help Vladimir walk. "It's fascinating, thanks for showing me those."

They continued to the farm house as Sveta went and knocked at the door. Maria expected an old haggardly woman to appear, but to her surprise, a young lady answered the door. She had curly red hair, blue eyes, prominent cheekbones and glowing skin.

"Is that Natalya?" She asked Vladimir quietly.

"Da, that's Natasha." He said as Natasha walked toward them. Maria felt embarrassed by what she had previously thought. Here was a vibrant young woman with a friendly smile and warm eyes. How she could have ever been called a witch seemed unthinkable.

"Zdrastvuite, I am Natasha," She said as she approached Maria.

"What happened to you, Vlad?" Natasha said in shock.

They walked toward the back of her house as he told her about the soldiers, and how Maria and Sveta had taken care of him. She set him down in a chair near her banya, and checked his bandages, "Excellent stitches Maria" She said, "And I see someone is using honey to prevent infection, Molodets!"

Vladimir winked at Maria, as Natasha went into her house for a moment. She returned with a cup and sprinkled something in it, "This is willow bark tea, it will help with pain." She said as she handed it to Vladimir.

Vladimir quickly drank the tea and handed the cup back to Natasha, "I'll have as much as you permit!" He teased.

She giggled as she went back for more, "Let's try for something stronger than just tea then." She said. "Sveta can you help me get a fire going in the banya?"

Sveta nodded as she headed to the banya to prepare the fire. Maria stood by Vladimir as Natasha returned with more tea. This time, he drank it more slowly.

Maria, will you help me prepare some herbs for Vladimir?

Maria followed Natasha back into her house, looking back at Vladimir for approval. He nodded with a smile and motioned for her to go along.

The inside of her house was unusual and exciting. All manner of plants and dried leaves were scattered around with their branches tied together. It was clear that she had an organization of each kind of substance, from herbs, leaves, and powders.

Maria had never seen such a system; the room formed a giant kitchen, capable of preparing any substance including food. Natasha laid out a cloth, and then took a bowl and set it on the table in front of Maria. "Crush this into a powder." She said as she handed Maria variegated leaves and stone.

Maria hesitated, wondering if she was unknowingly performing some kind of witchcraft.

Natasha noticed and stopped gathering things together for a moment, "What's wrong dear?"

"Not sure I can do this, I've never...conjured anything." She murmured.

"Conjured?" Natasha said as she laughed, "Well I haven't either; let me know how that works out. For now, I just need the leaves crushed to make a poultice."

Maria felt embarrassed and slowly began crushing the leaves, breaking them into small pieces then rubbing them with the stone inside the bowl.

"Let me guess, someone told you I was a witch?" Natasha asked as she picked several more things and brought them to the table.

Maria hesitated, knowing she had been warned not to bring this up. "Well, I don't know anything about..." she paused.

Natasha gently stopped Maria's hand and looked her in the eyes. "Maria, I believe in Jesus, just like you do darling. But the church has banned all manner of medicine and therapies. Should we call for their surgeons to bleed him in hopes he will improve?" She asked.

"No, I don't see how that will help," Maria replied.

"I know what they say about me, How I'm a heretic or witch. Why? Because I use herbs and medicine instead of prayer? I don't know why the church insists that anything new or unknown must be witchcraft, but that's how they view anything they can't control." Natasha added. "I'm a physician just like Saint Luke," Natasha said as she broke several dry leaves into the bowl.

Maria continued working as she listened to Natasha; she found her statements to be enlightened and inspiring. She had never thought to question what defined witchcraft before. It had always been presented with such outrage and shock in her village that no one would speak of it.

"Where I grew up, they accused several women of witchcraft and then they ran away or were killed. But they never said what their crimes were, just they were witches." Maria said as she worked the leaves into a powder.

"I had similar experiences, but they leave me alone here because there are several other sects in the town who protect me. The Christians visit in secret when they are ill." Natasha said. "My guess is the witches in your city were simply women with a secret that was a threat to someone with power."

Maria shrugged her shoulders as she listened and continued her task.

"That looks perfect!" Natasha said as she reached for the bowl of crushed leaves. She poured the powder in a long line on the cloth and then folded it over several times. Natasha handed it to Maria, "Take this and I'll bring the water for the steam and something for the pain." She said.

The returned outside, where Vladimir sat calmly, feeling the effects of his tea. "Let's go into the Banya," Natasha said.

They helped Vladimir up and walked into the banya where Sveta was adjusting the fire. It was roasting hot inside, as the walls began to heat up from the intense fire.

Vladimir sat down slowly in the middle, as Natasha poured the water over the rocks creating an instant curtain of steam. "Wrap that poultice around him, directly over the wound," Natasha instructed Maria and Sveta.

Within seconds Vladimir began to laugh, as the effects of the herbs set in. "I don't feel anything! He giggled, what's in this?!" he asked.

"Oh, herbs, plants and the usual witchcraft." Natasha teased as she winked at Maria.

The four of them sat together, enjoying the sensation of the banya and helping Vladimir's lungs to clear.

"He will be able to cough harder if he doesn't feel pain." Natasha said that's what we want in here."

The steam began to loosen Vladimir's congestion, and he produced more fluid, like before. Natasha took the kerchief from around her head and handed it to Vladimir, "I don't need this back!" she joked.

They all burst out laughing as he hacked and coughed into it. "I'm just glad you can do it by yourself this time." Sveta teased.

Vladimir smiled, "Da, I know…it's disgusting." He said as he coughed again.

The steam put everyone at ease as the room became increasingly dense with water and heat. Each lady took turns stepping outside to prevent themselves from being soaked in sweat. This was for Vladimir's benefit, and they still had to walk back to the ship.

Soon Vladimir's cough faded, and he spoke as if he was going back to work that afternoon. The effect of the poultice had made him forget his injury completely. Natasha cautioned him that this was to help him recover and rest, not for him to go back to work.

The fire in the banya began to mellow as Natasha brought a towel for Vladimir to dry off. His face was full of color, and his skin had a healthy glow.

Natasha wrapped some herbs for Maria to give to Vladimir to help him breathe easier and reduce his pain.

"I wish I could come back and learn all about these herbs from you," Maria said

"Natasha smiled, you are welcome here anytime."

Vladimir and Sveta looked at each other and smiled, impressed with Maria's open-mindedness.

Vladimir reached in his pocket and gave some money to Natasha, "It's not enough I know, but you have my gratitude, and

I'll bring you something from Neva on my first trip down the river in the spring." He said.

Natasha smiled, "It is more than enough!" She said, "But if you could bring me some amber and salt from the Baltic?"

"Absolutely, consider it done!" He replied with a smile.

They waved goodbye to Natasha and headed back to the ship, Vladimir walked as briskly as the ladies, making the return trip brief and easy. They laughed and told stories along the way, each becoming closer friends than they were at the beginning of the day.

# A Kiss under the Northern Lights

The Kupala headed across Lake Onega as the sun began to set. A steady breeze filled the sail and kept the ship gliding steadily southward toward the mouth of the Svir River. Vladimir returned to his cabin and rested from the day's activities while Sveta headed into the kitchen to check the items Gennady had purchased and then prepare the evening meal.

Maria rested on her bed as she thought about the day's events. She was very impressed with Natasha and her knowledge of natural healing, it reminded her of how her mother always knew what to place on a cut or bruise. It seemed a valuable skill for a woman to know such things and after her experience with Vladimir's injury and recovery, she wanted to know more.

The sounds of the happy crew erupted downstairs, they were free from rowing and had their time in the taverns that afternoon. Maria also felt a sense of excitement as the voyage was moving much faster as the days onboard were coming to a close. She decided to head downstairs to help Sveta in the kitchen.

When she arrived, Sveta was peeling potatoes and looked frustrated. "Can I help?" Maria asked.

"Da, I'm about halfway through these potatoes. If you could do the rest, I can start on the meat Gennady bought." She said.

Sveta began to hand the knife to Maria then giggled and set it down. Maria laughed as she picked it up, both of them amused by their mutual superstition.

"Is something bothering you?" Maria asked. "Ever since this morning, your mood has been different."

Maria waited for the answer afraid she might not like what she was going to hear.

"I started my cycle this morning," Sveta said in frustration.

"Ah," Maria said in relief, "Ya ponimayu."

"Natasha gave me some herbs to put in my tea. I haven't tried them yet, but they're supposed to help with the pain." Sveta said.

"Davai, take them now," Maria said. "I'm curious if they work! I can hardly get out of bed on those days."

"Mda!" Sveta agreed, "It's awful! We should have asked Natasha for a poultice!" She said as they both laughed hysterically.

The two ladies continued cooking while their conversation continued. The smell of roasting vegetables and beef invited the men to check in frequently asking when it would be ready. Sveta took full advantage of her irritable mood and chided each man who dared come into her kitchen.

As soon as the man began to ask about the meal, she pulled an answer from her repertoire of responses to this famous question, each response grew in intensity as each poor sailor made a mistake of stepping in and opening his mouth.

"Why do you interrupt me?... You think it will cook itself?... Oh, I'm not cooking fast enough for you?... If once again you come in here, you will get nothing but a bowl of steam for the rest of the trip!" She snapped.

Finally, the captain himself came into the kitchen, "It smells delicious in here!" He said.

"Da?" Sveta replied as Maria held her breath expecting him to ask the same question.

"I was just going to ask..." The captain began as Maria closed her eyes expecting him to be chewed to pieces by Sveta's wrath. "How did we get so lucky to have a beautiful cook like you?"

"Ne nado!", Sveta replied as she heard the men outside burst into laughter.

It was obvious they had convinced the captain to try his luck. She pushed the captain out of the kitchen, "Idi, Idi!" She said as she turned red from embarrassment.

Dinner was finally ready, and the men devoured it in their usual fashion. Maria nibbled on some vegetables in the kitchen as the two of them began to wash the dishes.

Sveta became sleepy after drinking the tea Natasha had prescribed. Maria agreed to finish up the dishes for her so she could go and rest.

Sveta took a plate of food for Vladimir as she headed to her cabin. He was asleep, so she left it by his bed. Her steps to her cabin felt like an effort just to move forward. Finally, her exhaustion was quenched as her head touched the pillow in her cabin, sending her into a deep, immediate sleep.

Maria set the final dish aside to dry and wiped hands on a washcloth as she took off her apron. She quickly mopped the floor, noticing only a small amount of food had been spilled. "I guess they really liked it." She thought.

Gennady entered the galley with a few dirty plates, "From the captain's cabin." He said as he set them in the sink.

Maria nodded and finished mopping. She noticed Gennady had remained in the room as she went to blow out the lantern. "Are you staying in here?" She asked.

"No, I was waiting for you." He replied.

"Why?" Maria replied, realizing she sounded a bit harsh.

"I want to show you something." He said with uncertainty.

"Show me what?" Maria asked, not realizing how fragile he felt to approach her like this.

Gennady pointed above the deck toward the stairs, "It's...outside."

"Davai." She replied as he nervously stepped aside to let her lead the way.

As they made their way up each flight of stairs, his heart raced with anticipation. He had admired Maria from the moment she set foot on the ship and was so overcome by his attraction that he could hardly speak in front of her. But Vladimir had noticed and encouraged him to take her on deck tonight to fulfill a promise the quartermaster had made earlier.

As Maria reached the top of the stairs, she turned back to see Gennady following her. "So what is it?" she asked impatiently.

Gennady paused as he looked into her eyes. He was completely spellbound by her beauty. The wind caught her hair as she looked at him waiting for an answer. He fidgeted for a moment, then cleared his throat and pointed toward the northern sky.

Maria turned and gasped as she saw the fantastic array of lights dancing in the starlit sky. "What is it?!" She said in amazement. "Vladimir told me there would be something, but I didn't imagine this!"

Gennady felt compelled to impress the young lady as he walked toward the back of the ship motioning for her to follow him.

"Severnoe Siyanie." he began, "When I was a boy, growing up on the White Sea, they told us so many legends about them. During winter they make a brilliant light across the sky!" He said.

"They look beautiful to me now!" Maria said in excitement as she marveled at the colors and movements in the sky.

"Some people look at them and see the hems of ladies dresses like they are dancing." He said as Maria nodded in agreement.

"My village believed it was more spiritual, like the dead leaving the earth for heaven." He added as he looked over at her.

She stood with a big smile and crossed arms from the cold wind.

"You're cold?" Gennady asked.

"Ochen" Maria replied as she shivered from the night air.

Gennady nervously slipped his coat off and draped it around her, fearing she would reject it or be offended.

The jacket felt warm inside, and it soothed Maria's body as she pulled it closer to her. She was instantly relieved from the cold and looked at Gennady with appreciation, "Spacibo." She said.

"Pozhalysta!" Gennady replied. "The captain has been teaching me the constellations." He said. "Sailors on the open sea use them for navigation."

"Really?" Maria replied as she looked at the stars. "My father showed me a few, there is a bear somewhere and..."

Gennady instantly pointed out the points of the bear and narrated his way across the sky giving numerous details about each constellation. As he spoke, Maria began to look more at him than the stars and realized his attention had a romantic purpose.

"You are so smart, Gena!" She said in a flirtatious voice. "I can barely find one star, and you know them all!"

Gennady turned red as he smiled. "Well, there isn't much to do at night on the ship." He continued, "But I plan to captain my own ship one day after I serve my time onboard."

"Is that how it works?" Maria asked, "You have to serve under a captain to become one?"

"Yes, as an apprentice you can learn everything you need to know while you wait for the chance to come" he replied.

"Captain Gennady." Maria teased.

"Not yet! But one day." He said as he laughed.

"Thanks for showing me this! You're really sweet." Maria said.

"It was my pleasure." He replied. "I have the watch now, so I have to take my station."

Maria nodded and walked back to the staircase. Gennady watched her moving like a dream with her hair blowing in the wind. He wanted to say something, do something, but was so afraid she would be offended.

She turned to wave at him before walking down the stairs and suddenly he shouted, "Wait!"

Maria smiled, hoping he might have more in mind as he walked toward her.

"Yes?" She said as her eyes lit up as he approached.

"I'll need my jacket, it's…going to be cold tonight." He said with reluctance.

"Oh, of course, I forgot I had it on. Thanks for letting me wear it" She said with a laugh as she quickly slipped it off her shoulders and handed it to him.

As he reached to take it, Gennady leaned in and kissed Maria's lips very gently. She didn't expect it but at the moment she saw him coming closer, she didn't resist him and pursed her lips in return as they touched.

Her eyes sparkled like the starlit sky as she smiled and nervously tried to say something, "Good night." She said, turning to go down the stairs.

Gennady watched her walk away, excited that he had dared and succeeded to kiss the woman of his dreams. "Good night." He whispered.

Maria walked down the hallway toward the cabin, the sensation of the kiss still on her lips. She entered the cabin and noticed Sveta was sitting up in her bed.

"What have you been up to?" She said, seeing Maria's blushing smile.

"Gennady was showing me the northern lights." She replied as she sat on her bed.

"Oh really? Is that all he showed you?" Sveta teased.

Maria smiled even more brightly, feeling embarrassed. "He kissed me!" She said energetically.

"Gena kissed you!" Sveta shouted. "That sneaky devil! She said with a laugh, "How was it?"

"Nice!" Maria replied. "He's quite smart, and wants to be a captain one day."

"Oh really, does he?" Sveta teased as she watched Maria smiling.

"I'll be watching Gospodin Gena now," Sveta said in a motherly voice. "I see he is not the shy boy I took him for, after all."

Maria laid back on her bed, reliving the moment when he kissed her. It was sweet and gentle and exactly how she imagined a kiss should be. She didn't want Sveta to know, but it was the first time a young man had kissed her.

Sveta blew out the candle as the glow from the Northern lights pulsed through their window, creating colorful shadows as they both fell asleep.

# Down the Svir River

The sounds of the oarsmen setting up their stations rattled through the boards of the ship, as the Kupala began to enter the Svir River at sunrise. The captain's voice shouted over the other men as the ship navigated around other ships and boats at the South East corner of Lake Onega.

Sveta and Maria sat up in their beds, looking around for confirmation that it was already morning. Sveta slipped from her bed and put her dress and shoes on while pinning her hair behind her head. "Time for breakfast." She said in sarcastic enthusiasm as she headed out the door.

Maria changed her clothes and brushed her hair. She wanted to go above and see what the commotion was all about. She wondered if Gennady would be on deck since he had the night watch. She braided her hair and checked her face in the mirror, wanting to look her best. She smiled as she headed up the stairs. The cold wind from the lake rushed down the stairs as she ascended to the top deck. The smell of smoke was in the air from nearby ships and camps along the coastline.

There were ships of all shapes and sizes waiting their turn to enter the river while others made their way out. Each captain struggled to keep his ship from getting too close to the others. Along the shoreline ports and harbors were in a constant state of motion as they loaded and unloaded their cargo. She watched the fishing ships drop their nets as they moved farther out into the lake. Then she heard the captain barking his commands to the helmsman.

"Bring us around that fishing ship to port, they just dropped anchor." He shouted.

"Yes, Captain, hard to port!" Shouted Gennady voice as the ship began to turn.

Maria turned and saw Gennady steering the ship behind her. She smiled and waved at him, but he was serious about his duties and didn't want the captain to see him noticing her as he smiled back at her.

Maria walked over to the captain who stood at the front of the ship. "Dobroye utro!" She said.

"And a good morning to you lass!" The captain responded as his eyes stayed vigilant.

"So many ships here!" Maria said.

"Da, too many for my liking!" He grumbled, "We are trying to get into the river now."

"How do you know when it's your turn?" She asked.

"The rules are simple out here, the bigger the ship, the more others should get out of your way. But there are many idiots in the water this morning, and we can't risk a collision so close to the current." The captain said as he turned back toward Gennady, "Get those oars in the water or we will clip them for sure!"

Gennady ordered the men to put their oars out as the Kupala turned around a fishing boat that had stopped ahead of it. "Prepare to reverse on port!" Gennady shouted as the oars dipped in the water, "Reverse on port!"

The oarsmen made a long stroke in the reverse direction causing the ship to turn safely around the fishing boat and its nets. Maria looked over and saw the other captain waving to the Kupala in gratitude.

"Da, you're welcome your stupid bastard!" The captain shouted, "Who fishes at the entrance of the river?"

Maria laughed at the sarcasm and turned to watch Gennady at the helm, he looked so handsome to her, and she wondered why she hadn't noticed that before.

"Look here lass, want to see two ships wreck?" The captain asked.

Maria looked in the direction the captain was pointing, "See those two over there?" he began "They are both headed for the same point at the same speed. One of them will have to slow down or speed up because they can't be in the same place at the same time. Make sense?"

Maria nodded as she tried to understand how the captain could understand this before it happened. "Oh, they just figured it out, look at them!" He laughed.

Suddenly the sails on one of the ships dropped as its anchor splashed in the water. Moments later both ships came within feet of hitting each other as they shouted in voices loud enough to be heard across the lake.

Maria was impressed, "How did you know that was going to happen?" She asked as her curiosity perked.

"Simple!" said the captain as he pointed to a ship off the right side of the Kupala. "You see how we are moving straight ahead?" He asked.

Maria nodded as she watched him pointing at the other ship.

"And you see how that ship is heading to the same place as us?" He asked again.

"Da, I can see that." She said not sure she understood the equation.

"As long as our boat and their boat stay at an equal degree of the direction were heading, we will crash at the moment we arrive there." He said calmly.

Maria felt nervous, "Should we do something then?" She asked.

"Not yet." Replied the captain, "Let's check the angle a few times and see what's going to happen."

Maria stepped closer to the bow, wanting to understand this magical ability the captain seemed to have been predicting the future. She watched the ship as the captain asked her questions, "Is the ship still on the starboard side?"

"Da!" she replied.

"And would you say he is closer to the point ahead than we are?" The captain asked.

"I would say we are about the same distance as they are." She answered.

"And what does that mean?" he asked in a voice that reminded her of her mother's teaching.

"Collision?" She said with concern.

"Da, Collision!" The captain said with excitement like it was a game.

Maria's eyes grew big as she looked at the captain for more answers. "Should we drop our sail at the other ship?" she asked.

"That tactic is for stupid bastards who don't pay attention." He said with a smile. "Besides, we are the bigger ship and right about now they have taken notice of us." The captain said as he pointed to the other ship as it began to lower its sails.

Maria smiled, as the captain chuckled with his ability to teach her. "Now, how can we know we will not hit that ship?" The captain asked.

"The distance to the middle point should be closer to us than for them?" She asked.

"Correct, the angle should change, and it should be obvious that we will arrive first." The captain said pointing again at the other ship. "See how he is getting farther off our bow?"

"Yes! Amazing!" She said as the captain patted her on the back, "You'll make a good captain one day!" he praised as he turned to give his next command. "Gennady, take us into the river! Be mindful of the smaller boats and bring the oars in!"

Gennady ordered the oars pulled in as he steered the ship into the river's channel. The ship picked up speed as the current carried it swiftly down the Svir River.

Maria watched along both sides of the ship as the port and small settlements whisked by. It was a different feeling than the previous rivers they had traveled as they had ridden against the current until now.

Maria began to shiver from the cold wind and decided to head below to warm up. She made her way to the kitchen, delighted to find a hot bowl of oatmeal waiting.

"Are we in the river yet?" Sveta asked.

"Da, so interesting how it all works up there!" Maria replied

"Good! We should be in Neva in two days then." Sveta said.

Maria was surprised that the trip would be over so soon. She thought another week perhaps, but now she realized her long journey was in its final days.

"So what part of Neva does your aunt live in?" Sveta asked.

Maria realized she wasn't confident of her aunt's exact location in the town. She knew she lived near the water and that there were many ships nearby. "I'm trying to remember. I thought my mother would be with me when I arrived…" She said as she sat down.

"Don't worry, if you only know her name you can visit a few churches, and I'm sure one of them will know her," Sveta replied.

Maria felt relieved, "Da, I think that's a good idea." She said. "My uncle was a lawyer there, but he died two years ago."

"I'm sure you will find her, and if you need a few days to locate her, you can stay with me and my mother until you do," Sveta said.

"Thanks! I'd be lost in that city without your help!" Maria replied.

The ship moved quickly down the Svir River as the day went by. By evening the Kupala was sailing across Lake Ladoga as the sun set. The captain had the anchor dropped for the evening, to celebrate the last night on board.

Sveta cooked a large meal and made enough of the captain's favorite apple pie for everyone to enjoy. All around the ship, the crew talked about their plans for the winter, how happy they were to be finished for the season and what they would do in the spring.

For Maria, it was a bittersweet moment. This had become her home and family after the horrific events in her hometown. She knew she could trust each person on the ship with her life and that they would protect her at all costs. It was difficult to imagine her future without the friends she had made on the trip. As she sat in the galley, eating with the crew, the captain, the quartermaster, Gennady and Sveta she felt the sense that this precious moment might never come again.

She excused herself to the kitchen, as she began to cry. Sveta followed her, knowing what she might be going through. They hugged and assured each other of spending time together during the winter which relieved the sadness she was feeling.

After dinner, Maria offered to help Sveta with the dishes. Sveta protested and insisted Maria go and watch the northern lights before the ship traveled too far south to see them. Maria was surprised as Sveta never turned down help before, but she did as her friend wished.

She went to the cabin, put on her coat and headed up the stairs to gaze at the stars. Once on the deck, it became evident why Sveta had insisted she not help with dishes. There was Gennady, waiting for her at the front of the ship.

Maria smiled and walked over to him. "Hello again." She mused.

Gennady smiled, "Come to see the show?" he asked pointing at the night sky as it began to grow darker.

"Da!" She said with excitement.

Gennady felt more confident with her now, he reached and took her hand, and guided her to the upper deck where the captain usually watched out over the ship. "I had to get permission to bring you up here," he said as she saw two chairs and a blanket waiting for them. "The captain doesn't usually let anyone in his roost," Gennady said with a smile.

Maria felt so charmed by the gesture; the chairs, a blanket to keep warm and all the preparation. Gennady had made her feel like a special woman.

She shared her new knowledge of avoiding collisions as they talked about ships, the stars, and the future.

"What will you do this winter?" She asked Gennady.

"I'll be returning to my home village on the White Sea." He said. "My parents are there, and they are getting older. It's a hard winter without someone to cut wood and do the hunting."

Maria nodded, "You take care of your parents, it's good." She said, feeling regret that he would not be in Neva. "Perhaps in the spring you will return?" She asked.

"Da, I'll be sailing on this ship again in the spring. The captain has promised me a letter after that to submit my name for my own ship with the trading companies." He said with excitement.

"Captain Gennady," Maria said again with admiration in her voice.

"I like the way you say my name." he whispered, "It has a special meaning when it comes from you."

"Why is it special?" Maria asked.

Gennady paused for a moment, "Because you know who I am, you know my name."

Maria didn't understand at first but took it to be a sincere thought. "Everyone on this ship knows your name," she replied.

"Yes, but I don't dream about them or admire the way the sun dances in their hair. And I definitely don't stay up all night thinking about how soft their lips are after I kissed them." He said slowly.

Maria blushed as she felt her heart melt from his kind words. She looked into his eyes and felt her heart race with anticipation. He touched her cheek and guided her willing lips to his as they kissed in a slow, soft motion. She slid her arms around him as he pulled her close. The two of them cuddled under the blanket as they pulled each other closer and closer under the neon sky.

Gennady's shoulders felt strong and powerful in her hands as she stroked her hands up his back. She liked how he fit against her as she moved off the edge of her chair to be closer to him. Her heart filled with emotions she could not define; it was as if she was out of breath but adored the sensation. She wanted everything to remain at that moment as if she was living her entire life inside a single kiss.

Their lips brushed softly, again and again until she felt him open his mouth slightly. She sucked at his bottom lip, feeling a hunger wash over her. Then she felt his tongue slipping between her lips, it felt amazing, erotic, so passionate and intense. She did the same to him and felt him moan softly from the sensation.

Suddenly she felt unexplainably afraid, it was so fast, so much, she pulled away a little bit and laid her head on his shoulder. "Gena, I need to go slower." She whispered.

Gennady put his arm around her and kept her close and warm as they watched the stars in the sky. He was on fire for her completely, but wouldn't dare push her as he was so grateful to be near this angel from his dreams.

"I could stay out here all night," he said.

"Me too!" Maria replied.

A while later the oarsmen began to set up their beds on the deck, making it an awkward place to have Maria in view. Gennady guided her down to her room and kissed her once more before she went inside her cabin.

"I'll see you in the morning, but I'll think of you all night." He whispered as his fingers gently stroked her cheeks.

Maria melted from his sweet words, she could feel herself growing hungry for him but wanted to stay in that safe place of kissing and feeling warm next to him. As she lay down to sleep that night, she imagined how life might be as a captain's wife. She kept her thoughts to herself, knowing Sveta would tease her.

Sveta only smiled and blew out the candle for the last time on their voyage.

# Mermaids in Lake Ladoga

The front of the ship dipped firmly into the water as it picked up speed in the morning sun. The sail was stretching to its limit as the wind across Lake Ladoga pushed it from the North down toward Neva. The sound of men working and preparing for the final destination could be heard in all directions.

Maria looked over at Sveta's bed and saw she had already gone below to the kitchen. She looked around the cabin taking in every detail, this would be her last day on the Kupala. She quickly got dressed and pulled her shoes on as she headed for the door. She was curious how the lake looked and headed up the stairs as she pushed her arms through her coat.

The lake was enormous, even larger than Onega, on the left, she saw the distant shore and several boats entering from the rivers that flowed inland. On the right and the Lake extended as far as the horizon with islands populating the view in all directions. The captain was giving commands from the front of the ship as Gennady handled the steering from the helm.

Maria walked toward the sail and placed her hand over the patch she had made weeks before. "It's still holding; you did excellent work!" She heard the quartermaster say behind her. She turned to see Vladimir carefully walking across the deck. "And I have first-hand experience of that!" he said with a laugh as he ran his hands over his chest.

"Nice to see you up and about!" Maria said, "How's the cough?"

"I'm feeling much better but not quite ready to go back to work." He said, "Just in time for the winter season."

Maria smiled, "How long until we're in port?" She asked.

"By nightfall, maybe sooner with this wind." He replied.

Maria felt as if an hourglass had been turned over and the grains were quickly pouring from the top to the bottom, she wanted to make the most of her last day and prepare for what lie ahead in Neva.

The captain called her to the front of the ship, waving excitedly for her to hurry, "Ever seen a mermaid?" He said with enthusiasm

Maria rushed to the side rail and looked in the direction the captain was pointing. There in the water something appeared and quickly slipped beneath the waves. She shielded her eyes from the morning sun desperately looking to see if it would appear again. "They come out to catch the sailors and pull them into the water!" the captain added.

She knew she had seen something but began to doubt as nothing appeared a second time. Then suddenly a smooth shape curled just above the water's edge and disappeared followed by a fin that flicked the water before going under. She eagerly pointed with excitement, "There I just saw one!" she shouted. The captain laughed as the quartermaster ambled over to join them.

More shapes began to appear, distinctive fins and smooth bodies spinning about in the water as the ship rolled by. Maria was astonished how calm the captain and the quartermaster were, "I thought they were just a myth!" She said as she watched to see them again. "Do they ever show their face?" she asked.

"Da, big dark eyes and bald heads with whiskers!" The captain said with a laugh.

Maria looked at the quartermaster, confused by the captain's comment. "The captain is having a bit of fun with you, those are seals, not mermaids," Vladimir said.

Maria felt embarrassed and punched the captain in his arm for tricking her. He let out a big laugh and patted her on the back, "Ladno! For a moment you believed it!" he said chuckling as he turned back to monitor the Kupala's route across the lake.

Vladimir and the captain began to talk about their plans when they arrived in port. Maria felt out of place among such business and headed back to the stairs to go below. She looked up at Gennady, her charming sailor, and waved to him as she walked down the stairs.

Gennady watched her intently, following each step she made down the steps. Maria felt the ship begin to lean firmly to one side as she steadied herself against the wall. The captain's voice began to boom from above the deck, "Gennady, eyes on the horizon ya horny bastard!" as the ship steadied back to a level position.

Maria laughed at the thought of her distraction causing the entire ship to tilt. She felt complimented and embarrassed at the same time. The crew were busy below decks, everything had to be moved out of storage once the ship was across the lake and into port. They were staging the cargo to be brought up in a particular order so it could be offloaded quickly. Maria shuffled past all the commotion and made her way down to the kitchen where she could hear Sveta cooking.

"Good Morning!" Sveta said as she saw Maria come down the stairs. "Hungry?"

"A little, maybe some oatmeal?" Maria asked as Sveta handed her a bowl already prepared.

"You know me too well," Maria replied as she blew on it to cool it off.

The ship turned sharply to one side then steadied, as they both reached to steady themselves against the wall. "Ah, it's impossible to cook when your boyfriend is at the wheel!" Sveta teased.

"He's not my boyfriend!" Maria contested, we're just friends.

"Oh, is that what you call it on the farm?" She said with a giggle.

Maria felt her face turn red as she tried to explain, "We like each other, but he is going to the White Sea, and I'll be in Neva looking for my mother, so it can't be more." She replied.

"I understand, but romance is the enemy of all practicality," Sveta said as she tended to her cooking.

"I really do like him, he treats me nice and makes me feel safe," Maria said as Sveta rolled her eyes.

"Oh, here we go!" Sveta said as she smiled. "Chosen your children's names yet?" She said sarcastically.

Maria laughed, "Stop! You're mean!" She said as they laughed together.

"Do you know what I don't understand, though? I've been on the ship all this time, and we just started to talk. Why now? Why not 3 weeks ago?" Maria said in frustration.

"I used to think how cruel life was to tease us with only a taste of something sweet, but then I realized it happens to prepare us for something that comes later. Those perfect moments at the wrong time leaving you wondering what if it had been sooner, or he wasn't married, or whatever it is that keeps it from lasting." Sveta said as she looked hopelessly at the ceiling.

Maria nodded as she ate her oatmeal, "How does it prepare us for later?" She asked.

Sveta turned and pointed at the stove as the fire burned inside. "See that handle there on the firebox?" Sveta replied, "My first day on the ship I burned my hand while trying to open the door. After that, I always used my apron to cover my hand when pulling at it."

Maria looked puzzled, "I don't understand your meaning." She said.

Sveta showed the scar on her hand, "It only took one of these for me to learn how to handle myself with the stove. And each time we get that taste of something bitter or sweet, we should learn from it, so next time..."

"We don't get hurt?" Maria replied.

"Yes, but it's not just about avoiding being hurt, it's about taking a chance the next time one comes along," Sveta said as she stirred the oatmeal on the stove. "A broken heart can heal but regret is the scar that never fades."

Sveta became quiet as she reflected on the past moments that had inspired her advice. Maria watched her and understood this was not just a philosophy discussion, it was Sveta's way of reconciling past regrets.

"Those perfect moments at the wrong time, what if it had been sooner, or someone wasn't married, or whatever it is that keeps it from lasting. We go through it so the next time, we don't hold back, or wait, or let the fear keep us from jumping when we think we should be still." Sveta said as she turned away to wipe her tears.

Maria looked at the wall, thinking about the many things she would have done differently if she could go back in time, "That makes a lot of sense, but I don't care for the bitter taste of such lessons." She said sadly.

"Me neither," Sveta said as her voice shook a bit in remorse.

There was a long pause between them as they each gathered their thoughts and emotions.

"So what's for lunch?" Maria asked to change the mood.

"Borsch!" Sveta said Gennady got some lovely beets at the last stop!

Maria smiled, "I'll help you make it!" She said with a happier voice.

They began sorting through the dishes and preparations as they cleaned and cut everything for the lunchtime meal. This would be the last meal served on the ship, and they wanted it to be perfect. The scent lifted from the kitchen as they cooked their magic brew of beets and vegetables in the classic Russian style. The men began to line up in the galley as they waited for it to be served.

Finally, both ladies emerged with large bowls and ladles to fill each man's cup with soup. The men were very polite and appreciative as their mood was turned to returning home and the winter rest that awaited them. Maria looked around for Gennady but noticed he wasn't there.

"Have you seen Gena?" She asked the quartermaster.

"He's on watch, take him something!" Vladimir said.

Maria smiled, she knew this meant he would be alone at the top of the ship. She rushed into the kitchen and quickly grabbed a bowl, filling it with soup. Then she took off her apron and braided her hair as Sveta walked in.

"Ah, soup delivery service?" She teased.

Maria shook her head in annoyance as Sveta walked toward her. "Look up." She said.

Maria looked up as Sveta smoothed her hair with her damp hands and wiped her face. Then she went behind Maria and pulled the ties on her dress tighter.

"Much better!" Sveta sighed "Try not to crash the ship?"

Maria laughed, "I'll do my best." She said as she headed up the stairs.

When she arrived on deck, she turned to see Gennady at the helm. He looked bored until he saw her, then he jumped to his feet and smiled as she walked up the ladder to join him. She felt excited to be bringing him something she had made and wondered if he would like it.

Gennady looked at her as she moved toward him. She was a vision to him, and if she had brought him only sea water, he would have been grateful. The brisk wind from the lake pushed her dress against her skin, revealing the slight outline of her breasts and petite figure.

When she climbed up beside him on the helm, her eyes sparkled like the bluest sky he had ever seen, filled with stars that sparkled even in the daylight. He reached for the bowl, letting his hands wrap around hers.

Their eyes met in that moment, and as he leaned in to kiss her without a single word spoken, the ship began to bank to one side causing him to quickly grab the wheel and laugh as he tried not to let go of her or the cup she had brought.

She liked his smile and kind eyes. And as she looked at him she felt herself melt with admiration. It was a magical feeling just to be near him, and she wondered if it was the same for him.

276

He sipped the soup and quickly voiced his approval, "Sveta did a great job on this!" He said. "Thanks for bringing it up here."

"I made it!" She said proudly, "It's my mother's recipe."

"Really? This is excellent!" Gennady replied. "I'm impressed!"

The wind gusts pushed them back, as Gennady handed her the cup to keep his balance. He put his hand on the lower part of her back to keep her close to him, then said, "Let's try this again." As he leaned down to kiss her.

She felt his lips reach hers, and she instinctively stretched her arms around his neck to hold him closer. She felt warm where his body pushed against hers and wanted to stay there for as long as possible. His tongue slipped into her mouth again, and she felt herself burning from the sensation, it was so pleasant and erotic. She felt it all over her body with a passion that made her want to continue so much that she slowly pulled away for fear it would consume her.

"Too much for you?" He said gently as she held on to him.

"Yes...no....I mean..." She whispered as she pressed her lips to his again, unable to think clearly. She knew she couldn't let the day go by without seizing each moment that might never come again. She thrust her tongue inside his mouth, learning as she went, unsure what was proper or expected, but the burning she felt was more intense than anything she had ever felt by her own hands. It was a delicious, hot wave of excitement that she wanted to feel again and again.

The crew began to emerge from the lower decks, as their kisses grew more intimate. Gennady gently backed away, motioning a look at the men walking on the deck. Maria didn't care, but she understood this was his duty to be serious when steering the ship.

"We'll talk when we get into port, yes?" Gennady asked.

"Konechno," Maria said as she smiled and headed down the stairs.

Gennady admired her every move as she headed below deck and noticed that every man watched her as she walked by, she was such a beauty, and he felt a special honor to be the focus of such a woman's attention. The moment she was out of view, he felt himself counting the seconds until he could see her again.

# Farewell Kupala

The ship began to slow as it completed its track across the lake making a southwestern turn toward Neva. Everyone came on deck to watch the ship make its way into the port. An island sat in the middle of the port entrance guarding the valuable passage down the Neva River that led to the Baltic Sea. As the ship passed the small island, the men began to remove their hats and stood silently.

"What's happening?" Maria asked the quartermaster as he also stood still and silent.

A few minutes later, everyone resumed their conversation, and Vladimir answered her question.

"We pay our respects to Saint Sophia. She protected the Russian sailors from the Swedes during a battle for this area over 40 years ago. Our fathers and grandfathers were sailors so we show our gratitude for a safe return home each time we arrive." Vladimir said as he crossed his hands over his heart. Maria followed his gesture and felt honored to be with such men who were not as barbaric as she had thought them to be when she came on board.

Neva was a busy port filled with ships traveling between Lake Ladoga and the river. There was anticipation in the air as the ship moved closer to its final port. It seemed they would stop any minute, but there was still much work going on.

The crews rolled everything on the top deck, preparing for the final docking. Maria went below to help Sveta as she had to place everything in storage for the winter. She was separating all vegetable into bags when Maria arrived.

"What are the bags for?" She asked

"The crew!" Sveta replied, "We can't keep food on board during the winter or we'll have rats everywhere!"

Maria understood and helped distribute everything evenly. "Are you glad to be done for the year?" She asked.

"Of course, it's been a long summer, and I haven't seen my mother since the spring," Sveta replied.

"Are you sure it's alright for me to stay with you until I find my aunt?" Marias asked

"Yes, I think it will be fun, don't you?" Sveta replied.

Maria smiled, "Da, I am already excited about it." She said.

"I can finish here; you should go and pack your things," Sveta said. When we get in they let us off first, then they go to unload in the storage area where the ships wait out the winter."

"Ah, I thought we were the last off," Maria said as she headed back to the cabin to pack.

As she gathered her things, she remembered each item she had brought or received on the trip. It was as if she had spent a lifetime onboard and now she had to take it with her in the few things she had to carry it in.

She wrapped the scroll from her home in Rostov, her brush, the knife Sergei had given her before she boarded and the bag of coins from the Oxana in the Tavern. Finally, she placed the small pot of honey Sveta had given her in the bag and felt overwhelmed by such memories and dear people.

The quartermaster knocked at the door as he carefully looked in to see if he could enter. "I'm just packing; you can come in," Maria said.

"You will be getting off before me so I wanted to say goodbye, good luck and thank you for saving my life." He said in a kind sad voice.

"You saved mine first, thank you for everything!" Maria said as her tears ran down her face.

"Ladno, we saved each other, now go and live your life! We are all here if you ever need us." He said as his eyes welled up. "You have become like my own daughter, and I will miss you." He said.

They embraced for a moment as Maria felt overwhelmed with appreciation and care from this man who been like a father to her. "I'll miss you too Vladimir! I wish you good health and happiness with Alexia and your daughter." She sobbed as she tried to speak clearly.

"No more tears." He said as he gently wiped her cheeks and headed for the door as the captain entered.

"Devochka, you're a fine young woman, and I wish you good luck! I've got to get back on deck so this will have to be short!" the captain said as he gave her a hug.

"Thank you for getting me here safely, I owe you my life!" She said sweetly.

"You're welcome, and you can come back with us anytime." He said as he patted her on the back and tried not to show his emotions. "I'm off, good luck to you Maria, we'll miss you!" he said as he left the room.

Maria felt as if her whole world was slowly being taken away, one person at a time. She had come to a ship of strangers but now felt her place among them was fading quickly. She put her bag on the bed and heard footsteps coming down the hall as noises of docking the ship began. She thought it would be Sveta, but then looked up and saw Gennady entering her cabin. Her heart sank, as she had dreaded this moment the entire day.

He walked to her and took her in his arms, "I'll be on my way to the White Sea in a few hours, if I had known about you, I would have never agreed to leave so soon after returning, but it's done."

Maria nodded, "I understand, it all happened so fast with us, but you will come back in the spring?" She asked

"Yes, I'll be here, and I will look for you when I return. Just tell Sveta where I can find you and I'll come for you!" he said as he pulled her close and kissed her deeply.

She held onto him as if her life would end if she let go. It was so bittersweet to find someone who could make her feel this way and then have to watch him walk away. "I'm scared Gena!" She said as she cried in his arms.

"It will be all right Masha, I will count the days, the minutes, the seconds until I'm holding you like this again. Please remember me, because I will never forget you!" He said as he squeezed her tightly.

"I'll remember!" She said as her voice shook from crying.

"Until the spring then..." He said as his hands loosened from around her. He reached and guided her mouth to his and kissed her one last time, softly and tenderly. He looked into her eyes as he pulled away and backed toward the door, wanting to remember her face until the very last second. Then he stepped into the hallway and was gone.

Maria collapsed on her bed, she felt betrayed by love, by life, by fate. Everything dear was taken from her, and she couldn't bear the thought of waiting an entire winter without this man who had inspired such beautiful feelings inside her.

A voice above the deck shouted, "Passengers and merchants ashore!" as the sound of the gangplank shuffled across the top deck.

"That's our call!" Sveta said as she rushed into the room. She took one look at Maria knew what had happened. She walked over to her and put her arms around her. "Dorogaya, I know you are upset, but this is life, we come and go, and that's how we meet new people. Now it's time to take the next step." Sveta said, wishing she could comfort her.

Maria nodded, knowing she was right, as she stood to gather her things. "I came here to find my mother; I know I should not forget that." She said as she wiped her eyes and picked up her bag.

Sveta reached for her belongings also and followed Maria up the stairs and to the gang plank.

The entire crew was there to say goodbye and wish her well as they stepped off the ship. Maria waved and wiped her tears as she tried to smile.

"See you in the spring!" Sveta said as she waved goodbye as well.

The ropes loosened off the poles in the dock as the ship drifted back into the river, heading for the cargo dock. The Kupala looked so different when watching it from the dock, it seemed bigger than when she had first seen it.

"My house isn't far from here, let's get a carriage and I'll show you the sights!" Sveta said as she walked toward the street looking for horses nearby.

Maria took one last look at the Kupala as it gracefully pulled into the current of the river. She missed everyone already and imagined it was spring time, and they were just coming in rather than leaving. She took a deep breath and turned to notice the evening lights of Neva welcoming her. The city was beautiful with all the ships lighting the lake and a warm glow from the windows along the shore inviting everyone inside as the cold air began to blow inland.

It felt romantic and bittersweet as the thoughts of Gennady mixed with finding her mother, her aunt's house and continuing alongside Sveta all ran together. A buckboard rolled by and stopped as Sveta motioned to Maria to climb aboard. The driver placed their bags in the back and helped them step up onto the bench seat.  Moments later they were rolling through the streets of Neva as Sveta patted Maria's hand in excitement whispering, "We're home!"

# The Mirror from Kiev

The buckboard went through the streets of Neva as the sun quickly fell below the horizon. Sveta pointed at landmarks to help Maria understand the primary points of the town, "This is Aleksandrovskaya Ulitsa, it's the main street, and everything connects to it, so if you get lost just ask how to get back to Aleksandrovskaya." Sveta said as she smiled at the sight of her hometown. "I used to play there with my friends when I was a little girl." She said pointing toward a grove of trees near the water bank.

Maria noticed several churches and shops along the busy road. The town seemed so much bigger than Rostov, with small homes and buildings stretching into the distance. The streets were filled with people walking in all directions, some buying food while others made their way back from the port. Two Tatar soldiers stood on a corner at the edge of the port entrance. Maria looked at Sveta with concern, "Should I hide in the back?" She asked.

Sveta smiled, "They do not have as much power here as in your town, it's an international city and commerce is the ruling power, not politics." She replied.

Maria felt herself breathe easier as the soldiers looked in their direction and continued talking as if they had no interest in her. "So they cannot arrest me then?" She asked.

"If they could show something like you had broken a law, then yes. But otherwise, there is nothing a soldier can do so far from his general." Sveta replied, "I would be more nervous about bounty hunters than soldiers." Sveta said.

"Oh wonderful, now I have to think about that?!" Maria sighed.

"Masha relax; how can they prove you're the one they are looking for? They can't! And it would cost them a lot to transport you back to Rostov, with no assurance they would get paid, plus winter is coming!"

Maria laughed, "You're right, I'm from Yaroslavl now, never been to Rostov!" She giggled.

"That's the idea!" Sveta shouted as the cart came to a halt. "This is it!" She said as she began to get down from the buckboard.

Maria looked around and saw an inn with several floors above the entrance. Sailors from the port were making their way inside, as the driver set their bags on the side of the street. "Skolko?" Sveta asked.

"Nichevo" He replied, "I was coming here anyway."

"Spacibo!" Maria said as she and Sveta headed inside with their bags.

The inn smelled like the galley on the ship as men sat and ate or drank around small tables. A man played a bayan while some sang familiar songs. It had a festive mood as everyone celebrated being home or in port for a few hours.

Sveta lead Maria up a narrow staircase into a hall and then another staircase until finally she stopped at one door, and knocked," Mama, ti spiish"? Sveta shouted as her voice echoed in the hall.

An elderly woman came to the door, her face lit up when she recognized Sveta and hugged her tight. The woman began to speak excitedly in another language, as she welcomed them both inside. "Da mom, ladno!" Sveta kept repeating as she giggled at her mother's excitement and attention.

"She is Finnish, but I'll ask her to speak Russian instead," Sveta said, as she chatted with her mother and set her bags down.

Maria looked around the room, it was bigger inside than she expected. The main room with a small table for preparing food and some chairs, then two adjoining rooms. Sveta turned toward Maria and guided her mother's attention;

"Mama, this is Maria, she will be staying with us for a little while. Maria this is my mom, Irja."

"Ochen priyatno Irja," Maria said kindly as Irja said something in Finnish.

"Da, she does" Sveta replied, "She says you look like my cousin Anna in Vyborg."

Maria smiled, feeling the awkwardness of the moment but hoping to adjust to her new surroundings.

Sveta motioned to the left-hand room and invited Maria to bring her things. "I'll show you where we will sleep." She said as she walked into the room.

Maria followed and looked inside as Sveta lit a lamp inside. The bed was large enough for two, with a large washstand in the corner and a mirror that stretched from the floor to the ceiling. "I missed my mirror!" Sveta shouted as she walked in front of it, "Papa brought it from Kiev a long time ago, before I was born." She said as she smiled.

Irja began to speak in a limited Russian dialect, "Sveta's Papa buy this for me when we get married." She said as she held her hand to her chest. "He tell me, 'Irja! What I can give that is more beautiful than you?" She said as she lowered her voice to sound more masculine. "And so here is my reflection."

Maria giggled as Sveta agreed, "Da! Papa had a strange way of expressing his heart."

"I no need be reminded how I look now; Sveta can use better," Irja said as she walked over and hugged Sveta.

"Kushat, Kushat!" Irja said excitedly as she led the two ladies back to the other room, where she began to place food on the table. They sat together, eating, sipping wine and sharing stories of their lives. Maria told how her father had died and how she was to meet her mother there in Neva. They agreed to visit the churches in town the next day to find out where her aunt lived.

As the hours passed late into the night, they made their way to the bedrooms to sleep off the wine's relaxing effect. Irja brought some towels to Sveta's room and kissed both girls good night. It reminded Maria of the care and nurturing spirit her mother had always put into everything she did.

Maria sat on the bed and sighed, "Oh my, it's really soft compared to the one on the ship." She said as she slid her hands over the mattress.

Sveta slipped out of her dress and washed as she looked at herself in the mirror, "Uzhas, I got fat this time. Too much apple pie." She said as she pinched herself at the waist.

"Nonsense, you have a slim figure and everything in proper proportions. "Maria contested as she reached for a cloth to wash her face.

Sveta turned, inspecting every angle of her naked body in the mirror. "Do you think my breasts are sagging?" She said as she pressed her hands underneath them.

"Sveta!" Maria shouted, "That mirror will drive you mad! I can see why your mother didn't want it in her room!" She said laughing.

"I just want to keep my magic alive, you know?" She teased "I'm not going to the nunnery with a body like this."

"The nunnery?" Maria asked in surprise.

"What options do we have as women? Wife, nun or fun? "Sveta said as she burst out laughing. "I'll take the life of a ship's cook, kholop and all for now."

"You know" Maria began, "It's not what every girl dreams of, but there are worse things."

Sveta nodded as she stumbled over to the bed, feeling the wine in her steps and words, "Da! Letting some man control what you do in exchange for a meal and a fuck." She blasted.

Maria felt shocked by her response but didn't disagree with her, "I was thinking about having no one to love or love you in return. On the ship, you are all like a family."

"I suppose," Sveta said as she slid beneath the blanket and wiggled to one side of the bed.

"You're going to sleep like that? Naked?" Maria asked.

"Why not? You can keep me warm." Sveta said in a drunken slur as she began to doze off.

Maria changed into her bed dress and blew out the lantern. She slipped beneath the blanket staying on the edge of the bed to place as much space as possible between them. It was awkward sleeping with Sveta like this, and she missed her private space on the ship.

Maria took a deep breath and felt herself relaxing slowly as the bed warmed up. It was very comfortable, and the familiar lumps in the ships mattress were no longer irritating her delicate body. The feelings of being in a home made her feel safe and cared for, even if it was not the home she had known growing up.

Sveta rolled over and got closer to her. "I'm cold," She said in a pouty voice as she put her arms around Maria.

Maria felt nervous, wondering if this was Sveta's way of starting something more intimate. She felt Sveta's hand move up her side, and then cup her breast. "Your tits are so firm, I wish mine were still like that." She said in half sleeping voice.

"Sveta!" Maria protested, as she pulled her hand away and nudged her to back away from her.

"Oh relax" Sveta replied. "You can touch mine if you want!" She said with a giggle.

"Can we just sleep?" Maria asked, feeling herself without an option to change the situation.

"Konechno," Sveta said as she rolled back over to the opposite corner of the bed.

Maria calmed down and began to think about the next day's plans. Finally, after so many weeks of travel, she could find her aunt, and hopefully, her mother was already there also. Everything felt surreal and hard to accept as actual life from the moment she had stepped off the cart in Rostov, it was as if she fell into a dream and hadn't yet woken up. Her confused thoughts wove a fabric of distressing dreams that haunted her as she fell asleep. She imagined herself walking through a castle going room to room, searching for someone and always the rooms were empty.

Then a soldier appeared, she saw armor, a sword, and metal shields. He walked towards her and drew his sword and held it over his head to strike. The blade began to swing towards her and just as it reached her neck, she woke up.

Her eyes opened as if she had slept all night, but it had only been an hour. She felt hot, her body was wet from sweating as if she had been running. She walked to the wash stand and wiped herself off. She felt a chill as she saw her reflection in the dim lit mirror, it was the same image from her dream; she was wearing a sheer dress and appeared lost in a castle.

She wondered if the threat of being chased by soldiers was truly over, was she safe there in Neva and could she finally stop running.

She slipped back into bed and felt Sveta cuddle up behind her. Sveta put her arms around her, and whispered, "Shh, you're safe." as they drifted back to sleep.

# Two Churches in Neva

The morning came, and the scent of blini drifted into the room as Irja cooked breakfast. Sveta stayed in bed while Maria got up to go and help.  She walked into the main room and greeted Irja as she reached for plates to set the table. Maria made herself at home as she squeezed juice from the extra fruit they had brought from the ship.

The sounds of clanking dishes and cookery brought Sveta out of the bedroom; she smiled at the idea of not having to cook and being able to enjoy her mother's care. Sveta sat at the table and chatted with them as they finished preparing the meal. Irja suddenly remembered a letter had arrived and brought it to Sveta as she told her about it in Finnish.

"What is it?" Maria asked curiously

"It's from the kholop guild." She replied as she opened it. "It came after I left. Can you read it for me?" She asked as she handed it to Maria.

Maria smiled and gladly took the letter and read it aloud, "Svetlana Nikolayevna Popova, according to the agreement on record between Nikolai Popov and Neva River Shipping, the balance of your debt will be satisfied on November 1, in the year of our Lord 1390."

Maria paused, realizing the date and meaning of what she had just read. There was absolute silence as Sveta's eyes widened in shock.

"Present this release to the captain of the Kupala for signature then record the document at the Kholop guild in Neva straightaway...Edictum, Konstantin Petrov", Maria concluded as she began to smile and watched for Sveta's reaction. Irja sat in suspense, unsure of the legal words and what it meant for her daughter.

Sveta softly began to say the words she had waited a decade to announce, "I'm free... I'm free!... Mam, Olen Vapaa!... I'm free!" she continued as her voice grew louder in excitement.

Irja and Sveta burst into the conversation as they hugged and cried. Maria stood and hugged them also. She knew this was a huge moment for them both. They all sat and ate with huge smiles on their faces. Sveta seemed to be a different person, her face lightened, her eyes sparkled, and she couldn't stop smiling. She had a new energy that made everyone excited.

"How long has it been?" Maria asked.

"Ten years this month! I was just 20 when Papa died and now..." Sveta said as she felt the reality of her freedom washing over her. "I thought it would be another year or two, but I guess they increased payments as wages went up for free men."

"What will you do?" Maria asked in excitement. "Maybe return to visit a particular farmer?" she teased.

"Maybe!... I've gotten so used to building my life around the ship; I don't know what to think. I just want to make sure my mother and I are able to take care of ourselves." She said as she stuffed blini into her mouth and chewed energetically.

Irja spoke excitedly about everything as Sveta smiled and quickly translated certain words for Maria. "She wants grandchildren." She said laughing.

"Ladno, the captain, still has to accept this, and it has to be recorded in the guild." Sveta said, "I can do this in a few days, let's find your Aunt first." She insisted.

Maria smiled and shook her head in agreement, "It's good to have some positive news for a change. Something uplifting." She said as she stood to put the dishes away.

Irja motioned that she would take care of the dishes, "I will do dish, go find Aunt" She said still smiling from the news in the letter.

Sveta and Maria got dressed and set out to visit the churches of Neva. The air was crisp against a bright blue sky as they walked along the street, back toward the port where Maria believed her aunt lived.

They came to an Orthodox church that was made of stone and painted white. At the top golden onion-shaped domes glistened in the sun with crosses positioned atop each apex. As they walked inside, Maria felt a sudden memory of the last time she had been in a church building, it was the night her father was killed by the Tatar soldiers.

She saw a calendar hanging by the door and walked toward it, counting the days backward. She placed her finger on the present day and looked at Sveta as She said "40." Maria's eyes welled up as she looked at the altar where she could light a candle for her father on this special day.

She looked around for something to cover her head but had nothing in her coat. The priest approached them as Sveta walked over to speak with him. A few words were exchanged, and he nodded as he walked over and handed them both a lace cover for their heads. He then lifted his hand inviting them to the altar to light a candle. They both approached and knelt at the altar where others had lit candles that morning.

It was a calm and peaceful place, with golden adornment and beautiful paintings of the saints along the walls and ceiling. The priest waited until they both had taken their time for the dead and met them near the door. Sveta slipped a coin into the contribution box as they talked.

"Are you in need of confession my children?" He said kindly.

Maria felt she was not ready to talk about her ordeal with a priest she did not know and declined. Sveta smiled and said, "I'm not the confessing type." with a nervous laugh.

The priest seemed very understanding, "It can bring you some peace my dear, please return anytime you wish." He said.

Sveta agreed and then presented the reason for their visit, "Father, my friend Maria has come in search of her Aunt, and perhaps you might know where we could find her?"

The Father looked at Maria with curious eyes, "What is your aunt's name?" He asked.

"Nina Kamarova" she replied.

The priest thought for a moment but said the name was unfamiliar to him.

"I know that she lives near the port," Maria said.

"Are you sure it's the port and not the shipbuilder's dock?" The priest asked.

"My uncle was a ship builder!" Maria said excitedly as the memory of her uncle's craft jumped into her mind.

"Ah, well we mostly get sailors and merchants through here. However, there is a large church down by the shipyard. Brother Timofei has been there many years, I'm sure he will know your aunt." The priest added.

Maria and Sveta turned toward the door and reached to return their head coverings. The priest gestured that they could keep them, "For next time." He said with a gentle smile.

Sveta thanked the priest for his help as they walked back onto the street and headed toward the shipyard. They took their coverings off as Maria felt the excitement that she would find her aunt very soon. They walked along the street with their eyes focused on the distant scaffolding of the shipyard. The sun had warmed the air since the early morning, and more people began to appear as shops and markets opened for the day.

Maria noticed the variety of food and clothing as they walked, she felt ready to make Neva her home and come each day to this market. "Perhaps we will meet here sometimes and go shopping?" Maria said to Sveta.

"Oh there are so many markets in Neva, I'll have to show you all of them!" Sveta said with a smile.

They soon arrived at the shipyard and walked toward a similar dome-topped building where crosses were placed. It was a large church with a graveyard on the side. "My father is buried here," Sveta said as she pointed to the stone garden. They both crossed their hearts and stood silently for a moment.

Sveta turned and reached for the handle of the Church's main door. The thick wooden door creaked on its hinges as she pushed it open. They looked at each other and quickly placed their coverings back on their heads as they giggled nervously. The sensation of the church overwhelmed them with the scent of candles and incense filling the air as they walked inside. Adorned columns rose from the floor to the lofty ceiling, covered in exquisite details of gold, tile, and carved wood. The sun cast a downward beam of light through the expired incense vapor, gracefully reaching for the floor as if a stairway of light had formed at the center of the room. The sense of calm and peace was beyond description. Maria noticed Latin text that marked scriptures and saint's names that she remembered from her home church in Rostov.

Maria looked around the room, taking in all the detail as Sveta noticed an elderly priest sweeping a broom across the open floor. She walked toward him as he looked up to see her.

"Zdrastvuite, are you brother Timofei?" Sveta asked.

"Da, have we met before?" He asked.

"Net, this is my first time here, I've come with a friend, she is from Rostov and searches for her Aunt here in Neva," Sveta said, trying to get the answer as quickly as possible.

The priest looked at her and paused while he thought for a moment. Maria walked over to join them as he looked at Sveta while thinking. His eyes were pale blue and shined brightly in spite of his old age. He lifted his hand to his chin as he recalled something he seemed eager to remember. "Nikolai!" He said excitedly.

Sveta's eyes widened, as she gasped. "Nikolai was my father." She said in shock.

"Da, indeed he was. He was also a good friend. We grew up together, and before I was a priest, he and I were sailors. Oh, such memories. Do you know it was I that christened you?"

Sveta was speechless, her father had never mentioned his friendship with this man. He had merely gone to church there a few times when he was in port.

"I can see his face in yours," Timofei said. "I remembered you at his funeral ten years ago, I wanted to tell you about him then, but I thought it best to wait for happier days to introduce myself. I was hoping to one day tell you some stories of the man I had known before I wore the garb of a priest. Then I heard you had joined the guild and you were gone."

"Da, I became a kholop to support my mother," Sveta said as her eyes teared with memories of her father. "I must confess; I only know a few stories of my dad. He worked until he dropped dead on the ships, and was never home after I was eight years old. My mother said he lost everything when the Tatars invaded, their house and his ship were destroyed, and he had so many debts."

"He lost more than that. The war broke his spirit and made him afraid to hold anything close for fear of losing it." Timofei said as his voice shook with regret.

"I wish you could have known him as a young man. He was wild, fearless and always chasing the girls." The priest began, "But then I suppose we all were." He chuckled.

Maria smiled, "Sounds a lot like you." She teased Sveta.

Sveta nudged Maria with her elbow, hinting not to embarrass her as they both laughed.

"Ladno, this one seeks her aunt, da?" Timofei said as he tried to regain his composure.

Maria began, "Da, if you could tell me if you know a woman named Nina Kamarova? Her husband was a shipbuilder, who died 2 years ago, and she has a son, Dmitri, who works the ships on the Volga?" She said trying to remember all details of her aunt's life.

Timofei nodded as she spoke, immediately recognizing the woman she described. "Nina comes every Sunday; she lives in an old farmhouse farm by the dry dock." He said confidently as he began to walk toward the back of the church. "I'll have my scribe show you the way."

"Spacibo!" Maria said excitedly.

As Timofei walked away, Sveta turned to Maria, "This is so exciting, he knows your aunt, he knows my father, I wasn't expecting all this!" Sveta said.

"You should come back and visit him, I think he wants to tell you more about your father," Maria said as she saw Sveta's eyes filled with tears.

"Da, I will," Sveta said shaking her head as she wiped her eyes.

A middle-aged man returned with Timofei, he was wiping his hands of ink as he greeted the two ladies. "This is Brother Boris; he will guide you to Nina's house." Timofei said as he paused, "Boris is mute, so he will speak with his hands only. He is also the best Latin scribe I've ever seen." Timofei said as he patted Boris on the back.

Boris smiled and pointed toward the door.

Sveta and Maria thanked Father Timofei for his kindness as Sveta promised to return and talk more about her father. It was clear that her father and Timofei had been very close. They all walked toward the door as Maria and Sveta greeted Boris.

"Ochen priyatno, Boris!" Sveta said slowly in a loud voice.

"He's mute, not deaf my dear," Timofei said as they all laughed.

As they exited the church, Timofei paused in the doorway and waved goodbye to them. "Udachi Maria, please say 'hello' to Nina from me."

# Finding Nina Kamarova

Boris led the two ladies down the street, walking calmly in front of them. Maria wondered what it was like to suffer from such a limitation, to have no ability to speak seemed beyond comprehension. She had never met a mute before and felt compelled to communicate with Boris somehow.

"Boris, I studied Latin in my hometown." She began, "Do you do a lot of writing?"

Boris turned and nodded, as he looked unsure what the point of her comment was.

Maria felt embarrassed and thought she might have offended him. She decided not to say anything more as her thoughts turned to finally seeing her aunt.

"Are you ready for this?" Sveta asked.

"Seeing my aunt? Of course!" Maria said excitedly.

"I meant about telling her why you are here alone," Sveta murmured.

Maria paused, she wasn't sure how she would even begin to explain. "There is so much to tell about my father, mother, Dima…unless my mother has already arrived. That will make it easier." She said, knowing the chances of that were very unlikely.

Boris listened carefully, realizing something tragic must have happened. He stopped and pointed at a woman walking toward them in the distance. She was carrying a basket with loaves of bread stacked inside and seemed to recognize Boris from far away.

"Is this Nina?" Sveta asked.

Boris nodded with a smile, as he waved to her.

The woman waved back as her voice carried from the distance, "Boris, privet!"

"When was the last time you saw your aunt?" Sveta asked.

"About 5 years ago, she visited us in Rostov. I thought I would recognize her but… yes, I believe that it's her!" Maria said as she began to walk toward Nina.

Sveta began to walk with Maria, but Boris caught her eye and motioned that perhaps she should wait. Sveta nodded and stood with Boris as Maria walked to greet her aunt and tell her the sad news.

They watched as Maria began walking quicker toward Nina, they could hear her voice as she recognized her,

"Masha?!", Nina shouted as she ran to embrace Maria.

Sveta watched knowing that the initial happiness would soon be replaced with the saddest words anyone would have to say. The sounds of laughter and giggling soon faded as Maria's body language and gestures told the story of her father's death and the unknown condition of her mother. There was a long pause and then Nina embraced Maria as they both cried.

Boris crossed his heart and said a prayer in silence, as his lips moved. Sveta bowed her head and whispered, "I wish I knew what to say to them."

Boris patted her back and motioned with his hands. Pointing to his mouth then waving his hand away. Sveta tried to understand, "I know, you can't speak. I didn't mean anything by that." Sveta said awkwardly.

Boris smiled and shook his head, then repeated the gesture with his hands, pointing at Sveta's mouth.

Sveta paused, "Oh, you mean, I shouldn't say anything?"

Boris pointed at her mouth again, then shrugged his shoulders while holding his hands open.

"Right, I don't know what to say!" Sveta agreed

Boris waved his hand as if to stop. Then pointed at Sveta and then to the ground.

Sveta curiously asked, "So, I should kneel and pray?"

Boris sarcastically rolled his eyes, as if her response was completely ignorant.

"What? I don't understand. I don't know what to say to them! What does the ground have to do with anything?" She said in frustration.

Boris smiled and tried again. He pointed at himself waiting for Sveta to acknowledge him. "Alright, um Boris." She began

He raised an eyebrow and quickly applauded her. His sarcasm began to make her smile and feel more comfortable with him.

He then pointed his hands to the ground. Then took a few steps and pointed to the ground again.

"I'm not sure I understand, you're here then you're there. Chto togda?" Sveta said hoping he would give up.

His face lit up as She said what he tried to explain. He pointed at her and motioned for her to repeat herself. "What? Here or there?" She asked.

He held his hand up to stop her in mid-sentence, gesturing for her to say the first word again.

"Here?" She said without understanding.

Boris applauded and repeated the entire meaning to her in gestures as she spoke out loud. He pointed to her mouth as Sveta recited;

"Um, I don't know what to say?" She began

Boris motioned his hand to stop as she continued speaking,

"And I shouldn't tell, or...?" Sveta asked unsure of the direction to take.

Boris rolled his hands encouraging her to keep talking.

"I don't need to know what to say?" Sveta searched as Boris waved goodbye to her as if he didn't like her answer.

"Who cares what I say?" Sveta asked excitedly.

Boris rotated his hand side to side as if she had almost gotten the point.

"It doesn't matter! ... It doesn't matter?" She asked.

Boris' eyes lit up as he walked closer to Sveta with excitement. He nodded his head in agreement. He held his hand to his heart, then pointed at her and then the ground.

Sveta paused, "It doesn't matter what I say...it matters that I am here?" She said slowly.

Boris smiled and put his hands together in a gesture of prayer, and bowed slightly to Sveta. She had understood his advice perfectly.

"You're right. I don't remember anything people said to me at father's funeral. I just remember who came." She replied.

Boris placed his hand on Sveta's shoulder and nudged her to go to Maria and Nina. She began to walk as he waved goodbye to her.

"Thank you, Brother Boris, that was...really something!" Sveta said, feeling as if she had just learned something deeper than any words could have taught.

Boris smiled as he turned to go back to the church. He paused after a few steps to watch the three ladies come together and comfort each other. The bittersweet reunion of loved ones during sadness was a scene he had admired many times in his life, but it was no less beautiful each time it unfolded.

The ladies walked together, returning to Nina's home. Nina opened the door to her small cottage at the edge of the shipyard. It was an old farmhouse that had been there for many years before the arrival of the ship building trade. She set her bread basket down at the table and invited Maria and Sveta inside.

"So you haven't heard from Lena since that night?" Nina asked.

"No, I was hoping she had already made it here or is right behind me on another ship," Maria said. "We looked for Mom in several cities, but had to stop asking about her when the soldiers began searching for me."

"Lena was always the smartest one in our family, I'm sure she will figure something out," Nina said. "I'm so sorry to hear about Alex, he was such a good man."

"Da and he would still be alive if I hadn't gotten off the cart that night," Maria said as she felt the reality of her father's death becoming more real in her aunt's presence.

"Masha, you think you can control the world? How many men were killed in your town for any reason that suited those soldiers? You didn't cause this; you should accept that!" Nina said firmly. "We should concentrate on the living now, and that means finding your mother."

Maria did not find comfort in her aunt's words but felt she was correct in her view. Still, the responsibility weighed heavy on her mind as she wondered where her mother might be.

"Dima will finish his work and come soon for winter break. I am sure he has been looking for Lena also. Perhaps she will come with him?" Nina said as she smiled.

"You think so?" Maria said as she considered the possibility.

"Of course, he knows the ships, the ports and how to get around soldiers," Nina said proudly.

Maria nodded in agreement, "Da, he got me out safely." She said.

"I think you two have a lot to talk about, and I need to take care of some business at the guild," Sveta said. "Masha, you are welcome to stay with us, if there is no room here." She added.

"Of course, there is room!" Nina said with a sharp interruption. "We can send to have her things picked up."

Maria felt embarrassed by her aunt's arrogant tone. "I'll come over later to see you and get my things." She said kindly to Sveta.

Sveta nodded and walked toward the door as Maria followed her outside.

"I don't know why she is like that," Maria said, trying to apologize. "She just doesn't know you or how much you have done to help me."

Sveta nodded, "It's fine, once she heard me say 'guild' she saw me as kholop or a prostitute. I'm used to that attitude when I'm here. Everyone has to be better than someone else."

"Well, she is wrong!" Maria insisted as she realized the people who had helped and cared for her was quite foreign to the conservative family she had been raised in. "I've forgotten how it feels to be told what to do or what to think." She added.

"Well, you can think for yourself now," Sveta said as she gave Maria a hug. "I'll see you later when you come back for your things."

"Thanks, and good luck with the guild. I hope the captain agrees to everything." Maria said.

"He will, but he might try to hire me to stay on with the ship. Still, if Ivan comes in the winter, I might be tempted to return with him to Mologo. I have a lot to think about." Sveta said as she waved and walked back toward the street.

Suddenly Masha realized her journey was complete, she had arrived at her aunt's house and was to begin her life here. After so much along the way, it seemed as if nothing fit in her new life. Her aunt seemed strict, and there was no farm to tend here. She walked back inside and felt her previous accomplishments and new knowledge fading away with only the hope of her Mother's arrival very soon.

"Your friend is a kholop?" Nina asked in disgust.

"She was, she just completed her agreement with the guild," Maria said as she looked around the house, taking in the new surroundings.

"Well the women are nothing but whore's if you ask me, they trade their life for a little money and then they just exist for men's pleasure." Nina snapped.

310

Maria felt enraged by the comments and took them as an attack on her friend. "She became kholop to pay her father's debt, and keep her mother off the street. I would do the same for my mother!" Maria said in defiance. "You don't know anything about her, and you would judge her that harshly? She is the reason I am alive and here right now!"

Nina paused and dismissed Maria's comments as those of a young girl who did not understand the world. The maturing of Maria had not yet happened in Nina's mind, nor did she recognized the young woman that had replaced the fourteen-year-old girl she last saw in Rostov five years ago. "When you are older, you will understand!" Nina said in conclusion.

Maria felt the vision of a perfect life in Neva quickly fading as she began to see how conservative her aunt was. She began to realize why her cousin, Dima, had chosen to work the ships on the Volga rather than Lake Ladoga. "If his mother only knew of the Taverns he often visited." She thought to herself, "She would have him committed to a Monastery in Siberia!"

They were both silent for a while, then Nina tried to make peace. "Masha, let's not fight. You've been through a lot, and I don't want to have such disagreements while you are here." She said.

Her aunt's voice sounded familiar, almost identical to her mother's and Maria felt herself relax as she listened to her speak. "You can sleep in Dima's room for now," Nina said as she opened a door revealing a bed and nightstand. A few items were stored there that Dima had collected on his travels, some winter clothing, and a few ship tools.

Nina looked around the room, "He is building a ship one part at a time I think." She said as she laughed and set the tools out of the way.

Maria sat on the bed and looked around the room. It felt familiar even though she had never been there. The sense of being in her Aunt's home began to appeal to her more than the initial greeting.

"I should go and get my things," Maria said, feeling an awkward sense of what to do next.

"That's fine, I'll walk as far as the market with you. I still need to deliver the morning bread." Nina added.

They both headed out of the house and back up the street, with few words between them. Maria felt she needed to keep her opinions to herself and not cause trouble at her aunt's home, this was her only family and she needed to respect her aunt's wishes.

"Do you make bread each day?" Maria asked as she tried to fill the silence.

"Da, it's the only thing I can do to survive. Dima helps me with things when he is here, but the money doesn't last forever, and I need to pay for food and taxes for the house. Once a month the Tatar soldiers come by and relieve us all of our hard earned money. Those who don't pay lose everything as an example to the others." Nina replied.

"I am afraid of them," Maria said. "They almost caught me on the ship, and someone got hurt trying to keep me hidden."

"They just want money here; they don't carry off brides like they do in the villages," Nina stated. "You will need to find something you can do here for work."

"Da, I noticed there is no farm, so I am wondering what I can do to help with money," Maria replied.

"I'll ask around the Market, perhaps someone needs a cook or dressmaker," Nina said.

"If there is something with herbs or medicine, I would enjoy learning that," Maria replied.

"Uzhas, you want to be a witch? Those things are the devil's craft!" Nina said in shock.

Maria laughed, "It's not witchcraft! It's just natural things to help the sick. I saw some of it during the trip, and it actually worked." She said.

Nina scoffed, "What kind of daughter has Lena raised? A friend of kholops and witches?" She said condescendingly. "You should learn things that make for a good wife. That is the only way for a woman to survive in this world." She added.

Maria reflected on her experiences, the women who had all made their own way without a man to depend on. How they considered men for love but not support. It was as if all she had learned was being thrown away and the strict views of her village life were returning but in a world where they no longer worked.

"I'm sure we will find something that meets your approval," Maria said as her aunt nodded in agreement.

They reached the market and agreed to meet later at Nina's house. Maria watched Nina leave and then retraced her own steps past the churches and to the tavern where Sveta and her mother lived. She smiled as she approached the building, "Aunt Nina would scream if she saw me walking in here." She thought.

It was as if Maria saw the world with new eyes, an ability to compare the virtues of the conservative and liberal mind she had developed. She could feel the constriction of her Aunt's morality choking at the unknown, judging and dismissing people or ideas that didn't fit her approved agenda. Her friends, occupation, and destiny all seemed to be on a trial rather than met with optimistic adventure.

"Is there a way to live virtuously without forbidding the fullness of life to unfold around you?" She wondered.

Maria walked up the stairs and knocked at the door, greeting Irja as they both waited for Sveta to return from the guild. From the moment she entered Irja's home, she felt complete relaxation and a sense of being truly home. It was the only time she had sensed such a calm since leaving Rostov, making the value of her aunt's conservative lifestyle decline quickly when compared to those who lived with generous hearts and common flaws.

# Quot Annorum Es?

The sounds of footsteps outside the door slowed as they approached Irja's room at the Inn. Maria and Irja smiled as they heard the door handle turn, knowing it was Sveta, returning with news of her freedom from her father's debt. The door opened, and Sveta walked in with a bright smile as she saw her mother and friend waiting for her.

"Yra!" She said in a happy voice, "I'm officially free!" Sveta announced as she waved a small piece of paper in her hand.

The three ladies hugged and cheered, as tears rolled down their faces. The positive energy between them was overwhelming as the joy of Sveta's long journey had come to an end. It had been 10 years since the young woman had signed her name to repay her deceased father's debt, and now she was free to go and do whatever she wanted in her life.

Irja spoke excitedly in Finnish as Sveta tried to translate for Maria. "She says she is going to get some wine from downstairs and will be back!" Sveta said as her mother left the room.

Maria looked at Sveta, genuinely happy for her friend's new life. "Did the captain agree to everything then?" Maria asked.

"He thought he had two more years, but when they presented the records, he agreed that he had lost track of time."

So there was nothing he could do. "He wished me well and asked me to come back as a paid cook in the spring," Sveta replied.

"Will you do it?" Maria asked.

"Honestly, the Kupala has been my home for 10 years, and it's all I know. But I think about how many times we pulled out of port, and I felt myself wanting to stay, to be part of a life that doesn't float away." She said as her eyes took on a romantic glow.

"You're thinking about Ivan!" Maria teased.

"Da! I admit, I had several other men, some I wondered why they didn't love me or want me enough to make an offer, but Ivan, he was the one I felt happy with, I was myself with him." Sveta said.

"Will you wait for him in the winter?" Maria asked.

"I would like to see if he would make that trip to see me, it would give me proof that he really does want me," Sveta replied.

"Like a test?" Maria asked.

"I suppose. More than just words. It's easy to enjoy the convenience of me visiting him when I am in port, but will Ivan be the one to make the journey, and come to me?" Sveta said calmly.

"Well, he doesn't know you are free, so hopefully he will come and find out the good news," Maria added.

Sveta nodded in agreement, but it was evident she was considering the idea of going back to him, "Masha, I've spent ten years waiting; I don't want to wait anymore." She confessed.

"Then go to him! Why should you test someone who clearly adores you as he does? I saw how the two of you were! He loves you!" Maria insisted. "It's time to get off the ship!"

Sveta smiled, enjoying the pleasure of Maria's words as she listened. Irja returned with a bottle of wine and brought cups to the table. "We drink!" She said insisting with a smile.

They began to toast to Sveta's freedom, to her father, to love and everything in the universe until the day and the bottle were gone. Maria felt unbalanced as she stood to collect her things. "Oh dear, I believe I am drunk." She said as she giggled, stumbling slightly as she tried to walk around the room.

Sveta laughed, "We all are!" She said as she stood to help Maria gather her bags.

"Stay the night, you can go to Nina the nun tomorrow." Sveta said as she burst into laughter at her own joke, "Nina the nun, that's perfect!"

Maria also laughed, "Nuns would be offended, they are less conservative." She said as she laughed between her words.

Irja mumbled as she slowly made her way to her room. Sveta helped Maria to the other room as they both collapsed on the bed. Sveta wrapped her arms around Maria as if she were holding a doll. They laid together without a sound or movement for the rest of the night.

The next morning, they awoke and slowly began to stand, feeling hung over from the wine. Maria kept her head down and shielded her eyes to the light, while Sveta supported herself by placing her hand on the wall as she walked.

They made their way to the table and sat with Irja.

"Chai budish?" Irja asked as she pushed a cup toward them.

The girls sat and slowly sipped the tea, hoping it would bring relief from the wine's lingering expense of celebration.

"I'm sure Tetya Nina is wondering where I am now," Maria announced.

"She knows you're with a friend, but I think she hates me," Sveta said.

"She hates everything; I don't understand how anyone could live with her. And my family was planning to come stay with her here as if life would be so perfect for us." Maria said as she starred in her cup.

"She lives alone; she can afford to have rules for everyone when there is no one to offend her," Sveta replied.

Maria agreed as she silently contemplated the life her aunt intended for her in Neva. She retraced the conversation they had the day before about finding work and wanted to tell Sveta about it, "I told her I wanted to find work, maybe something with medicine or herbs like Natasha in Besov? Can you imagine... She called me a witch!" Maria said in outrage.

Sveta shook her head in disbelief and then her eyes opened wide, "Wait! When I was in the guild, there was a guy there who kept the records and contracts. He said he needed an assistant who could write in Russian and Latin! You should go there and ask for work!"

Maria thought for a minute, "How much do you think he would pay?" She asked.

"We can go ask him! The guild gets a percentage of all contracts, I am sure it's more than what you would make in the market." Sveta replied.

"Why would they hire a woman when there are monks who can write in Latin perfectly?" She said in objection.

"Selling yourself into slavery is not something a monk will be a part of, they think the guild is an evil thing. But honestly, they keep the masters from taking advantage of the innocent." Sveta assured as she held Maria's hand. "For those who don't ask, the answer is always 'No', da?"

Maria smiled, "Alright, we'll go and ask!" She said excitedly.

Irja prepared a small breakfast for everyone as they discussed ideas for Maria to find work and where she might live in Neva. It was evident, without discussion, that the conservative nature of Maria's aunt would present a lot of conflict for Maria to establish herself.

"Is your mother going to want to live with your aunt when she arrives?" Sveta asked.

"We never talked about living with her, only to make our home in the same town. But with Papa gone, I don't know what will happen. Her cottage is not big enough for all of us." Maria said as she smiled from the implied relief.

Irja listened and asked Sveta a question in Finnish directing it toward Maria, "Mom says there are many places you could live on basic wages if it's just you and your mother." Sveta translated. "Just outside the city, they rent dachas that can handle the winter and in summer you would have enough space for a garden."

"A dacha would be perfect, it's what we are used to, especially growing our own food," Maria replied.

"Well, first we need to get you working!" Sveta said as she stood to return her plate to the dishpan.

"Da, let's see what they say," Maria said as she stood and handed her plate to Sveta.

Irja returned to her bedroom to recover from the previous night's drinking. The two girls exited the apartment and walked across the city as Sveta guided the way to the guild. The building was close to the center of the town square and boasted large wooden beams extending through the outer walls, to support the external roof. It was well maintained compared to the other buildings around it.

"So clean," Maria said as they walked toward the entrance.

"Da, the guild has a lot of money and access to slave labor ... they can afford to have someone sweeping the floor all day and night if they want." Sveta said with slight sarcasm.

They walked through the door, revealing the large inner rooms, the placement of chairs and desks gave it a formal feeling that serious business was conducted here.

"I expected something similar to the slave traders on the docks, but not this," Maria said

"This is a guild, kholops are not sold into slavery against their will, they make a contract in exchange for their service. And once made, the guild can enforce the slave going to work or the master to provide food, clothing, shelter and so on." Sveta explained.

They walked to a desk where an older man sat, surrounded by books and papers. He had a stocky build, with a wide frame. His tanned face revealed a character of being outdoors and rugged, with reseeded hair along the sides of his head and a few grey wisps covering his scalp. His piercing blue eyes gave an intensity to his stare, revealing a superior intellect as he looked up from his work as they approached him.

"Kostya," Sveta said in a friendly tone.

His face shifted from concentration to a pleasant smile as he recognized Sveta.

"Svetlana!" He said enthusiastically. "You were free yesterday, are you back so soon to make another contract?" He teased.

Sveta laughed, "Konechno net!" She mused as she looked toward Maria who stood beside her.

"Maria this is Konstantin, cleric of the guild." Sveta said as she pointed at Maria, "And this is my friend Maria, she is an expert in Latin and Russian, just arrived in Neva and needs to find serious work. Can you hire her?"

Konstantin looked at Maria with a defiant glance, studying her appearance and concluding she was not as impressive as Sveta had described, "Quot annorum es?" He asked quickly watching her response to his impromptu interview in Latin.

321

"Undeviginti" Maria replied softly as she looked at the floor, feeling intimidated by Konstantin's hard manner.

Sveta looked at Maria and shrugged her shoulders unsure of the conversation, "He asked my age." Maria said quickly.

Konstantin grunted, expecting her to get the answer wrong, he fumbled through his papers and pulled a blank page out and slapped it on the desk in front of her. "Complete this calculation" he grunted as Maria rushed to reach for a quill.

"A man agrees to work eleven years for a wage of 10 silver denga each month. How much will the guild make on such a contract at the end of each year and overall, when we receive fifteen percent of each payment?"

Sveta scoffed at the idea of such a calculation, then she watched Maria quickly write two lines of numbers down the page, cutting the number in half on one side and doubling it on the other. She then drew a line through one set before making a quick addition of the doubled column.

Within seconds, Maria held the paper in her hand and asked confidently, "Do you want the annual or total profit amount first?"

"Annual" Konstantin barked, sounding annoyed.

"Duodevigenti...." Maria began.

"In Russian!" Konstantin demanded.

"Prostiti" Maria replied as she continued, "18 silver denga each year, and over the 11 years a total of 198 silver denga to the guild."

Konstantin's eyes looked upward as he completed the math in his head. Then he paused and looked approvingly at Sveta, "You've brought me someone clever." He said with a smile.

"Where did you study, under the nuns?" Konstantin asked in disapproval.

"No sir, my mother was the town school teacher, she taught me at home," Maria replied.

"Horosho," Konstantin said as he looked over his paperwork. "I need someone who can read, write and calculate for me during negotiations. You have to think fast and be confident with answers. Can you do that?"

"Yes sir, I think so," Maria said, realizing her confidence was not strong enough.

Konstantin laughed, "Ladno. We will work on that."

"Oh thank you! I will try very hard!" Maria said with excitement as she walked around the desk to hug Konstantin.

"Net, net, everyone will take one look at you and think I've taken a mistress instead of an assistant" Konstantin mused as he extended his hand and shook Maria's briefly. "You can start tomorrow, come at mid-day." He said.

"Podezhdi!" Sveta interrupted, "How much will you pay her Kostya?" Sveta teased with a smile.

Kostya hesitated, "You are too young to have experience, so let's make it 4 silver denga each month." He said firmly.

"Five!" Sveta shouted as she looked at Kostya with judgmental eyes. "She's all alone here, she has to pay for everything herself, so don't be greedy!"

"Horosho, Pyat! But more confidence, and soon!" Konstantin said as he stood up.

Maria nodded in agreement as she smiled. "Spacibo bolshoe, Konstantin."

Sveta tugged at Maria's arm suggesting they leave the guild now. As they walked outside Maria extended her arms and spun in circles, "Ura! Ura!" she sang. She stopped and hugged Sveta in appreciation. "Spacibo Sveta, you have helped me so much." She said.

"Pozhalysta" Sveta replied, "We help each other!"

They strolled back home as they discussed the possibilities for Maria's future when her mother arrived.

"What do you think your aunt will say when you tell her about working at the guild?" Sveta asked.

"I'm sure she won't approve; she seems to prefer I sell fruit in the market while my brain goes soft," Maria replied

An hour later they were in Sveta's room, packing Maria's things for her to return to her aunt's house.

"If it gets complicated, you can always come back," Sveta said as Maria headed toward the door.

"Thanks, I plan to stay only until my mother returns, and then we will build our life here." Maria said, "What about you, what will you do?"

"I'm actually thinking about catching the last of southbound ships and spending the summer with Ivan. Do you think it's crazy?"

"No! I think it's romantic! Of course, I will miss you, but this is your life, you need to live it now!" Maria insisted.

"I'll come see you before I go, mom will go with me, so if you need a place to rent, this one might be open soon!" Sveta teased.

"I'm excited for you Sveta; I will come see you there when things are calmer here. Maybe in the spring?" Maria said

"That would be wonderful, you can bring your mother also, and we will all be together!" Sveta said as her eyes began to fill with tears.

Maria tried not to cry, it was everything she could do to be supportive of her friend even though she secretly wanted her to stay nearby. "I'll see you before you leave, so no tears yet." She insisted.

They hugged, and Maria carried her bags out the door and out of the inn. She turned for a moment and looked over her shoulder, realizing the source of her comfort and confidence in her new life was going to leave soon. She suddenly felt alone as if she had been placed in a battle against the world and she had to fight for herself.

The walk down the street to the shipyard seemed longer than ever. As she walked past the church, she looked for the familiar face of Brother Boris or Timofei, but none were in sight. Her eyes looked forward, seeing the cottage where her aunt lived. With each step closer she felt more uncomfortable and unsure of her decisions, more defensive about how she would explain her new work.

Finally, she reached the door and slowly opened it, expecting her aunt to ask where she had been all night. She rehearsed what she would say as she stepped inside, but saw her aunt sitting at the table crying. Her aunt nervously looked up with eyes of joy and ran to her.

"Masha! I thought I had driven you off" she exclaimed, "I searched all night for you but couldn't find you."

Maria felt terrible, all this time she had been celebrating with her friend while her aunt was upset. "I'm sorry, I decided to stay with my friends as we talked until very late and it's not safe to be on the streets at night," Maria said, hoping it would explain everything in a pleasant way.

Nina wiped her eyes, "Ah, well, that makes sense. I'm just relieved you are well!" She said as she hugged Maria several times.

Maria set her things down, wondering how she would begin to discuss the news of her job at the guild.

"I should know not to worry about you so much; you've been on your own all this time. I forget you are a woman now." Nina said. "Perhaps we can go look for work in the market tomorrow morning? I hear they make as much as two silver denga a month when the season is busy."

Maria stared at the wall, thinking how hard it was not to announce she had made a much better arrangement to support herself. "I appreciate your help, but I feel I should find a job on my own, I hope you don't mind." She said.

"No, not at all, you're very assertive, just like your mother, I admire that," Nina said.

They talked while preparing their dinner, Nina told Maria stories about her mother when she was younger and how her mother was very popular with the boys in town. Maria was surprised her mother had never told her such tales but then it made sense that the less virtuous chapters of her mother's life would be concealed for fear of being repeated in her daughter.

# Konstantin's Apprentice

Each morning for the next four weeks Maria left the cottage to look for work, always insisting her aunt allow her to find a job on her own while she rushed to the guild to assist Konstantin with his contracts. Each evening she would make up stories about greedy merchants who didn't want to pay her enough, or that she walked farther into the city to try other markets away from the port. Her aunt often scolded her for being too selective and spoiled regarding finding work, which Maria accepted as proof her story was believed by Nina. She felt it was a necessary deception to keep the peace, but when her mother arrived, she would be bolder in revealing her chosen occupation at the guild.

Once a week, disputes between slaves and their masters were heard by the guild. Konstantin was appointed as arbitrator to ensure the contracts were respected, and any changes to the agreements could be recorded. On this particular day, a landowner and an older farmer were waiting to see Konstantin when she arrived.

Konstantin emerged from a small room where the cases were reviewed and motioned to Maria to come in with the land owner and slave. "Bring the log from ten years ago." He instructed as she walked by his desk.

Once inside the room, Maria sat in the corner with the log book on her lap as she watched Konstantin review the case. Each man stated his position, the landowner wanted to reduce the slave's pay, and the slave insisted he should receive more.

Konstantin nodded and reached for the book as Maria handed it to him. He flipped through the pages until he found their contract. He paused, reading it carefully and then placed it in front of the men, do you see what each of you signed here?

They both looked at the book as the slave spoke first, "Sir, it's in Latin, I don't understand it."

The landowner shrugged his shoulders, "I haven't read Latin for many years, perhaps you can translate it?" he said.

Konstantin handed the book back to Maria as he looked both men in the eye, "Maria, what was the agreed upon wage when this agreement was made?"

Maria quickly scanned the Latin text, and announced the amount in Russian, "Seven silver denga to the man's family in exchange for farming duties."

Konstantin nodded as he looked at the slave, "Are you lazy? Do you work hard?" He said aggressively.

"I work all day, Sir! I only stop to eat and then go back in the field!" He insisted.

The landowner interrupted, "You are old and slower than the others, the young ones work twice as fast as you!" he snapped.

Konstantin interrupted, "And you think paying him less will cure this?" he said as silence filled the room.

Maria felt sympathetic to the slave, he was a farmer, much like her father and she knew how hard they worked.

Konstantin looked at both men, trying to make up his mind. "My assistant is very skilled in math; do you mind if I ask her opinion?

Both men shrugged their shoulders without objection as Konstantin turned toward Maria, "Should we pay this man less because he is older or slower than the others?"

Maria paused and considered her words carefully, "This agreement was made with the understanding it could not prevent old age, so this should not be held against the man." She began as Konstantin nodded in agreement, "But if he does not work fast enough, more money or less money will not help."

The landowner and Konstantin nodded in agreement, expecting her view to satisfy them as she kept analyzing the case.

"Can I ask the land owner a question?" Maria asked.

Konstantin motioned his approval with delight as he enjoyed listening to Maria's thought process.

"Do you have more crops now than when you made this agreement for his labor?" She asked the landowner.

"Yes, my farm is twice as big now as it was then." He replied

"And did this man help to make it bigger?" she asked.

"Yes, he is responsible to get the planting done in the spring and then the harvest in the fall, why?" The landowner asked curiously.

"Well, it seems to me the agreement was made when the farm was at a size much smaller than it is now." She stated as Konstantin listened.

"She has a point!" Konstantin said with a smile.

"Yes, but I have hired more workers to help, he simply doesn't do enough work." The landowner insisted in a defensive tone.

"Sir, a skilled farmer, can get twice the crops from half the work," Maria said as she remembered hearing her father tell her that many times. "You pay him for more than heavy lifting, you pay for his knowledge, and you've admitted he grew your farm to twice its size?" Maria said in a rhetoric tone.

"Your assistant presumes too much!" The landowner scoffed.

"Chto? She has become your enemy for telling the truth?" Konstantin said with a chuckle. "I agree with her, you cannot reduce this man's wages. He has proven his worth."

"Your sympathies for the kholops is beneath your station Konstantin, you know damn well they will all hear of this and work less as a result." The landowner snapped as he stood to exit the room in disgust.

"Indeed, and the masters will hear of it also and wonder why a man with twice the crop is depriving his servants of their fair wage," Konstantin said as he paused waiting for his words to take effect.

The landowner stopped at the door and paused as he contemplated the gossip about his reputation among the other landowners. Many of them envied his success and would enjoy seeing him in a less favorable view. This was the politics of the town, and he had seen it in action many times.

"I suppose your point is valid." He said as he turned toward Konstantin in an appealing gesture. "But what of the request for more money than agreed on?"

Konstantin looked back at Maria, hoping she could continue to provide perspective.

"Money is not the only thing of value to the farmer, you could assign the heavy tasks to the younger workers and give him a portion of the crops to feed his family. This way your original agreement could stay intact, and the case could be dismissed." Maria said with persuasive charm.

The landowner nodded to Konstantin, "Can we dismiss the case then?"

Konstantin ripped the documents in half with a smile, "What case are you talking about sir?"

The landowner smiled, feeling he had spared his reputation as he exited the room. The servant's face lit up as he reached to shake Konstantin's hand. "Spacibo, Gospodin Konstantin, Spacibo bolshoe!" He said eagerly.

Konstantin smiled and said, "Don't thank me, thank the bee keeper's daughter, she made your case for you." He insisted.

The farmer quickly walked to Maria and shook her hand also. His firm, leathery hands reminded Maria of her father. She could feel an entire farm in a single touch, so much effort and patience to bring food from the ground. She respected the man and felt unworthy of his appreciation. "I only spoke the truth." She said kindly.

Konstantin guided the servant out of the room as he looked to see if any more cases were waiting. He returned and closed the door;

"That was very impressive, young lady. Your father would be very proud of you." He said.

Maria smiled; she had told Konstantin her life story over the past month and confided her wishes to take care of her mother when she arrived. He had become like an uncle to her and encouraged her to learn as much as she could about the guild and negotiations. He felt she would someday be in a position where diplomacy and knowledge would serve her well.

"That's the last of them for this week." He said as he sat at his desk. "You can go for the day."

"Spacibo!" Maria said excitedly, "I am going to visit Sveta on my way home, she will leave tomorrow for Cheropovets!"

"Ladno, tell her to make that man marry her!" Konstantin urged as he watched Maria leave the room.

Maria rushed across town, eager to spend time with her dear friend. She had only seen her a few times in the last four weeks, and now this would be goodbye for an entire season. She stopped in the market to buy some fruit to take as a gift before heading to the inn where Sveta and Irja lived.

She rushed up the stairs and knocked on the door, hearing them talking inside as soon as she arrived. The door opened, and Irja's eyes lit up, "Masha! Idi suda!" Irja shouted.

Sveta walked from her bedroom and laid several bags in the center of the room as she saw Maria enter. They hugged and set the fruit down, ready to eat it immediately. The three of them talked about their trip plans, then Irja left to take care of some details before departing in the morning.

"So this is it? Are you nervous?" Maria asked.

"Konechno, more for my mom than me. I know Ivan will be happy to see me, but for her, this will all be new. She hasn't traveled on board a ship since she met my father." Sveta said.

"I'm sure she will be fine; she is an experienced woman," Maria assured.

"Da, she's been in this place too long, she needs to see new things," Sveta said. "How's life at the guild?"

"Good, Konstantin is very supportive and wants me to learn everything," Maria replied.

"Did you tell your aunt yet?" Sveta teased as she nudged Maria.

"Konechno net!" Maria said with a laugh, "Not till my mother arrives!"

"The last of the northbound ships are coming in now, she should be here soon." Sveta said, "We are catching one of the last one's heading south for the winter."

"Da, no one wants to be on the river when it freezes," Maria replied.

They nibbled at the fruit and swapped ideas about the future. Sveta spoke of her imaginary wedding and Maria talked about a farmhouse where she and her mother could soon live. Suddenly the door opened, and Irja rushed in, speaking out of breath in Finnish, as Sveta tried to understand her.

"Shto Mom, shto? Sveta said trying to get her mother to speak slower."

"A big ship just came in from Yaroslavl, it's the last one from that far south!" Sveta said excitedly. "Your mother is probably on it!"

Maria felt a rush of energy shooting through her body, she jumped to her feet and headed for the door. "I have to go!" She said excitedly. "What time do you leave tomorrow?"

"First light. But I will go with you! Mom can finish packing." Sveta said as she reached for her coat.

The two girls ran down the stairs on their way to the port. Several ships were docked, and they struggled to find the right one. Sveta asked each dock hand which ship had just come from Yaroslavl until they found someone who knew and pointed the way.

Maria's excitement made her run faster and faster as they approached the dock. A quartermaster was directing the offloading of barrels as they got closer to the gang plank. Sveta caught his attention and asked if the passengers had already gotten off. He nodded in agreement and pointed to the same dock they had arrived on when they left the Kupala.

"They are probably already at my Aunts house then!" Maria said as she started to walk in that direction.

Sveta hesitated, knowing how unwelcomed she was around Nina. "Perhaps you should go alone, this is a family time," Sveta said as she hugged Maria.

"You are my family too!" Maria insisted, "But you're right, my aunt will be difficult as always."

"It's fine, I'll see you in the morning before we go then?"

"Yes, I'll meet you at the dock and bring my mother!" Maria said excitedly.

"I can't wait to meet her! See you in the morning!" Sveta said as she turned to walk home.

Maria rushed down the street, imagining her mother's face, the stories they would share, and how this would be their first chance to comfort each other after her father's death. With each step, she felt more and more determined to arrive sooner.

She reached the cottage and rushed into the door, expecting to see her mother. She immediately saw Dima sitting with his mother. "Dima! You're here! Where is my mom?" She said as she looked in each room.

A sudden coldness began to creep over Maria's heart as she realized her mother was not there. And Dima looked sorrowful and afraid to speak to her. "What's going on? Shouldn't she be here? It's the last ship from Yaroslavl, right?" Maria insisted.

Dima stood and hugged Maria without saying a word.  She pushed him away, fearing the dreadful news he was holding. "Where is my mother, Dima?!"

"Masha, sit down, I need to tell you something," Dima said in a shaking voice.

"I don't want to sit down!" Maria shouted, feeling her nervous energy boiling the fear inside her.

Nina's eyes were dripping with tears as she placed her hand on Maria's shoulder, she guided her to sit as she nodded to Dima to explain what had happened. As Dima began to speak Maria felt her entire world was about to change, before a single word had been said, she knew this was a moment where everything would never be the same. She braced herself for the worst of her fears and waited for him to say her mother had died.

"Masha, your mother, is not on the ship, and she won't be on any others. She was taken prisoner by Tatars the night you escaped. They are keeping her as a slave to work the farms in Rostov. They took your father's farm also."

Maria felt relieved that her mother was alive, but as the idea of her dear mother being subjected to the brutal slavery of the Tatars sank in, she felt responsible for making this happen. She sat silently for a few minutes as Dima explained to them both what had happened since the night of Maria's escape.

"There was a reward for both you and your mother that went out all over the region. To deny the khanate a bride was bad enough, but the soldiers were humiliated when they were caught in the bee swarm and let your mother escape. She made it to another ship, but they caught her in Yaroslavl and took her back to Rostov. When the news of her capture was announced, they doubled the bounty for returning you as a lesson to everyone that it's better to cooperate with Alchiday." Dima said.

"Da, they searched for me all the way up the Volga," Maria said as she sat in shock.

"I thought they had caught you but when I arrived, Mom told me you were here and safe, it's a miracle!" Dima said happily.

"Not such a miracle for my mother," Maria said as her body began to shake from the grief that erupted inside her.

The three of them sat quietly for a while, crying and trying to make sense of the tragedy that had fallen on Maria's family. Maria cried endlessly until she fell asleep. Dima carried her to his bed and let her rest while he slept on the floor. All through the night, her sobbing could be heard through the house, her broken heart carried a pain beyond words.

# A Ship with Three Masts

An early morning light flickered through the window and caught Maria's eyes. She was exhausted from her troubled sleep but realized her best friend would soon be leaving for the season. She sat up on the bed and walked to the door without any attempt to change her clothes or prepare her hair. She was still in shock as the cold morning air blew across her face.

She walked to the dock and saw a crowd of people waiting to board a ship, she could see Sveta standing in the line and walked toward her. Sveta saw her approaching alone and then noticed how puffy her eyes were as she rushed to Maria. "What happened?! Where is your mother? Tell me!" Sveta said.

Maria explained the entire story as her tears returned. Sveta also cried, feeling as if she was abandoning Maria at a time when she really needed her.

"I'll cancel this trip; we can go in the spring," Sveta said.

"No!" Maria insisted, "I have to handle this on my own, and you have a life waiting for you! Please don't stay, go and live your life!" Maria said in a strong tone. "Where is Irja?"

"She went to get amber and sea salt for Natasha, we will stop to see her on the way," Sveta said.

"Oh, tell her I hope to visit her one day," Maria said as she looked into the distance. Irja walked through the morning fog with a small bundle in her hands that contained the amber and salts.

Sveta spoke to her mother, telling her what had happened in Finnish as they collected their bags.

"She says we can stay if you need us to remain here," Sveta said.

"I appreciate your kindness, but both of you should take this trip. I don't know what I will do yet, but I'm not going to sit here waiting for a miracle." Maria said with confidence in her voice.

The quartermaster called for the passengers one last time, looking at Sveta with an impatient gesture as the rest of the ship waited. "Come with us!" Sveta begged.

"I can't, my family is here, my work is here, and I have to find a way to help my mother. I am no use to her if I am captured by the Tatars on the river." Maria insisted as she resisted the impulse to walk onboard the ship at that very moment.

"Ladno, there will be a few more ships going south, if you change your mind we will be waiting for you there. And if not, we will come back in the spring!" Sveta said as she kissed Maria's cheek and looked at her sweetly one last time before turning to go to the ship.

Irja gave Maria a hug and said something in Finnish that sounded comforting. She wiped Maria's tears and then blew her a kiss as she stepped away toward the ship.

Maria watched as they boarded and quickly cast off. It was almost dreamlike seeing her dear friend whom she had been so close to, drifting off into the mouth of Lake Ladoga. The morning breeze caught the ships sail and soon they were out of sight and over the horizon. Maria turned to walk back to the cottage, feeling each second of time that passed made her farther from everyone she was close to.  Her aunt and cousin were relatives but her friendships and her mother were the people dearest to her, and now they were all far away.

As she entered the cottage, Dima sat at the table sipping tea. Nina was still sleeping, and he motioned to Maria to speak quietly as he pointed toward her bedroom. Maria sat at the table as Dima made her a cup of tea. She was still in a daze from everything that had happened.

Dima returned to the table and looked at Maria with serious eyes. "Masha, we don't have much time."

"For what?" Maria asked.

"To get your mother out of Rostov!" he insisted.

Maria took a moment to comprehend what he had said, as she didn't understand him.

"Get her out?" She said.

"Da! The longer she is there, the worse it will be for her. The cold winter for slaves is unforgiving. I've seen how the Tatars make them live, their horses are treated better." He said.

"What can we do?" Maria asked.

"The Tatars sell slaves all the time, it's just a matter of paying the right people to get her out!" Dima said.

"How much do we need?" Maria asked, thinking she had saved enough to solve the problem.

"I have enough to get back to Rostov and then return with your mother. But not enough for the slave traders and bribes." He said. "We need five hundred silver denga more."

Maria felt overwhelmed, "Five hundred, it might as well be five thousand!" She thought.

"I have a little bit of money, but nothing like that." She said.

"I know, and I need to give some to my mother so she can afford to live here while I am away," Dima said.

Maria thought quietly and then felt she should talk with Konstantin; the smartest man she knew to get his thoughts. Maybe he would even give her the money.

"How long until the next ship leaves? She asked.

"Three days, maybe four. If we miss that one, it will be too late for the winter." Dima said sadly.

"I need to get ready for work," Maria said as she filled with energy and stood up.

"What work? Mom said you were still looking?" Dima asked in surprise.

"I can't tell her everything, I think you know why," Maria said as she went to brush her hair. Dima nodded, knowing how conservative his mother was, but unsure what kind of work his cousin was doing that required such deception.

Maria quickly prepared herself and headed out the door on her way to the guild. It was earlier than her usual time to arrive, but she felt her needs were urgent enough that Konstantin would be able to help her. As she arrived, several people stood outside waiting to make contracts with slaves and have them recorded at the guild. This was usually done before Maria came to work, as Konstantin preferred her absent from the men who came there.

She worked her way through the crowd and found Konstantin talking with several men. He noticed her right away and interrupted his conversation, "Masha, you are early today?" He said.

"Kostya, I need to speak with you, it's urgent!" Maria said.

Konstantin could see how red and swollen Maria's eyes were, he knew she had suffered some kind of emotional trauma as he dismissed the men from his office.

"What's wrong Masha, are you sad because Sveta has left?" he asked.

Maria told him the entire story about his mother and the attempt to buy her freedom from the Tatars. He was shocked and felt distressed for his young assistant's family. He went to his desk, and opened a locked drawer, revealing a bag of coins.

"This is all I've been able to save after taking care of all the bills around here. It's yours, consider it a gift or an advance on your salary, whatever you want to call it." He said kindly. "But it's only two hundred denga!"

Maria hugged Konstantin and thanked him for his generosity. She knew the money she had already saved plus his contribution would make two hundred fifty.

She apologized for interrupting his business and said she would return at the regular time later that day. Konstantin nodded as he motioned for the men to come back to his office as she walked out the door.

A handsome man with sandy colored hair and deep brown eyes stopped her at the door. He spoke with a Finnish accent similar to Irja's voice and asked where he could find Konstantin.

"He's in a negotiation now, you'll have to wait with the others." She said as she tried to leave.

The man stopped her again, "Perhaps you can help me? I'm Captain Tanner of the Ukko, my cook has died, and I'm to put out to sea tomorrow for England. I must find a replacement quickly, and everyone in the port recommends this guild." he insisted.

Maria felt annoyed by the man's persistence, "Konstantin does all the negotiations, you'll have to wait." She said as she pushed past him.

Within a few steps, Maria stopped and turned back to the captain. "How long is the journey to England," she asked.

"6 weeks, each way, with a few stops at the ports on the Baltic and the North Sea." He replied, "Why do you ask? Do you know a cook?"

"Is it a large ship?" Maria asked again, ignoring his questions.

"Yes, new construction with 3 masts, enormous compared to the river ships here." He said proudly.

"Then the pay for a cook would be quite good, even for a kholop." She said as she walked toward him.

"The last cook made ninety per month, but he was not very reliable. The crew hated his cooking." Captain Tanner said.

"For one hundred per month, I can arrange for someone with experience, who makes tasty meals," Maria said, feeling nervous at how quickly she boasted herself.

"One hundred is too much!" The captain said, "Maybe I should try in town."

"Ha!" Maria snapped sarcastically, "Why do you think there is such a line here? If one hundred is too much, then good luck to you." She said as she turned to walk away, feeling herself bargaining like Sveta but relieved that her idea had failed.

"Wait." Captain Tanner said, "I can pay one hundred."

Maria stopped again, feeling herself in a position to raise all the money and negotiate the contract for the work. In three months her mother would be free and in Neva, just as she would be returning from England. "It could work, it had to work, this was the answer!" she thought.

"The guild will add fifteen percent to the price, but we can avoid that if I write the contract between you and the cook without their knowledge, as long as you pay up front." She said confidently.

"Three hundred up front?" The captain contested.

"Plus fifteen percent if you go through that door," Maria said calmly.

The captain hesitated but was apparently interested in a quick solution. "Fine, three hundred up front, but the cook had better be amazing!" he said as he began to write down some details on a small piece of paper.

"Bring the cook and the contract to the port tomorrow morning at daybreak. We will be taking on provisions at that time and can sign everything before leaving. The Ukko is the only ship in port with three masts." Tanner said.

Maria nodded and kept her strong negotiation stance until the captain walked away. As soon as he was out of view, she felt herself gasp as she had just made a deal that could raise the money to free her mother.

She walked back to tell her cousin of the news as she tried to think of what she was getting herself into. She had studied Sveta's habits on the Kupala and was sure she could duplicate them for 6 months. She knew how to cook, shop for food and negotiate, surely this was all she would need.

She met Dima at the cottage and handed him the money she had received from Konstantin, then she went into her bag and gave him the coins she had kept from Yaroslavl. He quickly counted it out as she explained how she would get the rest the following day.

"A woman onboard a sea ship?" Dima protested. They don't allow that!

"I've seen women cooks on river ships, it's no different." Maria protested.

"Sea ships are very different! The captain will never agree to it, and you're so young!" Dima said, feeling frustrated by the idea.

"Well, I have to try! My father died so I could escape, my mother is a slave for the same reason. You think I'm afraid of working on a ship?" Maria shouted as her aunt walked into the room.

"Who is working on a ship? Dima?" Nina asked.

They changed the subject and dismissed the comments as just talking about nothing.

"Well, I think it's time you got serious about finding work, Masha. The situation is different now, and you can't be so selective about the work you can find. This is survival." Nina said.

"I agree with you completely," Maria said as she stared harshly at Dima, knowing he would understand how she took the meaning for her own purposes.

Dima waited until Nina was out of the room to continue the conversation, "I still haven't told her I'm leaving in two days. It's best that it happens all at once, or she will make it impossible for us." He said.

"Agreed, I will be gone by tomorrow night, and you can leave the next day. I think it's best she finds out what I've done after I've left, not before. In time, I think she will understand I did what I had to do." Maria said. Dima agreed and hid the coins from sight, to avoid further questions.

Maria returned to the guild that day and looked through several contracts that had previously been made, to get a sense of how she should write her agreement with Captain Tanner. She looked through several books and smiled when she found the one between Sveta and the captain. 10 years for only 8 denga per month, "How awful!" she thought. She copied the text as closely as possible to fit her own needs and hid the document, along with a copy, from view.

Konstantin was absorbed in his papers and discussions with visitors. He asked Maria what she was doing a few times, and she pretended to be organizing documents to make them easier to find in the future.

Before leaving that day, Maria talked with Konstantin to make sure she was not thought of in a poor light after she left. "Kostya, I have a problem." She said.

"There's no more money dear, I'm sorry," Konstantin replied.

"No, it's not that. Not exactly. I have a chance to make the money, but I need to leave for three months, as early as tomorrow, if it is all agreed. Would you be upset with me if I go but promise to return to pay back the money?" She said sweetly.

"I'll be sad to see you go, Masha, repaying the money is not necessary. A promise to return is all I want because I will miss having you here." Konstantin said as his eyes seemed to sparkle with tears. "Whatever it is you are about to do, please be careful. I've grown quite fond of you, and now I'll wonder what has become of you."

"You're not going to try to stop me?" Maria said in surprise.

"Stop you from doing whatever you can to free your mother? No, how could I?" He said wisely.

At that moment Maria realized how much this man understood her and had helped her. She felt guilty for keeping him out of the contract she would make with Captain Tanner, but now it was too late to take that back.

She hugged Konstantin as the day came to an end and told him she would never forget him as she promised to return.

As Konstantin closed the guild that day, he looked around the room and felt empty by all the success he had when compared to the charm and inspiration of his young apprentice. As he walked home to his family, he felt reminded that work was not everything that made life enjoyable. In fact, it seemed a great distraction.

# Exodus from Neva

As the morning sun rose over Neva, Maria quietly got up and packed her belongings. Dima came into her room and handed her some hot tea as they spoke in whispers about their plans while trying not to awake Nina from her sleep. Maria insisted Dima come with her to meet Captain Tanner so she could give the money to him and know he had everything he needed to free her mother.

"I still don't think he will take you. This is not some dilapidated river cog, it's a sea ship, they are much more severe, and they never take women on board!" Dima insisted in a heightened whisper.

"Then you can watch me fail!" Maria said, "But you won't see me give up!" She said forcefully as she handed him one of her bags to carry. "And don't tell your mother which ship I'm on, say I went south to be with my friend Sveta or something else, make up a story, I don't care."

"I'll be gone tomorrow too, she won't have time to make trouble, but she will try, no doubt about that," Dima replied.

They quietly exited the cottage, carefully closing the door as Maria slipped her coat on and carried her bags in both hands. She had a fierce determination, and it was evident she would not be talked out of her plan. Dima walked beside her, feeling unsure about her decision and carelessness for her own safety.

"Dima, are you sure you can get my mother out of Rostov?" Maria asked as the reality of her decisions began to take shape in the presence of the ships that were docked before them.

"Nothing is sure, but I've known others who got out by bribing guards and making deals like this." He said without confidence.

"You are her only hope, do you understand that? I can't go back there, or they will arrest me. My father is gone, so that means you have to do this!" Maria said as she stopped and looked firmly into his eyes.

Dima paused as Maria's words settled in his mind. He knew everything she was saying already and how difficult this would be. "Masha, I lived at your house more than my own mothers when I was in Rostov. Your father taught me to fish, and your mother was always kind to me. I won't betray their kindness. I'll get her out, I promise!" He said as his voice shook from the energy in his words.

Maria felt much more convinced as she reached into her pocket to make sure she had the contract she had written the day before. She felt the folded parchment with her fingertips and knew, she was ready. She picked up her bags and looked for a three masted ship among the many moored at the dock.

"There!" Dima said spotting it at the end of the dock. "At least you'll be free of Tatars for a while, they haven't conquered the Baltic yet. He added.

"Yes, I think that's why so many people are leaving Russia to live elsewhere, even the slaves are asking for contracts outside the country now," Maria said as they walked closer to the ship.

As they approached, a line of passengers stood, waiting for a chance to go aboard. Many of them were wealthy, but some appeared to be peasants who were spending all they had to find a life beyond the Tatar dominated kingdom.

"Look, women on a ship, imagine that!" Maria said sarcastically pointing at the passengers.

Dima remained silent as he studied the ship and the crew, knowing the types of men who might be on board. He had learned a lot about sailing over the years he had worked on the river, and he felt uncomfortable with sea going sailors as they were less accountable to the ports they visited. "The crew are not like those you find on the river, these can be hired from prison, don't trust anyone!" Dima cautioned.

Maria dismissed his advice, she had been told the same thing before getting on the Kupala and in her experience, everyone was very kind to her, even protected her. As they arrived at the dock, the actual size of the ship became apparent. It was four times the size of the Kupala, with sophisticated sails and many more decks. The wood was clean and smooth as if the ship had just been made and never touched the ocean. Maria felt a sense of adventure as she pointed out the captain.

They walked to him as he stood by a loading ramp, talking with the Quartermaster. "Ah, the cook is here I see!" The captain said as he looked up and down at Dima. "You look a bit young, have you fed a crew and passengers of 50 before?" he asked. "Oh and we're pulling out earlier than expected so we'll need lunch served in 3 hours."

Dima hesitated to speak, unsure why the captain was asking him such questions, then he realized Maria had not explained that she would be the cook. He began to reply as Maria interrupted him, "Captain Tanner this is Dima, he also works for the guild and will be holding our contract while I'm onboard." Maria said calmly.

The captain looked a second time at Maria, "You? On board? For what?" he said in shock. "Where is the cook?"

"I am the cook sir, recently finished my apprenticeship on the Kupala which is now in dry dock. I only work at the guild during the winter season." Maria said trying to convince the captain of her qualifications.

"Is this a joke?" The captain snapped? "There are no women cooks on ships!"

Dima began to shuffle his feet, feeling they should leave immediately and end the humiliation that was about to come. He reached for Maria's arm to coax her away from the captain but she pulled her arm from his grasp as she walked closer to the captain. She was determined to convince him in the same manner she had seen Sveta challenge the captain of the Kupala.

"And just how have male cooks worked out for you, sir? Bad food? Miserable crew? Nothing tasty to motivate the men? You need a woman's touch with food, everyone knows that. Did your father cook for your family when you were a boy? No, it was your mother, of course, a nurturing hand understands these things, and I have experience cooking onboard. I know how to plan meals, keep the stove hot, wash the dishes and shop for provisions in port." She said waiting for him to respond.

The captain paused while Dima felt he didn't recognize his cousin at all. She was strong, confident and no longer the innocent farm girl he smuggled out of Rostov.

The captain looked at Maria without speaking. Her delicate looks and beautiful face distracted him as he tried to imagine her as his cook. The quartermaster shouted from a distance, "We're loaded sir, time to put out!"

"Young lady, you are out of your mind if you think I can seriously trust the feeding of my ship to a little girl like you. I thought you would bring me a cook, not pretend to be one." He said as he walked away.

Maria felt a humbling sting from his words made worse by the presence of her cousin, who watched her make a fool of herself. But she imagined her mother freezing in a slave barn in Rostov. For Maria, there was no level of shame she would not subject herself to if it meant her mother's freedom.

"Good luck finding a cook while your fully loaded ship waits for you to return!" Maria snapped at the captain as he stopped in his steps. "How much will it cost you to stay tied to the dock for another day or two or three? And with all passengers aboard? Someone will have to feed them!" She yelled feeling she had nothing to lose.

The captain turned around to face her, his face was red with anger.

"All because I stopped looking yesterday when you promised me a cook!" He growled as he walked back to her.

Maria reached into her pocket, "Captain, you're a bright man. You can solve this problem right now and delight your crew with the best meals they ever had. You'll be a hero to them. Just sign here and pay Dima 300 denga." She said, imitating the mannerisms she had learned from Konstantin.

Dima watched in shock as the captain took a small quill from his pocket and signed the contract. He then opened a large bag of coins and shuffled several into his palm. "Count it," He said to Dima as kept his angry eyes on Maria.

Dima took the coins and quickly counted the value to three hundred. "It's all here," He said to Maria.

Maria handed the contract to Dima and smiled, "Congratulations, you've made a wise choice." She said to the captain.

"Lunch, three hours, move your arse!" the captain barked as he turned back to the quartermaster and said, "Prepare to disembark! Raise the sails on the mizzen mast and guide us out."

Maria hugged Dima quickly, "This is it, no matter what, rescue my mother!" Maria said with fear in her eyes.

"I will, and we will be back here in the spring when you return!" Dima said, still in shock by what he had just seen.

He watched his young cousin, the girl he had grown up with, take her bags and run to the ship as if she were going on a fun voyage. She had just sold herself into slavery for 12 weeks' worth of wages, and she didn't even hesitate. Such courage to save her mother.

As the ships ropes were withdrawn, he watched the large vessel drift from the dock and hoist her sails as it began to drift swiftly westward on the Neva river. "She will be on the Baltic by sundown," he thought during his walk back to the cottage. He slipped the contract and coins into his pocket and began to consider how he could get back to the Volga River as quickly as possible. The cold wind that blew reminded him of the coming freeze that would halt him halfway if he wasn't fast enough.

# Life Aboard the Ukko

Maria made her way beneath the decks, smiling at the passengers as they passed in the halls. She saw the quartermaster directing the storage of freight and asked him where she would be staying, "How the bloody hell should I know?" He barked at her. "The captain's got no servants quarters for women, go to the galley and stay there until your told otherwise." He shouted as he walked off.

"Welcome aboard!" She sarcastically said to herself.

Maria walked down a few flights of stairs, searching for the kitchen. She discovered it below, as much larger space than the one on the Kupala with a separate cooking area and a window between the dining and kitchen area. She looked around at everything, feeling the familiar placement of dishes, cookware, and provisions.

She set her bags in the corner and walked to the stove, it was cold to the touch and needed to be kindled as her first act in the role of ship's cook. She found a flint and sparked a wad of wood shavings to get the fire going. After a few minutes of blowing and poking, the timbers burst into a steady flame.

Then she turned and looked through the provisions.

"Three hours and fifty people," She said under her breath.

She opened a large storage bin of potatoes and onions and counted how many she would need to peel and prepare. Then set herself into motion of developing a meal plan, trying to make a good first impression.

The ship tossed and turned a bit, reminding her of life on the water and the challenges of keeping her balance in each step. Soon she had several pots simmering with vegetables as she sliced pork for baking.

"This is why I don't eat meat." She said feeling disgusted by the sensation of animal flesh under her knife.

The captain appeared for a moment, taking a look around and seeming pleased with her progress. He noticed her bags in the corner and remembered the issue of where she would sleep. "We have a single bed in the adjoining room, it's reserved as an infirmary, but we can locate that elsewhere. You can sleep there, so you'll be close to the kitchen." The captain said.

"Thank you, sir, that will be fine for me," Maria said as she stirred the pots.

"Just so we are clear, you're not to venture on the other decks or mingle with the passengers while we are at sea. You are to accompany me in port when we buy provisions, and you will stay out of the crew decks, that's no place for a young girl like you." The captain commanded as he walked away.

At that moment Maria began to feel the difference in being a passenger and a slave. She couldn't do as she pleased at any given time, she would be in the kitchen always it seemed. She felt afraid of how she would handle such harsh conditions but pushed herself to be strong, even as the tears began to roll down her cheeks.

The heat from the stove began to fill the room, reminding her of sweeter days on the Kupala.  She set a large pan of pork and vegetables in the oven and filled large pots with water to boil the rest of the potatoes. She slowly began to feel she was making progress in her new life as a ship's cook. She stacked metal plates to make the meal preparation faster as she served everyone.

An hour later an elderly man stepped into the kitchen, he seemed surprised to see a young woman behind the noise and smell of the ships galley.  "I've come for the passenger meals, are they ready?"

Maria looked at the stack of plates, thinking the guests would come and get them as she had seen on the Kupala. "I thought the passengers would be eating in the galley?" She asked shyly.

"With the crew?" the man scoffed. "Passengers dine with the captain, not in the galley!" He barked.

"Ladno, I'll make them now, how many should I prepare?" She asked as she reached for a plate.

The man understood she was not trying to be difficult, and only didn't realize her responsibilities.

He also reached for a plate, "There are six officers, including the captain, five servants and twenty-one passengers on this passage. Passenger counts change with each stop between here and Poole. The crew number is always eighteen including our new cook." He said with a patient smile.

"Spacibo, what's your name?" Maria asked sweetly.

"I am Edik, ochen priyatno," he said.

Maria felt a sudden sadness as his name made her think of her father. She paused as her memories of him rushed back into her mind.

"We'll need thirty-two plates, Miss...?" Edik said impatiently.

"Maria! Prostiti, I was just thinking about my... thirty-two? Do I take them to the captain's galley or...?" She said as she tried to refocus her mind.

"I take the plates and bring them back. You have enough to do with the crew dining." Edik said as the sounds of men laughing and shouting came from the stairway. Their languages were a mixture of Russian, Finnish and German.

Maria opened the stove and filled each plate with a small portion from the roast, handing them one by one to Edik. He set several plates on a platter and carried it over his head, comfortably working his way through the crew as he walked up the stairs.

A man stood by a small window that opened between the galley and kitchen, waiting to be given his food.

"Oi, let's have it then!" he shouted with a thick German accent.

Maria turned and walked to the window, seeing a long line of the hungry crew behind him. She remembered the looks that Sveta often got on the Kupala, but this time, it was her turn. The men were surprised to see her and not the former cook in the kitchen, as a sudden quiet swept over them. She could hear them make vulgar sounds as they talked among themselves. She remembered the feeling of being a trophy among such men, the same night her father was killed, how they all looked at her with wolve's eyes.

She reached into the oven and grabbed the pan to quickly get the food out and ready. The moment her delicate fingers touched the hot pan, she heard a light singe as she snatched her hands back, realizing she had just burned her fingers. She gasped and quickly held it in, not wishing to appear weak to the men who waited just out of view. Her eyes teared as she looked at the red marks on her hands.

She shook her head, knowing she was smarter than this, and slid her hands beneath her apron, using it to protect her fingers as she lifted the heavy roast and vegetables, setting it by the window. The men who could see it seemed to calm down and began pushing each other to hurry as Maria set a plate down and quickly filled it for each face that appeared in the window. She tried to keep the portions correct so she would have enough for everyone.

Her hands hurt just to the touch but being near anything warm made it even more agonizing. Finally, the last man was served, she turned and dipped her apron into a pail of water and wrapped it around her fingers. Within seconds, she felt the pain leave her hands, and a sense of relief came over her.

Edik returned for more plates and noticed her hands wrapped in her apron.

"Are you cut?" He said nervously.

"No, just...stupid actually, I burned my fingers on the pan." She said, pointing toward the remaining pork and vegetables by the window.

Edik looked over in shock, "Is this all that is left?" He asked.

"No, I have more vegetables on the stove," Maria answered.

"Good, because they loved your cooking upstairs." He said with a smile. "Now about your hands, let's have a look."

Maria took her hand from her apron and showed him the injured areas. The pain immediately returned with more intensity when she took her fingers from the cool, wet apron.

"You need to keep them clean and not put pressure on them. It will only get worse. I'll prepare the plates." He said, as he quickly stepped around her to get the meals ready.

"Spacibo, Edik," She said as she handed him the plates.

Soon the platter was full with the last round of meals for the passengers. The sound of the metal plates began to clang as the men returned them to the window. Maria filled a sink with water, dreading the task of washing so many dishes with sore fingers. She walked to the window to pick up a stack of dishes as a man added one to the pile.

"Vkusna!" He said as he set it politely on top.

"Spacibo bolshoe" Maria replied, enjoying her first compliment from the crew.

The kitchen seemed a disaster, food, dishes and a dirty stove made her remember how many times Sveta would be all day and night there. Her mind was distracted by the new surroundings, faces and memories of her family and friends. She felt completely out of place and awkward.

"It's going to be a long three months." She thought to herself.

She was pleased to see most of the dishes were empty, a good sign the men liked her cooking. She dipped a plate into the sink of hot water and slowly went through each one, using her injured hand to wipe them clean while trying not to aggravate her injured hands.

Edik returned with all the plates from the captain's galley. "You're very popular upstairs," he said. The passengers are remarking they've not tasted such good cooking onboard other ships.

"Spacibo, I am just a simple farm girl," Maria replied humbly.

Edik set the dishes by the sink and placed the leftover food by the stove. "What do you think, maybe something to add to dinner?"

Maria gasped, "I haven't even thought about dinner! But yes, I can make soup and put the pork and vegetables in pirozhki.

Edik smiled as he agreed with her idea. "Something sweet for the passengers after dinner would be welcome. They will sit at the table and talk for hours about how rich they are, and it helps to put something in their mouth." He joked as they both laughed.

"Ladno, I'll see what we have for fruit and some honey," Maria said as she washed the dishes.

Edik left to go and clean the captain's galley, as Maria finished clearing the kitchen. She felt tired and walked to the room adjacent to the galley. As she walked into the galley, she saw the floors and tables were dirty. She stood in shock for a moment, "Such pigs!" She thought as the idea of grown men being so careless sank in.

She returned to the kitchen and took a cloth to wipe the tables. Then she swept the floors and straightened the chairs. It looked more presentable now, but she felt this was not necessary for her, "The crew should know how to behave, they never did this on the Kupala." She thought as she wondered how Sveta had gotten them to always return their chairs and keep their tables clean.

Finally, everything was done, and she could rest. She walked to the room set aside for her and saw a small bed and washstand in the corner.

"No window." She thought.

She laid back on the bed and felt herself relax for the first time since setting foot on board the ship. Footsteps echoed down the stairs as someone approached. She didn't have the energy to look for who it was until she heard the captain's voice from the door of her room.

"Well done Maria, you've delighted the passengers, and that's the first time I've heard such compliments onboard this ship. Edik told me you burned your hands, how bad is it?" He asked.

Maria held her throbbing fingers out for the captain to see the large white swollen blisters covering three of her fingertips.

"It's not bad, just makes it difficult to be near anything hot." She replied. "I'll be ok in a few days."

The captain nodded as he looked up the stairs for a deck hand. A young man noticed the captain's stare and walked closer to the top of the stairwell.

"Aye Captain?" the young man asked, knowing the captain's gesture without prompting.

"Stewart, fetch us a few of the small ballast stones from under the forecastle, I need the coldest you can find." The captain commanded, speaking in English to Stewart.

Maria was impressed that the captain spoke English and Russian even though he was clearly from Finland.

"The stones at the bottom of the ship make it cold enough to store meat on long voyages. They will help with the pain." The captain said as he looked up the stairwell, waiting for Stewart to return.

An awkward silence prompted Maria to ask a question, "Why do you have stones at the bottom of the ship? Doesn't it weigh you down?" She pondered out loud.

"The sails put a lot of twist on the ship, side to side, fore and aft, the stones act as a ballast to keep us from tipping over when we run empty." The captain replied nonchalantly.

Maria nodded, concerned that it was possible for any ship to tip over. She had only learned basic things about ships while on the Kupala, but the Ukko was a tall sailing ship meant for the open ocean without a river bank or coastline nearby for safety.

Stewart appeared, slightly out of breath, with several river rocks in his hands. He gave one to the captain as he stood in the doorway of Maria's cabin.

Maria tried to understand the captain's discussion on ballast while he handed her a palm-sized stone to hold. The stone was ice cold, smooth and polished like the ones in the river where she played as a child in Rostov. The moment she touched her burned fingertips to it, the pain vanished.

Maria gasped as the relief swept over her, smiling with a nod of gratitude and comfort.

Captain Tanner smiled briefly, then turned and reached for the remaining stones in Stewart's hands. He set them on the floor by Maria's bed and asked Stewart to bring a dry washcloth from the kitchen.

The captain handed the washcloth to Maria instructing her to hold the rocks through the cloth, letting only her bare fingertips touch it.

"It will stay cold much longer this way," he instructed.

"Spacibo bolshoe!" Maria replied.

"We'll need you to have dinner ready by seven bells, can you work like this?" The captain asked.

"Da, it will be ready." She sighed as the one-hour bell rang once in the distance.

The captain and Stewart exited her cabin, returning to their duties. Maria sat on her bed and let her eyes close for a moment, feeling the exhaustion set in from the sleepless nights and hard work in the kitchen. Her mind flashed through images of Neva, the guild, her family and the Kupala. So many new experiences and emotions, as if she could not process it all at the moment and now her mind was catching up.

She fell asleep in seconds but awoke within a few minutes when the pain in her fingers returned as her hand slipped away from the stone she held. She ached to sleep but knew she had to prepare a large meal soon. She began to appreciate the strength Sveta had to always be up early and go to bed late just to feed an entire crew.

She rested on her bed, staring at the coarsely hewn cypress boards in her ceiling, realizing she was far from everyone and everything she had ever known. She knew she had to decide between an impossible situation and collapse from the reality it presented or take one incredible moment at a time just as she had done along the Volga.

She stood and walked into the kitchen, keeping the cold rock within reach, and began organizing the evening meal. With each ingredient and each pot, she felt herself exchange the tragic death of her father and imprisonment of her mother, for the simple task of cooking. If this were the way to free her mother, she would never complain, she would embrace any injury, any exhaustion as a small price to pay for her mother's return to Neva.

Within hours she had created everything necessary for the evening meal, keeping her fingers against the stone for comfort from the hot pans. Edik arrived and assisted her in serving the crew as the ship rocked its way out of the Neva River into the Gulf of Finland.

# Reval

The red-roofed towers and heavy walls of Reval grew larger as the ship made its way toward the first stop in port. The sounds of cargo being shuffled onto deck and men shouting, echoed down the stairs into the kitchen. The deck hands threw ropes to the dock, easing the ship into port with a light thud as it brushed against the pier.

Maria was finishing the morning's dishes as the captain walked in, holding a piece of ice he had picked up from the dock. "Look what I have?" He said teasingly. "Fresh from the docks of Reval!"

Maria held it in her hands to show her appreciation. "The pain subsided while I slept, thanks to the stones you gave me. It's still tender but thank you!" She said.

"Da, wish we had the ice yesterday, it's the best for burns, but we don't always have what we need when we need it most." The captain sighed.

"So true," Maria said, hoping she had not offended his kind intentions.

The captain looked around the kitchen, noting she had cleaned it very well. "You perform your duties well," He said, "Very impressive work for a young lady. We will take on provisions in an hour, and I need to inspect them before loading.

It's customary for the cook to inspect the food, are you ready?" He asked.

Maria remembered how she and Sveta had walked through the markets, bartering for the best deals and fresh food for the ship. She felt her experience had prepared her well for this as she replied, "Konechno! Poshli?"

"Davai." The captain replied with a smile.

Her positive attitude was very charming to him, and he felt excited to spend time with her in the city. They began to walk to the stairs as he noticed she had only her dress on. "It's not as warm as the kitchen out there, you'll need a coat and warm shoes." He insisted. "I'll meet you on deck."

Maria quickly ducked into her room and pulled her tunic and boots from her luggage. She hadn't had to wear boots since last winter, but she was glad she thought to pack them when she fled Rostov. She wrapped herself in her tunic and emerged from her room with a sense of adventure.

When she walked on deck, she saw the captain waiting by the gang plank. Behind him lay the city of Reval, it looked like a town made of stones and fairy tales. Towers lined the border, making it even more interesting to discover what was inside the forbidding walls, while ships of all sizes filled the port with tradesman, cargo, and passengers.

The captain led Maria through the harbour, as they walked to a building where he signed some papers. She felt a lot of respect for him, he was younger than the captain of the Kupala and commanded a newer, larger ship that traveled internationally. She watched him skim documents, each in a different language with instructions for cargo and passenger lists.

His voice sounded different as he spoke in German to the clerk of the port. Then the clerk pointed to an office down the hall that the captain seemed to be excited to visit. He waved to Maria to come with him as they walked to the door.

"Oleg!" Tanner thundered as he entered the office with Maria shyly following.

"Tanner! My favorite captain is here! Oleg replied as he stood from his desk.

Maria peered into the office as the two men shook hands. Oleg was a heavy set man with a bald head and greying beard. He reminded her of Konstantin as she saw his desk with papers spread across its surface. Behind him was a map, attached to the wall, with the names of countries and ports from all over the world. It was the first time Maria had seen such a detailed map of anything beyond her countries origin.

Tanner turned toward Maria, motioning for her to step closer.

"And this ... is our new, fantastic cook, Maria!" Tanner said proudly.

Oleg's eyes traveled up and down Maria's body like a farmer examining cattle before slaughter. As he extended his hand, he was already undressing her with his gaze and imagining more than she cared to know.

"Ochen priyatno, Maria. I am Oleg!" he said with a naughty sparkle in his eyes that felt surprisingly charming to Maria as she shook his hand. His charisma was disarming in spite of her immediate reservations about him.

Oleg turned his attention back to Tanner as the two men talked about business and negotiations with different ports. Maria felt an awkwardness about her place in the room, where to stand and if she should try to follow the conversation or simply stand and be pretty.

Her eyes began to travel around the room, eventually fixating on the map behind Oleg's desk. Oleg noticed her intrigue in the map and interrupted his discussion with the captain in hopes of impressing her.

"It's beautiful isn't it?" He said as he walked toward the map. Soon Reval will be part of the Hansa Guild and guess who will be in charge of the port?"

The captain smiled and decided to explain, "Oleg is a gifted Russian, he is within months of getting Reval into the protection of the Hansa, which will change everything about trade in this region."

Maria didn't understand what the captain meant, she simply continued to walk closer to the map, searching for Rostov. At first, she didn't see it until she followed the path from Lake Ladoga backward to the Volga. Each city along the way became an image in her mind, memories along the path, connecting from a high view. Finally, her hand traced to Yaroslavl and followed the river south until she saw it, Rostov. She felt excited to see her hometown there.

Oleg stood beside Maria and narrated various facts about the drawing of the map and how long it took to create as the captain impatiently waited to get Oleg's attention back to business.

"Where are we?" Maria asked with a smile.

Oleg's reached carefully in front of Maria, gently wrapping his hand over hers while she pointed at Rostov. She knew what he was doing and smiled nervously at his subtle attempt to charm her. He then guided her hand diagonally across Russia and the Baltic, stopping at Reval.

"Here we are, Reval. You're a long way from home, beautiful lady." Oleg said as he slowly slid his hand from hers.

"Da, hard to believe." She said, feeling lost on the map of endless cities and ports.

The captain staged a cough, "Ahem, sorry to break up the seductive lessons in old cartography my friend, but are we agreed that the guild will control the ports without interference from local authority?"

Oleg immediately changed his character back to a businessman and turned to respond. "Mda! The ships and ports will have international favors and protection on a bilateral basis. Once you are in the guild, all ports are home." Oleg said with pride.

"Excellent, no more taxes or corrupt port masters eating our profits." The captain snarled.

"Negotiation has been tedious with the locals in Reval, I have … expenses." Oleg replied.

The captain hesitated and then reached into his pocket, leaving several gold coins on the desk.

"Even free trade comes at a price," Tanner said.

"Spacibo Tanner, I will remember your generosity when I'm the head of the Hanseatic in Reval," Oleg said.

The captain turned to leave, chuckling at Oleg's claim as if everything was understood.

"Time to go, Maria, I fear for your safety in a room with such a wolf." He said.

Oleg burst into laughter as he quickly slid the coins out of view.

"Wait, can you show me the rest of the route we will take?" She asked sweetly.

Oleg smiled as he admired her innocent curiosity and beautiful face.

"Go on Tanner, show the young lady!" Oleg insisted as he stepped out of the way.

Captain Tanner rolled his eyes as he walked around the desk and pointed at the map.

"Here is Reval," he said "We will go south to Pomeralia, and port in Danzig for offloading passengers and then on to Kopenhaven. We will take a short rest there before making the turn south to Poole, which is here at the bottom of the Britains. Then we return the same way." He said as his fingers traced imaginary lines to dots along the coastlines.

The span covered in a few inches on the map meant months of time and distance, all taking Maria farther away than she ever imagined possible.

"It's the other side of the world." She said in a guarded voice.

"Most people never see anything beyond the village they were born in, you are lucky to live a life that opens the world to you!" Oleg said as Maria and the captain prepared to leave.

"When I return in the spring, I'll expect to see guild colors on this port!" the captain said in a flattering tone to Oleg.

Oleg laughed, "And then we will all celebrate old friend!" he said as he looked hungrily at Maria.

Tanner guided Maria from the room hastily, "Poshli, let's get out of here before he shows you his compass."

Maria giggled and flushed red with embarrassment as she and Tanner exited the building and headed to the market. She sensed a bit of jealousy between the captain and Oleg and felt a secret pleasure of being a maiden with multiple suitors challenging each other for her attention.

The captain's mood seemed to focus back to business once they were on the street.

"We need to inspect the food before it's loaded, these merchants will fill your ship full of rats and rotten food if you're not standing on the docks when they arrive." He warned.

They walked across the port and found a market similar to the ones Maria had seen on the river ports. The merchants all held their fruit and vegetables out as they walked by, trying to get interest from the captain. The captain looked around and decided to test Maria's skills.

"So, my young cook... Your meals are good, but you burned your fingers on the first day in my kitchen, which makes me wonder how much experience you really have. We need enough food to last the week-long journey to Danzig. I already know how much I usually spend here, so...show me what you can negotiate." Captain Tanner said as he motioned toward the market filled with merchants.

Maria smiled at the chance to prove herself. She walked to a merchant who was selling apples and remembered how Sveta had taught her to play this game. The merchant handed her a large red apple and encouraged her to taste it. She gave it to the captain instead and whispered: "Taste it, but spit it out after I ask how much."

The captain grinned and did as she asked. "How much for 3 barrels?" Maria asked.

The merchant quickly responded, "Fifteen silver!"

She then turned to the captain as he tasted the apple and spit it out.

"Prostiti, not very tasty. We can only have the best apples." She said as she turned and guided the captain to walk with her toward another display of apples in the distance.

"Wait! Maybe just one bad? Try another!" The merchant insisted as he followed and handed Maria a second apple.

Maria took one bite, it was delicious, perfect, but she held her enjoyment as she swallowed, "They are not quite ripe, I think I would only give five silver." She said capriciously as she turned away again.

The captain followed her as they walked to the next display. "Fifteen per barrel is reasonable," Tanner whispered.

"It's the end of the season and no one wants to carry all those apples back to their farm. Wait and see what happens while he thinks about it." Maria said confidently.

"Fourteen!" The merchant shouted as they walked a few steps away. Maria smiled and felt proud of her skills.

"Seven!" Maria replied.,

The merchant shook his head in disapproval while Maria remained immune to his tactics.

"Poshli, there are better ones down there," Maria said to the captain, making sure the merchant heard her.

They turned and walked toward another fruit stand as the captain watched in enjoyment at the process this young girl had apparently perfected.

"Right now he is asking himself if he would rather go home with some money than to keep his apples and watch us buy from a competitor."

The captain shook his head, feeling she had overestimated her skills. "He'll never sell for seven."

"Twelve!" the merchant shouted as they arrived at the other cart.

"Don't look!" Maria insisted, just take one of these apples here and ignore him.

The young boy at the second cart smiled and handed an apple to the captain.

"Just smile and nod your head as if you've never seen such an apple," Maria instructed.

The captain played along, keeping his back to the merchant who began to approach them.

"Eleven each for three barrels?" the merchant asked cautiously, keeping his distance from the other vendor.

The captain's eyes opened wider in astonishment, he had never bargained such a price for fresh fruit.

"Ten" Maria quickly replied, "But I'll take all four of your barrels if you can deliver them to the Ukko within the hour."

The merchant smiled and quickly extended his hand for the money.

"Payment on delivery!" Maria cautioned.

The merchant smiled and nodded in agreement, turning to go and pack the apples for shipping.

"Unbelievable, do you know how many times I've come here and paid fifteen per barrel?" The captain marveled.

Maria continued her way through the market, teasing the vendors with her dissatisfaction and then getting a better deal than the captain had ever negotiated himself. He was impressed and couldn't hide his genuine pride in having her beside him.

As they made their way back to the ship, they stopped at a merchant selling amber. Maria had never seen the warm colored stones, strung into beautiful necklaces and figurines. The captain noticed her intrigue and how she kept returning to touch a necklace with a single strand of polished stones.

The captain made eye contact with the elderly lady sitting at the table and mouthed the words "How Much?" to her.

"Ten silver." She whispered quietly.

He nodded in approval as the woman stood and lifted the necklace from the table, draping it around Maria's neck, unexpectedly.

"You have an eye for the best, these stones are rare, pure with no imperfections!" the woman said as she fastened it around Maria's neck.

Maria looked in a hand mirror at the beautiful stones around her neck, "Well it's beautiful of course, but I couldn't possibly afford…" She began.

"Here you are." The captain said kindly to the lady as he placed ten silver coins into her palm.

Maria was surprised, no one had ever given her such an ornate gift before. "You shouldn't buy this for me!" She said in shock as reached to take it off.

"Nonsense, you saved me ten times that today, besides Amber is good for healing. Maybe it will help with your hands." The captain said as he stepped back admiring how it looked around her neck.

Maria held the smoothly polished stones between her fingers, as she smiled by the surprise of such a gift. "I really didn't expect I would have something so nice, thank you." She said as they walked back toward the ship.

"Does it actually work? The healing?" Maria asked.

"Some have a lot of faith in it, I think it is more the luck that a sick person would recover anyway" He replied

"Ah, but why take chances, right? Faith and Luck?" Maria mused.

"Exactly!" The captain laughed while Maria looked down to admire the necklace as they walked. "Where does this stone come from?" she asked.

"We used to pull gems like that out of our nets when I worked on the fishing boats." The captain said, "But you can also find them laying on the beaches, especially after a big storm."

"It's breathtaking like honey turned to stone." She replied

"There is a legend about those stones, would you like to hear it?" He asked as they walked toward the ship.

"Yes, of course, I want to hear it, tell me!" Maria insisted as she smiled at the attention she was getting.

The captain smiled and began to tell the story.

"Long ago on the bottom of the Baltic, there was a beautiful queen named Jurata. She was a kind queen and always gave back to the ocean, even the fish she ate, would only be consumed by half, and the rest returned for the creatures of the sea to finish.

But one day she learned that a fisherman was catching the very fish she had returned. This was a great offense and Jurata was furious! She decided to find the fisherman in his boat and kill him. But when Queen Jurata found the fisherman, she fell in love with him instantly because he was very handsome.

Every evening after that day she swam to the shore to see him. Their love grew quickly, and they were very happy but the god of thunder, who had always wanted Jurata for himself, became jealous. How could Jurata choose a simple fisherman over him?

So, he caused a great storm over the ocean, the sky turned black, and the water crashed in all directions, destroying the amber palace and carrying Jurate off to another sea, where she would never find her way back to the Baltic.

The fisherman waited for days along the shore, but Jurata never returned. He soon began to find pieces of amber scattered along the sand and knew something tragic had happened to his beloved. He took his boat out into the Baltic and dove to the bottom of the sea, searching for Jurata. Nothing remained, but broken pieces of amber on the sea floor and he has been searching for her ever since. This is why we find amber on the seashore after a storm, it is the fisherman casting the broken pieces of the palace into the waves, hoping they will make a trail for Jurata to find and return to her lost love.

"How sad!" Maria replied as she felt disappointed in the story. She slid her fingers over the stones in the necklace, "Poor Jurata, poor fisherman!"

"Well, love isn't only about happiness. It's also how you remember those you held dear when they are gone." The captain replied.

Maria nodded quietly, as she felt thoughts of her father coming to her mind.

They arrived back at the ship, where new passengers and cargo waited to be inspected by the captain. "Provisions are yours, I'll deal with passengers." The captain said as they split up to attend their duties. The merchants delivered everything as expected and then went to the captain for payment. He would only look over at Maria and wait for her to nod that they should be paid.

Maria noticed that the captain really trusted her, and she felt comfortable with him. The chemistry between them was pleasant and slightly romantic. She didn't see him as a man, but more like a leader, a reliable person to take care of everyone.

A cart arrived with large animal carcasses hooked to the top of it. Maria looked at it with disgust, she knew this was the meat delivery for the ship but dreaded having to inspect it. She walked to the cart and greeted the butcher. His clothes were dirty and covered in blood. Even his hands looked red, with dark lines around his fingernails where the dirt and blood had collected.

"These are all fresh, just finished them this morning." He said with pride as the ship hands came to load them onboard.

Maria felt sad for the animal that had been killed and skinned and now hung in front of her. Her stomach turned as she felt sick from the sight of their hacked remains. Every memory she had of animals being butchered rushed to her mind as she felt responsible for cooking such things even though she didn't wish to see an animal killed for food.

The butcher noticed her reaction and calmly said, "I understand how you feel miss, my wife is the same way!"

Maria thought to herself, "Wife? You mean somewhere there's a woman who lets this man touch her…knowing what he does all day?"

The last of the cargo was loaded, and the passengers rotated on and off the ship as the captain gave the crew time in port before pulling out at sunset. Maria sat on the main deck, waiting for the sunset and the order to cast off. She didn't have to cook for the evening and planned on getting some rest before breakfast the next day.

The crew quietly returned as the sun moved closer to the horizon. Soon the ropes were dropped from the dock and the Ukko set sail for Pomeralia. As the orange sky faded to dark, she touched her necklace and imagined Jurate, following a trail of amber stones, swimming to the fisherman as he waited on shore.

# A Familiar Face

Maria made her way to her cabin as the ship rocked on its course Southward through the Baltic. She walked to the kitchen to see that everything had been stocked while the ship was in port. She reached for an apple from the storage bin and remembered the negotiating that had taken place earlier that day. As she hungrily devoured it, she heard footsteps coming down the hall.

The captain walked into the kitchen and smiled, she greeted him and wondered if he wanted something to eat. "Kushat budish?" She asked politely.

"Chut chut." He replied as he shuffled his feet appearing slightly nervous.

She reached into the bin and retrieved another apple, "These are delicious!" She said as she handed it to him.

He smiled and seemed to relax as he took a bite. "I was wondering if you enjoyed reading?" He asked.

"Of course!" Maria replied, "But books are so expensive and hard to find."

"Come with me." The captain said with a gleam of intrigue in his eye.

Maria followed him up several flights of stairs, working their way to his cabin. She wondered what he would show her there, perhaps a book, or maybe he had some other ideas. As she walked behind him, she began to worry this might be an awkward situation.

As the door to his cabin opened, Maria saw his elegant cabin, complete with large windows, his own dining area, a table filled with maps and along the wall, little shelves, all filled with books.

"Since you're limited to moving around the ship, which is for your own safety, I thought you might enjoy reading when you're not cooking?" The captain said as he pointed to the rows of books on the shelves.

Maria's eyes grew big in excitement as she glanced along the thick binders that held the books together. Different languages, colors and sizes, each book with an interesting character all its own.

"So many!" she gasped as she picked one to see what it contained.

The words were foreign, a Latin style text with Germanic sounding context. She returned it to the shelf and continued searching.

The captain pulled a book from the collection and placed it in her hands. "If I could suggest the most useful books in this library, it would be the ones that teach another language. This one was written to prepare Russian monks for translation of scriptures from English. Your ability to negotiate will be enhanced by the number of languages you speak, so I recommend starting with this one."

Maria opened the cover to see what the wording looked like. The familiar Latin text formed words she had never heard before, as she tried to sound them out.

The captain smiled, "I need to get back to charting our course...take good care of that book? He asked politely.

"Of course!" Maria said excitedly as she headed toward the door. "Spacibo!" her voice repeated multiple times as she excused herself from the cabin.

She rushed toward the stairs, excited to have something new to learn in her hands. She looked down trying to read the first few words as she walked but a man stepped out of his room, and she walked directly into him. Her book fell to the floor, and the man reached to pick it up before she had time to retrieve it. Her eyes followed his hand up to his face as she began to thank him. His face was recently familiar to her as she remembered the golden cross around his neck, it was the monk, Brother Boris from the Church in Neva.

"Boris?!" Maria said excitedly as he also realized they had met before. He smiled as he returned the book to her open hands. "We're on the same ship? I didn't even see you earlier!"

Boris shrugged his shoulders as he pointed to his cabin. "Oh, you've been in your cabin all this time?" Maria asked, trying to follow his gestures.

Boris nodded, then opened his hands toward Maria as he tilted his head curiously.

"Oh me? I took a position as the cook to raise money for my mother's release. She is a prisoner in Rostov and my cousin has gone to help her escape." Maria explained.

Boris's eyes showed his amazement at Maria's confidence to take on such risks. Then he smiled and pointed at her and then to his stomach inquisitively.

Maria paused, "Am I pregnant? No! I'm still a maid, of course...!"

She began to defend her virtue as if in confession when Boris shook his hand to stop her and pointed to his stomach again as his hand moved in a circle.

Maria gasped at her stupidity, "Oh, am I the cook?!" she laughed, "Yes, that's me!"

Boris nodded and gently patted her on the shoulder to share his appreciation for her cooking.

Maria blushed at the compliment, "Spacibo, na zdorovie!" she replied.

"So what brings you on this long trip?" Maria asked as she realized how strange it seemed to find a monk traveling onboard.

Boris pointed at himself, then motioned his hands as if he were writing a letter, followed by his two fingers walking along an imaginary line, then he put his hands together as if praying as his eyes looked up.

Maria felt intrigued by the challenge of his gestures, she wanted to get it right the first time, and began to speak aloud what she saw. "You write a letter and then walk...no, travel...to...pray...?"

Boris rolled his eyes, knowing the statement made no sense. He often felt frustrated that people would not think about what they said as they spoke aloud. He repeated the set of gestures slowly, waiting for Maria to guess each part correctly.

He began pointing to himself as Maria followed.

"You?" She said as he nodded in agreement.

He motioned his hand as if holding a pen.

"Write letters?" she asked.

Boris shook his head no, as he pretended to seal the letter and roll it up.

"Ah, someone else wrote the letter, and you are taking it somewhere?" She stated.

Boris smiled in enthusiasm.

Then he motioned his hands together as if praying, very strongly, very seriously.

"Hmm, you take these letters to pray...or someone who prays..." She replied as Boris motioned his hand in a circle to get Maria to continue speaking about the idea.

"Someone who prays, or...someone people pray to?" She asked, knowing she wasn't quite there with his answer.

Boris made a motion to pray and then held his hand very high.

"God!" Maria shouted in excitement. Boris smiled, then nodded negatively as he lowered his hand a bit and looked at her to see if she could follow.

"Someone people pray to, but not God, wait. It's not about prayer, it's someone in the church...high level but not God...the Pope?" Maria asked in astonishment.

Boris clapped his hands and smiled as he pointed to Maria to emphasize her correctness.

"You take letters to the Pope?" She said in amazement. "That's a tremendous responsibility, why did they pick you for that?"

Boris shrugged his shoulders and then pointed to his mouth, waiting for Maria to understand.

"Ah, they know you won't say what is in the letters! Very shrewd." She said with a giggle.

Boris nodded and pointed toward the staircase as he waved goodbye to Maria.

"Ah, you need to go, I understand. See you later then." Maria said sweetly as she held her book tightly in her hands.

Boris motioned his hand up down and across, blessing Maria as he departed. She felt suddenly safer than ever knowing Boris was on the ship. He had a calming way about him, his personality and gestures were friendly and approachable. In many ways, he didn't even seem like a priest, more like an uncle or family friend.

Maria headed down the stairs back to the kitchen. She found and carried one of the kitchen lamps to her room to give more light for reading. She jumped onto her bed and quickly opened the book, eager to learn another language.

Her eyes looked over the Latin styled letters, as she tried to pronounce the words they made. The Russian introduction of the book explained its purpose of presenting phrases from the English language and then showing how they translated into Russian.

She sounded each syllable out softly as she used her knowledge of Latin to quickly begin reading in English. "Hel-low" She said as she looked across the page for the translation, "Eto Privet! Ladno; Hel-low" She said excitedly.

The hours of the night flew by as she continued to read from one page to the next, she was too excited to sleep, but soon her eyes dimmed, and she slept with the book laying on her chest.

# Breakfast

Edik walked into the kitchen and immediately knew something was wrong, he didn't hear any noises, nothing was set out, and Maria was nowhere in sight. He walked to her room and saw her still asleep in her bed. He shook his head in disbelief as he walked toward her to wake her up quickly.

Maria was still dreaming, she kept seeing the same scenes over and over of her life on the farm in Rostov, scenes of her father working in the garden and her mother cooking continued to appear and pass her by. Then she would sense a dark presence, someone after her and each time she moved closer to her parents she felt safe but then as they faded from the dream the dark character returned. It was an evil presence, someone determined to harm her in every possible way. She felt a hand reaching for her, a flash of a sword and a shout as the sound of men fighting echoed in her mind.

As Edik touched her shoulder to wake her, she jumped from the bed, fearing the character had finally reached her. Her eyes were wide open as she stepped back into the corner of the room, still shaken from her dream. "What do you want!?" She demanded as her breath gasped.

Edik stared at her for a moment, trying to understand what was happening, then he cleared his throat and calmly said, "The passengers are waiting for their breakfast, miss. And soon the crew will also be..."

Maria began to realize where she was, and that she had slept too late. She walked to the corner of the bed where her dress was laying and looked at Edik, as he quickly left the cabin and closed the door. She could hear his footsteps going toward the kitchen as she changed her clothes and put her shoes on. She pinned her hair back and quickly walked to the kitchen.

Edik was cutting some fruit and arranging it on the platters. "This should keep them occupied while you get something going," he said calmly as he lifted the tray over his head and exited the kitchen.

"I can't believe I overslept!" Maria said as she rushed into the kitchen. "Spacibo Edik!" she shouted as the sound of his steps left the room.

Maria turned to the stove and quickly got a fire going as she filled two pots with water to boil. "Eggs and oatmeal with fruit should be enough." She thought as she began gathering everything she needed. She placed a lid on each pot to get it to boil quicker as she cut fruits to lay out for the crew. Her mind still remembered her dream, the continuing scenes and how they repeated. "Who was this character, chasing her? What was the sound of the sword and fighting?" She wondered.

Edik returned and took some more fruit, and noticed the other dishes being prepared. He seemed satisfied with her decision as he nodded and smiled. Maria liked his calmness, nothing appeared to make him nervous, he just went about his work and helped when he was needed.

The crew began shuffling in, their loud voices echoed in the hallways as they pushed chairs around the floor and whistled to get everyone to be quiet. The quartermaster was making some announcements before they ate, and assigning tasks to each man. As she stirred the oatmeal into the hot water, she could hear the men asking questions. Then she could hear a conversation with one man, asking about the cook, it sounded crude as if he was suggesting she be available for more than cooking. All the men laughed at the end of his question.

Maria felt sick at the idea of their talking about her. She immediately remembered how Sveta had several men after her onboard the Kupala, but she worked everything to her advantage. The idea of one of these men touching her made her nervous and afraid.

She listened to see if anything more was said, then she heard the quartermaster say in a loud voice, "Don't forget the captain's orders, the cook is a member of the crew, so show her proper respect."

"So, off limits then?" one man shouted.

"Exactly," said the quartermaster.

"The captain's got his eye on her already!" Another man shouted over the other voices.

"You'll not be questioning Captain Tanner!" the quartermaster shouted as the room became deadly silent. It was evident the respect for the captain was taken very seriously.

Maria smiled, she felt flattered and safer, knowing the captain seemed to like her, and he was an intelligent man who was clearly very accomplished and generous.

She turned and opened the window between the rooms and set the fruit out, as the crew began to form a line. Then she carefully lifted the oatmeal and brought it closer so she could dip some onto each man's plate as he passed. "I'll have eggs in a few minutes if anyone wants' some." She said, wondering which man had made the rude comments about her. They all appeared the same to her, different ages but the same empty look in their eyes. It seemed they only came to life while in port.

Edik returned and took several eggs along with a smaller pot of oatmeal to the passengers. Maria nibbled on a few items as the line calmed down and she prepared to clean everything.

The empty plates began to return and soon she had a large pile of dishes to wash as she stored the uneaten food for later. She noticed she had a headache that would not go away no matter what she did. It made everything harder as she felt the urge to lay down, even though she could not. Edik brought the last of the dishes and noticed her rubbing her head.

"You have a headache?" he asked.

"Da, it seems worse now that it's hot in here." She said.

"It's very cloudy today." He replied, "Lot of pressure in the air."

"Ah, konechno," Maria replied.

She began washing the dishes and was surprised to see Edik remain to help her. He picked up all the heavy pots and cleaned them to make her work less difficult.

"Edik, I met a familiar face onboard yesterday, do you know this priest, Brother Boris?" she asked.

"Everyone knows Boris, imagine, a priest among sailors, good thing he can't repeat what he hears in confession," Edik replied.

"Da, he is taking letters to the Pope from Neva." She replied. "I think because he can't speak they trust him not to repeat what is in them."

"That's not why he carries the letters." Edik scoffed. "Boris was a captain of soldiers when the Tatars invaded. He was captured and tortured to reveal the location of his regiment, but he never told them. So they cut out his tongue to make the other prisoners talk.  After that, he escaped but a captain that can't give orders is a risk in battle, so they put him out of the army."

Maria was astonished, she had never even guessed Boris had such a fascinating and tragic past. "I thought he had been a priest his whole life!" She said.

"No, he caught the attention of Rome after his torture, so they offered him something others could not. An education, travel around the world and their trust. I think, becoming a priest was more of a formality than a calling." Edik said.

Maria was in shock, the same kind man who she had spoken to the night before was a hero and very brave. She felt saddened by his hard life but realized he had made the best of the situation and was being rewarded for his work. "Such an impressive story, I'll have to ask him about it the next time I see him." She said.

"I don't recommend bringing it up, I think he prefers people see him as a simple monk rather than a former soldier. It's part of his vow of humility." Edik cautioned.

"Yes, you're right. If he brings it up, I will ask more." Maria replied.

The dishes and remaining food were quickly managed as the two of them continued talking and getting more acquainted. Maria felt the familiar sense of being connected to the people on the ship, much in the way she had experienced on the Kupala, but there was a sharp difference in the formality and seriousness of the crew. It seemed the men were more careful not to offend the captain as orders were vigorously enforced.

Everything ran in a particular timeline as she understood she needed to meet expectations of the captain and crew. Her only concern was not being prepared for a meal when it was due. She remembered how Sveta worked around the clock, many times to have meals ready, and now she also had to be as diligent.

# Night in Port

The days began to pass with a normal rhythm of meal preparation, serving and cleaning. The frustration of cleaning, only to begin cooking again, began to wear on Maria's patience. Her only recreation was reading the book that the captain had loaned to her. She practiced the words until they felt natural to her mind; she even began calling the names of the vegetables and cookware by their English terms. Sometimes the captain would stop in and hear her, and then offer a corrective pronunciation to help her speak more accurately.

Maria rushed to finish her duties so she could return to her new found interest in learning English. She felt it was such an exotic language compared to Russian, with so many rules complicating the process of constructing a sentence. But she was determined to have a conversation one day with an English speaker, just to feel the satisfaction of expressing thought in a new language.

At times, when she read her book at night, she remembered her mother teaching her Latin, and how many of the words appeared in English as well.

"Intellect is at its highest when a conversation takes place." She remembered her mother saying.

Many nights went by as she sat on her bed brushing her hair and reciting phrases in English. She had a secret wish to impress the captain with how much she had learned.

The captain stopped by one evening and asked, "Are you tired of English yet?" He teased.

"No! It's very...interesting for me!" She said in English.

"Let's try a few phrases...'What's your name?'" The captain asked.

Maria hesitated, unsure if she was ready to respond as she translated the words she had learned. "My name Maria." She said with a giggle.

Captain Tanner smiled, impressed she had understood him. "Is, my name is" he instructed.

"Mm, ladno, my name is Maria." She returned.

"Lovely to meet you, Maria, my name is Tanner." He replied, sounding brilliant and charming.

"Lovely?" Maria asked while flipping through the pages to find the word.

Tanner chuckled, enjoying her intrigue. He knew it would take a while for her to get enough vocabulary memorized, so he translated the word for her.

"Eto tak...priyatno... krasivaya." He said, returning to Russian.

Maria blushed, thinking he was complimenting her rather than translating. The captain realized he sounded flirtatious and wanted to clarify.

"Uh…. Lovely to meet you… Ochen priyatno s vami poznakomitsya." He affirmed with a smile.

"Ahh," Maria quipped, understanding he was polite, not complimentary.

"Lov-e-ly," she read aloud as she found the word in the book.

"Molodets," he praised as he began to walk up the stairs.

"Lovely!" She repeated aloud to practice.

"Ochen." The captain said to himself as he ascended the stairs, returning to his duties.

Maria had grown fond of the captain and his attention. He was very gentle with her and seemed to want to protect her from the other members of the crew. Occasionally she would overhear someone would make a vulgar comment about her, but she was not insulted as she dismissed it as typical sailor talk.

As the ship moved closer to the Pomeralian coast, the frequent conversations with the captain made her wonder if something more might happen between them. She had not forgotten Gennady and remembered how things onboard the Kupala happened all at once and then faded quickly, as everyone scatters in port. The captain seemed more confident and experienced, perhaps he was simply accomodating her, but she imagined his interest was more than kindness.

Edik appeared in the kitchen in preparation for the evening meal. He organized everything to fit on the trays to prevent them from sliding as he carried them up several flights of stairs. Maria quickly placed a serving of each portion on the plates, making sure each passenger got the same meal. The captain knew how petty passengers could be, and insisted they get the exact same servings, as one person with an extra piece of bread became the favored one and all others would complain.

Edik finished loading the tray and looked toward Maria to get her attention, "I don't know if anyone has told you, but we will be in Pomerania late tonight, and it's the captain's birthday, tomorrow."

Maria's eyes lit up, "Really? Will we make a party?" She asked with excitement.

"We will be in port, so I imagine the men will take him into town for a drink and the usual recreation," Edik said as he lifted his tray to his shoulder.

"Usual recreation?" Maria asked.

"Women and gambling," Edik said with a sarcastic smile as he turned to leave the room.

Maria felt her heart sink, "Somehow everything changes in port. The crew step off the ship and into another life, another person." She thought.

She paced in the kitchen, wondering what she might do to keep her mind off the idea of the captain with some strange woman. Her mind returned to what she saw in Yaroslavl, the sailors spending the night in the tavern, even her cousin was known well there. She wanted to believe the captain was different, and not as simple as those men who traded all their money for a few moments of pleasure.

She began to realize that her jealousy was dominating her thoughts, she felt out of his reach and wished she could be the one he would seek in port.

Her eyes searched the shelves, as she noticed the bags of milled oats and wheat. "A cake!" She thought, maybe it would impress him or remind him of her. She tried to remember the recipe her mother had taught her for baking a honey cake, it had been so long since she made one and this one had to be perfect.

As she finished setting out the food for the crew and washed dishes, she imagined what his reaction would be when she surprised him with a cake on the morning of his birthday.

She heard footsteps in the stairwell and looked to see Boris entering the kitchen. She smiled and greeted him but now imagined him as a soldier and hero, it was as if he had become a different person to her. She wondered what stories he might share if he could speak now.

"Boris!" She said excitedly, "Are you hungry?"

He patted his stomach and nodded disagreeing, she understood he had just had his dinner.

Boris looked around and inhaled deeply with pride as if approving of her work and orderly kitchen. He walked to a bowl of apples and admired them. They were his favorite food, and he couldn't resist taking one into his hand as he turned and headed to the stairs. He waved and began to walk away.

"Were you just coming to check on me?" She asked playfully.

Boris stopped, nodded with a smile and then held up the apple in gratitude.

"Na zdorovie!" She giggled as he exited the room.

The ship began to rock more slowly, as the sound of shouting men and shifting freight began above deck. She could hear unusual voices as the crew offloaded the ship and passengers.

"I guess we are in Pomeralia." She thought.

She went up the stairs to the top deck to see how it looked in port. The lights were bright in port, ship masts were in all directions, and the wind was surprisingly high for night time. It had a unique scent, the air was warm but not as fresh as in the northern Baltic. Crew members continually passed around her as she realized she was in everyone's way.

She remembered her idea to make a cake and headed back to the kitchen to get it ready. She set out all the ingredients and retraced the steps she had learned as a young girl. The eggs, wheat, and honey, were all mixed and set into a pan for baking. She pushed an extra log into the fire to get the oven hot as she continued mixing.

Her mind still fixated on ideas of the captain with the crew in some dreadful tavern later that night or tomorrow. She felt angry and jealous at the same time, even though she had seen plenty of sailors doing the exact same thing in each port.

She placed the cake in the oven and slid the iron door closed to keep it hot. She knew it would take a while for the cake to bake, so she heated some water for washing herself off after a long night of cooking. The dim light from the stove fire and one lantern lit the kitchen in a softer glow than when the crew was there, and all lamps were lit. She felt everyone was leaving the ship, and she would be alone until tomorrow.

She took a hand towel and dipped it in the warmed water as she began to wipe her face and arms off. She felt instantly relaxed from the sensation, as she continued to scrub her neck. She looked around to see if anyone was there, but she was completely alone. Only the muffled sounds of cargo and crew in the distance.

She slipped her dress over her head and quickly made an effort to finish cleaning herself. The warm water felt amazing as she glided the cloth down her neck, across her chest and torso. She dipped it again and again, enjoying that it was hotter each time. Finally, she bent over to run the cloth down both her legs, taking her time to be thorough and relaxed.

Her long hair cascaded onto the floor as she quickly shook it and stood back up. As she nodded her head back, her hair snapped into place behind her, like a blonde whip. Suddenly she sensed something out of place. The floor boards creaked in the galley, she gasped, realizing her body was exposed for anyone to see.

She scrambled to pull her dress back on, but her damp skin made it difficult for the fabric to slide smoothly. She pulled harder, almost ripping it as she tried to cover herself and look to see who was in the galley.

She reached for the lantern and bravely walked out of the kitchen, unsure who she might find there. But no one was there.

She sighed deeply, hearing more noise from above the decks. She realized it was just the crew working in other parts of the ship. She remembered her cake and turned to rescue it from the hot oven.

She rushed to the oven door and peeked inside. It was perfect and ready to be taken out. She opened the door wide and went to reach for the cake. The heat of the oven reminded her to cover her hands or risk getting burned by the edges of the pan. She grabbed the hem of her dress, and used the fabric instead, reaching inside the oven and carefully picking the cake from the hot surface.

As she lifted the cake to the counter, her dress also lifted, exposing her bare legs completely. She felt the draft blowing through the ship and again, the sound of the floor creaking, in the same way as before. She set the cake down and quickly brushed her dress into place.

"I'm imagining things." She thought as she cut the fire down in the stove and headed to her bed to rest. But as she turned to leave the kitchen she saw the shadow of an unknown man quietly walking up the stairs.

Her blood ran cold; she was in shock. Who was it? Did she imagine it? What were they doing all this time? She went to her room and closed the door. She pushed her chair against it, hoping it would prevent whoever that was from getting in while she was asleep.

The familiar sensation of fear returned to her heart. It was as if she was hiding from the Tatars again. She spent the night with her lantern lit while holding the knife that Sergei had given her, eventually nodding off to sleep. Every sound on the ship became an alarm sending her into a panic.

She finally fell asleep from exhaustion and didn't realize it until she heard a knock on the door. She walked slowly to the door, sliding the chair away from the handle. She kept the knife in her hand, holding it behind her back.

"Kto tam?" She said as her voice sounded dry from a rough night of no sleep.

"Good morning!" the captain said in English from the other side of the door.

"Good morning!" She replied, as she smiled and quickly unlatched the handle

The captain immediately saw how her face had changed, she looked upset, even though she smiled at him. He looked around her cabin, and then at her. "We're in port, you don't have to cook today." He said calmly.

She felt the fear slipping away from her mind as he stood in her doorway. She realized that nothing had happened to her last night, and now she could focus on the needs of the day. But her face showed she had something on her mind, and between the mysterious shadow last night and the idea that he would spend time with the crew in a brothel today, she was covering it all with a forced smile.

"I know, but someone is having a birthday today, and I made them a cake." She said playfully.

The captain paused, the charm of her voice and unexpected attention caught him by surprise. "You made a cake for me?" He asked with a smile.

"Da, c Dnem Rozdeniya!" She said sweetly, as she walked toward the kitchen with him following.

"Here it is!" She teased, as the simple cake was sitting in the pan from the night before.

Maria felt somewhat foolish suddenly. Maybe she looked like a little girl to him, not a woman to be taken seriously or to fall in love with. Her mind could not stop imagining him with another woman. She stared at him as the conversation slowed, thinking to herself that she should know her place and not dream so big. He was a captain of a ship; she was a mere farm girl working in the galley. And that was all she would ever be to him.

The captain paused as he looked at the cake and then at Maria, "20 years at sea, and no one ever made me a cake on my birthday." He said in an unexpected tone. He seemed to be genuinely touched by her gesture.

She dismissed his kindness and reached for a knife. "Oh, it's nothing special, just a honey cake. Have a taste?" She said.

"No!" he interrupted, save it for tonight! I want to enjoy it after we come back from town.

"Ah," She said in a disappointed tone. In her mind, it was a polite notice. First, he would have his fun in port, then he would have time for her simple cake.

"Well, maybe there will be enough for you and some of your crew." She said as she set the knife down.

"Crew?" He replied. "I meant you and me, let's go into Pomeralia today, there are so many interesting places here. They even have a library!"

Maria was astonished but needed to confirm her understanding, "You're not going with the crew today? It's your birthday, and I thought you all went to…" she began.

"Konechno net!" He laughed, "I don't care for heavy drink, it's never improved anyone from my experience. The men will toast to my health and everything else they can think of. It's enough."

Maria's felt her mood shift from keeping her distance, to wanting to be closer to him. He had come to invite her to spend the day in town, and he had no intention of being less than the man she had initially admired.

Footsteps came rushing down the steps as a voice from the crew shouted out, "Captain, they're ready for you on deck. Everything is offloaded!"

"Be right there!" he shouted as he turned to leave, "Well, get ready! We leave in ten minutes!"

Maria smiled as she rushed to her cabin. Reaching for her hair brush and sorting through her few dresses to look her best. Her joy was like an energy racing through her body. She wanted to leave at once but kept changing her mind on how to fix her hair and what clothes were best.

Half an hour later, she walked onto the deck. She had a thin braid of her banding around the side of her head, then blending into the back. The captain gasped with pleasure as he saw her, "You look like an angel in that white dress." He sighed as he guided her toward the gangplank. Every man within view was watching her, this was surely not the cook, she was a princess; delicate, beautiful and graceful.

Edik walked toward her and nodded to the captain, "All the passengers are off sir, and I'll be seeing you on your return to Danzig in a few months."

"Spacibo Edik, enjoy your time with your family." The captain said.

"You're not coming with us to Poole?" Maria asked as Edik motioned to shake her hand in farewell.

"I only assist when there are passengers on board, the next part of the trip is cargo and crew only. Until your return, have a safe journey!" Edik said politely as he walked toward the gangway.

Maria hadn't expected that Edik would not stay on board, she felt nervous to complete all her tasks without his help. The captain noticed the concern on her face and didn't want to detract from the fun they were about to have in port.

"It will be much easier when you only cook for the crew." The captain assured, "Shall we go?" he asked.

"Da, poshli!" Maria replied, feeling her concerns as a momentary distraction from the overwhelming curiosity of the city and being with the captain on his birthday.

408

# Pomeralia

It was well into the afternoon as the captain and Maria walked along the pier, like a sailor rejoined with his bride. They smiled and talked openly as they ducked around moving cargo and ship workers. Their path led them away from the harbor onto modern city streets, lined with shops and a large stone church in the distance. Maria marveled at the cleanliness of the town, it seemed so new compared to other ports.

"It's so clean here!" Maria said in intrigue as she looked in all directions.

"They've come a long way, now that the fighting is over." The captain said.

"Fighting?" Maria asked.

"You name it, Mongols, Danes, Poles, everyone wants to own the town because the port is a gateway to the region. Luckily, they didn't destroy it all in the process." He said as they arrived at an old building. "I give you, the Library of Pomeralia."

Maria's eyes lit up as the large wooden door creaked open to expose the view of books stacked up to the ceiling. She rushed in and raced to see what she could find, there were so many languages, different sizes and the warm smell of the paper was like its own perfume.

"Take your time, look around," The captain said as he smiled and walked to the librarian's desk. The two of them engaged in conversation quietly as Maria pulled books randomly from different stacks. Some contained maps, others had drawings of churches and city ports. A multitude of languages in all directions, many she couldn't recognize.

The captain and librarian went over several maps and discussed issues for over an hour before he returned.

Meanwhile. Maria slid her hand inside a large heavy book and pulled it open. The words were unrecognizable, but the illustrations were highly detailed works of the human body. As she turned the pages, she saw instructions on how sculptors took slabs of granite or marble and created masterpieces for the Roman church. Her hand slowly traced the outline of a woman's body as depicted by the sculptor.

"Find something you like?" The captain asked as he returned to her side.

"It's amazing how they bring such art out of pure rock." She said as she looked up and closed the book.

"If you ever make it to Rome, you'll be even more impressed. That book is from the chapels there." He said. "Would you like to take something with you to read? I've made arrangements with the owner, he has several of my books here as well so it's fine to take one."

Maria looked around so many choices and not so much time to decide. "You know I think I'll get one next time, it's your birthday, and there are still many books on the ship I can read." She said

"As you wish," the captain said as he motioned toward the door.

They walked along the streets moving closer to the large church.

"I need to light a candle here." The captain said as began walking up the steps.

Maria nodded and said, "I'd like to do the same."

The elaborate threshold surrounding the door replicated concentric outlines cut into the stone like echoes moving closer to the opening. Metal bands wrapped the wooden door panels with large steel bolts and hinges to support its substantial weight. The captain pushed the latch and the door slowly opened with a familiar creaking that only church doors could make.

They stepped inside as an elderly woman began to exit the building. Maria looked at her and remembered she had nothing to cover her head with.

"Podozhdi, ya ne mogu!" Maria halted at the door.

The captain realized her concern and turned to the older woman.

"Psheprashaam?" He beckoned as he motioned toward her veil.

The elderly lady nodded, understanding instantly and removing her veil as She said something unrecognizable in Polish. She handed it to Maria while still talking.

Captain Tanner gave her a silver coin to calm her obvious annoyance with their lack of preparation to enter the church.

Maria donned the veil quickly, "How can I say thank you?" She asked.

"Djenkuichi," The captain said with a smile as he turned to walk into the church.

"Djenkuichi!" Maria replied, "Uh...minuta?"

The woman nodded, understanding they would only be there for a moment and stood by the door to wait.

Maria followed Tanner down the center of the baroque church, toward the flicker of altar candles near the pulpit. The high ceilings and stained glass windows created a sensation of being in a separate world as if a warm blanket of safety had been wrapped around her.

Without a word they both lit candles and quietly bowed for a moment. Maria thought of her father as she watched the candlelight dance in the draft of the building. The church was the only place she felt a sense of being closer to him. She prayed for her mother's safe return to Neva and asked God to let her father watch over her and her mother.

The captain sat quietly for a moment, taking a deep breath and exhaling slowly as he closed his eyes and whispered a soft prayer. He looked up a few minutes later and stood to leave the altar. Maria hesitated to leave but knew this was a brief stop in their day, and she needed to continue on with the captain.

As they returned to the streets, Maria removed her head covering and returned it to the elderly woman at the door. They waved goodbye to her and continued walking through the town.

Maria wondered who the captain was thinking of but wasn't sure if asking would be appropriate.

"My father," She said abruptly.

"Pardon?" said the captain

"Back there, the candle…" she hinted.

"Ah, my condolences." The captain said awkwardly.

There was a brief pause, then the captain's voice became softer and quiet. "My wife." He said.

Maria was shocked, "You were married?" She asked without thinking how it sounded.

The captain's eyes looked into the distance, he spoke slowly with great regret in his voice.

"She took sick while I was at sea," he said. "I only returned in time to bury her."

Maria felt she had pushed the conversation into a depressing level and should have tried to keep the day more positive as it was the captain's birthday. This explained a lot about his manner with her, his kindness and careful distance.

"I'm sure you did all you could," she comforted.

"Did I?" he asked rhetorically. "I'm not so sure, in my quest for rank and wealth at sea, I left the one more deserving of my attention at home."

Maria nodded, unsure if she should continue the conversation.

"Time is such a curse in this world, we would sell our future away to change the past while ignoring the moments in our hands. Yet, looking back, we see the wisdom in every turn of events, blessings and curses." He said.

Maria felt his words run through her, she had ached over losing her father and felt responsible for his death. And every moment since her life had seemed to twist and shake her without mercy.

"You're right." She said. "I would give away 10,000 tomorrows for one yesterday."

"Still..." The captain continued, "Are we naive to think a single moment changed, will unfold the rest so perfectly? Had I been at my wife's side, I'd also be dead from the plague that took her.... Or, so I remind myself when I think about it all."

Maria held her words, she could still see her father being killed on the street by the soldiers. She wondered if she had not left the cart, would any of it have been avoided.

They walked without words for a while, then the captain's voice seemed to perk up as he wanted to put the sorrow aside for the day.

"Today I am 41 years on this earth!" He said as if speaking to the entire street. "Time to celebrate!"

A small Inn was set at the end of the street, alongside the river. The captain led Maria to the door and said, "Best food in all of Europe. Seriously, I've checked." The door swung open, and the innkeeper recognized the captain immediately taking them inside.

"Have you come for the ritual?" The innkeeper said excitedly in Russian.

"Ritual? Oh that's today isn't it!?" The captain laughed as he realized what was happening.

The innkeeper guided them to a set of tables set along the river bank. Guests were dining and watching as the sun began to set in the distance.

"What's happening?" Maria said with intrigue.

"One of the benefits of being born on the shortest night of the year. There is always a party." The captain joked as they sat facing the river.

Young men were rushing to build a fire by the bank as girls holding wreaths began to arrive. It seemed the whole town was coming to this place as the crowds grew.

The innkeeper brought wine and two plates of vegetables. "We have shashlik tonight, it's still cooking." He said as he rushed back to the kitchen.

The scene by the water became more interesting to watch as the young men took turns jumping over the fire.

"Isn't this dangerous?" Maria asked.

"Nah" The captain dismissed, "It's tradition! Don't they have this ceremony where you live?"

What tradition? She asked curiously.

The captain smiled as he knew he was about to share an interesting story.

"Well my dear, this is a fire and water ritual. You see those lads there, they are trying to prove who is the bravest and most skilled. While those girls by the river have made wreaths from nine herbs that they set afloat on the river." He began.

"Oh, this is Kupala!" My parents never let me attend it, they said it was pagan. "I can only imagine their reaction to the name of my last ship." She joked as she realized she had interrupted Tanner's story.

"So ...The men then try to jump through fire and then fish the wreath from the water before it floats away, and if he is successful, he can consider the girl his fiancé." Tanner explained.

"Ah I see, well it doesn't seem so hard to catch a wreath if you're willing to get wet," Maria replied while she watched the young girls tossing their wreaths far into the river.

"Indeed, but it wasn't so easy for Jacek" the captain continued in a mysterious tone.

"Another legend?" Maria teased.

"Of course, what kind of sailor would I be without stories to tell?" The captain replied with a smile.

"Davai, tell me your story." Maria encouraged as she watched the ritual along the river bank.

"The legend goes that a weak and clumsy man named Jacek could neither handle the fires or the water. So he sat, frustrated beneath a tree when a fairy appeared to him."

"Go into the forest!" The captain said in a strange voice "Find the flower that blooms only tonight for its magic power can grant any wish!"

"And did Jacek find this flower?" Maria asked playfully.

"He did!" The captain insisted, "And he made his wish but instead of love he wished for wealth. The fairy was disappointed and warned him, that his greed for money, instead of seeking love, would come at a price. His fortune was granted, but he could never share it with anyone."

"What happened to him?" Maria asked in complete suspense.

The captain dramatically told the end of the story, "Jacek awoke in a great palace. He had more money than he could count but he missed his family, so he returned to his village. Unfortunately, when he came to his father's poor home, no one recognized him in such fancy clothing. He remembered the fairy's warning and returned to his palace, without giving a single coin to anyone, not even his family.

As years passed, his homesickness grew, and he came back again to his village only to find all his relatives had died of hunger. In remorse, Jacek became as thin as a twig, and in his prosperity suffered alone, realizing that the happiness he missed would have come from sharing, not possession."

"I like this story!" Maria said smiling, "It's better to jump through fire and water for love!"

The local people sang songs around the fire as the evening came to a close. It was relaxing to be outside the ship for a change, but soon the captain stood, and Maria knew it was time to return.

"There's a cake waiting for me in the galley, let's see how it tastes!" The captain said as they turned to make the walk back to the harbor. There was a new sense between them, more familiar and kind. A common bond in their respective loss, a beginning of real friends and possibly more but for now, a comfort simply from being together.

Maria slid her hand around the captain's arm, laying her head against his shoulder briefly.

"Thank you for today." She said with a relieved sigh.

She could feel the strength in his arm as she held on to him. She felt so safe and cared for next to him and wanted to stay in that moment forever. The captain turned toward her and gently guided his hand under chin, lifting her face to his. Without hesitation, his lips found hers and the entire world seemed to stop turning. She felt the tenderness of his touch as his hand slide down her arm and around her back to pull her closer to him.

Their lips parted, and the warmth of his welcomed tongue slid erotically into her mouth. She felt as if she were made of fuel and his tongue was the fire, setting her ablaze. She held her breath, hanging on to the lingering pleasure of being touched like this, so completely immersed in the moment. Her heart raced with excitement as she tried to anticipate what it meant, where would it go, what he might expect from her after this.

She gently pulled away, wishing to continue, but wanting to go slowly as her shyness made her rush to a cautious place. "You make me shy...." She said as her breath failed her.

The captain quietly replied, "Forgive me if I offended you."

"Oh no! not offended just...shy." She replied, feeling like a girl without experience or the words to explain her hesitation for more.

"We should get back to the ship." The captain affirmed as if there was no need to stay in this awkward moment any longer.

"Yes, we should!" Maria agreed as they began to walk back along the streets.

"I'm glad we went to the church today..." Maria started as she wished to clear away the lingering silence between them. "My father's death was recent and very tragic."

"I understand; I don't talk about my wife very often, but it helped. I still feeling like she is waiting for me in Kotka sometimes, then I remember she is gone."

Maria paused, taking in the depth of his words as she continued their walk toward the ship.

She struggled with the right response and decided not to say anything. She could see the faraway look in his eyes, a look she often had when thinking of her father.

"Surely, he must have loved his wife a lot," she thought.

The trip back to the ship was soon over with few words spoken. There was a tension between them, but as they arrived, the captain made her feel more comfortable with him, "Does this mean I don't get to try the cake?" he said playfully.

Maria burst into a relieved laugh, "Oh that cake? It is gone, forget about that cake!"

"I need to meet a new member of the crew, and then I'll be down to see you." He said.

"Very well, I'll try to save you some..." She teased.

Maria walked on board and headed to the stairwell. She noticed the captain speaking with a strange man who stood by a large trunk on the dock. The man looked up at her, and as their eyes met, she felt a chill in her heart, as if someone had splashed cold water on her.

Her mind flashed back to the church in Rostov when the guard pulled her into the room and set her life into turmoil from that moment. Her face began to burn with the sensation of cold and heat all at once. It was as if she was in danger but she had no reason to feel that way.

She rushed to the galley to prepare the cake for the captain and try to bring a positive conclusion to their day in port.

The captain soon came on deck and greeted Maria as the man from the dock followed closely behind him.

"Masha, meet our new quartermaster, Paul Beneke." He said, gesturing for the man to shake Maria's hand.

Maria hesitated to reach out to the man, still nervous about the effect his initial glance had given her.

Beneke extended his hand in a formal manner, "Pleasure to meet the famous cook the captain has been telling me about." He said.

Maria slowly shook his hand but avoided making eye contact with him.

The captain noticed her hesitation but kept his thoughts. "Now, there is a birthday cake around here with my name on it!" the captain said proudly.

"Care for some?" He asked Beneke.

"I need to get sorted in my cabin, but thank you, sir," Beneke replied as he made his way from the galley.

As Beneke's footsteps retreated up the stairs, the captain reached to taste the cake Maria presented him.

"Oh, this is an excellent cake!" He said with his mouth full. "I didn't really want to share it with him anyway."

"You're in a good mood!" Maria said curiously.

"Ah, yes!" the captain began. "Beneke is going to help with the ocean crossing to Poole, it's one thing to drive a crew through the Baltic, but once we pass Kopenhaven, it will be more work than one person can tend."

"I see." Maria replied, "What does the Quartermaster do?"

The captain hesitated, "I thought you had been on a ship before? He asked.

"Oh, it was a river vessel, nothing as grand as this." She continued, "We had a quartermaster, and he was excellent. But he was second to the captain, not sure how it works here."

"It's the same, Beneke will be my second and able to direct the crew in my stead, including the galley." He teased.

Maria felt the same chill run through her as she tried to hide her reservations. Something about this man took all pleasure from being on the ship and made her feel like a prisoner suddenly.

"Not to worry, he only does that when I am off the ship or unavailable. Can't have two captains, right?" The captain reassured.

"Right!" Maria agreed quickly as she cut a slice of the cake and set it on a plate.

"Is that for you?" The captain asked.

"No, for you of course!" She replied.

The captain took a fork and lifted the entire remaining cake into his hand. "Captain size" he teased.

Maria burst into laughter as she reached for the smaller piece, "Fine, I'll have this one then....C dnem rozdeniya!" she toasted with her plate.

"Mda! ... Spacibo!" The captain said as he shoveled more cake into his mouth.

The awkwardness vanished between them as they talked of less dramatic events in their lives and found common ground in a romantic friendship that left each word between them like a sweet invitation to hope and wonder.  A blissful, torturous, anticipation filled with longing for the moment the next kiss might come.

# Trouble in the Baltic

The ship hoisted anchor as the moorings were cleared and set a course west to Denmark. The sun had just begun to appear on the horizon as the crew hurried about the deck, preparing for a day at sea. The wind was strong and offered a chance to move quickly on the course. Below decks, Maria cleaned the dishes from the morning meal and began sorting food for the rest of the day's cooking.

Unfamiliar footsteps clogged down the stairs as Maria turned to see who it was. Quartermaster Beneke stood in the door, watching her work.

"I missed breakfast, anything left to eat down here?" he asked.

Maria nodded hesitantly without a sound. She took a plate and began to place oatmeal and potatoes on it. Her sense of fear was fading slightly as she focused on her work. She handed the plate to Beneke quickly looking at his face then looking away.

"Is this all we have?" Beneke smirked.

"Yes sir," She said politely, "That is what is left."

"Hmm, maybe you have something special set aside for the captain?" He teased.

"Excuse me?" Maria questioned.

Beneke began to stuff his face and talk while chewing, he was clearly not the refined type of man she had gotten accustomed to after spending time with the captain. "No more cake then?" he teased.

Maria felt his words were hiding a much darker intention. "No sir, the captain finished the cake last night." She said firmly.

"Mmm, is that all he finished?" Beneke said chewing his food.

Maria felt pulled between shock and outrage.

"Is he suggesting I slept with the captain?" she thought.

Beneke snapped the empty plate down on the table and headed to the stairs. "Oh, Tonight the crew will be throwing a little party for the captain since he didn't show at the tavern last night. Be sure to plan on feeding the men on the main deck."

Beneke's commanding tone was arrogant and harsh. Maria felt herself as a small doll in the hands of an angry child. She wondered why the captain had taken such a disgusting man into his trust.

She continued cooking throughout the day without any visit from the captain. She wanted to speak to him to see if he knew how Beneke had talked about him and his offensive manner with her.

The day passed and soon the sun set over the southern Baltic. The Ukko was far from shore with only a distant line along the south horizon as a reference to how far they were from civilization. The orange sky and fading sun beckoned them further westward toward Kopenhaven.

Maria was dutiful in delivering the men's dinner on the main deck. The crew seemed excited to have their meal on the main deck, but their excitement was not entirely about the meal. As the plates were collected up, Beneke stood and addressed the men.

"Lads! We got a captain here who's worth his weight in gold! Every one of you owes something to Captain Tanner, and it's only right we celebrate the day of his birth with a little indulgence and festivities." Beneke shouted as he paced the cheering and whistling crew.

I've got permission to allow a quick toast to our beloved Captain, and then we'll be playing a few rounds of chance with the dice to see who can win his pay back after losing it on shore last night!" Beneke joked as the men laughed out loud.

Beneke reached for a large bottle that sat on the captain's table and began to fill the glasses of all the men. It was awkward to watch as Maria had never seen the crew drink while on board. The captain seemed to enjoy the attention and made no reservations about the celebration.

She headed downstairs with the dishes, quickly returning to see what else was in store for the captain's party.

As she walked on deck, the men were toasting the captain repeatedly between cheers. Music erupted from an accordion one of the men had on board, with all the men singing along to the tune. Some sat on the benches drinking while the rest shouted at the fate of each rolled dice, followed by a quick coin exchange of wins and losses.

Suddenly she felt her arm pulled into the center of the deck as Beneke began to dance and spin her around. She felt awkward and was eager to step away, but then the captain joined in and rescued her from Beneke's grasp.

Beneke objected slightly as his voice sounded slightly drunk, "Of course, only the captain gets the girl!" he said.

One of the shipmates stuffed his shirt with small ropes and put a dry deck mop over his head. "Quartermaster! You can dance with me!" The man said acting like a flirtatious woman.

The men whistled and laughed as the two danced about comically.

Maria felt much better being near the captain. "Perhaps, Beneke was simply the kind of man who connected well with the men which would be useful to the captain." She thought to herself.

Tanner moved gracefully as he led Maria in a waltz-like turn, stepping and guiding her with the music. Maria had never danced formally, but she liked how it felt to have her arms on the captain's shoulders. He held her hand in his palm and looked into her eyes with charming, soulful, affection.

"Perhaps I should allow parties more often?" Tanner said as his dimpled smile emerged.

Maria was speechless, she felt swept away by the energy of this man, so accomplished and respected with all his attention on her. The warm salt air breezed across the bow and lifted her hair like a sail torn free. She could feel herself wanting the moment to last, to somehow spend a lifetime being spun about the deck by

Captain Tanner, serenaded by the warmth of the accordion's song.

The sound of shouting began to overpower the music as fighting erupted from the quarter deck. A crowd of men began to surround a brawl between two shipmates. One accused the other of cheating as their voices grew stronger and angrier.

"And that's why I don't allow drinking on my ship…" The captain said sarcastically, clearly disappointed as he released Maria's hand and turned to tend to the crew.

The captain started to walk toward the fight as a body slipped from the decks and fell into the ocean.

"Man overboard!" Began to echo from the mouths of all the men.

"Dammit!" The captain shouted as he began to bark orders.

"Drop the sails! Turn us about, and put that man in irons!" he shouted as he pointed at the other man in the fight.

The sound of the party was quickly lost as men rushed about the decks in an attempt to turn around and save the lost man.

The waves crashed against the ship as the water resisted the ships turn.

Beneke stood aft watching the man in the water.

"Do you have him?" Tanner asked as he ran to see where the man was.

"No sir, he was there a moment, now he's under," Beneke replied in a serious tone.

"Who was it?" The captain snapped at the crew.

"Gressi!" One of the shipmates replied.

The captain nodded and turned looking back over the turning waves.

"Anything?" He asked Beneke.

"Maybe there!" Beneke shouted as he pointed at the sight of a single white spot floating in the darkening water.

Maria rushed to look over the edge. The captain reached and caught her arm.

"Careful there, we don't want a woman overboard as well." He said calmly.

She looked back, his eyes were bright and strangely intense. She could see the full weight of the captain's position on him as the crew turned the ship.

"Damn wind is contrary; we won't be able to get to him in time," Beneke said. "Sir we might lose him."

The captain turned, quickly searching around the deck. "Twenty years at sea and I've never lost a man. Not starting today!"

Beneke looked puzzled as he stood watching the captain.

"Secure that line!" The captain barked as a man quickly picked up a rolled rope and tied it to a cleat on the railing.

Without another word the captain ran across the deck holding the rope in one hand as he dove off the edge of the ship.

"Is he mad?!" Beneke shouted.

Maria ran to the railing, watching the captain swim toward the white spot. It seemed like forever, but soon he reached him and turned him over; waving for the men to take action.

"All right! Pull him in, you gutless maggots!" Beneke chided as the men began heaving on the line that had been routed around the capstan for leverage.

"Anyone of you could have gone after him, but you wait for your captain?!" Beneke continued, announcing their shame with his own.

The emotions of the men were visible; Maria could read their faces. They felt ashamed and eager to redeem themselves by bringing the captain back quickly.

Finally, the captain's voice was close enough to be heard.

"Throw another rope!" Tanner insisted. We'll have to pull him up with this one, and I'll take the other.

The lifeless body of Gressi flopped against the side of the rocking ship as the men worked to lift him from the water line. The ropes dripped with frigid sea water as the men pulled quickly to bring Gressi onboard. Their hands eagerly reached for his body, grasping at his clothing to transition him over the railing and onto the deck.

They set him gently on his back, pulling the ropes away while Beneke assisted the captain's climb up the side. The captain ignored the chilled water and soaked clothing as he stepped over the rail and immediately walked toward Gressi's body.

The men were completely silent, filled with respect for their captain who had risked his life to save a member of the crew. As the captain inspected Gressi's body, Maria looked away, she knew he was dead.

The captain listened carefully to see if any chance of a breath remained. He looked up at the men, who waited with hope, only to nod and drop his head in sadness.

Beneke walked over to the captain. "What would you have us do Captain? Burial at sea?"

"Yes," Tanner replied, "After the trial."

"Trial?" Beneke questioned. "It was an accident from what we all saw."

The captain reached and pulled a knife from his belt. "I found this in his back. This was murder, not an accident." The captain said as the men stepped back from the knife.

Maria stood in shock, she couldn't believe someone could take life so quickly. She watched the captain's manner with the men, she felt proud of him for his composed manner. The men were entirely devoted to him, and this was why.

Tanner stood, "There will be a trial at sunrise. All men will be present and available for questioning. Now get this ship on course, secure the prisoner and store Gressi's body in the forecastle."

"You heard the captain!" Beneke shouted, "Move your arse!"

The captain began to remove his soaked clothing, his body shivered from the icy water that clung to him from head to toe.

The men helped him undress as his hands shook from hypothermia.

Beneke turned and addressed Maria, "Captain needs some privacy, get to your duties below!"

Maria nodded in agreement and hasted down the stairs. The entire evening had been a shock to her. On one hand, she was proud to have such a captain as Tanner but also terrified that a murder had taken place in plain sight. As she cleaned the dishes, she could hear the men escorting the prisoner to the lowest level of the ship where they clapped irons on his hands and feet.

She closed her door and put her chair under the latch to keep it closed. She felt unsafe in her room and slept with her hand holding her knife.

# Trial at Sea

The men were assembled on the main deck as the sun rose over the Southern Baltic. They stood in line at each side of the hull while the captain sat in a chair on the quarter deck with the quartermaster at his side. Maria walked up the stairs and watched from the steps, wanting to keep herself out of sight.

One by one, the captain called each man to give an account of what he saw. Each told one or two details, rebuilding the story that led to the Gressi's death. They described how the two men often fought and frequently commented about one's fortune over another.

The men explained that the game they played involved a lot of money and one felt cheated by the other when he lost. The captain produced the murder weapon, and all the men confirmed it belonged to the prisoner.

Maria heard someone coming up the stairs below her. It was the prisoner, led by Brother Boris.

Boris motioned for her to step aside as he escorted the prisoner on deck.

"Is there anyone here who can give testimony in the defense of this man?" The captain asked.

The men quietly looked down, knowing the man's fate was inevitable and justified. He had taken a life of a fellow crewman.

The man sobbed as Boris nudged him toward the captain.

"What is your name?" The captain asked.

"Victor." The man said, shaking in fear.

"Victor." The captain replied, "I find you guilty of murder and as Captain, hereby sentence you to death."

"No!" the man pleaded, "I didn't mean to kill him, truly it was an accident! Please sir, cast me in prison, sell me as a slave, I'll do whatever you ask, but not death!"

The captain took a deep breath, feeling the burden of his words. He looked up at the men and addressed them briefly. His voice made Maria cry as it cracked from the cold, harsh sea he had swallowed the night before.

"Men, you are a crew and as such you must place the life of your shipmates over your own. And they must do likewise. You will esteem others better than yourselves and accept the same honor from them. That's what a crew is! Not a captain or a mate, but a team devoted to the task! When we forget that, when we turn on each other, we rot from within, until we are hollow, filling the emptiness with greed, lust, jealousy... even murder.

Victor fell to his knees, sobbing. His chains rattled against the wooden deck as he cried heavily, begging for forgiveness.

"Bring the body of Gressi!" the captain commanded.

The men carried the limp body of Gressi and laid it on the deck. A sheet was placed beneath him, as the men began to wrap the body.

"Wait!" The captain shouted as his voice scratched.

"This burial at sea, it is also an execution... tie Victor face to face with Gressi." Tanner demanded.

"Captain!?" Beneke said in shock.

The captain's hand motioned for Beneke to obey without question his orders.

Beneke seemed resistant but complied. Victor's voice shrieked as they took him and laid him on top of Gressi, tying the two men together face to face.

Maria looked at the eyes of the men, most cried, others looked away, knowing the justice was harsh and swift.

She understood the captain's need for discipline, but this seemed so cruel and callous. Had she not seen his real character all along? Was he a monster?

The men looked at the captain for sympathy as they finished tying the two together.

"Sir, I believe you've made your point," Beneke added, hoping to change the captain's mind.

"Really?" The captain replied quietly. I don't think Gressi would object.

"Let each of you remember this day. You have witnessed how bitterness, envy, and anger consumed a man until it was all he saw, and now it will be the last thing he sees before breathing his last." The captain said as he walked toward the two bodies tied together.

"Gressi, you will be missed. You were a loyal shipmate, and I'm sorry I couldn't save you. May the sea carry you home." The captain said with remorse, "Victor, I will spare your family the shame of knowing your actions ... we will only say that you died at sea."

The captain looked at the men standing nearby and nodded, instructing them to throw the two overboard.

Brother Boris motioned a blessing over the two of them as the men carried them to the edge of the railing. The shouts and cries of Victor haunted everyone aboard as he was cast into the sea, silenced within seconds, never to be heard again.

Maria closed her eyes and spread her hand against her chest, she felt as if she were drowning with him. The silence on board was deafening, no one spoke. The captain had made his authority absolute, and no one wanted to question the wisdom he had demonstrated.

Maria looked at the men as they were dismissed. Each seemed a bit gentler with the other, and none complained in their usual ways as they got back to work.

The captain walked toward the staircase where Maria stood and nodded to her without speaking. She felt he had somehow moved higher in status on the ship, and she was not to question this.

As he passed her on the stairs, he slipped one step and reached for her hand to steady him. She looked into his eyes, they were red and swollen. "I may not be able to walk to my cabin." He said under his breath.

Maria realized he had given all his strength as captain but now needed to rest. As they walked down the stairs, she stayed at his side. He coughed, and his chest made a rattling sound. His hand felt cold, and he had no energy to pick up his feet as they slid along the corridor.

"You're ill!" She insisted.

"I just need to sleep it off." He rebutted. "Not my first dip in the Baltic."

Maria nodded, knowing the sound of sickness all too well. "I'll bring you some tea and honey." She said.

Maria helped the captain to bed and headed back to the galley. Beneke met her on the way and asked what she was doing in the captain's room. She explained his illness and went to get the tea.

She boiled extra water to take as well and cut some fruit to make a compote to sip. When she returned, Beneke was in the captain's quarters along with the head members of the crew.

The captain was giving instructions as he coughed and cleared his throat.

"Beneke will assume general operations so route your work assignments through him until we reach Denmark. We need to get all the cargo from Pomeralia offloaded before we can take on the payload for Poole, that's a lot of load time, and we don't have much to spare." The captain said.

Maria hesitated at the door but Beneke motioned for her to come in as the captain spoke.

"Right then." Beneke said, "As the new captain, I'll be familiarizing myself with how you handle freight preparation over the next two days. We may make some changes along the way but..."

"Aye, slow down Pasha, you're still quartermaster. I'm the captain till they take me off of this ship in a box." The captain said chuckling.

"Forgive my presumption sir, it's just when one is not able to perform their duties, they usually..." Beneke said.

"I'm performing my duties right now, and that's how we'll run it. Run routine stuff through the quartermaster, for higher issues come to me, just like always. Clear?!" The captain demanded.

All the men quickly nodded their heads.

"Fine, now get out of here, I have tea waiting!" The captain said as he looked in Maria's direction.

Maria smiled and waited until the men left the cabin. Beneke remained as if he wished to continue talking.

"You have your orders, Pasha." The captain said, dismissing his hesitance to leave.

"Aye, sir," Beneke said as his eyes looked around the room and finally to the door.

Maria brought the tea to the captain's bedside.

"Tough meeting!" She jested.

"Yes, never, ever hint that you're giving up command, or the vultures will circle," Tanner said as he sipped the tea.

"Vultures?" Maria asked.

"Vultures..." Tanner replied, "Nasty birds that eat dead animals...?"

Maria shrugged her shoulders abandoning hope of understanding.

Tanner nodded, realizing she had never seen a vulture. He leaned back in the bed and set the tea on his bedside. "Thanks for this, I'll be fine in the morning." He said.

Maria stood and turned to leave, then decided she should be more confident in caring for him. She placed her hand on his forehead and felt the heat radiating from his skin, "You have a fever!" She said.

Tanner dismissed her concern, "Ah, it's the tea, it made me hot. Don't worry." He said.

Maria nodded in disagreement and turned to leave. "I'll be back after lunch to see how you are." She said.

Tanner motioned with his eyes in agreement, he slipped into a heavy sleep before she reached the door. She turned to take a look at him in his bed and felt nervous that he was not able to protect himself or the ship in this condition.

She hoped the loyalty of the men would remain while Beneke seemed so eager to take over the ship.

# The Magic Tea

Maria finished the last of the dishes after serving lunch, the galley was empty as the men rushed back to their posts. There was an anxiety among them, rumors of the captain's illness had spread, and some thought it was a curse from Victor for being put to death in such a horrific way. Others looked toward the passing through Denmark, into the Atlantic, as a way to leave it behind in the Baltic.

Maria set a kettle on the stove, to catch the last of the heat until dinner time. She knew the captain would be ready for more tea and hopefully his fever had already broken. The sound of Beneke's heavy boots clomped down the stairs toward the galley, Maria looked and saw him walking with a handful of carrots that he extended to her as he came closer.

"For the captain!" He said in a voice that was strangely louder than necessary.

"Carrots?" Maria asked cautiously.

"They're wild carrots!" Beneke insisted. "Old medicine from Pomeralia, cut small pieces and put them in tea. It works like magic."

Maria turned her head to one side, unsure of such a potion.

"I've never heard of such a thing. It actually works?" She said, hoping the claim was indeed true.

Beneke shook his head in frustration and gasped as he turned to leave the galley.

"Just try it!" He said as his voice faded up the stairs.

Maria took a knife and cut a small piece of the carrot. She tasted it and spit it out.

"How old are these?!" She shouted up the stairwell.

She chopped another piece and mashed into a pulp, adding it to the tea for the captain. Then she doubled the amount of honey to hide the bitter taste. She made her way quickly to the captain's cabin, hoping he would be feeling better.

She knocked on the door but heard no answer. She reached for the latch and waited. What if he is sleeping, or naked on his bed? Maybe I should wait. Her thoughts rushed through her mind and before she could sort them her hand was on the latch opening the door.

The captain was still in his bed, right where she had left him. She secretly felt disappointed he wasn't accidentally naked in some way, just for a moment to see him out of his clothes and conveniently blame the tea. She set the kettle and cup next to his bedside, reaching again to touch his forehead. He was still hot but seemed to be sleeping well. His eyes fluttered as her hand touched him, he awoke and spoke with a dizzied voice as if still dreaming,

"I'm fine Ira, just let me sleep, ok?" he said in a frustrated voice as he rolled away from her exhaling deeply as he fell back into his dream.

Maria paused and realized, he had mistaken her for his deceased wife, Irina. In her mind, she pictured a time when she had tended to him in the same way. The reality of his love for his wife was so evident to Maria at that moment, even though his wife had died, in his fevered dream he imagined her right there with him.

She felt warmed by the moment, to see how a man can love a woman, even in her absence. On a ship surrounded by sailors who live different lives in every port, the captain was so devoted, even after losing her to a dreadful plague. He had clearly kept his wife in his heart during their time together, and now she lived in his dreams, still beside him.

Maria felt sadness for his tragedy and accepted she could never compete with an immortal memory. Her affection for the captain had grown quickly, but now she needed to see him with new eyes and focus on his care. She straightened his room, folding his clothes and took the old dishes with her as she left.

As she walked through the lower deck, she heard a loud banging just around the corner. It grew louder as she approached. As she came around the corner, she heard another bang, and suddenly something brushed across her feet.

"What was that!?" She said, afraid of the answer.

"Rats!" said one of the crew as he held a dead rat by the tail in one hand.

Maria shivered as she quickly looked away. "Ugh! Disgusting!" she replied. "Is it dead?"

"This one is." The man laughed. "We picked up a few in the last port, Beneke has us hunting them down."

Maria realized she had just felt the other one that got away. "I need to go." She insisted.

The men laughed and continued their rat hunt, banging away with hammers as she rushed to get down the stairs and wash her feet.

"Eww, eww, ewww!", she repeated as she took the hottest water she could find and scrubbed her feet."

Her eyes raced around the room, checking every corner for potential refugees from the hammer patrol. She reached for a broom and swept the entire floor multiple times until she was convinced she had scared any of them away.

She returned to the kitchen to begin the work of the evening meal. She made an extra effort to bang the pans louder than normal, in hopes the sound would work as a perimeter of safety from the rats.

Hours passed and soon the men returned for their dinner. Maria wanted to go and check on the captain, but her duties kept her in the kitchen for several more hours. She saw Brother Boris at the table and walked over to talk to him. It was rare that Maria ventured out of the kitchen when the men were present, and their conversations dimmed quickly as she walked to Boris.

"Could you see how the captain is doing?" She asked, trying to keep her voice down in the unexpected silence.

Boris nodded and understood correctly.

"I'll make some more tea, would you mind taking it to him?" she asked sweetly

Boris nodded again and turned to finish his plate quickly.

Maria returned to the kitchen and went to the bin where she had placed the wild carrots. As she opened the hinged door to the bin a large, dead rat fell onto the floor with a hard thump. A deafening shrill of horror echoed through every board of the ship as Maria's scream caused the men to rush toward the kitchen.

Maria backed into the galley, as the men stood behind her, looking over her shoulder. She was breathless from the spectacle of the rodent's carcass laying on the floor.

"Ra.. rat..." was all she could say as she felt her skin crawling over her body.

One of the men she had seen in the hallway emerged from the crowd, holding his hammer.

"Saw one, did ya?" he said comically as the other men burst into laughter.

Maria went to stand near Boris, the safest place on the ship as far as she was concerned.

"Wait for it!" one of the crew shouted as everyone continued laughing. But there was only silence, no familiar ring of the hammer or knock on the floor boards.

The crew began to shift forward trying to look around the corner, as the man returned holding the rat, by its tail, in one hand and the hammer in the other.

"Uff" it's hideous!" Maria said as the men joked and whistled.

"Aye, that's a proper Pomeralian rat!" the man jested. "Nice work on killing him Miss, saved me from having to chase him down."

The men returned to their seats as Maria began to understand what was happening, "But I didn't kill him, he was dead already."

The men hushed instantly as they looked at each other. A dead rat could mean disease and they had all been exposed.

"Get that rat off the ship!" Beneke shouted as he burst into the room. "Priest, I have need of you in the captain's quarters."

Boris looked into Maria's eyes and quickly rushed with Beneke up the stairs.

The men began to whisper amongst themselves. It was evident they feared the worst if a priest was being called to the captain's quarters.

Maria rushed to catch up to Boris, she wanted to know if the captain had become worse or if something else had happened.

When she arrived, they had already gone into his cabin and were standing by his bed. Maria approached slowly. The captain was pale, his eyes looked hollow, and his breathing was labored. It was shocking how fast he had declined since lunch.

Brother Boris looked at the captain's hands and feet, searching for clues to help heal him.

"I called you here as a priest, not a doctor, in case there is no time for either," Beneke said confidently.

Maria felt very suspicious of Beneke, it was more like he was rushing a clandestine plan into action rather than trying to save the captain.

Maria pushed her way through the men and touched the captain's head. His fever had gone, and now he felt cold. He looked at her and forced a smile to calm her.

"Masha," he said, "I'll be fine, and could you get me some more tea?"

Maria nodded agreeing, "Right away, I'll get it now and be right back."

Maria rushed down the hall and straight to the kitchen. She lit another fire and quickly got her kettle to a boil as her mind raced with the fear of losing Captain Tanner. "He seemed unstoppable, indestructible and suddenly he can hardly speak." She thought as she paced waiting for the kettle to boil.

She grabbed a knife and reached for the carrots in the bin, no longer thinking of the rat she had found there. Maria laid the carrots on the chopping block, cutting a few pieces until she saw chew marks on one of the carrots.

She paused for a moment, realizing what the marks were, then pushed the knife and carrots away from her hands. She picked up one of the carrots that appeared untouched by the rat and rinsed it in her washing pail.

As she turned back to her cutting board, a chilling awareness washed over her, freezing her in place as she saw everything perfectly. Her entire being knew what had happened. The rat ate the carrots and died. But she had given the same thing to the captain in his tea, hiding the bitter taste of the carrots with extra honey.

"That's why he got worse so quickly." She said to herself. "These carrots are some kind of poison."

She wiped her hands on her apron and lifted the cutting board from the edges, dumping everything into the waste bin. She turned to make her way back to the captain's cabin. She needed to tell him what had happened, and perhaps Brother Boris could help her save him.

When she arrived, the captain's door was closed, and a crewman stood at the door.

"I need to go inside." She insisted

"Sorry miss." The crewman answered, "No one goes in, too risky with the chance of a plague on board."

"Plague?" She said in shock.

"Captain Beneke's orders, first the rat, now the captain. Who knows who else might get sick?" He said nervously.

Maria turned to see Beneke standing at the end of the corridor.

"Plague?" She said sarcastically, not realizing he assumed she would believe it.

"Indeed, very dangerous on a ship and you need to go and clean that kitchen top to bottom. Scrub the entire thing and throw out all the food. We'll put in port tomorrow and restock." Beneke said barking as if he were on the top deck.

"All men, to their mops, clean this ship fore and aft!" He commanded.

Maria stood in front of Beneke, ready to confront him about the carrots.

"What if it's not the plague?" She said resisting his expected compliance.

"Did you forget the rats we had onboard? They can spread disease faster than a leper!" Beneke snapped.

"Oh, I remember the Pomeralian rats, especially the big one," Maria said accusingly as she looked directly into his eyes.

"You got something to say, kholop?" Beneke retorted.

"What if the captain was poisoned? Has anyone considered that?" She demanded, ensuring others could hear her.

"The only person who gave the captain anything is standing in front of me, so unless you're ready to give a confession I suggest you get your arse in the kitchen and carry out my orders!... And I got irons below for any of the crew not cleaning this ship right now!" Beneke barked while pushing past Maria and walking toward the stairwell.

The men scattered and began pulling everything apart to clean it. Maria realized this was not the time to make her case against Beneke, who clearly had the upper hand and could implicate her as the one who poisoned the captain.

She made her way down the hall and stopped at Brother Boris' room. She knocked at the door which was quickly opened by Boris. He pulled her inside and closed the door, knowing something nefarious was taking place onboard.

"I think the captain was poisoned!" She said in a booming voice.

"Beneke gave me some wild carrots, claiming they would help him get better, I put them in his tea and ...now..."

Boris motioned for her to talk quietly as he pointed cautiously to the walls. She nodded, calming her voice into a whisper and watched him for gestures.

Boris reached for a book on his desk, flipping through the pages until he found what he was looking for. He turned the book toward Maria and laid it on his table. A drawing of the same wild carrots she had received from Beneke was illustrated on the page, captioned in Latin text beneath.

Maria began to read it, "Conium Maculatum...?" She asked.

Boris pointed to a cup on his desk and then to the book, making an inquisitive gesture with his face.

"Yes!" Maria exclaimed, "That's what I put in the tea. I can show them to you, they are in the galley waste bin right now."

Boris slid has hand slowly down his face, pulling at his beard in dismay. He knew Maria was unaware that the wild carrots were actually a lethal poison known as hemlock. He motioned for her to follow him back to the kitchen.

When they arrived, several men were at work in the galley, mopping the floors. Maria was surprised, as she was the only one who had ever cleaned the kitchen area.

"Captain said to make sure the galley is completely sorted," the crewman said as he poured sea water on the floors.

"Where's the food...and trash!?" Maria asked.

"All overboard, can't take any chances with plague, Miss." Said the crewman.

Maria looked at Brother Boris, as they both realized there was no longer any proof, only her word against Beneke.

Boris nodded, understanding everything and patted her hands in reassurance.  He turned his back to the other men so that only she could see his hands. He motioned his fingers in a circle of time.

Maria quietly followed his gestures. "Time...tomorrow?"

Boris nodded, and his eyes closed in the hope she would whisper.

Boris pointed up, "God?" Maria asked. He quickly nodded no, then immediately saluted her.

"Captain?" She gasped quietly.

Boris nodded again as his fingers walked across his arm.

"We'll be in port; will he be taken somewhere? A doctor?" She asked.

Boris nodded and slowly held the hand representing the captain as he pointed at himself and Maria and waved goodbye.

"He will have to leave the ship, and we'll be going on." She said, knowing it was true before the words crossed her lips.

Boris' hands refreshed.

"But?" Maria guessed.

He nodded as he pointed to the hand representing the captain and made one thumb go up.

"He will recover," she said in relief. "But what if someone wants to make sure he doesn't? You should go with him, you're the only one who knows what has happened!"

Boris nodded in hesitant agreement, knowing she was right.

She felt a calm come over her that soothed the thought of leaving the captain in Denmark. She looked at Boris and paused, she could see his concern for her in his eyes.

"I'll be fine, and we'll be back in Kopenhaven in two months." She said confidently.

Boris exhaled in a frustrated breath of agreement. He nodded quickly and walked into the kitchen, opening the stove and reaching his hands into the wood box. He sifted through the ash and pulled small pieces of partially charred wood. Maria watched in amazement as he set the pieces on the counter and shaved the charcoal from the bark, creating a pile of black powder.

Boris motioned for a cup, which Maria quickly gave him. He held the cup below the counter line and pulled the entire pile of charcoal off the edge, letting it fall into the cup below. "Hmph," Boris grunted as he pointed at the pail of water behind Maria.

Maria understood and quickly dipped a ladle into the pail and turned to pour it into the cup.

"Will this work?" Maria asked, assuming it was some kind of remedy for the captain.

Boris swirled the mixture in the cup and looked at Maria. He motioned as if drinking it then placed his hand over his stomach and made a sound as if vomiting.

Maria recoiled but realized that was the only way to slow the effect of the poison.

"We'll be mopping in the kitchen also; can you give us a hand?" One of the crew said as they watched the two of them.

Maria nodded to Boris to go quickly with the charcoal as she reached for a broom to clean up the debris on the floor.

Boris advanced up the stairs, holding the cup steady to keep it from spilling. When he arrived at the captain's quarters, Beneke was hovering over the bed like a predator watching his prey.

"Ah, more tea!" Beneke said excitedly. "Come right on in, he needs as much as he can swallow."

Boris knew Beneke thought it was the last of the poison to finish the captain off. He walked around to the captain and hesitated to indicate Beneke should move. Secretly hoping he would not see the charcoal mixture in the cup.

Beneke quickly removed himself, knowing he should not be present when the captain died.

"Well I have a ship to run, I'll leave you in the priest's care and come back later to check on you, Sir!" Beneke said, in a false sentiment that now seemed obvious to Boris.

As soon as the door closed, Boris lifted the weak captain's shoulders to help him drink from the cup.

"What is this?" the captain said in a dazed voice. "Where's the tea?"

Boris grunted with insistence at the captain, pushing the cup into his mouth. The captain took one sip and spit it out.

"Oh, that is vile, are you trying to poison me old friend?" The captain chuckled as he looked up at Boris.

Boris's eyes spoke volumes in a single glance as he pushed the cup to the captain's mouth with insistence.

"What?" He asked.

The captain paused as he realized everything in a moment of

clarity. His eyes began to look across the room at the details of his situation connected in his mind.

"Poison? But who would poison me? ..." He asked rhetorically.

Boris nodded toward the door, but the captain already knew. "That evil bastard! The league warned me he was sneaky, but I never expected this." The captain said in astonishment.

He drank the mixture entirely, gagging as he tried to swallow the thickened ashes that had settled at the bottom of the cup.

Boris walked to the corner of the captain's cabin, picking up an empty bucket and walking back to the captain's bed.

"What happens now?" The captain asked as he laid back onto his bed.

Suddenly he sat up and vomited. Boris placed the pail in his lap just in time. The captain's week body convulsed until he was completely vacant. He fell back on the bed and passed out.

Boris took the bucket to the window and dumped it into the sea. He returned and sat by the captain's bed, knowing the captain would soon awake and repeat purging for several hours. He began to whisper prayers for strength and blessing over the captain as the ship tossed its way through the Baltic toward Kopenhaven.

# Farewell at Kopenhaven

The ship quietly moved through the outer edge of the Baltic as the morning wind began to stir, lifting the sails toward Kopenhaven. The distant coastlines began to merge like a narrowing, dark hallway, lit by dim shore lights that peered through the dark. The bow pointed toward a passage into the Atlantic, just past the port harbor.

Maria awoke to the shudders and thuds of the crew as they prepared the cargo for offloading. She knew the ship would soon dock and her chance to see the captain would be brief before he was taken to a physician. She arose, quickly dressed and walked up the dark stairway to see if the captain's cabin was still guarded. Her eyes lit up when she saw his door partly opened and no one in sight.

She rushed down the hallway, peeking through the crack in the door to see if anyone was inside. She saw the captain asleep in his bed and Boris sitting by his side. Boris looked up and saw her in the door and motioned for her to come in.

Maria darted to the captain's side, touching his forehead to see how he was. His skin was still pale, and his breathing seemed labored and arduous. His eyes slowly opened when he sensed her touch. He reached and put his hand on hers, gazing up at her with a lost look as if searching for an answer.

"I'm so sorry Masha, I thought we would finish this voyage together," he said in a crackled voice.

Masha patted his hand, "I'll be fine and back here to see you in eight weeks!" She insisted.

"They'll appoint another captain; your contract will be assigned to him." He said with regret in his voice. Boris watched Maria's face as the captain tried to prepare her for the changes she would experience.

"I wish Boris would stay on board, but he's as stubborn as a mule and determined to protect me." The captain teased.

Boris nodded in agreement.

"He needs to make sure you get taken care of, we can't trust anyone at this point," Maria said.

The sound of the gangway rattled outside, signaling the ship was docked and ready for cargo to move.

"They'll come for me soon." The captain said, "Beneke will want me off the ship as soon as possible. But I'll have a word with the shipping line in port, Boris will help in turning the tables on that mutinous bastard." The captain whispered.

"Tanner, what if I never see you again?" Maria said as tears filled her eyes.

"Shh, let's have none of that." The captain said, "Something wonderful waits for you, I saw it in my dreams."

Maria held the captain's hand to her chest, the reality of not having someone she felt safe with began to fill her heart with fear. Without him and Boris, she was easy prey for those who could harm her.

Captain Tanner could see the vulnerability in her face, he remembered the words a priest had told him upon learning of his wife's death.

"God hasn't forgotten you Masha, so don't forget him." Tanner said, "The path you are meant to follow is filled with critical turns, disguised as a tragedy."

Maria sobbed and nodded, comforted by his kind words.

The sound of heavy footsteps drew closer toward the captain's cabin. The door swung open wide as Beneke entered followed by two men, wearing cloths over their faces to prevent infection. They carried a full-length cravat to transport the captain's body off the ship.

"Be gentle with him, lads, he's delirious and may not live the day," Beneke said in a rehearsed tone.

Tanner sat up on the bed, making himself appear robust and capable.

"Aye lads, be gentle!" the captain said in a coughed laugh, "It's my first time being poisoned by a shipmate."

Beneke pretended not to understand the captain and noticed the other men looking at him.

"It's the sickness talking, let's get him to our physician on shore," Beneke replied.

"Boris will accompany me and arrange my doctor!" The captain insisted as Maria stood out of the way, while the men laid the cravat beside the bed.

"Now, wait outside until I am packed and ready," Tanner commanded as the men gladly exited into the hallway, apparently wishing to minimize their exposure to the plague.

"Priest, you want to delay your passage to Rome and remain here?" Beneke asked in a nervous tone.

Boris nodded as he stood and began packing the captain's things into a chest. Maria assisted Boris as they tried to avoid making eye contact with Beneke. They knew he still had charge of the ship and could affect their plans to get the captain to safety.

Beneke began picking up the captain's personal items to speed up the process.

"The contracts and invoices are in this pouch," Tanner said as he pointed to a leather wrap filled with papers.

Maria knew her contract was among them and felt set adrift in the ocean as she watched Beneke scoop the documents up with greedy enthusiasm.

"Complete our business here in port and the ship will be yours when you depart this evening," Tanner said as he wished to get Beneke out of the room.

"Aye," Beneke said as he looked around the room and then left toward the main deck. Outside his voice echoed as he hurled commands in all directions to get the ship offloaded.

The captain's chest was filled to capacity. All his books were neatly stored inside along with his clothing and money. He stood and slowly walked over to the chest. He reached into a small compartment in the lid of the chest and pulled out a beautiful hair ornament carved from solid jade.

"Masha," he gasped, breathing heavily from exhaustion as he looked at Maria to come toward him.

Maria came closer as the captain handed her the pin. It looked very expensive, gilded with lines in the shape of wings and jade tipped pins that formed a butterfly when inserted.

"I bought this babochka for my wife but before I could give it to her..." Maria nodded, feeling unworthy of a gift meant for his dead wife.

She tried to hand it back to him, knowing it was too much to accept.

The captain was insistent, pressing it into her palm and closing her fingers around it.

"I got it from an unscrupulous Japanese merchant, it's um... not just to decorate that pretty hair of yours..." the captain said as he slid one of the pins from the ornament.

With a flick of his wrist, the pin flew across the room and stuck firmly in the wooden beam where Boris stood. Boris shuddered as the thump of the pin startled him, then a satisfied, approving smile crept over the former soldier's face.

"Practice...mhm?" The captain whispered as Boris seemed to giggle while pulling the pin from the beam and then placed it in Maria's hand.

Masha smiled for the first time in days, she knew Tanner wanted to protect her, and it filled her heart with love for him. Here was a man facing death, losing his ship and yet he paused to care for her. He reached to embrace Maria one last time and began to slip where he stood as his energy was gone.

Maria held him in her arms, gladly supporting him and wanting to remain there but she knew he had to get to a physician quickly.

"We're ready!" She shouted as the men returned from the hall and guided him back to his bed where the cravat had lain.

Boris put his own bag over his shoulder and closed the lid to the chest. He then turned and put his hand over Maria's head, whispering a prayer of protection over her. She could only guess what he might be saying but appreciated his benevolence.

Boris motioned a cross with his hand and then pulled Maria close to hug her. His brute strength made for a crushing embrace that left her breathless. He was equally torn over leaving her behind but knew that Tanner needed him more. He motioned to the men to bring the captain as he dragged the large chest by the handle, letting it slide behind him.

Maria followed them from the empty cabin, once filled with the charm and intellect of Captain Tanner, now a vacant and lifeless space. As the men ascended the stairs, she slid her fingers through her hair, taking several locks and pinning them in place with the ornament at the back of her head. She then slid the two lethal pins into place and followed the men onto the main deck.

They carefully carried Captain Tanner across the deck and down the gangway, where a horse and carriage waited to take them to the port physician. Maria followed them to the edge of the deck, intending to go with them, but Beneke knew she might say something about her suspicions of poison.

"No one but the priest is permitted in port, we're suspected of carrying plague," Beneke shouted as the crew sadly remained on board and waved farewell to their captain.

We'll be wanting our breakfast now, cook!" Beneke insisted, wanting the crew to see how he commanded her. "We've never cooked in port!" Maria said defiantly, turning to leave the ship.

"New captain, new rules. Now get below or you'll be cooking in chains." Beneke barked, ensuring everyone heard him.

Maria watched the carriage pull away as she hung her head and felt the mixture of sadness and anger rush through her entire being.

"And just what does the new captain wish for me to cook? All the food was thrown overboard due to your plague!" Maria snapped.

"Supplies have already been arranged by the ship line. They'll be delivered soon enough. Until then you'll remain in your quarters." Beneke barked.

Maria nodded, knowing this would be the norm from now on as she headed down the stairs. She refused to cry, he would never see that from her, ever. She closed the door to her cabin and took the ornament from her hair, sliding a pin into her hand and hurling it at the wall.

To her surprise, it stuck firmly into the wood and made her pause, realizing she had to be on guard now and able to take care of herself. She sat on her bed and looked at the delicate ornament, so emotionally precious to her. She thought of the captain's last words and their last embrace.

Her tears, so carefully guarded from Beneke, began to  flow effortlessly for Tanner. Losing him reminded her of the others she cared about, now gone, at the hand of a cruel world that took far more than it ever gave. A deep despair swept over and consumed her like a storm at sea, blocking the sun and plunging everything beneath it into darkness. Her heartfelt emptied of all hope, so many unknowns, did her mother escape?... Would Tanner survive the poison?... What will happen to her now that Beneke was the captain of the ship?

She wanted to believe God had abandoned her, but the captain's words kept echoing in her mind. What could God possibly do with an enslaved cook, a simple farm girl, on a ship ruled by a tyrant? She closed her eyes and prayed until the despair moved through her like a drug, putting her to sleep in her bed.

Hours passed in silence as the men spent the day cleaning the ship and loading cargo. She began to awaken as sounds from the deck indicated the provisions for the galley had arrived. She stood and saw the hairpin still stuck on the wall. She pried it loose and put the ornament away in her things.

She opened her door and began to walk up to the main deck. When she arrived, she could hear an argument between two men, one was Beneke's voice, and the other was a man she had never heard before.

She stood mid stair, just out of sight, watching them argue as the other man held a large piece of paper that he continued to point at. Suddenly he cussed in Norwegian and shoved Beneke, pushing him back on his heels.

She thought Beneke would surely fight back, but instead, he seemed oddly obedient. Bowing his head for a moment and then nodding in agreement to whatever the dispute was.

A pause fell over the men who had watched their exchange and waited to see how the altercation resolved.

"Attention all hands, the line has sent Captain Tanner's replacement. This is Captain Svendsen of the Norwegian guild. He'll be commanding the ship henceforth. I'm staying on as quartermaster. Give him your respect and follow his orders, as I will do, also." Beneke said in confident protest.

The words came like an apology from the broken lip of a man who lost a fight. Beneke had not calculated the shipping line to work so quickly in replacing the captain. He intended to set sail before any decisions could be made, but obviously, word had spread quickly once in port.

Svendsen looked the crew over, quietly assessing them without comment. He walked with Beneke behind him as a tour of the ship was given. As they headed below decks, he saw Maria standing on the stairs.

"No harlots onboard, Beneke! You know that!" He said as he passed her without interest.

"Oh, no sir, this is our cook, she's a kholop from Russia, onboard for the trip to Poole and then back to Neva," Beneke replied.

"Female kholops as cooks?" Svendsen jeered, "What kind of ship was Tanner running? It's bad luck to have women onboard, they're a curse!"

The two men continued down the halls to the captain's cabin, with Svendsen listing his objections to the ships cleanliness with each step.

A man slowly climbed down the stairs, carrying the captain's chest on his back. He had dark skin and a kind face. Maria looked up at him, moving off the stairs to make room for him to get past her.

"Namaste," he said, as he followed the captain's direction.

Maria didn't know what he had said and just nodded. Clearly, things were quickly changing but a new captain, who didn't like her, seemed more appealing than one who had lied and poisoned his way to take over the ship.

The men loaded the provisions and cargo into the holds and soon set off the dock to move toward the Atlantic. Maria stood at the back of the ship, watching the port of Kopenhaven fade into the evening mist. She hadn't felt such loss since she left her Mother in Rostov.

She knew the men would be expecting dinner soon, and she headed below to get started. As she made her way down the stairs, she passed the crewmen who had chased rats earlier. They shushed their talking when she came near, so she stopped when she rounded a corner to hear what they were saying.

Within seconds they continued their gossip:

"What do you mean he lost his last ship? Was it pirates?" The first man asked.

"No, not pirates. A witch!" The other man replied.

"A witch? C'mon, that's daft." The man retorted.

"The last time we were here, there was a guy from the North Sea line in the pub. Told us about picking up Svendsen on their way into Reykjavic. Said that the Line has been trying to get rid of him ever since and look who we got?!" The first man said.

"And he lost a ship because of a witch? Sounds like a sea tale or some harbor gossip," the other man replied.

"Well here's what I heard:

*They was five days out of berth in Iceland, returning from Norway with a cargo of live farm animals. One of the rabbits gets loose, and the cargo master is chasing it around until it runs under a tarp, he goes after it and finds a beautiful young woman...stowaway.*

*Of course, he tells the captain, Svendsen, who brings her up on deck to find out who's been keeping her there. The whole crew is questioned, and the woman says, 'It wasn't any of them,' she was running away to Iceland to escape an arranged marriage to the local pig farmer.*

*Naturally, they all laugh it off and figure, what's the harm, in a few days they'll be in port. So Svendsen lets her stay in an empty cabin. But of course, these men start getting ideas, a pretty lady on board, lonely nights and you can imagine the rest. But this woman, she's kind of strange right? She tells each man that when they get into the port, she wants to get off the ship with him and be his wife. And with her own cabin, well, who knows how many of them came to her bed.*

*But the men start figuring out that she's telling them all the same story and then the fights start. But get this, each man wants her for himself. They never stopped to ask if maybe she was playing at some kind of game with their minds.*

*By the time the captain finds out, he's got an entire crew at war with each other. So, there they are, less than a day out of port when the ship hits a rocky shoal. The men were ignoring their posts, obsessed with this one woman and fighting over her. They're taking on water, so the captain put her in the lifeboat first, all while they fight over who goes with her. Then without warning, she cuts the rope and drifts away, alone in the boat.*

*By this time, they're all trapped on a sinking ship. Svendsen ropes together some barrels and floats out from the wreckage then gets picked up by another cargo ship in the lane. He tells them the whole story, and they ask him if this girl had the pox? He's asking..."What pox? Why?"*

Turns out there was a village in Norway where everybody was infected with the pox and dying. The surrounding towns had to set it on fire to stop the plague. Everyone was killed except this one girl, the most beautiful woman in this city. The men who did the burning, they just couldn't kill her so they let her live as long as she left on the next boat...that's how she ended up on Svendsen's ship. This girl stayed alive by seducing men then convincing them she loved them, but she was really infecting them with the pox."

"So how does that make her a witch?" The other man asked.

"She never had the pox, no marks, no boils, no rotting skin, she looked perfect." He replied.

"Do you think Svendsen, you know...had a go at her?" The second man asked.

"He was the only survivor, he lost a ship and 45 men. I think that's his curse, if he had given in to her, he'd be dead as well by now. Instead, he's more like a living ghost. She cursed him for not taking her to his bed, then slipped away to Iceland or Hell or wherever it is witches go." He replied.

"I think she knew if anyone found out she had the pox, she'd be dead. So she covered her tracks and floated into port or found another ship." The second man said.

"Aye, clever girl." The first man said.

Beneke came, stomping up the stairs toward Maria, as she listed to the tragic story. "Captains' expecting his meal, move your arse!" He shouted.

The men quickly scurried up the stairs, unaware Maria had overheard them. She rushed to the galley and started the stove.

She looked over the new provisions, everything looked proper for their voyage, with plenty of food to last the weeklong trip to Poole, England.

As she finished preparing a roasted chicken for the captain, she saw the dark skinned man come down the stairs. She gathered he was the captain's servant.

He kindly smiled and said "Namaste" again, holding his palms together vertically. Maria tilted her head curiously, indicating she didn't understand.

The man realized her pause, "Hello, I am Aybak" he said. "What is your name?"

"Maria," She said smiling as she studied his skin, he was tanner than anyone she had ever seen. The Tatars were more yellow skinned, but his skin was truly bronze like. "Where are you from?" She asked.

"My home is Mamluk, India. But I haven't been there in many years." He replied.

Maria placed the food on a tray for him to carry. The men began arriving for their meal which distracted them both to return to their duties. But there was a common thread of being a servant between them, and they both felt they would become friends.

# The Man from Mamluk

The men cleared from the galley after eating their evening meal. Maria completed her usual tasks of cleaning up, washing dishes and setting anything left uneaten to be served tomorrow. She grimaced at the remains of the chickens she had to butcher and prepare, it was a bloody and violent task that never became routine for her. It was at least fortunate that the harbor sent them with the feathers already removed. Otherwise, her work was triple the effort.

She looked over the provisions and set aside the things she would cook in the morning. A soft set of footsteps came down the stairs, she didn't recognize them and turned to see who it was. She saw Aybak, carrying the empty tray from the captain's cabin.

It seemed strange on this voyage, no guests or passengers, only crew and cargo for the trip to Poole. And here was Aybak, probably the only person who ate alongside the captain.

"Your meal very good, captain happy!" Aybak said.

Maria nodded and thanked him, "Did you get anything to eat?" She asked.

"Not yet, maybe a potato or some rice if you have?" Aybak asked politely.

Maria smiled, "You can have more than that, it's fine." She said.

She took a plate and put half a baked chicken on it with a potato on the side. Then pointed to the table where the men had just left. "Go ahead, I'll join you." She said as she took a potato for herself.

Aybak quickly finished the potato, it was evident he was famished, but he never touched the chicken.

"You don't like chicken?" Maria asked.

"I eat vegetable, fish only." He replied, hoping he had not offended her.

"Me too!" Maria said excitedly, "My mother was the same way, never could stand the sight of dead animals, or be able to eat them."

"My people believe negative action, especially kill, more bad action follows. This chicken...was it afraid when killed? Of course, yes. Now man eat, take fear into body, very bad for soul. What become of man eat fear and violence?" Aybak said.

"I never thought about that, it's very interesting, is it a religion like faith?" Maria asked.

"More like path, seek enlightenment, not riches or reward," Aybak replied.

"What about Heaven? Don't you want to go there?" Maria asked, trying to reconcile her Christian faith with Aybak's.

"Heaven only possible after many lifetimes, must first perfect path," Aybak said as he looked at the large plate of potatoes by the kitchen.

Maria stood and grabbed two more potatoes, returning to the table and sharing one with Aybak. "So you believe people can live more than one life?" She asked.

"Indeed, many life, not just man, but animal, insect." He answered.

"Wow, imagine that I could have been a bird or a horse or a queen in a castle someplace!" Maria said with a little giggle.

Aybak nodded in agreement. "Each life give lesson, make next path better, until perfect."

Maria marveled at the philosophy of this humble servant, he seemed more like a priest or magician than a man subjugated by the captain.

"It sounds like a long journey, so many lifetimes, trying over and over," Maria said as she stared into the dim shadows of the galley.

"Man greatest journey between mind and heart," Aybak said in a calm, reflective tone.

"So, what is this life teaching you? Your time with the captain, is it difficult for you?" She asked.

"I sold, slavery before fifteen birthsday. Had brother, sister, good parent. But debt to pay, father or me. I choose me so family not have life without father." Aybak said in emotionally charged words.

"I understand you completely," Maria said, refraining from telling her similar story.

Beneke clamored down the stairs and saw the two of them sitting at the table. "Boy! The captain needs his cabin prepared, get to it!" Beneke barked. "And you, get this galley cleaned up, the captain was furious with the condition of the floors when he saw them." He said to Maria.

Maria looked surprised as she looked at the floors, they were absolutely clean and always had been. But she realized Beneke was taking pleasure in ordering them around, as he no longer had the run of the entire ship.

Once Aybak had left the room, Beneke stood watching her take the plates back to the kitchen. It was clear he wanted to say something to her about what happened to Captain Tanner, but he was unsure how to go about it. Maria decided to ignore him until he spoke to her, as she felt uneasy around him now that Boris and Tanner were no longer on board to protect her.

Beneke stepped into the kitchen, he paused as he watched her working. Maria felt a cold sensation running down her back. It was the same way she felt when she was almost captured on board the Kupala. While Beneke said nothing, she felt he was acting something out in his mind and preparing to take action.

She set the last of the plates aside after washing them. She looked for a knife in case things went badly, but there was only a paring knife within reach. She quickly tucked it inside her palm trying to conceal it from his view while her back was turned. She turned with her apron over her hands, as if drying them but keeping the knife tightly in her grip.

Beneke set his hand on the counter and leaned as he spoke, trying to look relaxed and non-threatening.

"This new captain doesn't like women on his ship, so you best stay down here and not be any trouble to him." He began. "I also think we should set some new rules for how things are going to be for the rest of the voyage." He said.

"Oh?" Maria said trying to sound confident as she kept the hidden knife ready.

"Yes. Well, now that Tanner's gone I think you'll find the crew will be friendlier to you." Beneke said, "Unless of course, you prefer some kind of protection?"

"Protection?" Maria asked knowing what he meant.

"Well these sailors can get lonely, and you're easy enough on the eyes to make them think they could come visit you down here...late at night...when everyone's sleeping..." He said as his voice became darker.

"And this protection? What would it cost me?" Maria asked feeling irritated by the idea.

"Oh c'mon lass, I think we both know how this works. I'm second in command of the ship. One word from me and no man will touch you. Of course, in return for that, I expect certain favors, and I don't mean extra food at meal time."

Beneke began walking toward Maria, his eyes grew cold, and his breathing was deep and lustful. "In fact, you could start paying me right now..." he said as his hand slid down her back and reached around to grope her breast. Pulling her body firmly against his.

Maria gasped at his brazen lust, quickly pulling away from him as she backed up against the wall.

"I'll cut you like the pig you are!" she shouted, aiming the knife at him. Her hands trembled with fear, making her grip it tighter to show her resolve.

Beneke shushed her, "Shh, calm down girl, no one's cutting anything with that tiny knife."

He walked toward her unafraid and snatched the knife from her hand, then looked at her with disdain as he snapped the blade in two pieces with his bare hands.

"You think you're too good for me? Is that it? Oh, but you were ready to spread your legs for Tanner weren't you?

"Get out!" Maria demanded, knowing she was powerless to stop him.

"It's time someone showed you that your only place on this ship, is on your back," Beneke said in a voice so evil that his words made Maria shiver in terror.

He put his hands around Maria's neck and began pushing her backward toward the floor of the kitchen.

Her hands slid along the side of the counter, trying to balance as Beneke pushed her harder toward the floor. Her hand passed over the salt pouch, instantly her impulses reacted as she grabbed a handful of ground salt and tossed it into his eyes.

"Ahhh you bitch!" Beneke screamed as he stopped in his tracks to clear the salt from his tearing eyes.

Maria ran to her cabin, latching the door and searching for the knife she kept under pillow. She shuffled through her blankets and saw it beneath the bed on the floor. She stretched her arm to reach it in time but then heard her door burst open. Beneke had kicked it in, ripping the lock from the door frame. Splinters flew all over the floor as she turned to defend herself, empty handed.

At that moment she saw the ornament Tanner had given her, sitting beside her bed. She quickly pulled the hairpin from it and threw it directly at Beneke's face. He growled at her as it stuck in his cheek like a pin in a cushion. He pulled the pin from his face and threw it on the floor. Blood dripped profusely from his cheek as he moved toward Maria. She backed onto her bed and pushed herself into the corner, trying to get as far from his reach as possible.

A wicked anger mixed with revenge filled Beneke's eyes. Maria screamed hoping someone would help her, but there was no one. She feared he had ordered the men away to the other side of the ship. He reached and grabbed her by the arm, pulling her toward him. His breath wreaked of alcohol as his course beard pushed against her cheek.

"Go on, fight!" He shouted.

"I'll enjoy it more!" He said as he ripped her dress down off her shoulder, exposing her breasts.

Maria felt sickened by his touch, angry, fearful and helpless to stop him. She pushed to get herself away, dreading the idea that he would rape her in her own bed. But his hold on her was too strong.

He pushed her to her knees and let go of one of her arms to reach for his belt. Maria turned her head away as he reached inside his pants. His blood dripped down his face and fell on her head and chest, staining her white torn dress. She knew what he intended, and she thought she would vomit any second while she continued to struggle.

Suddenly, a rush of footsteps thundered down the stairs, and within seconds she heard the sound of her wooden chair crashing over Beneke's back. It was Aybak!

Aybak's eyes were wide and full of fear as Beneke turned to face him. Beneke stammered but was still twice Aybak's size and seemed ready to kill him for interrupting. Beneke grabbed the lapel of Aybak's coat with one hand and reached back with the other, preparing to strike him in the face.

"Another rebellious servant in need of an ass beating!" Beneke said cruelly as he began to throw his punch.

Aybak stepped slightly forward and made a fast chopping movement with the inside edge of his palms on both sides of Beneke's neck. "Shaa!" Aybak shouted as his hands hit their mark.

Beneke stopped and looked curiously at Aybak as if amused by the futility of his defense.

Maria felt there was no hope for either of them, then she watched in amazement as Aybak confidently exhaled slowly while pushing Beneke backward with one hand.

Beneke collapsed on the floor like a drunken sailor. His eyes were closed with no breath in his body.

Aybak quickly turned to Maria, seeing her condition. She was covered in Beneke's blood, her dress was torn almost completely from her upper body. Her face was flush with fear as she tried to hold her shirt closed while she cried.

Aybak slipped his coat from his shoulders and wrapped it around her, knowing she was not completely aware of what was happening.

"Maria, Maria!" he said as he tried to get her to look in his eyes.

"Is over!" he said calmly, "Look me, is over."

Maria's eyes welled with tears, she was unsure what to do, what to say and nothing seemed an appropriate response. Aybak helped her to her feet and guided her out of the cabin, stepping over Beneke's lifeless body. He sat her in the galley and sat beside her while she cried.

The captain and some of the men were coming down the stairs, stepping inside Maria's cabin to see what had happened. He noted the busted door and Beneke on the floor. The captain seemed annoyed, and shouted out to Aybak, "Come and wake him up!" he ordered.

Maria was surprised no one was concerned for her wellbeing, it was as if she was no more important than the broken door.

Aybak stepped into the cabin and pulled a handful of Beneke's hair, lifting his head high. A loud smack was heard as Aybak struck the back of Beneke's neck to wake him.

Beneke slowly came back, groggy and unaware of his surroundings. The captain sat on Maria's bed, looking at Beneke's condition.

"What the hell happened to your face?" The captain asked as he noticed the jade pin on the floor. He picked it up and looked around the room, nodding his head, as if seeing the entire scene were played out before him.

"Clap him in irons." The captain said casually.

The sailors drug Beneke from Maria's cabin and took him below to the confinement space at the bottom of the ship.

"You've cost me my quartermaster." The captain said as he walked to where Maria sat.

Maria swallowed, still catching her breath and unsure how to respond.

"Nothing poisons a crew like a woman onboard." The captain said as he glared at Maria, "Get this mess cleaned up."

The captain headed up the stairs without hesitation. Maria was relieved to know Beneke was locked up, but the captain's reaction was almost as vile as the attack. She was innocent and yet he spoke to her as if she had some blame to bear.

Aybak helped Maria straighten her room, he then left and returned with tools to move the lock on her door where it could still function.

Maria sat on her bed, still wearing Aybak's coat. She looked at her floor, covered in salt, blood, and splinters. The stench of Beneke still remained in the room, she could even feel it on her clothes, in her hair, and on her body.

She cried softly as Aybak mopped the floor, he was her hero and without a word had saved her from that Pomeralian devil.

"You saved me..." She said through her tears. "Thank you."

Aybak stopped mopping and turned to look at her. "I save virtue, only you, rescue you." He said.

Maria wasn't sure what he meant but took his words as a kind intention.

Aybak took the mop from the cabin and returned with a bucket of water and a large pan for bathing. "Lock door behind me," he said, "I'll come in morning."

Maria nodded, feeling grateful that he understood she would want to wash everything off.

She locked the door and turned to see her room, returned to its original condition. It had been restored to its original condition but would never be the same, nor would she feel safe there.

She set Aybak's coat aside and slid her torn dress off. The blood had soaked in and made it look like rags from a surgeon's ward. She threw the dress to the corner of the room and stepped into the pan. The water was cold, but it quickly rinsed the blood and sweat of her attacker away. She poured water through her hair, again and again. Seeing it run red made her feel nauseous, it was as if it would never come out, but finally, the blonde returned, and the blood was gone.

The pail was filled with red-tinted water, her washcloth appeared pink, even after rinsing. There was simply too much of him left in the room with her.

She left her lantern burning, put on her gown and slept, sitting against the wall on the far corner of the bed, watching the door. One hand on her knife and the other wrapped around the jade hairpins.

She drifted in and out of sleep the rest of the night, imagining the door bursting open again. Images of the captain accusing her, rumors of poisoning his men, and the story of the witch the men had been telling earlier.

# Confined to the Galley

The morning came slowly; Maria awoke to the steps of the men coming down the stairs for breakfast which she had not yet prepared. She rushed from her bed, changing into only clean shirt she had left.

She quickly made her way into the kitchen and set the fruit out so the men could eat something while she heated the water for oatmeal.

It was silent in the galley. The men spoke only in whispers as she set the prepared oatmeal out for them to serve themselves. She tried to ignore them, hoping Beneke's threats about the men trying to get her in bed were false.

She saw one man speaking with another as they looked at her then saw his lips say "Witch" as she passed by. She thought perhaps she imagined this as her mind was still very confused about what had happened.

A dark suggestion had taken root in her subconscious, the idea that she was somehow to blame for the attack. Had she truly played a part in it? Was there a time when she might have said or done something that could justify the actions of Beneke?

Aybak appeared in the galley and asked for the captain's breakfast. Maria set it on the platter and thanked him again for coming to her aid. The men in the galley watched as she returned his jacket to him. Their eyes became judgmental as if she was playing one man against another. She could feel their thoughts running through her like daggers.

"Aybak," She whispered, "I want you to know I didn't do anything to encourage Beneke, he attacked me."

Aybak nodded and whispered so only Maria could hear him, "I know, but he convinces Captain that you offer service for money. Say you invite him to cabin and then change mind."

"That's a lie!" Maria snapped, "You saw my door!"

Aybak motioned to Maria to calm down, "Yes and the captain also see. Beneke say I kick in when I hear fighting. Captain believe him ... for now."

Maria felt her face run hot with anger, that monster had lied, conspired, attempted to kill Tanner, and now he was making her out to be some kind of witch or harlot.

"Captain speak you later, for now, he say, you stay, galley only," Aybak said.

Maria nodded, feeling like the world was closing in around her and no one could save her from the corruption of Beneke's lies and conspiracies. She needed to think how to outsmart him before she fell victim to his next trick or attack.

Maria cleaned the galley and waited for the captain. Hours passed by as she read the English book, left by Tanner. Finally, footsteps clapped down the stairs as the captain arrived followed by Aybak.

"You signed a contract with this ship, did you not?" The captain asked.

Maria nodded, unsure why he would ask that.

"You say you're a kholop, but there's no copy of your contract in the captain's quarters, no evidence to prove you're anything more than an indentured servant, sold at auction just like I came to purchase Aybak." Svendsen charred.

"Captain Tanner gave my contract to Mr. Beneke. It was right before Captain Tanner was taken off the ship, he gave him a pouch with all ship's contracts and invoices..." Maria said as she realized Beneke must have destroyed the only proof of her status.

"It's also recorded in Neva at the guild office, I wrote it myself," Maria assured, realizing she had not registered it at all, other than a copy held by her cousin.

"A cook that can write, how charming, more lies to consider in your eventual fate... Well when I meet with Captain Tanner on our return to Kopenhaven, I'll ask him about this magical contract, written by a slave cook in my galley. Assuming Tanner survives of course... Meanwhile, you'll be confined to the galley until we reach the port of Poole in 5 days. You're not to come out for any reason. I don't want you around the rest of the crew, so have the meals set out before they arrive and clean after they've left. Understood?" Svendsen demanded.

Maria nodded, "Yes sir."

The captain turned and began to ascend the stairs.

"Sir, I'm not a witch, and I'm not trying to seduce your men. Beneke attacked me when I wouldn't give him what he wanted." She said in a sad voice.

The captain stopped and turned. "Who said anything about witches?" He stated in a haunted voice. "And what do you know of witches? Do you think they're some haggardly old lady, living in cave...? Well, they're not!" "They look just like you... innocent. Innocent and cunning while they work their craft to seduce and corrupt the hearts of men." He said with contemptuous anger.

The captain paused, calming his voice and regaining his stature in the room. "Just keep your face out of sight until we get to Poole!" the captain snapped as he turned to continue his exit.

Maria hesitated, knowing her fate was in the balance of anything she might say or do.

"I know about the curse. I know how you lost your ship, but I swear I'm not a witch! I'm just a farm girl from Rostov. No matter what Beneke has told you, Sir... I'm a simple Bee keeper's daughter who needed money and came to work on this ship!" She said as her eyes began to tear.

The captain stood with his back to Maria, unmoved by her genuine pleading. "I did *not* lose my ship!" He said as his words filled with rage. "She sank beneath me while my crew fought over the whore we put in our only lifeboat." The captain said as he stomped up the stairs and out of sight.

"Aybak!" the captain shouted from the deck.

Aybak gave a sympathetic nod to Maria as he rushed to follow the captain.

Maria cried as they left, knowing the situation was getting worse. She had to be invisible to the crew, complete her duties and never step outside to see the sky or feel the spray of the ocean on her face. And what would happen in Poole, why didn't the captain mention the return home?

Maria went to the kitchen to prepare the lunchtime meal. Her hands shaking as she tried to cook and sort through every scenario, every outcome, hoping to resolve what she could do but every conclusion was the same. A slave has no choice, no hope, only her contract protected her, and Beneke knew that.

Time became a silent torture as she spent the next 5 days hiding in her cabin during meals. Only Aybak came to see her and give her some company, a brief conversation, a human presence in a floating prison aboard the ship.

She reflected on what Tanner had told her, the idea of bad things putting her on a path she might not see. Was this in his dream? If so, would he have told her?

The ship tossed its way southward across the Atlantic, moving toward the port of Poole, England. With each passing hour, the fear of what would happen there felt more intense as dread and depression consumed Maria's thoughts and heart.

Sleep abandoned her, as she felt the passing of every second, laying in her bed, waiting for the eventuality of fate regardless of her eyes being opened or closed. There was no reality, only the buffering waves outside the hull, the cycle of meals and cleaning, followed by deafening silence.

# The Port of Poole

The dim light beneath the deck had become day and night without transition. The small window in the galley had become frosted by salt spray leaving no hint of land or sea. Maria rose each morning to cook and then hide away in her cabin, waiting for the men to leave.

Her English book was her only escape, her only doorway to the world outside of the creaking wood and rocking floors of the ship, that had taken her so far from home. Even home as she remembered it was no more. The simple farm she grew up on had become a paradise beyond this world, leaving a void filled by the hope that her mother had survived and could make the journey up the Volga before the winter set in. If she could only know her mother had survived, it would all be worth it, her suffering at the hands of Beneke would have meaning and justification.

She prayed to God for an answer, a remedy, a solution to fix her situation and reunite her with her mother. On the night before arriving in port, she dreamed of being at home in Rostov, the smell of the garden, the feeling of moist dirt between her toes as she picked blackberries from the bushes her father had planted. She remembered the way the hairbrush felt in her hair when her mother combed it each night, and the sound of her mother's voice when she recited the Latin words from the illuminated script. Visions of Rostov scrolled through her mind, riding on the cart with her father, taking honey and candles into town to sell at the market...a once perfect life, fading.

She awoke as the ship shuddered from being moored in port. They were in England, and she feared her life would never be the same, nor would she return to the simple farm life she had felt in her dreams.

She got up and prepared the meal for the men, even though it wasn't customary when in port. She simply didn't want to give the captain any reason to be more cross with her. As she finished laying out the plates, she saw Aybak's familiar face coming into the galley.

He looked happy and smiled at her. "Captain wants you put on best clothing, go into port!" he said with his charming accent. "I think he not angry anymore."

Maria felt a gargantuan weight lift from her soul. Could it really be so simple? Perhaps he found her contract or discovered all of Beneke's lies. Whatever it was, her prayers had been answered!

She rushed to her room and put on her cleanest gown, a full-length white linen that had been smoothed and softened in sea water before rinsing. It was the finest clothing she owned, and she put her hair up using the ornament given to her by Tanner. She couldn't stop smiling as she walked to the door of her cabin, then she turned and had thought to take the illuminated script with her. She intended to show the captain her reading abilities if the opportunity came. She lifted the lid to the cabinet in her room and saw her knife along with the amber necklace Tanner had bought for her in Reval and the script beneath them. She gathered everything in her hands, put the necklace on and tucked the script and knife into the broad belt of her dress.

She took one last look at her cabin, feeling that when she returned everything would be different, better, her prayers were answered.

She walked on the deck and saw the captain waiting at the gang plank. He seemed to be less angry than the last time they had spoken. He motioned for her to approach him, as Aybak walked with her. Then he led them into the port.

Maria felt strange walking on land after so many days at sea. The ground seemed to firm and dead, but the scent of the harbour was wonderful. She could smell baking and fresh seafood, even the smell of the cargo ropes seemed pleasant. She smiled as the captain walked alongside her without speaking, only pointing their way.

"Are we buying provisions? We're out of almost everything in vegetables, spices, salts and we ran out of meat two days ago, except the bones I use for soup. Do they have fruit here?" She asked, remembering the days when she used to barter for food with Sveta onboard the Kupala.

It was all coming back to her as she marveled at the view in this strange country, England, where the language she had studied for weeks was spoken natively. Even the signs on the shops and streets were all in English.

The captain turned back to Aybak, "Did you get all of that?" He asked.

Aybak nodded nervously, hoping he could remember all the items Maria had mentioned.

"Go and make the arrangements for provisions. Tell the merchants I will pay them upon my return." The captain said, keeping his back to Maria.

"Should I go with him?" Maria asked innocently.

"No, we're going this way." The captain replied as he pointed toward a small building with a stage beside it. The grass was worn down from all the foot traffic around the building. Metal bars defined the walls of a large cage that sat behind the stage area. Carts and traders were gathering as the captain led Maria inside the building.

A desk sat inside the single room structure with an opening at the rear leading into the cage. Bales of straw were laid around the edges of the caged space where poorly dressed people sat as if waiting for something to happen.

Maria looked at the captain, "What do they trade here? Horses? That will be a hard journey for them back to Kopenhaven" She said.

A savage looking man entered the room from the cage, he was dirty and looked as if he hadn't bathed in weeks.

"Selling or buying?!" The man asked in a thick English accent.

"Selling," the captain said, responding in English while avoiding eye contact with Maria.

Maria's command of English was still developing, she could not discern the conversation between the captain and the merchant. She began to look around the room nervously,

"What was happening? If this is a trading post, where are the animals?" She wondered.

"Three hundred!" The captain insisted.

The slave trader walked around the desk and looked at her from head to toe, nodding his head in agreement.

"Got all her teeth?" He asked as he reached into his pocket and began counting coins.

"Uh...yes." The captain replied, feeling the awkwardness of the scene unfolding. "Uh but, no English, only Russian." He added.

"Probably better." The trader replied. "Got a name?"

"Maria." The captain replied.

The first word Maria understood since their conversation had changed into English, and it was her name. She felt the room begin to close in on her. They were not buying horses in this place, this was a slave trader, and she was being sold off, dressed up by her own will, to fetch the highest price.

The betrayal burned her face like hot oil pouring over her. The captain had all too casually brought her here to discard her into slavery, abandoning her in a foreign land with no paperwork to protect her. Her heart began to beat so hard that her pulse made her lips quiver.

At that moment, a man entered the room from the front door, leaving it open to a view outside that felt like a message. Within a second she knew what she had to do. She bolted for the door, lifted the hem of her dress to let her legs run freely. She ran across the yard, hearing the trader and the captain chasing behind her.

She ducked between two shops, feeling her way in an unknown port, trying to hide, to evade, to disappear. She knelt down behind a barrel and saw the captain run by on the street. She knew she had a chance if she ran around the back in the other direction, she turned and ran but slipped on the wet cobblestone. Her shoes ripped, cutting her toes slightly. The dirt and mud smeared on her dress, but she continued to run. Picking herself up and limping as she rushed to get away from the captain and his treachery.

She turned the corner and moved down an alley, working her way out of the port, into the countryside. The slave trader appeared between the hills and chased after her.

"Maria! C'mon don't run lass!" he shouted.

The path into town was formed by two dirt lanes, beaten smooth from carts and horses. Maria followed the path away from town, hoping to find a hiding place in the woods or tall grass, while the slave trader followed behind her.

Two men dressed in chain mail with swords on their belts walked toward her on the path. They appeared to be soldiers, arriving in town, but she sensed no concern of running past them. Her wish was to reach a cart that rode much further behind them.

An elderly man drove the cart, he looked kind, and she hoped he could help her.

Maria dashed between the two men, her hair coming undone as her ornament fell from her head, unleashing her silken blonde hair, splashing the face of one of the men as she passed.

"Oi," the first man said laughing as he picked up the ornament. "You dropped this!" he playfully shouted as he turned to his friend. "Story of my life, eh William? They just go on running."

"Aye, Robert," William said, "And …Here comes the … husband?"

They both looked back at Maria and then to the slave trader, knowing there was no chance these two were together. The merchant continued to pursue Maria, following her path between the two men.

"What ya think?" Asked Robert as he studied the delicate quality of the ornament.

"Feels wrong." Said William as he nodded with a smile of agreement of an unspoken action.

"Aye." Said Robert as he extended his steel wrapped arm outward, catching the slave trader by the neck as he ran between them. The trader's body lifted into the air, sailing several yards before he fell onto the ground like a giant sack of grain.

William walked over to the trader, "Sorry about that mate, but that one is definitely in need of a head start." He joked as he and Robert turned to see Maria running to the cart.

The trader coughed and slowly stood as the two men walked away, talking and laughing as if nothing had happened. They were clearly soldiers of some sort and not the type of men he wanted to engage.

The men reached the port and saw the captain on a horse, racing down the path toward Maria.

"What's this ...? Father maybe?" Robert joked.

"Nah, I'd say she's on the run," William replied.

"How come Gustav never has girls like that back in Meridian?" William asked.

"For the same reason, we're going to France to marry you off to the lady Celine. England has to import beauty." Robert replied.

"Aye, and royal blood, to keep the peace," William added.

"Well, there is that, also. What was the name of our ship?" Robert asked as he patted his friend on the back.

"Algadon," William replied, "I think the captain is a Spaniard."

The two men walked out of view just as Maria reached the distant cart. Her accent was never so heavy as this moment when she needed to communicate in English.

"Sir, please help me?" She begged.

The man smiled and stopped his horse. He helped her step up into the cart.

"Bonjour," he said, "Je m'appelle Gustav."

Maria didn't understand his words and looked up to see the captain rushing his horse toward them as the trader walked angrily closer, rubbing his throat as he coughed.

"Please, can we go the other way?" Maria begged, knowing the captain would find her.

Gustav began speaking in an irritated tone, pointing in both directions toward and away from the city. Maria could not understand him and looked around desperately for anyone else who might help her, but the path was empty.

Within seconds the captain arrived, his face was red with anger as he dismounted his horse and walked toward the cart.

"That slave belongs to me; I'll take her now!" He commanded.

Gustav began cursing in French and pulled a knife from the floor of his cart, holding it at the captain's throat as he reached for Maria.

Maria felt relieved, finally a protector, someone who didn't have to do the captain's bidding.

"Je suis désolé." The captain said calmly as he carefully backed away.

Maria's eyes grew big as the captain began to converse in the same language as Gustav. They pointed and nodded toward the port and the trading post, and within minutes the old man pushed her out of his cart toward the captain.

"Aller!" He insisted.

The captain put his hand on the back of Maria's neck and squeezed it harshly as he guided her back to the trading post.

"Let's go, witch!" He commanded.

The merchant gathered the horse and followed them. Maria began to cry, she felt everything in her life was coming to an end. She had given up her freedom for money, and now she had lost everything. Her life would be for sale, her service like a commodity to be traded and no one would know what had happened to her. Something in her soul seemed to retreat and hide, she felt herself fading from her own body, watching her hands being tied by the slave traders as she was pushed and goaded into the cage like cattle. The captain counted the money they gave him and smiled as he turned and left the post, never looking back.

Several other girls were there, some older, some younger. Their clothes were tattered and dirty. They all looked at Maria for a moment, then turned their attention back to the ground in despair. It appeared this was not their first time at the trading post. Some had tattoo marks on their hands or a single pierced ear, indicating their slave status. Many of them cried, others just sighed and looked off in the distance.

Maria stared through the bars of the cage, past the crowds toward the edge of the port, where the sea disappeared into the horizon. She imagined if only she could find a ship, a boat, a raft, she would peddle home to Neva and never set foot on a ship again.

"No one will know that I am here." She gasped as she cried and shook all over, leaning forward with her face in her hands.

Her hair spilled over her shoulders and hung over her head like a blonde veil.

An older woman came and sat beside her, she only brushed her hand down Maria's back as she cried. Maria kept her face in her hands, wishing the world would change when she opened her eyes. Hours passed, and the yard became noisy as traders gathered to buy slaves. She sensed the older woman getting up and then heard her whisper, "Vso budit horosho…"

Maria's eyes snapped open as she looked up to see that the woman beside her had gone, but the whisper was in Russian, not English. A comfort came in her heart as she felt her mother or an angel had just sat beside her and touched her.

The gate to the cage swung open, and one by one, the older women were led onto the stage where people bid on them to work as servants, cooks, maids and midwives. The young girls were held until the end and brought out all at once. The crowd had thinned some, and only a few men remained, including Gustav, the man with the cart.

He spoke with an accent and walked over to the traders. They seemed to argue and made gestures with two fingers, then three as if the price and the purchase were being negotiated. Eventually, the traders came over and looked at Maria and the other three girls.

"All of you are going to Meridian, you'll be… really popular." The trader said as he looked at their bodies with a sexual stare.

He threw a bag of coins up in the air, catching it again as he turned to the man with the cart, waving him closer.

"What's going to happen to us?" One of the girls cried.

"I expect you'll be working in Gustav's tavern, he needs barmaids for his tables and girls for his beds." He said, "And he paid extra for the spirited one, they're always more fun to break." He chuckled as he pulled at their tied hands leading them to Gustav's cart.

Maria could not understand anything being said, her studies in English had failed to prepare her for such an ordeal. She moved compliantly with the others, feeling unsure what recourse she had.

The girls looked at each other as they sat together in the back of the cart. Gustav tied them all together to keep them from running and showed them his knife to make it clear he was not to be tested. He snapped the reigns, and the horse pulled forward, heading back up the path that had once looked like the way to freedom, but now represented an unknown and dark future.

Tears rode down Maria's face as she and the other ladies, drifted into the hills as the port faded from view.

The captain returned to the ship, where Beneke stood on deck waiting for them. He was still clapped in irons with chains dragging behind him as he walked toward the gangplank.

"Captain I want to commend you on your decision, that girl would have brought nothing but bad luck to this ship," Beneke said in a sycophantic tone.

"Indeed." The captain said as he stepped on the ship. "Release him." The captain ordered as the chains were removed.

Beneke rubbed his wrists in relief, the marks of the iron still imprinted in his skin. He smiled, feeling victorious over Maria and keeping his position on the ship.

"Now." The captain began, "Get off my ship."

"What?!" Beneke said in shock, "But sir I'm your quartermaster, your second in…"

"You're a coward, you attacked that girl and poisoned Tanner. God knows what else you had planned. Get off or return to Kopenhaven in chains. If you show your face there, I'll press charges for attempted murder and rape." The captain said pushing Beneke toward the gangplank.

"But sir, this is madness, Poison? How could I possibly?" Beneke pleaded.

"I met with Tanner and his priest before we set sail. He told me everything. Including his devotion to that girl, I could see the lust in his eyes, just as it was in yours and the men on my last ship. I'll never make that mistake again." The captain said as he motioned to the crew to push Beneke down the gangplank.

"Let's shove off this rain covered rock, we're off to Spain, new orders and a new home port!" The captain ordered.

The men who had dealt with Beneke's treachery gladly pushed him more than needed, pulling the gangplank sooner than he could complete his steps. He fell, hitting his face on the edge of the dock before slipping into the cold water below.

The Ukko pulled into the Atlantic once more, as Beneke struggled to climb the slimy barnacle covered dock poles, his hands and clothing ripped from the jagged edges as he pulled himself onto the central platform, soaked, bleeding and humiliated.

He looked over his shoulder to see the Ukko, his once, and future kingdom, now lost as its' sails filled and took it to the horizon without him. He had lost everything, disgraced and abandoned in a land where he had no friends, no money, no one.

Meanwhile, the tied up servants shook and swayed in the back of Gustav's cart as the city of Poole grew smaller on the path behind them. The women remained silent, some cried, others looked at each other, wondering what would become of them. They spoke different languages and began to share their names.

A young brunette girl with green eyes and pale complexion pointed to herself with her hands still tied, "Diana" She said, looking in the eyes of the other three ladies.

"Tara," said another with long red curly hair, blue eyes, and light freckles.

"Francesca," said a tan skinned woman with black hair, brown eyes, and a kind smile.

"Maria," said a voice through a veil of long blonde hair, and tear filled grey eyes.

The ladies seemed to bond quickly, without more than each other's names. They knew they would be reliant on each other to survive whatever life waited for them at the end of the path they rode on.

Maria dried her eyes and did her best to brush her hair back, while her hands were tied. She took a deep breath and tried to make sense of the procedural tragedies that had befallen her since leaving Kopenhaven. Now she sat in a company of more women than she had seen in months since working on the ship.

Tara reached her hands over to Maria's necklace, touching it delicately, admiring how fine it was made.

"So lovely." She said smiling.

Maria smiled for the first time since realizing she had been sold into slavery. She remembered learning this word from Captain Tanner and the memory of the moment warmed her heart.

"Thank...you," she affected her reply in English.

As the hours passed, she sat up straighter and tried to regain her inner strength as her hands rested in her lap, brushing against the knife, still tucked in her belt...

# End of Volume, I of V

◆ ◆

The saga continues:

Vol. ii, The King's Body Guard, January 2017

Details: www.kingdomofmeridian.com

We appreciate your reviews and feedback on Amazon, Nook, Kobo and iBooks

# Translation Index

| Anglicized Word/Phrase | Russian Word in Cyrillic | Translation |
|---|---|---|
| Aller | Aller (French) | Go |
| Babochka | Бабочка | Butterfly |
| Banya | Баня | Steam room |
| Bar | Бар | Bar |
| Bayan | Баян | Accordion |
| Bleen | Блин | Shoot |
| Blinchiki | Блинчики | Crepe -pancake |
| Bolshoe | Большое | Much or Big |
| Bonjour | Bonjour (French) | Hello |
| Boyus | Боюсь | Afraid |
| Budish | Будешь | Awaken |
| Chai | Чай | Tea |
| Chut chut | Чуть-чуть | A little |
| Da | Да | Yes |
| Davai | Давай | Do it |
| Deti | Дети | Children |
| Devochka | Девочка | Girl |
| Devochki | Девочки | Girls |
| Dacha | Дача | Summer home |
| Dorogaya | Дорогая | Dear |
| Dobroye | Доброе | Good |
| Dyadya | дядя | Uncle |
| Duodevigenti | Duodevigenti (Latin) | 18 |

| | | |
|---|---|---|
| Eto | Это | This |
| Gospodin | Господин | Mr. |
| Gospodi | Господи | Lord have mercy |
| Horosho | Хорошо | Good |
| Idi | Иди | Go |
| Interesno | Интересно | Interesting |
| Izvinitye | Извините | Excuse Me |
| Je m'appelle | Je m'appelle (French) | My name is |
| Je suis désolé | Je suis désolé (French) | I am sorry |
| Kholop | Холоп | Indentured Servant |
| Konechno | Конечно | Of course |
| Kashmar | Кашмар | Nightmare |
| Kto | Кто | Who |
| Kushat | Кушать | Eat |
| Ladno | Ладно | Fine |
| Magu | Могу | To do |
| Molodets | Молодец | Good job |
| Namaste | Namaste (Hindi) | Greeting & Farewell |
| Na zdoroviye | На здоровье | To your health |
| Ne | Не | Not |
| Nichevo | Ничего | Nothing |
| Ne Nado | Не Надо | Don't |
| Net | Нет | No |
| Normalno | Нормально | Normal |
| Ochen | Очень | Very |
| Olen Vapaa | Olen Vapaa (Finnish) | I'm Free |
| Pirozhki | Пирожки | Pastry-Meat/Vegetable |
| Pochemu | Почему | Why |
| Podozhdi | Подожди | Wait |
| Poka | Пока | Bye |
| Ponimayu | Понимаю | I Understand |
| Ponimayesh | Понимаешь | You Understand |
| Poshli | Пошли | Let's go |

| | | |
|---|---|---|
| Pozhalysta | Пожалуйста | You're welcome |
| Preyatnoga apetita | Приятного аппетита | Enjoy your meal |
| Psheprashaam | Przepraszam (Polish) | Excuse Me |
| Privet | Привет | Hello |
| Priyatno | Приятно | Nice |
| Producti | Продукты | Produce |
| Prosto | Просто | Simply |
| Prosti | Прости | Forgive me |
| Pyat | Пять | 5 |
| Severnoe Siyanie | Северное сияние | Northern Lights |
| Seriozno | Серьезно | Seriously |
| Shto | Что | What |
| Skatina Takoy | Скотина такой | Dumb Animals |
| Skolko | Сколько | How Much |
| Sladki | Сладкий | Sweet |
| Slishu | Слышу | I'm listening |
| Snov | Снов | Dreams |
| Spacibo | Спасибо | Thank You |
| Spiish | Спишь | Sleep |
| Suda | Сюда | Here |
| Svinya | Свинья | Pig |
| Takoe | Такое | That |
| Tam | Там | There |
| Ti | Ты | You |
| Tobak | Табак | Tobacco |
| Togda | Тогда | Then |
| Tolka | Только | Only |
| U nas | У нас | Our |
| Udachi | Удачи | Luck |
| Ulitsa | Улица | Street |
| Undeviginti | Undeviginti (Latin) | 19 |
| Utro | Утро | Morning |
| Uzhas | Ужас | Horror |

| | | |
|---|---|---|
| Vkusna | Вкусно | Tasty |
| Vse | Все | All |
| Vso budit horosho | Все будет хорошо | Everything will be good |
| Ya | Я | I |
| Yra | Ура | Hooray |
| Zdes | Здесь | Here |
| Zdrastvuite | Здравствуйте | Greetings |

Copyright © Aurous Publishing, 2010 – Present

ISBN-13: 978-0997129113 // ISBN-10: 0997129115